Tor

The Command

Book

The Holy Land in the year 1193. Guillaume de Born, an unscrupulous Templar Knight on a secret mission to meet with the Assassins, acquires in Jerusalem what he believes to be the holiest relic of Christianity: the fabled Ark of the Covenant. On his way back to the port city of Acre, he is ambushed by his Templar brothers. They rob him of the treasure and leave him badly wounded in the mountains of Galilee. Deeply humiliated, he swears revenge. With the help of a young Muslim man, an unconventional Jewish woman and two daring Christian knights, he sets out to reclaim the sacred relic from the powerful Order. But the precious artefact is now in an impregnable Templar fortress, guarded by a ruthless enemy...

Author

Tom Melley was born in Germany in 1962. He has been passionate about medieval history since boyhood, in particular the era of the Crusades, and he writes gripping historical novels about this eventful period.

Also published by Tom Melley in 2021:

THE WARRIOR OF THE LORD

Tom Melley

THE COMMANDMENTS OF THE TEMPLAR

Historical Novel

"Some believe they wish for their advantage
and wish for their detriment"

from 'Yvain' by Chrétien de Troyes,
French poet, ca. 1180

I

Jerusalem, the Holy City of Miracles, certainly deserved its epithet. Although great miracles hadn't happened here for a long time, only small ones that weren't always recognised as such. And yet they did happen.

Ishmael leaned back contentedly, wiped his overworked, watering eyes and admired his work. The delicate bracelet he had fashioned for the first wife of the governor of Jerusalem, Emir Izz ad-Din, was finished. Three finely hammered, gold filigree snakes intertwined to form a lustrous circlet. Their heads were nestled close to their bodies, and tiny eyes of sparkling rubies glittered in the radiant afternoon sun falling through the open window of his workshop onto the wooden workbench.

It was only a small commission, but one of considerable significance for the Jewish goldsmith, who was a renowned master of his craft. This wasn't the first time the Emir had commissioned a costly piece of jewellery from him. The prince's goodwill drew further commissions from associates of his magnificent court. With every satisfied customer, Ismael's reputation spread, to the benefit of the city's steadily growing Jewish community.

As the senior teacher and Rabbi of Jerusalem, Ishmael oversaw the intake and housing of Jewish immigrants arriving in Jerusalem from all over the world. His positive relationships with the Muslim governor and his officials simplified many administrative procedures for the newcomers.

The powerful sultan, Salah ad-Din Yusuf, had recaptured the Holy City from the Christians six years prior. At that point, it was utterly depopulated, so he encouraged Jews in particular to resettle there. His call was answered by many of those suffering hardship and persecution in Christian lands, who wished to finally live in peace in the lands their ancestors. Ishmael was once one of them.

Meanwhile, his work on behalf of the immigrants took up so much time that he scarcely had time to read the old scriptures he so loved, of which there were dozens stacked behind him on a shelf.

Ishmael stroked his thick, white beard, and a smile deepened the creases in his face. He gazed, blinking, through the window, and listened to the twittering birds and children's laughter. A gentle breeze wafted into the tidy little workshop on the second floor of his house, carrying with it the sweet scent of the blossoming almond tree rooted in the small courtyard below.

Fate has truly favoured me, he thought with a smile. It had only been two years since he arrived here himself as a homeless refugee.

The journey from the cold lands of Alemannia had been arduous and dangerous. He had spent almost fifty peaceful summers in Cologne, until fanatical Christian pilgrims had accused the Jews of being Jesus-murderers and jointly responsible for the loss of the Holy City to the Muslims. Wild bands of rapacious mercenaries, too poor to embark on a pilgrimage to the Holy Land, had begun to plunder and lynch his friends and neighbours. The citizens of Cologne and the nobility proved powerless, allowing the butchers to rampage unhindered. Partly because it conveniently released them from their debts to the gold-lending Jews. Ishmael escaped the carnage with a few other survivors and, despite his advanced years, saw no alternative other than to flee to his younger brother Esau in Jerusalem and start a new life there.

Esau was a widower who lived alone with his daughter Leah and ran a lucrative money-changing business. He had invited his brother long before these terrible events to live with him in the city of their forefathers. Unfortunately, they never saw one another again. Ishmael's journey was long and arduous, and a few days before he arrived in Jerusalem, Esau died of a heart attack, bequeathing him his house in the Jewish Quarter and a considerable sum of money.

Ishmael assumed guardianship of his unmarried niece Leah, as there were no other relatives in the city to take care of the young woman. Her two older brothers had left long ago to trade as wool and grain merchants in distant Antioch.

Ishmael opened a goldsmith's workshop in the house, and his business soon flourished thanks to his excellent craftsmanship and reasonable prices. His fellow Jewish citizens admired his knowledge, wisdom and godliness and quickly appointed him as their rabbi.

He was no longer pursued or humiliated in his new homeland. Here, he was under the protection of the Sultan; he paid the jizyah – a kind of poll tax that all tolerated non-Muslims in the realm had to pay – and experienced a happiness he'd seldom known before. Cologne and its bloodthirsty citizens slowly faded in his memory. But he could never forget them.

An impatient knock at the door jolted him out of his reverie.

"Uncle, uncle! Open the door please!"

Ishmael prized himself up from his stool and shuffled to the firmly barred wooden door of the workshop. Many valuables were stored here on the upper floor of their modest house: a supply of small gold and silver bars, rough diamonds, solder, lead balls, copper wire and rare tools for fashioning jewellery. There were also priceless old papyrus scrolls in which the history of the Jewish people was recorded in its entirety.

As a precaution against thieves and intruders, he had heavy hardwood bolts installed inside and out, which he now lifted out of their hasps.

The hinges creaked as he opened the door a crack and looked into his niece's dark brown eyes.

"What is it, child? I want to use what's left of the light to read by. If the food is ready, please bring it to me in here."

Leah shook her dark brown, shoulder-length locks. "No, uncle, you have a visitor. There's a Muslim at our door, and he urgently wants to speak to you."

Ishmael raised his ash-grey eyebrows. A Muslim. That was unusual. Perhaps a messenger from the governor. The bracelet wasn't due to be delivered until tomorrow, but the Emir was known for his impatience.

"Please invite him in. I'll be down in a moment. Offer him sweet tea and see that he's comfortable."

Leah nodded and hurried downstairs.

Good child, thought Ishmael, locking the window's heavy wooden shutters and crossbar. *Although she's hardly a child anymore.* His niece had seen eighteen summers, and he had to admit she had grown into a beautiful, graceful woman. Her mother had died when she was twelve. Leah had been responsible for her father's household from a young age, and had taken care of her two brothers until they left for Antioch, where they now lived independently. Leah had diligently attended to her father's bookkeeping. His sudden death after a brief illness hit her hard. Considerate, friendly and compassionate, she now took care of her uncle, who was delighted to have her capable assistance in his old age.

His creaking knees rankled, and walking was no longer easy for him. He shuffled across the workshop and laid the bracelet in a little walnut box lined with green silk, which he carefully stowed in a drawer in his workbench. Upon leaving the room,

10

he closed the door firmly behind him and carefully locked it with a padlock, before cautiously descending the stairs that led directly into the living room.

He saw at once that it was not an emissary of the great Sultan sipping his tea and lounging on the beautifully embroidered cushions that Leah had carefully arranged on a carpet in the centre of the room. The stranger wore a ragged, faded green robe. His dirty, grey turban and filth-encrusted wooden sandals made him look more like one of those dark, Syrian waste collectors who drove to the gate every evening to tip the city's refuse into deep holes and crevices outside the fortified walls. He looked very young. He was small, underfed, and his dark, restless eyes peered at Ishmael from under a mop of brown curls that fell in a tangle across his forehead. A faint shadow on his smooth cheeks and upper lip hinted at the beginnings of a beard.

When the Muslim saw Ishmael, he leapt up, and a heavy object wrapped in tattered rags clattered from his lap to the floor. He immediately picked it up, clasped it to his chest and bowed deeply. *Too deeply*, thought Ishmael, *even Muslim waste collectors usually treat Jews less respectfully than their cargo.*

"*As-salamu aleikum!*" the Arab rasped hastily, glancing humbly into Ishmael's crinkled face. Ishmael eyed the visitor with surprise. Muslims never greeted Jews first. Their pride toward the infidel scripture-readers didn't allow it.

"Shalom," Ishmael replied coolly, gesturing for the stranger to resume his seat.

"Are you Ishmael, the wise goldsmith, and the Ishmael that the Jews call the old rabbi?" asked the visitor. A hesitant smile revealed a row of gleaming white teeth, whose immaculate condition contrasted starkly with his ragged exterior. His dark eyes darted restlessly, as if he perceived danger in every corner of the room.

11

"No, I'm the Caliph of Baghdad," replied Ishmael gruffly. "Of course I am he."

"Yes, of course. Forgive me," The Arab bowed nervously. "My name is Harit ibn Tharit ibn..."

"Please spare me your family history! One name is enough for me," the rabbi interrupted rudely upon noticing the clumps of mud dropping from the man's filthy sandals onto his precious, silk-threaded carpet. It was the most beautiful item in the otherwise modestly furnished but well-kept house.

The man nodded earnestly. "Then just call me Harit."

"Well, what do you want from me?"

The Muslim glanced around, as if he suspected the walls had ears, and whispered, "I've come to offer to sell you something. Something valuable, I think – in fact, I believe it's very valuable!"

Ishmael stiffened. Another of these people who believed Jews would buy any of the old junk that piled up every day from the countless pilgrims who visited the eminent city.

"Leave my house, I don't want to buy anything. I don't care what you have!" he said brusquely.

Harit bit his lower lip in disappointment and lifted the bulging sack from his knees. "Please, just look at it! You won't regret it!"

Ishmael sighed and nodded. Mercy and compassion were rare enough in this world, and the young man before him was clearly in need of both.

Even though the two of them were alone in the room, Harit glanced around once again. Then he carefully unwrapped the package. A gleaming, dark grey figurine emerged, roughly a cubit long, half a cubit wide and half a cubit high. A winged lion with a human head, its feathered arms stretched out in front of it and its head slightly lowered. A cherub.

Astonishment flashed across Ishmael's face. It was clearly a very old, beautifully crafted effigy of one of the guardians God posted in front of Paradise to watch over the tree of life. The ancient lore described cherubim just like this. Christians and Muslims called them angels. For the Jews, the protectors of the sacred Ark of the Covenant were a symbol of their connection to God through their faith. The acacia reliquary contained the Ten Commandments of the Lord chiselled in stone, which Moses himself had received from the Almighty on Mount Sinai. The Ark bore two cherubim of pure gold on its lid and, according to the old scriptures, God's presence on earth was situated between them.

This holiest relic of his people was said to be lost, stolen thousands of years ago.

He carefully took the cherub from the Muslim's hands. The figurine was surprisingly heavy. Almost three pounds, he estimated as he studied it professionally from all angles.

Harit was pleased by the Jew's interest, and his eyes shone. "It might be made of stone or even copper. Isn't it pretty? I didn't promise too much, did I? Look, there's even a little gold on it."

Possibly cast in lead, Ishmael guessed, because his fingers blackened when he rubbed its surface firmly. *Or bronze.* Indeed, there were some tiny traces of gold to be seen in a few places. Its material value seemed low. Clearly, it was an expertly made replica of the original – the shape and size, at least, matched the descriptions precisely.

"Well, what do you think? It's worth something, isn't it? Will you buy it?" Harit was becoming impatient and the questions bubbled out of him.

"Hmm... it appears to be lead or bronze. A casting. I can't do much with it, but it's nice to look at. So that you quickly leave my house, I'll give you a dirham for it. Unfortunately, it's not worth more than that," said Ishmael, handing the figurine back. Harit held up his hands in a gesture of refusal.

"Three dirham and by Allah, it's yours. I have other things like it outside on my cart. Perhaps we could agree on a lump sum for everything?"

Ishmael shrugged. "Oh, I don't know. Where did you get them? I hope they're not stolen, because that would make me liable if I bought them from you."

Harit secretly rejoiced. It seemed he had found another buyer, after having sold a similar figurine for a dirham that morning to a Frankish pilgrim in the *suq* – the city's large, bustling, covered market. That infidel had also asked about the origin of the half-human, half-bird statue, but seemed quite satisfied with Harit's explanation.

"I work for the Emir of our magnanimous Sultan, Izz ad-Din Yurdik, may Allah grant him good health! He commissions me to clear away the debris left years ago by the infidel Jesus-worshippers, the damned Nazarenes. I perform my work in the huge cellars under *al haram ash-sharif*, the holy site from which Mohammed rose into the heavens. The mosque is currently being rebuilt, and below it are high vaults containing a lot of rubble and stones. The evil Templars – may Allah punish them for their crimes against us true believers – used to keep horses there until our glorious Sultan drove them out. If I find something that the infidels left behind in their haste, I must inform my overseer. He decides whether it's of value to our Emir. If not, then I can do with it as I will. Usually I cart the junk out to the refuse trenches."

He wasn't being entirely truthful. To supplement his meagre wage, he sold his finds. He didn't dare ask his overseer for permission. It wasn't theft in his eyes, nevertheless he was careful and took great pains to conduct his business as discreetly as possible.

Harit cleared his throat, sipped his tea and continued, "While I was working, I discovered an unremarkable door at the bottom of a staircase, which led to a small room. I stored this dusty figurine and other objects there. My overseer thought they were worthless, but I knew better, so I packed them on my cart, and here I am!"

Ishmael regarded him thoughtfully. The Arab dug around in the holiest sites of Judaism, which Jews had not been allowed to enter since the Christians conquered Jerusalem. Nor did the current Muslim rulers permit it. The place he spoke of so candidly must certainly be King Solomon's fabled horse stables. Al Aqsa mosque had been built on the foundations of the Jewish temple, which the barbaric Romans had destroyed over a thousand years ago. They subsequently drove out the Jews, scattering them all over the world. The beginning of a long road of suffering.

The place had served the proud and merciless Templars as their headquarters and church in the Holy Land since the conquest of Jerusalem almost a hundred years ago, until Sultan Salah ad-Din chased them out of the city. The vaulted Temple Mount had been shrouded since ancient times in legends of precious treasures – and still was, though nothing had ever been found.

Ishmael's curiosity was aroused. *Perhaps there's more to be found down there than just a leaden cherub? Perhaps... the mighty Ark of the Covenant? Impossible... That would be too good to be true.*

The thought made the blood rush to his head and he began to sweat.

"Trust me, rabbi. As I said, the refuse was searched by the overseer and handed over to me. I can do what I want with it. You can buy it from me without any misgivings. Come, I'll show you the rest!"

The anxious Harit had noticed the Jew's face suddenly flush red. Dealing in stolen goods was punishable by death in the Sultan's realm. The goldsmith would naturally be circumspect.

Ishmael nodded. "Alright, let's go to your cart. Show me what else you have to peddle." He placed the cherub carefully on the floor.

Harit rose cheerfully and helped the old man to his feet. Ishmael's knees cracked loudly as he stood up.

They left the house and stepped out onto the empty street that snaked through the small, convoluted Jewish quarter in north Jerusalem. All they heard was the chirping of cicadas and their own quiet footfalls on the sand. Evening was drawing in. The blood-red sun hung low above the gables and cast long shadows down the alley. Many of the city's inhabitants had finished their day's work and retreated into their cool houses.

The Muslim led Ishmael to his rickety handcart standing two houses further up the street by a locked gate. He continued to glance around him as if he feared he had been followed, but there was no one in sight. Reassured, Harit flung back the threadbare woollen blanket that covered the cart.

There were several rusty nails, a bent iron crucifix, gleaming silver chandelier parts, two well-preserved stirrups and a multitude of pottery shards decorated with Christian symbols. The most valuable-looking objects in this pile of junk were four dark, metal rings hanging from tastefully forged hinges.

"I'll leave it all with you for..." Harit swept his arm in an inviting gesture, "...for ten dirham."

He noticed the Jew's unenthusiastic expression as he sceptically surveyed the supposed treasures, and added, "Fine, I can see you're interested and I'm not unreasonable. Eight coins would suffice."

Ishmael's eyes wandered over the junk and stopped on two pale grey stone slabs, their corners jutting out from under the debris in the back of the cart. He stepped closer and carefully pulled one of them out in the red light of the setting sun.

It was two cubits long, one cubit wide, two thumbs thick, and when he picked it up, it felt about twice as heavy as the cherub.

He carefully wiped away a layer of accumulated dust with his hand, revealing small, engraved letters.

Squinting, he tried to decipher them. He knew this script. He had old, tattered papyrus rolls in his collection with similar lettering, which described the trade relations of a long-lost seafaring people during the reign of the pharaohs. His fingers ran slowly over the unusually warm stone, following the lines of the script.

I am YHWH, your God, who brought you out of Egypt, out of the land of slavery.

After translating the painstakingly engraved Phoenician characters, he shuddered. The Ten Commandments of God began that way! The first five were engraved here. He hurriedly drew out the second stone slab, studied it closely and shook his white head incredulously. Like the other tablet, this one had another five Commandments chiselled into it.

The rabbi's knees weakened, he staggered back and steadied himself with a hand on the Muslim's shoulder.

"What's wrong?" asked Harit, alarmed. "You look like you've just glimpsed the fiery pits of hell!"

Ishmael couldn't answer. The words of the *Sefer Shemot,* the second book of Moses, thundered through his head like a storm unleashed: *Thou shalt put into the Ark the testimony which I shall give thee. And there was nothing in the Ark except the two stone tablets that Moses had placed in it at Horeb, where the LORD made a covenant with the Israelites after they came out of Egypt.*

If he wasn't mistaken, what lay before him were the exceptionally well-preserved remains of the holiest of the holy: the contents of the Ark of the Covenant. The long-lost, most precious treasure in the world!

After it was delivered, the Ark is said to have been robbed by heathen Babylonians and has never been seen since. But... are these really the sacred contents of the Ark of the Covenant lying here? They appear to be... and, of all people, an unbelieving Muslim was the one chosen to find them? I must have certainty... Oh, God... If it's true...

Ishmael was speechless, torn this way and that by his turbulent thoughts. He heard the young Arab's voice as though from a distance, babbling about payment. As if money were important now! He reached irritably into the pouch at his belt and counted out twenty silver dirham with trembling fingers.

"I... I'll buy all of it. But there must be a second winged figurine. Did you find that too?" he wheezed.

At the sight of all the coins, Harit was momentarily lost for words. He held the gleaming pieces close to his eyes. He didn't earn this much in three weeks of hard drudgery. He wanted to beat himself over the head for not coming to the Jew earlier. Instead he'd sold the first figurine to a Nazarene pilgrim for a price that was clearly too low.

He pictured the tall man with the blue eyes; the way he smugly stowed the cheaply acquired statue into his pilgrim's sack, and quickly melted away into the thronging market crowds.

"Yes, there is a second figurine, and perhaps I can bring it to you. But that must be worth another..." Harit faltered "...shall we say... twenty dirham?"

"Fine! You'll have them... I must have the second cherub," said Ishmael, more to himself than to the surprised Arab, who immediately began pondering the fastest way to locate the pilgrim. For twenty silver pieces, he would search every corner of the city to reverse the bad deal he'd struck with him.

The goldsmith held his breath, carefully placed the stone tablets one on top of the other, lifted them off the cart and carried them like an armful of raw eggs into his home.

By Allah, I don't know what it is about this junk, but it appears to be very valuable to the old man. Harit refrained from enquiring. The crazy Jew might regain his senses and ask for his money back. He bundled the other objects in the dirty blanket and followed the goldsmith in silence.

Stopping in the middle of the living room, Ishmael pressed the stone tablets tightly against his chest and indicated with a nod for Harit to put the bundle down against the wall in a corner.

"Go now and fetch me the second statue! Bring it to me... as quickly as you can, please..." whispered the goldsmith. Fat beads of sweat glued his hair to his scalp, his voice became shrill and his eyes rolled in his head. "I'll pay you what you ask!"

"It's alright... calm yourself. I'll get it for you. But you'll have to wait until tomorrow morning," said Harit with a look of concern. *I hope he lives to see another day. The frail little man is swaying like a reed in the wind.*

"What? Yes, fine... until the morning... promise me!"

"I promise," said Harit doubtfully, not entirely sure he could keep his word. But he would certainly try his best to buy the second figurine back from the pilgrim – for three, maybe even five dirham. Then he would still have an incredible fifteen silver coins. He couldn't let such a lucrative deal slip through his fingers.

Harit was suddenly in a hurry to leave. He hastily bowed and said goodbye, leaving the Jew's house with a full money pouch and a confident smile.

Ishmael stood alone in the centre of the room, not wanting to put down the unspeakably precious tablets. He couldn't think of a better place for the Commandments than against his heart. Sweat ran down his cheeks and his head throbbed. Through the feeling of unspeakable joy flashed a nagging doubt. Doubts about the authenticity, doubts about reality, doubts about the truth.

What if it's just a replica? A fake? I have to find out. Today!

Leah entered the room, humming quietly. She had prepared warm flatbreads with olive oil, thinking she would invite the supposed Sultan's emissary to dinner. Hospitality was valued highly in the household. Although, she thought the stranger looked more like a young day labourer searching for work. But she had learned from a young age that you couldn't always judge a person's status by their clothing. Her uncle, for example, wore very modest, almost destitute-looking robes that revealed nothing of his excellent reputation in the Holy City, as an important rabbi and craftsman of considerable means.

She was startled when she noticed her uncle's waxen, sweaty face. He was clutching two grey tablets so firmly to his chest that his white knuckles looked like they might dislocate at any moment.

"Is everything alright? Where's our guest?" she asked with concern.

"It's nothing, my child. It's nothing, I'm fine. The little Muslim has gone," he replied vacantly, then stiffened. "I must go straight to my workshop! I mustn't be disturbed, do you hear? By anyone!"

He turned abruptly and trudged resolutely up the stairs.

Puzzled and a little worried, Leah watched him go.

II

His sins clung to him like leprous skin. He was regarded with fear and dismay by some of the other Templars at prayer time. A few even crossed themselves at the sight of him, as if in the presence of Satan incarnate.

For the last two weeks, the regular prayers at Sext in the religious Order's unadorned church was the only time Brother Guillaume de Born could leave his prison and move freely. At least they still permitted that.

His desolate cell, with its walls of rough limestone, was four paces long and two paces wide. After the service, he paced around it in restless circles. In one corner, a straw mattress on the compacted dirt floor served as a bed. The room was otherwise empty. A small, barred window let in scant daylight and the cold damp of a winter's afternoon.

Miracles no longer came to pass in the Holy Land, he was sure of that. The last had occurred here over a thousand years ago, and today he finally abandoned his half-hearted prayers for a personal miracle. He was the last person the Almighty was likely to answer. As so often before, he would have to help himself.

Guillaume bit morosely into a hunk of bread. It was as hard as wood and only passably edible after being dunked in water.

He carefully ran his tongue through the half-chewed pulp in his mouth. Grains of sand and small stones often found their way into the low-quality barley flour that was baked into cheap bread for the servants and squires. Only the noble Templar knights got to enjoy the pale, soft, tasty loaves made of high quality wheat.

Until his final hearing, he wasn't permitted to dine at a table with the warriors of the brotherhood, as decreed by Grand

Master Robert de Sablé. He received a little meat once a week in a cracked wooden bowl, and otherwise nothing but millet porridge, stale bread and water.

To think that he of all people should fall into such disgrace – the Order's *turcopolier,* in command of three hundred light cavalry for the last five years, who themselves had successfully supported the heavily armoured Templars with their bows and arrows in countless battles against the Saracens.

It was largely thanks to him that this ragtag bunch of mercenaries from all corners of the world had become such indispensable, experienced fighters. His position was now highly regarded within the Order, giving him power and influence. In times of war, even the sergeants – the serving non-noble members of the Templar brotherhood – reported to him.

Guillaume shivered, spat a small stone through the window and looked down into the courtyard of the Templar fortress to see a couple of squires erect three large table tops on trestles and then stack dozens of clattering wooden bowls on them. The daily preparations had begun for the feeding of the poor at vespers.

Not a single damned heathen has succeeded in killing me, but this pigswill might do it. Damn it, I can hardly choke the stuff down.

He swallowed the tasteless mass in disgust and hastily washed it down with a mouthful of cold water from a small clay jug. He turned away from the window and crouched again on the cold floor with his back to the wall.

Guillaume's uncertain fate gnawed at him. The Grand Master should have long since convened the Chapter of the brothers to pass final judgement on him. Clearly, they were still not in agreement on some of the sinful charges.

For a long time, there had been mutterings among the brothers that Guillaume interpreted the strict rules of the Order too loosely for himself, but they had made concessions for him. His close friendship with the Marshal, Raoul de Garlande, and Guillaume's reputation as a fearless fighter and prudent leader had thus far shielded him from repercussions.

But underestimating the conscience of the squire Pierre had been his biggest mistake. Guillaume wrinkled his nose and stared at the floor of his cell as he cast his mind back.

The milky-faced, pretty boy wasn't in his service for long. His innocent, subservient eyes, full lips and effeminate manner excited Guillaume. He tried to make a man out of him, but failed utterly. He ordered the boy to accompany him on one of his secret, boozy tours of the rank pleasure houses in the harbour, and filled him with sweet, red Cyprian wine until he could barely stand. Then he led him into the back room of a dingy tavern, where two fat, giggling girls were waiting for them on a straw mattress. Pierre promptly sank between the thighs of one of the whores and licked her loudly, as if slurping out a pot of honey. In doing so, he stuck his well-formed backside up in the air, and Guillaume initially mistook the squire for one of the girls.

At first, Pierre moaned sensually as he felt his master's cock in his arse. But then he began to whimper and cry out, unsure whether from shame or pain, and tried in vain to fend him off. Guillaume, too drunk and too horny to pay any attention to his howls, twisted the squire's arm behind his back and pressed his head hard into the giggling woman's snatch. He gave a shout as he came in the boy's anus, then slurred something and let go of him, to the whores' exuberant applause. The defiled lad grabbed his things and fled, half-naked, with tears streaming down his face and the girls' derisive jeering echoing loudly after him.

Pierre rushed, sobbing, back to the Templar fortress. Overcome with shame and disgust, he woke the chaplain and confessed his rape, out of genuine fear of hellfire and eternal damnation. He accused Guillaume as a corrupter and rapist of a subordinate, thereby releasing the clergyman from the seal of the confessional.

The chaplain was shocked. He calmed the trembling lad and sent him to his chamber. The next morning he informed the Grand Master, who reacted swiftly, as if he'd been waiting for such an opportunity.

Guillaume was arrested on his return to the Temple. He instantly forfeited his white habit – the cloak of the Templar and the most visible sign of his high status. Thenceforth he had to wear rough, dark sacking. His sword, lance, shield and chainmail were confiscated and he was only permitted to leave his cell for the daily mass. For the time being, the Grand Master had not put him in chains. Serious accusations by a lowly squire against a noble knight called for thorough investigation before harsh measures were enacted.

Guillaume didn't hesitate to exploit this advantage. The naïve and unsuspecting squire visited his former master in his cell one moonless night. It was never his intention to accuse the turcopolier, he insisted with a stammer. The chaplain had pressured him. He only wanted to confess and receive absolution for his sin of sodomy. He never meant to harm Guillaume. He was so incredibly sorry that his commander was being punished so severely.

Careless words could inflict deeper wounds than swords. Guillaume looked at the witless squire with a sympathetic expression and took him in his arms as if to comfort and forgive him. But then he snapped his neck with a powerful wrench. With great effort, he dragged the body unseen up the church tower and let it fall.

Thinking back to that night, Guillaume scowled, and his face set in a fierce grimace. If the foolish lad hadn't come to him, he'd still be alive. *Little Pierre will never again open his loud mouth to accuse anyone. The blame for his death is not on me.*

Later, Pierre's night-time fall from the roof of the church was viewed by all as understandable self-punishment for his own sins. But the act was an unforgivable crime in the eyes of God – decisions of life and death were His alone. Now the boy lay in unconsecrated ground outside the city walls, as was customary in the case of suicides.

Through Guillaume's window came the excited hubbub of a large gathering of people. He stood again and gazed down.

The feeding of the poor had begun. Starvelings, layabouts and beggars gathered every day at noon in large numbers in the courtyard of the Templar fortress. They were now shouting, cursing and thronging around the tables that bore the remains of the warrior monks' midday meal in pots and willow baskets. Seven serving brothers distributed the food and poured weak beer. An armed Templar knight attempted to bring order to the ragged, filthy, vermin-infested crowd, who were in danger of upturning the tables in their ravenous desperation.

Guillaume had also performed this duty many years ago when he first joined the Order. They were still repellent to him – the diseased, the maimed and the stranded who had arrived in the Holy Land full of joy and hope and found nothing but a life of misery. Acre had decayed into a city of scum and rabble since the heathen Sultan Saladin had laid waste to the Latin Kingdom with his hordes of warriors, and thousands of refugees had spilled out into the narrow strip of coast that was still in Christian hands.

The needy people tore cups and bowls from each other's hands and hastily swallowed the contents, much of which was vomited back up on the spot because their starved, shrunken stomachs were unaccustomed to solid food.

Guillaume felt nauseated when he recalled the sour smell. He never wanted to end up like that, and turned morosely away from the window. Having lost his appetite, he wrapped the remains of the hard bread in a scrap of linen and flung it disdainfully on the bed. Then he crouched once more with his back to the wall.

He was again plagued by anxiety about how he would be dealt with. Sodomy called for dishonourable discharge from the Order; incarceration for life was also a possibility. Transgressions with women were punished with the loss of the white habit for a year and a day, if the Templar rules were interpreted generously. On the other hand, he had done everything in his power to avoid a conviction. And he was hoping for the support of his best friend, Marshal Raoul de Garlande.

Heavy footfalls rapped along the walkway outside his door, snapping him out of his reverie. Perhaps he was about to gain some certainty in all this. A Templar in full armour, with his helmet under his arm, entered Guillaume's unlocked cell without knocking.

The blood-red cross formée on the shoulder of the snow-white cloak looked as if it had been freshly sewn on, and caught Guillaume's eye immediately. He recently had such a magnificent habit to call his own. He scratched his itching throat, rubbed raw by the hard neck of his coarse tunic.

Nicholas de Seagrave, his temporary replacement as commander of the turcopoles.

Brother Nicholas had come to the Holy Land many years ago as part of King Richard's entourage, and had joined the Knights Templar soon after. Guillaume was baffled and aggrieved when he heard the Grand Master had appointed this pale yellow man to lead the auxiliary troops in his stead.

He had always privately mocked Nicholas' huge head, which reminded him with its close-set, sunken eyes of a gourd with two holes poked into the flesh. Guillaume considered him a cruel, vain sycophant, who grovelled before his superiors, told them what they wanted to hear, and bullied his subordinates. With men of equal rank, however, he was friendly and fond of telling bawdy jokes.

But he was a good warrior in battle – seasoned and brave – which was why Guillaume intended to help Nicholas find his feet in his temporary post, until he himself was reinstated. Perhaps he would be also able to control him, despite his reservations.

Nicholas glanced around the desolate room, noticed the leather whip beside Guillaume's straw bed and picked it up with a frown.

"You shouldn't do that. It's not part of your punishment."

Guillaume feigned a tortured smile and got to his feet, brushing breadcrumbs out of his shaggy beard. He stood two spans taller than Nicholas.

"It's a penance I've chosen for myself, Brother Nicholas. I'm praying to the Lord that, through the pain of the whip, he'll free me from the unbelievable charges against me, because I have nothing to blame myself for," he lied shamelessly. He wouldn't whip himself with that thing if he were paid to. It was gift from the chaplain, who had flung it into the room five days ago with an indignant glance, ostentatiously keeping his distance and muttering a prayer of protection.

The knight nodded sympathetically. "Many of the fighting brothers miss you. They say they would still gladly stand together under your command. No one really believes you committed those shameful acts. There's no evidence and no witnesses."

No, there are none of those, thought Guillaume. *The one who could have borne witness is dead.*

Nicholas threw the whip onto the bed with distaste.

"In any case, I don't know how I'll fill this post as well as you have. The responsibility weighs heavy, and every day there's an awful lot to be done. Until now, I've only had to take care of myself, and now I'm supposed to keep a wild bunch of godless mercenaries in harmony with the strict tenets of the Order and train them. Syrians, Armenians, Italians, Spaniards, converted Muslims. They won't move a muscle without being paid. The scoundrels are disorderly, voracious and greedy. I don't find it easy to control them. And then there's the problem of my inadequate command of the Saracen language. That's probably why many of them don't take me seriously. Perhaps our Grand Master has finally realised it was a mistake to take your habit from you and entrust me with the command of the auxiliary troops. I'm to take you to the Palace."

Guillaume looked at him in surprise, but Nicholas' gaze flickered past him to the floor. Guillaume had noticed this quirk often in the past few weeks.

"Ahhh... escorted by a knight. Is he going to banish me from the Order? Or throw me in the dungeon?"

Nicholas shook his head. "No, I don't think so. You've been a Templar for over twelve years, sent countless heathens to hell and fought in innumerable battles. You even survived the Battle of the Horns of Hattin, when Sultan Saladin pulverised the Christian army of the Kingdom of Jerusalem in a single day and had the hacked-off head of almost every Templar in the land impaled on his horsemen's spears. Together, we conquered Acre, and defeated the Sultan's armies at King Richard's side in the forest of Arsuf. You are highly esteemed among the brothers. I don't know of a better warrior than you!"

Guillaume was bored by this flattery and shrugged.

"You're probably right. My innocence will be proven. And don't worry, brother, I'll help you in whatever way I can with your difficult new duties, which I'm sure you won't have to shoulder for long. No one learns to lead these wild warriors overnight. It took me many years, and I had to learn the heathen language to train the men into worthy fighters for our holy cause."

Nicholas' face broke into a broad grin and he clapped Guillaume on the shoulders, visibly relieved.

"I'll be glad to accept your help."

They left the cell, descended to the ground floor of the building that contained the men's quarters, and crossed the courtyard. They passed the horde of paupers eating huddled on the ground, and strode to the Palace containing the chapter house.

III

The massive Palace abutted a thirty-foot-high defence wall, and was the largest building in the Templar fortress in northeast Acre. It served as a gathering place for the brothers, where new members were ceremonially accepted into the brotherhood and important guests were received. Built of pale limestone, it towered impressively into the overcast sky. The facade was adorned with six huge arches and at its centre were the usual pair of massive, iron-bound wooden doors, embellished with carvings depicting the stations of the cross.

Today one was ajar, and Nicholas leaned his shoulder against it to open it wide. They entered.

They were greeted by a cool stillness, and it took Guillaume a moment to adjust to the gloom in the high-ceilinged hall. Brother Nicholas bowed slightly and left without a word. The door clanged shut behind him.

At the rear of the hall stood a row of thirteen roughly hewn armchairs. These were for the Templars' Convent, comprised of eight carefully selected knights, four ministering brothers and the chaplain as the embodiment of the presence of the Almighty. A heavy, dark oak cross hung from the wall above the chairs, reaching all the way to the ceiling. Below it sat Grand Master Robert de Sablé. Guillaume was surprised to be received by him alone.

The Grand Master's pale, creased face slowly emerged from the half-dark as he leaned forward. His hair was shorn and a well-groomed, ice-grey beard fell to his chest. He was wrapped in a dark grey, woollen blanket against the cold, his hands hidden beneath it. Below a high brow, his watery, grey-blue eyes fixed Guillaume with a piercing gaze.

"Kneel!"

The stern command came without warning and echoed off the smooth stone walls. Guillaume obeyed, sinking to his knees and staring blankly at the rough floor strewn with reeds.

They couldn't abide one another. Guillaume was already turcopolier of the Knights Templar when Robert de Sablé was elected as Grand Master two years ago, at the insistence of Richard the Lionheart. De Sablé's predecessor, the impetuous and hapless Gérard de Ridefort, had fallen in one of the many battles around the city of Acre. For a long time, the Templars couldn't agree on a successor. They needed a leader who wouldn't throw himself into the front lines of battle, who wore the sword merely as an ornament of his post and who would guide the fate of the Order with a cool head.

In the end, the English king used his influence to insert the ageing admiral of his fleet, Robert de Sablé, into this high and influential position.

Much to the annoyance of Guillaume, who feared for his freedom and privileges, which had steadily expanded over the years. De Sablé took the rules and the holy mission of the Templars very seriously. Initially he had seemed amiable and understanding, but the brothers soon felt the effects of his firm hand. Anyone who didn't unconditionally obey him knew his days in the brotherhood were numbered.

The grand master slowly leaned back in his chair.

"Well, Brother Guillaume… Your conduct is almost too monstrous for the brothers to ever find it in themselves to forgive you," he droned. "Lying with a woman is a serious enough of breach of our rules. But to engage in sodomy with two whores and another brother, at the same time in the same room, is truly grounds enough for eternal damnation! It's a good thing Brother Pierre informed us. How regrettable that he had to be buried out in the open, in unconsecrated ground, as a heretical suicide."

Guillaume looked up and gazed steadily into the Grand Master's eyes. "I'm innocent! Brother Pierre, as I suspected, had long since succumbed to carnal lust. So I followed him as he secretly left the fortress, to catch him in the act. Which I did. Unfortunately, he saw me and shamelessly accused *me* of his own unspeakable crime."

He lowered his gaze in disgust. "It's a disgrace that the Order is more inclined to believe him than me! I…"

"Silence!" De Sablé cut him off harshly and, after a moment's icy silence, said, "Following the statement from Brother Pierre, I was justified in temporarily relieving you of your duties and your habit. Unfortunately, we've been unable to find those wicked women. In the whorehouse in the harbour that Brother Pierre named, no one could recall having seen them or the two of you. It's possible those two harlots could have confirmed the deed, and then you'd be banished from the Order for life!"

The Grand Master paused to catch his breath and then continued impatiently, "Now, as there's no one left to bear witness to the damnable sin, and as you continue to protest your innocence, I have to take the word of a Templar knight against that of a man who committed suicide. We now have to reconsider your case."

Yes, you do, Guillaume thought smugly to himself. *Breaking Pierre's neck was easier than I thought. But dragging him five dozen steps up the tower, quickly and unseen, and then throwing him down, was incredibly arduous. And you should know, as a former admiral, that there are more whores than fish in any great trading port. Anyway, the girls, like me, were full to the brim with rich red wine. Even if you tracked them down, they probably wouldn't remember.*

"So, hear my decision: you will have an opportunity to prove your worth to the Order. We know you speak the infidels' language. For this reason, you were previously in command of the heathens converted to the true faith who now fight on our side. Your knowledge of the old scriptures from your time at the monastery also counts in your favour. The brothers value your courage, your experience in battle and your good relationships with important Saracen merchants. I have an extremely urgent task for you. Listen carefully. What I'm about to say, you must reveal to no one. If you do, it will have dire consequences for you."

De Sablé's eyes bored into him. Guillaume fought to suppress his elation and meet the gaze of those moist frog eyes without showing emotion. The charges against him actually appeared to be off the table. Finally an end to his ignominy.

"Do you agree to undertake a strictly secret mission for our Order?"

"Wherever this mission for the Almighty takes me, I will fulfil his wish and keep silent," Guillaume replied. He paused demonstratively.

An easier mission would be to press your fat eyes into your wrinkly skull with my thumbs, you slimy toad, he thought, adding aloud, "Not to us, oh Lord, not to us, but to your name give glory. I will do whatever you demand of me."

The grand master nodded contentedly at the mention of the Templar motto. He raised his head imperiously. "We command you thus: ride to Jerusalem disguised as a pilgrim, with a rich fortune in gold and silver. There you will secretly seek out members of the heathen Assassins sect. Some of them are said to live there in secret while maintaining their connection to their leader Sinan, the Old Man of the Mountain. They have paid tribute to us in the past, as you know, and have served the Temple once before…"

De Sablé broke off. Guillaume mustn't know too much. The murder of King Conrad half a year ago had been his most daring and successful piece of work since becoming Grand Master.

Guillaume noticed Robert's hesitation. So, the suspicions might be true, that the English King Richard and the Templars had commissioned the assassination of the stubborn Conrad of Montferat, in order to maintain their influence in the Kingdom of Jerusalem. The Lionheart's nephew, Count Henry of Champagne, had married Conrad's widow only eight days later and reigned as king of Acre ever since. The rumours had quickly spread amongst the barons of the Holy Land and circulated in every tavern in the city.

"We require the services of the Assassins once again," de Sablé continued. "But we can't reach their leader, who is residing in the fortress at Masyaf in the far north, in the mountains near the city of Antioch. The road is blocked by the heathen troops of that damned Saladin. Jerusalem, however, was opened to Christian pilgrims by the Sultan a few months ago. You're sure to be able to track down the Assassins there. I heard you were in their fortress many years ago and traded with them, so you'll be aware of their sensitivities. You must come to an arrangement with them whereby they rid of a loathsome enemy of Christendom: Bohemond of Antioch. Commission them to kill the prince. If you succeed, you'll rejoin our ranks a Templar, regain your white cloak and be restored to your position as turcopolier."

The Grand Master leaned back and cocked his head to study the effect of his words on the fallen Templar.

Guillaume was glad to be kneeling and not standing when he heard this monstrous proposition. He swayed a little, but quickly composed himself and lowered his gaze in feigned humility.

What an abysmally duplicitous and heinous plan. The god-fearing Knights Templar actually wanted to commission the most dangerous of all heathens to commit a murder. Bohemond of Antioch, no less, a man of the faith, a prince and ruler over one of the last cities still in Christian hands. It was a monstrous violation of the Templars' code, which unambiguously obliged them to protect the lives of Christians under any circumstances.

"What crime has the prince committed that…"

De Sablé interrupted sharply, "That's not your concern. All you need to know is that he's conspiring with the heathens against us. And… he's been branded by our supreme leader, His Holiness the Pope, as a heretic. He has married three times, even though his first two wives still live. He's a stammering fornicator, doesn't pay his debts, and all attempts to guide him back to the righteous path of God have been in vain. He mocked, humiliated and incarcerated our emissary. We've pleaded with him time and again to refrain from his godless activities. Finally, we issued a warning, which he disregarded. He has no respect, no fear of God and no honour. There's no other way!"

The Grand Master had become so agitated that his long beard was flecked with spittle. He reached for the silver goblet on his armrest and drank a large mouthful of the undiluted red wine.

Guillaume nodded thoughtfully. He knew the stammering prince well, and he knew his beautiful, power-hungry wife Sibylle, who was also utterly insatiable in bed. He had met her years ago. Her sharp fingernails had left deep, bloody scratches on his back. It wasn't news to him that Bohemond was in dizzying amounts of debt to the Templars. He himself had voted in the Convent of the Templars four years ago to approve the funds for Bohemond, who had asked them for a credit to fortify Antioch against the Armenians and Turks.

Since then, the prince had roundly rejected the proposal that he hand over two castles in his realm to the Order, asserting that repayment was out of the question in these tumultuous times.

The stubborn and devious Bohemond was clearly trying to stall for time until the issue was forgotten. But Templars never forgot.

"In God's name, I will obey my orders and fulfil the mission to the complete satisfaction of the brotherhood," said Guillaume, bowing his head reverently.

The Grand Master gave a satisfied smile. This action would bring good fortune to the Order. Not only because the scurrilous, defaulting prince was a constant irritation, but also because his independent principality would be annexed by the dwindling Kingdom of Jerusalem. This was the subject of a secret agreement between de Sablé and King Henry. The King in turn would grant the Templars special privileges in the Christian-ruled, second-largest city in the Holy Land.

"Tomorrow, at the ninth hour, you'll join a pilgrim train departing for the Holy City from the House of the Knights Hospitaller. We will exempt you from our rules of attire during this time. Trim your beard a little and always wear a cap over your short hair, so that you're not recognised as one of us. You will be given a mule, a thousand gold bezants to pay the infidels and three hundred and sixty deniers in silver for your own expenses."

De Sablé lowered his voice and leaned forward. "Don't disappoint us, Guillaume. Let me be perfectly clear: you must speak to no one of your mission. Swear by the Lord God and by our brotherhood, that you will die before disclosing its secret. No one – not a beggar nor a king nor an infidel nor a Christian. Not even in dire emergency!"

"By God, I swear it!" Guillaume's voice was steady, as was his gaze as it met Brother Robert's narrowed, searching eyes.

"Rise, Brother Guillaume. And go with God." The Grand Master leaned back and waved him away as if he were a pesky fly. Guillaume stood, weak at the knees, and left the hall.

Once Guillaume was gone, the only sound in the cool Palace was the Grand Master's wheezing breath.

De Sablé slowly rubbed his numb hands. He was certain Guillaume had committed the crimes he was accused of, but he couldn't prove it. If he could, he would be rid of that irritating, pustular pimple on his arse. Sodomy was a deadly sin. Brother Pierre had tearfully reported the misdeed to the chaplain, down to the smallest detail. *A shame he flung himself to his death. Or foolishly allowed his unscrupulous bedfellow to kill him. I wouldn't put it past Guillaume to have had a hand in it.*

The former turcopolier divided the brotherhood. He still enjoyed the highest respect from some of the brothers. They didn't believe the horrendous accusations, assuming it was an attempt at defamation because Guillaume openly entered into profitable negotiations with the Muslims instead of bloody war. But others considered him a traitor for exactly that reason, and thought he deserved to be punished severely.

Removing the disrespectful sinner from the Temple for a while, and simultaneously assigning him to a dangerous mission from which he likely wouldn't return, was the best course of action.

De Sablé heard a clattering sound and looked around to see Brother Nicholas, who had crept in through a side entrance and hidden himself during the grand master's conversation

with Guillaume, behind one of the six mighty pillars that supported the hall's heavy, barrel-vaulted ceiling.

The grand master wasn't surprised. He rose from his creaking wooden chair and stretched his aching back. Since falling
from his warhorse, intoxicated by too much strong, sweet red
wine, he could no longer sit for long periods. Luckily, this happened to him alone on a pleasure ride around the city walls,
and no one had witnessed the embarrassment.

*No, I'm not too old, although I can feel my bones with every movement.
I can still control things here as I wish and as I see fit. I won't allow
anyone to bring the brotherhood into disrepute or challenge the influential
and peaceful position I have secured for my old age. Especially not a rat
like Guillaume, that feeble-minded liar and godless fornicator.*

He turned to Brother Nicholas and asked him directly, "Tell
me, will he do it?"

"Of course he will. He's a Templar knight and must follow
your orders at all times," he replied. "You're a clever man,
Grand Master. This mission rids you of him for a while, and
grants us some peace here. And what's more, a significant enemy of our Order will be dispatched to hell thanks to Guillaume's good relationship with the Assassins, and no one will
connect us to it. If they do, he can bear the blame alone as a
fallen sinner who's already been divested of his habit. No one
will believe him. Guillaume might even be killed and..."

"...and then his post will be yours permanently," finished de
Sablé with a nod. "You're right. He must not survive this mission. If he returns to Acre unscathed, he'll have to die here.
I'm making you personally responsible for it. It's about the
welfare and reputation of the brotherhood, and therefore
godly work. Guillaume's immoral conduct has long been a
thorn in our side. We know perfectly well that he has a weak-
ness of the flesh, and I suspect he personally eliminated all wit-

nesses to his shameful transgressions. He questions my decisions and undermines my reputation. Calls me a weak, old toad! I have ears everywhere! Probably thinks he can usurp my position because he's been in command of half the warriors of our Order and can supposedly negotiate profitably with the heathens! Pah!"

Saliva drooled from the corners of his disdainfully downturned mouth.

Guillaume is better than many, thought Nicholas, *much better than you. But not better than me, although he's a danger to us both. That's why his head must roll.*

"In the name of God, so it shall come to pass. Guillaume will never see the Temple again."

Robert de Sablé's lips twitched and stretched into a benevolent smile.

"It was a good idea of mine to appoint you turcopolier in his place, Brother. You are a truly loyal, virtuous and devoted to our holy mission, and you'll go far in our brotherhood. I'm already considering sending you to Antioch as a steward of the Order, as soon as the prince has been dispatched to hell by the Assassins. Go now. Make sure Guillaume receives everything he needs from the Komtur for his journey. And lull him into a false sense of security."

Nicholas could scarcely suppress his delight. He bowed deeply and walked out briskly, leaving the scornfully grinning Grand Master alone.

Meanwhile, Guillaume trudged slowly across the empty courtyard of the Templar fortress. The feeding of the poor was finished and the needy starvelings had already been ushered off the premises. The high entrance gate was firmly locked once more.

It was now evening. A cool, salty wind swept up from the sea over the high walls of the fortress. He drew the fresh air deep into his lungs and drew his robe across his chest with numb fingers. A vague suspicion dawned on him. De Sablé could have him killed after he had completed his murderous secret mission, and remove all traces of the Order's involvement in the sudden death of Prince Bohemond. Guillaume couldn't rule it out, and decided to take precautions to ensure it didn't come to that.

A pound of pure gold coins as blood money for this murder is a lot. I could do much better things with it. Old de Sablé shouldn't be so sure of himself.

A plan began to take shape in his head. He scratched his beard thoughtfully and sauntered sedately toward the brothers' quarters.

"I warned you."

The deep voice behind him belonged to Raoul de Garlande, the Marshal of the Templars, his superior. The entire Templar army, including Guillaume and his turcopoles, were subordinate to this man.

Guillaume turned and looked into the pale, pocked face of the knight whose powerful figure loomed half a head above his.

His light brown, almost red hair was cropped short. He had very unusual eyes below a high forehead – pale brown, with a small, black cleft dividing the bottom half of his irises, making them look reptilian. Guillaume thought of it as an advantageous birth defect, because those eyes often commanded fear and respect without Raoul even having to open his mouth.

The towering Marshal came from an aristocratic Frankish house near Paris. Among his ancestors and relatives were influential princes and high royal officials. Unlike Guillaume, who was a bastard born from a liaison between a simple knight and a pretty serving maid.

He and Raoul had arrived in the Holy Land around the same time, over twelve years ago, and joined the Knights Templar together. Side by side, they had survived many battles against the heathens. The hard life in the Order had created a bond between them, and Guillaume had often loyally and selflessly supported the somewhat forgetful and erratic Raoul as commander of the troops.

And yet Raoul had adeptly ensured his promotion to Marshal, with prudence, skill and exceptional eloquence. Two years younger, Guillaume was appointed as turcopolier under him. Raoul commanded the Templar army with remarkable fortitude and courage, and the men liked him for being approachable. He always had an ear for the concerns and wishes of his warriors.

Until recently, Raoul and Guillaume had been close friends. After the appointment of the new Grand Master, things between them had cooled off a little. Unlike Guillaume, Raoul got along excellently with Grand Master Robert. Since his entry into the Order and his election to the highest office of the Templars soon after, they were often seen together. The Marshal helped de Sablé find his feet in the strict brotherhood, and willingly performed any service for him. Guillaume found this disconcerting, and considered Raoul's behaviour excessively obsequious.

"I told you a while back to be careful. Not everyone here approves of your indecent, reckless lifestyle," said Raoul, scratching his angular chin.

"What are you talking about, friend? You've done things that weren't much better. I still stand firmly behind you, just as good comrades in arms should do," Guillaume said reproachfully. Since his arrest, Raoul hadn't spoken to him, let alone visited him in his cell.

"That may be true. But these are different times, and we must all conduct ourselves more prudently. Brother Robert is more powerful than you think," replied Raoul, ignoring Guillaume's puzzled look. "You can still count on my help. This secret mission – which *I* suggested to the Grand Master, by the way – is a final test. Execute it as instructed and you'll be allowed to remain in the Order. If you don't, I can no longer protect you."

Guillaume looked at him in astonishment.

Oh yes, you will. I know too much about you. That you're still legally married in France, that you left behind a wife and two small children, to whom you regularly send money, embezzled from the Order's coffers, through Venetian merchants I know. That alone is enough to have you banned from the brotherhood for life. And then there's your lustful affair with the man-hungry Ruzan.

The widowed Armenian farmer's daughter hired herself out in one of the city's many taverns as a servant and occasional whore, and Raoul paid her handsomely in silver for her carnal services. Guillaume had originally introduced the two of them and paid for Raoul's first night with her. That was at the end of a drinking binge in the tavern with a Pisan horse trader, who was celebrating the conclusion of a purchase agreement for half a dozen valuable warhorses.

Since then, the Marshal visited her once a week and fucked the soul out of his body.

"You know it's about the murder of a Christian prince?" Guillaume asked quietly and conspiratorially.

"I know that it serves the interests of our Order. Just do as you've been instructed," replied Raoul with uncharacteristic harshness, looking past Guillaume.

Guillaume suddenly felt the cold of the evening more keenly and his dry lips smiled uncertainly.

"I will, you can count on me, Brother Raoul. I'll succeed in my mission. And after that, I'll think carefully about whom I can trust, and behave with more prudence. You'll be my role model. The threat of harsh punishment has reformed me. I never want to experience such dishonour again. I only ask you to keep an eye on Brother Nicholas. See to it that he leads the turcopoles well in my absence. It seems to me he's a little out of his depth."

"That's... possible," said the Marshal hesitantly. "Don't worry. Go now, prepare for your journey. The Komtur knows and is counting the money as we speak."

"Of course. I depart early tomorrow. Brother Thibaut – that pinchfist – his heart will bleed to hand over so much money to me," said Guillaume in jest.

"He's a conscientious man," Raoul replied reproachfully.

Guillaume shrugged. "Yes, yes, he is. Please pass on my greetings to Ruzan when you see her." He couldn't resist that little jab.

The Templar's eyes narrowed at the mention of his secret lover's name. He nodded with a face like stone.

They shook hands in farewell. Guillaume moved off pensively toward the men's quarters, while a glowering Raoul de Garlande strode to the fortress gates.

IV

It was oppressively humid in the goldsmith's little workshop. The stifling air smelled of cloying sweat and burnt oil. For hours, Ishmael hadn't dared open the shutters facing the street, even though a cool evening breeze was now blowing past the houses. He was too afraid of inquisitive eyes seeing what he was working on.

Three oil lamps gave off bright light, but also sooty smoke. For better visibility, he had extended the wicks out fully, but now the large flames and smoke were making it hard to breathe. His face was beaded with sweat and the left sleeve of his robe was sopping wet from continuously wiping his forehead. His lumbar vertebrae ached as though an awl was stabbing into the middle of his spine. His eyes burned, and he was making slow progress in his examination of the precious items.

Once he had finally cleaned the plaster, loam and dust off the second tablet with a spatula and paint brush, he took it in his hands, leaned back and regarded it with disappointment. He was now certain it was a fake, and his initial joy at finding what he thought was a sacred artefact evaporated like an incinerated haystack.

The lettering engraved into the tablets was in the old Phoenician script, and it was indeed the Ten Commandments of God, but the tablets were of hard-fired clay, not stone, as described in the holy Jewish book, the Tanakh. But they were unusually heavy for ordinary clay tablets. Perhaps it was the material used. He had never seen grey ceramic, but then he wasn't well versed in pottery. They appeared to be replicas of the sacred tablets, perhaps having once stood in a house of God for illustrative purposes.

Utterly disillusioned, he flung the tablet carelessly onto his workbench. *All that sweat and strain for nothing,* he thought morosely, wrinkling his nose. It seemed that little Arab with the innocent, child-like eyes had foisted nothing but worthless junk on him.

He pushed his stool back, stood up, stretched and groaned. Glancing irritably at his workbench, he noticed he had damaged the tablet when he threw it down.

A piece the size of his palm had flaked off the top right corner. A different material shimmered slate grey in the light of the lamps.

Stunned, he took the tablet in both hands and examined it closely. *That's metal. The tablets are metal, encased in fired clay!*

Now he was curious. He held the piece directly under one of the lamps and saw that it was engraved with the same lettering as the clay. Hope sparked in him again. He immediately picked up his tools and carefully chipped off more of the pale grey clay with a hammer and graver.

An unusual, highly polished surface revealed itself. When he finished his work two hours later, he was finally convinced. He had the genuine tablets before of him. However, contrary to the scriptures, they were not made of stone but some completely unknown raw material. Dark grey, almost black, flecked with green, unusually warm. The Ten Commandments were set into their gleaming surfaces in elaborate Phoenician letters, five on each tablet.

How these intricate inscriptions had been carved into the hard element, Ishmael couldn't explain. He tried out every tool he owned. Hammer, chisel, graver – nothing made even the slightest scratch. This miraculous property convinced him once and for all. *These tablets were not made by human hands!*

After he had cleaned them both and rubbed them down with a rag, they softly reflected the light of the oil lamps and he could see his incredulous face mirrored back.

After the tablets, he started on the winged cherub, the first item Harit had sold him. A thorough inspection of the figurine brought another incredible discovery: it wasn't made of copper or lead – under its greenish-black surface it was gold, of a purity he had never seen before in his life.

His jaw dropped and he stared dumbfounded at the cherub.

Who would plate eight pounds of the purest gold in cheap lead, and cover ore tablets with ordinary clay, unless they wanted to hide something infinitely precious from the world!

What he had before him were parts of the most sacred relic of his people – the contents of the lost Ark of the Covenant, the Israelites' symbol of their communion with God. He had dispelled all doubt as to their authenticity.

As Ishmael gazed lovingly at the precious items, sudden tears of joy and horror streamed into his white beard. What incredible good fortune this discovery could bring to his mistreated people; hope of liberation from servitude and protection from the most terrible persecution; hope of the rebirth and reunification of the old Kingdom of David. But the Ark was also known to be a powerful, frightening weapon in the time of their forefathers. It was said that it could throw lightning bolts to transform the Israelites' enemies into living torches.

The thought made him shudder. He was convinced this incredible discovery would result in his death. All of the writings stated clearly: whoever gets too close to the Ark of the Covenant, or touches it, will forfeit their life.

In the Tanakh it is written that after the Ark was taken to Jerusalem by King David, a Levite named Usa touched it and was instantly slayed by the wrath of the Lord.

Why he himself wasn't already lying dead on the floor was a mystery to Ishmael.

Perhaps this discovery wasn't the end for him, but the beginning of a godly calling. Perhaps the Lord had something great in store for him.

But the second cherub was missing. Without it, the Ark was incomplete. It was only between *both* guardians that the Lord's presence on earth could manifest.

Ishmael's heart beat like a mufffled drum in his chest. He hoped fervently that the unsuspecting Arab would keep his word and bring him the missing figurine soon.

"Uncle?" Leah rattled the locked workshop door. "Uncle, open the door! I'm worried! Are you still alive?"

Ishmael was startled and quickly covered the precious items with a linen cloth.

"I'm coming, I'm coming!" he called, unbarring the door and opening it. Leah eyed him with a reproachful frown.

"What are you doing in here? You haven't had anything to eat or drink since yesterday evening, and now it's the early hours of the morning!"

She entered the workshop, glanced around and noticed the veiled workbench.

"It stinks in here like a smoky smithy. You should open a window. What have you been working on all this time?" she asked curiously, and before he could stop her, she flung back the cloth.

The tablets gleamed in the light of the flickering oil lamps. Leah froze. She knew at once what she was looking at. Every devout Jew knew the wondrous part of the Torah that told of the Lord's Commandments. The tablets of the Covenant!

"You're... making new ones? For our congregation? My goodness... oh, it's... masterful!" She clasped her hands in front of her face and gazed at the artworks in awe.

"I had no idea you could craft such wonderful things..." she whispered reverently. "They're indescribably beautiful." She turned to her uncle with a look of amazement.

"No, Leah, no..." Ishmael said hoarsely, looking her straight in the eye. "I could never make something like that. I would never do anything so sacrilegious. *Adonai,* it is his work, the work of the Most High. It's the genuine sacred relic."

Leah shook her head in disbelief and was about to pick up one of the tablets. Ishmael quickly grabbed her hands and squeezed them.

"Keep away from it, child! Never touch it, do you hear! No one should touch it. It brings certain death!"

"Uncle, this is impossible. The Ark and its contents have been lost for thousands of years. You must be mistaken... But if you didn't make these, where did you get them?"

The goldsmith lowered his eyes and slowly released her hands.

"The tablets are genuine, my child, as is the cherub. Look, they're made of a completely unknown ore. It's warm and incredibly hard. So perfectly and cleanly polished... there's no earthly tool that can work such hard metal. The engraved script is ancient and yet they are our letters. I understood every word as soon as I read it. And the cherub here... it's made of the finest gold, so pure and soft I can scratch off a piece with my fingernail." Ishmael's eyes lit up with delight and Leah looked at the cherub in awe.

"It can't be true. I simply don't believe it. Uncle, if it's true... Where did you... get these things?"

He answered her excitedly, "The little, enterprising Arab Harit brought them to me yesterday. You remember his visit. You thought he was an emissary from the Emir. But he works for the governor, under the new mosque on the Temple Mount and he found these items in a hidden room. He offered to sell me the cherub and the tablets, presumably to supplement his meagre wage. He assumed the figurine was copper or lead and the tablets cheap stone. And... he dug out more. Look, the four golden bearer rings... They surely belonged to the acacia wood casket... and there's a second cherub. He's bringing it to me later... I hope. Oh, child, I can hardly believe it myself!"

Ishmael spread his arms. "The tablets were covered in clay and loam, and the cherub was plated in lead, as were the rings. He doesn't appear to have found the Ark itself. But that's to be expected – wood could never last that long. The location corresponds to the old legends. There in the deep cellars of the old temple is where our ancestors are said to have hidden the Ark from the Babylonians."

He took a deep breath and continued. "I didn't want to believe it at first. Then, after cleaning the dust and filth of centuries from the treasures and liberating them from their disguise, I saw them in all their glory! This is the long-lost sacred relic of our people!"

Leah felt dizzy. The sacred, immeasurably precious Ark of the Covenant was here in their house, in her uncle's hands. That she, the daughter of an ordinary money changer, should be closer to it than almost anyone ever before, made her feel uneasy.

Fear suddenly constricted her throat. She was afraid the artefacts would bring death and misery if the knowledge of their present location became public.

Her face drained of colour until it was as pale as the linen under which she had discovered the precious objects. She whispered, "If it's true... if it's really true... what will you do with these things?"

The goldsmith floundered. He hadn't yet asked himself this simple question.

"I... I don't know." His reply was halting and he leaned against the door frame. "By God, I have no idea how, or whether, I should reveal these treasures to the world. Who would believe me...?" he faltered. "And... who would protect them from falling into the wrong hands?"

They both lapsed into a bewildered silence. Ishmael stepped up to the workbench and picked up the cherub, the golden pedestal of which he had freed from its protective layer of lead, so that it glowed mysteriously in the light of the lamps.

"We must keep this miracle to ourselves for now, until I'm sure of the right course of action."

He turned to Leah beseechingly. "You must tell no one, no one at all! I'll return these things to their previous condition, as I found them on the Muslim's cart. I want no one to recognise them. When he brings me the second cherub, I'll craft a worthy chest, place the relics inside it and bury it deep in our garden. Then we'll see."

Leah sighed with relief and her cheeks regained their colour.

"Don't worry, uncle. Not a soul will hear anything from me. You're the high rabbi in our Jerusalem and the Lord will en-lighten you. I have faith in his omnipotence. If he has led you to his Commandments, then he'll reveal himself and share his plan with you."

Ishmael shook his head almost imperceptibly and returned the cherub to the workbench. *Perhaps God will guide me, but per-haps not. The Lord hasn't shown his face to anyone since Moses. Surely I'm not worthy. It's presumptuous to hope for such a miracle. It is I who must determine what should happen with the Ark, so that it brings the greatest benefit to our people. But not until the second cherub has completed the sacred set.*

V

Peace still reigned in the Holy Land. The armistice Richard the Lionheart had brokered with Sultan Salah ad-Din a year ago was scrupulously observed by Christians and Saracens alike. Pilgrims were permitted to visit the holy sites in Jerusalem, but only unarmed, in small groups, and under the watch of Muslim soldiers. This brought to the shrunken Latin Kingdom and the Sultan's dominion an ever-increasing, stream of well-to-do pilgrims come to pray at the Lord's tomb for salvation from their earthly sins.

Dressed inconspicuously as a Frankish cattle merchant with two mules, Guillaume joined a pilgrim train that journeyed for a week from Acre to Jerusalem. The fifty-odd penitent pilgrims from Spain, Italy and Sicily were guided by three Knights of the Hospitaller southwest along the coastal road to the occupied port city of Jaffa. Outside its massive fortification walls, Muslim soldiers then took charge of the flock. The surly heathen warriors were clearly reluctant to guide these infidels, but they were obliged to follow the Sultan's orders. So they made the Nazarenes pay handsomely for their escort through the mountains.

Guillaume was familiar with the route. He had taken it into the Promised Land, became a Templar knight in Jerusalem, and then fled along the same roads to Acre six years ago when the Holy City had been forced to surrender to the powerful Sultan.

The pilgrim train arrived without incident in Jerusalem on a dreary, overcast day, and Guillaume found it scarcely changed. He entered the city through St Stephen's Gate in the north, on which fluttered a dozen green flags of the prophet, in place of the black-and-white banner of the Latin Kingdom. A newly repaired city wall encircled numerous small, two-storeyed houses built from loam and limestone. Their flat roofs crouched in the shade of impressive churches and monasteries that towered like giants in the tangle of small alleyways. The Muslims had knocked the crosses off the church roofs and replaced some of them with magnificent crescent moons. Many buildings were now empty or used as warehouses.

Immediately upon arrival, Guillaume separated from the pilgrim troupe and searched for accommodation near the suq, the huge, covered market at the centre of the city.

The price for an overnight stay in one of the plentiful inns had shot up since Christian visitors had once again been granted entry into the city. He found a small, overpriced room above a dilapidated tea room run by a stout but exceptionally friendly Armenian, who also provided for his animals in the inner courtyard.

Guillaume went to his bare, musty room on the second floor and hid the heavy saddlebags containing the gold coins under the pitiful bed, which was simply a pile of hay covered with a linen sheet. It would serve its purpose. He left the room and immersed himself in the bustle of the lively market. He hoped to meet a few Arab acquaintances here, with whom he had previously done favourable business on behalf of the Order.

The suq was originally just an alley containing a number of stalls. After the Christian occupiers conquered the city, they erected high stone arches between the houses and covered them with a wooden structure, turning it into a huge building that stretched from the fish market almost a quarter of a mile south to David Street. A dense crowd of men, women and children swarmed past the stalls. Poor, rich, servants, labourers, high officials, Christian pilgrims and veiled ladies merged into a slow-moving river of people.

At this market, you could buy almost anything the Orient had to offer, from expensive, colourfully embroidered silk cloth, magnificent carpets interwoven with gold thread and ornate ceramics, to rare spices, fresh fruit and vegetables. The scent of cinnamon, jasmine and frankincense mingled with the dust stirred up by hundreds of feet, making Guillaume cough. The sellers vaunted their wares loudly and eloquently, gesturing wildly as they haggled over quantities and prices and thrust samples at the market-goers.

Guillaume elbowed his way through the throng. He was looking for a potter known as Fat Muhammad. He had often acted as a helpful informant to Guillaume and maintained a secret relationship with the Assassins. Guillaume hoped he hadn't died as a result of his excessive eating habits.

He eventually found him in the usual spot near the market's southern exit, in his shop cluttered with crooked shelves on which bowls, jugs and pots were piled in alarmingly high stacks. The unshapely Arab, who despite his corpulence moved with astonishing agility between his towers of breakable wares, was haggling with a veiled woman over two oil lamps, and didn't notice Guillaume. He waited until they agreed on a price, after what seemed like endless bargaining, and the woman disappeared into the crowd. The disgruntled potter dropped a copper coin into his purse and Guillaume said to him in fluent Arabic, "I might have an opportunity for you to fill your purse much more lucratively."

The potter looked up, his eyes widening in surprise, and he hissed, "By Allah, *faris ar-ruhban al bayd,* the knight of the white monks. Impossible. How did you... Get in here, quick!"

He hastily pulled Guillaume by his robe into the back of his shop.

"Are you crazy? What if someone recognises you? A Templar in Jerusalem! Your life isn't worth a shard of pottery if they find you here! And nor is mine! By the Almighty, what are you doing here? After all this time?" His jowls flushed red.

"Is that how you greet an old acquaintance?" Guillaume smiled.

"What? No... I'm quite flustered. Please, sit on this stool. I can't let anyone see you with me," replied Muhammad, standing with his legs astride between Guillaume and the front of the shop. "Your boldness borders on idiocy, Templar, I must say, even though I'm happy to see you. Those were good times. I made a lot of money with your help, and I was able to buy a house outside the city. But that was all a long time ago. It's a miracle you're still alive. Listen, the Sultan has a predilection for publicly skinning and beheading your brothers. I've seen it with my own eyes. You're putting me in a very difficult situation, I..."

"Muhammad, that's the last thing I want to do," Guillaume interrupted. "I'll leave soon, but I need your help and I'll pay you for it. I need to meet with the Assassins as soon as possible. Preferably tomorrow or the day after. I'm sure they're still spying in the city on behalf of their leader, the Old Man of the Mountain. If you arrange this for me, you won't regret it."

Muhammad clicked his tongue and waggled his head as he weighed up the proposition. "They're not exactly friends of mine, those hashish eaters. Their minds are often clouded and they mostly talk nonsense, but they can kill with their daggers faster than poisonous adders. Very dangerous people, as you know. What do you want from them? It would have to be a lot of money..."

"A hundred dirham. Here and now. And no more questions."

Guillaume reached under his cloak and pulled out a full money pouch, which he dangled before the potter's eyes.

"I would need a hundred dirham just to keep me from screaming for help right now because a Christian dog is threatening me." Muhammad smiled sweetly and his eyes narrowed.

"A hundred and fifty. More than your shop and its contents are worth." Guillaume smiled sardonically back.

"By Allah the Magnanimous, you really are blessed by him. I'll do you this favour. Come back just before sunset, and I'll let you know."

The potter snatched the pouch and Guillaume counted another fifty silver dirham into his hand. Then he stood up and pushed past the ample paunch of the now cheerful Muslim.

"Thank you, Master of the potter's wheel," he jested, adding with an icy glare, "You know that if you betray me to the Sultan's soldiers, I'll slice open your fat belly and divide your stinking entrails amongst the pots here. I'll still have time to do that."

Muhammad appeared to shrink, and he bowed. "Don't worry, I haven't forgotten your reputation as a merciless swordsman and butcher of highway men."

Guillaume nodded, pulled his hood over his head and left the shop. Behind him, Muhammad swiftly tidied away his wares, locked his shop and hurried to the other end of the market, where the long-distance traders peddled their wares. Their caravans brought highly coveted goods into the city: liquorice root from Egypt, myrrh and frankincense from Arabia, peppercorns and cinnamon sticks from India and expensive saffron from Persia.

The rich merchants maintained excellent relations with the Assassins Sect – or hashish eaters, as they were disparagingly referred to by devout Muslims – and were happy to take their money and supply them with goods, or information about their arch-enemy Salah ad-Din, who pursued them everywhere as enemies of the faith. The merchants asked the potter only a few questions about his request for a meeting with the contract killers, which he answered to their satisfaction with a few silver coins.

Meanwhile, Guillaume was hungry, so he whiled away some time at the fish market. At a smoky cooking stand, he indulged in a smoked bass from the Jordan River and a soft, warm, wheat flatbread. The bread's sweet flavour reminded him of his meals with the Templars, and he saw the Grand Master's face in his mind's eye. He wasn't here to enjoy himself, he had a mission to fulfil. He stashed the remains of the bread in his pilgrim's sack and sauntered back to the potter's shop.

Muhammad was already waiting for him in front of the open door. He waved him in, panting, and closed the door behind him, sweat dripping from his high forehead. It wasn't often that he had to haul his rotund body to the other end of the market and back during the day.

"By Allah, Templar, the things we do for a few silver coins," he wheezed. "It appears you have luck on your side. Or perhaps not. You can meet the dangerous killers tomorrow just after midday. But not in the city – it must be outside the walls. Do you know the Lazarus monastery on the road to Bethlehem?

"Of course, about an hour on foot. The charitable monks healed many pilgrims and did godly work," replied Guillaume.

The potter cleared his throat sheepishly. "Well, our severe Sultan didn't see it that way. He had their heads lopped off and their home reduced to rubble and ashes just before he moved victoriously into Jerusalem. All that's left are abandoned ruins."

"Very sad. May God grant their souls peace," said Guillaume apathetically. He had never understood why so many Christians described the Sultan as magnanimous and chivalrous, just because he spared the inhabitants of Jerusalem when he conquered it. He charged them mountains of gold and silver for this supposed magnanimity. Anyone who couldn't raise the money was sold into slavery or killed. To Guillaume, he was nothing more than a greedy, cruel, calculating butcher.

"You're to go alone. On foot and unarmed," Muhammad continued, adding, "But *I* wouldn't chance it."

"Maybe you wouldn't, but I would. And not for the first time. I'll take my leave. Thank you for your efforts. And not a word to anyone."

"Obviously not! I want to keep my head on my shoulders. It was nice to see you after such a long time. I'd love to invite you to my house, but..." He gave the Templar a contrite look and raised his hands apologetically.

"But without a head, the most hospitable house is useless," finished Guillaume with a nod. "Maybe times will change and we can make up for lost time one day. May your god be with you."

"And yours with you."

Muhammad unlocked the shop door and let Guillaume out. He quickly merged and disappeared into the crowd of shoppers.

The potter wiped his brow with his sleeve and watched the Templar go with a mixture of relief and incomprehension. He shrugged and turned away. The money pouch under his robe pressed gratifyingly against his rolls of fat and he decided not to open his shop again that day.

VI

Guillaume sat on a wobbly stool in his room, appraising a dark grey, metal figurine he held in his hand. On a whim, he had allowed a pushy street vendor to persuade him to buy it on his way back from the market that day. Allegedly found in the ruins of the Temple Mount. When he fled Jerusalem all those years ago, he had to leave all his belongings behind, so a little memento from his time at the old Templar headquarters seemed apt.

The sculpture depicted an angel, its curly head bowed between two wings stretched out in front of it. It had the body of a reclining lion. He could make out the finest details: feathers, hair, claws, the closed eyes, and even a smile, as if it were experiencing a wonderful dream. One silver dirham was a bargain for this small artwork made of tin or lead. It may even be cast bronze.

It reminded Guillaume vaguely of something from his past.

The longer he weighed the figurine in his hand and studied it, the more his thoughts wandered back to his youth. Many years ago, as a student at the Dalon monastery in his homeland of France, he had been made to transcribe an old scripture containing a number of artistic illustrations depicting dragons, saints, angels and other wondrous things from the Orient.

The Book of the Prophets – that was the title of the tattered book, one of the older sections of the Bible. He remembered it clearly.

His face warped into a sour grimace. What exhausting work it had been. He spent weeks transcribing those parchments. His reward was cracked, raw fingers, watering eyes and constant chastisement from the merciless monks telling to put more care into his work. One incorrect letter or an unclean stroke of the quill and he was punished harshly. The parchment, ink and colours were rare and expensive. But he learned to translate Greek and Hebrew into Latin, and the words of these scriptures had engraved themselves on his memory.

One colourful illustration had especially impressed him. A gold shrine carried on poles, on top of which sat two golden, winged beings, part human, part bird. The cherubim.

They looked exactly like the figurine in his hand today. They guarded the Ark of the Covenant containing the stone tablets inscribed with the Ten Commandments – the beginning of all faith in the Lord. Anyone who touched them was struck by bolts of lightning, and the careless blasphemers were burnt to ash.

The Ark had stimulated his imagination as a boy. How he would have loved to possess such a fear-inspiring weapon. In his dreams he had used it to burn down the odious, miserable Cistercian monastery to rubble and ash, and then, like his older half-brother Constantine de Born, performed glorious, heroic deeds at the court of young King Henry of Aquitaine. Or finally convinced his father, the troubadour Bertran de Born from Pèrigord, that his bastard son had a higher calling than spending his life among dull-witted monks.

This wonderful story of the unattainable and powerful Ark of the Covenant, lost somewhere in the Holy Land, had altered the course of his life. The tale was a factor in motivating him to take up the cross and later enter the service of the Templars.

A few knights from the famous Order had stopped to rest at the monastery on their way south. They were travelling all over France at the time, recruiting warriors for their brotherhood, and Guillaume had listened enthralled to their tales of glory and honour garnered for the Christian faith on battlefields in the Levant – precisely where the Ark of the Covenant was said to be hidden.

Deeply impressed by their narratives, he fled the gloomy abbey a few days later to follow them and become a knight. Instead he found himself, hungry and ragged, as a cabin boy on a Venetian galley sailing from Marseille to Cyprus and later to Jaffa. When he finally arrived, he entered the service of the Templars as a day labourer and stable hand. Two long years later, he was finally accepted into the Order as a full ministering brother.

As a sergeant and the squire of an aging Templar knight, he learned to use weapons and later saved his master's life in a bloody skirmish with Bedouin bandits. Overcome with gratitude, he made him a knight then and there.

That was a long time ago. His memory of the Ark of the Covenant had been buried under his experiences along life's stony path, which was drenched in sweat, blood and hardship.

This cherub brought it all back, as clearly as if Guillaume were holding the book in his hands again.

He took a deep breath. A bitter smile twisted his mouth and he glanced through the window. It was now evening. The sun was setting behind the barren mountains surrounding Jerusalem. Its last, warm rays streamed through the iron window grate. Lost in thought, he rose and carried the winged figurine to the window to study it more closely.

He held the sculpture up to the light and saw fine gold flecks glinting on the cherub's grey feathers. The remains of gold plating, he guessed, and scratched it lightly with his fingernail. The gold didn't flake off. Instead, small patches of the dark surface came away, revealing more gold. He rubbed his eyes incredulously and scratched harder on another spot. More shimmering gold appeared. Excited, he fished his dagger from under his robe and pressed its point into the exposed spot. It left a deep impression.

Gold. The purest gold!

The discovery hit him like a blow from a club and he staggered back from the window. This wasn't a replica he was holding! This had to be one of the genuine cherubs of the Ark of the Covenant. Pure gold, covered in a thin layer of lead, judging by his blackened fingertips.

"God in heaven," he muttered. "This is not possible!"

Did that little Muslim really sell me part of the most sacred relic for one dirham?

He turned the figurine upside-down and discovered tiny Hebrew letters engraved on the base.

"YHWH." The Jewish name for God.

Guillaume had to sit down. He stared at the cherub in disbelief. He no longer doubted its authenticity.

Who would cast three pounds of pure gold into the shape of a winged creature and then cover it in worthless lead? And inscribe it with the unutterable name of the Jewish God? Only someone trying to hide a treasure from the covetous eyes of the world.

Everything suddenly fit together. The Arab had told him he'd found the figurine in the cellar of *al haram ash-sharif*, the Temple Mount. That was once the site of the holy Jewish temple, destroyed over a thousand years ago. They had kept the Ark of the Covenant safe there until foreign invaders had conquered the Kingdom of David, enslaved its inhabitants, taken them to foreign lands and robbed them of their treasures. That was how it was written in that old, precious book, and now Guillaume believed everything he had painstakingly transcribed all those years ago.

He had found solid evidence that the most sacred relic on earth was not lost. And he, Guillaume the bastard son, could find it and use the infinite power residing in it for himself. He would lead the Templar Order to unimaginable glory, unconquerable by the heathens. The Frankish Kingdom in the Holy

Land could be restored. Yes, the whole world would lie at his feet.

His breath came fast and his heart raced. He paced restlessly back and forth.

A golden winged creature on its own is no sacred relic. I need the other parts.

The second cherub, the gilt lid of the chest and the stone tablets with the Ten Commandments were also part of the Ark of the Covenant. Perhaps the naïve vendor, who clearly knew nothing about the treasure, had dug up other artefacts too.

I must speak to the young man before he foolishly sells the other pieces too cheaply. As soon as possible!

But it was too late to look for him that day. The market had long since closed and Guillaume would have to wait until tomorrow, for better or worse. Clasping the cherub close, he paced in circles around the cramped room. He whispered the Lord's Prayer a few times and prayed that he would find the Arab in the suq after daybreak.

Overwrought, he went to bed and slept restlessly. He tossed from one side to the other on his hard bed and was glad when the muezzin woke him at dawn, wailing across the city roofs to call his fellow believers to morning prayer.

"Allahu akbar!" – God is the greatest, he called four times, and then, *"As-salatu khairu min an-naum"* – prayer is better than sleep.

Guillaume yawned, prised himself·off the straw bed and rubbed his gummy eyes. He'd heard this heathen call to prayer many times before, and understood the words. He reluctantly had to agree with the Muslim with the powerful voice.

He knelt, crossed himself and sent his own prayer to the Lord. "Almighty God, gift me this sacred relic. I intend to use it in your honour and for your glory. Help me, that I might find the Arab quickly at the market, that he knows the location of your holy Commandments, and that he will reveal it to me."

He got to his feet, drank a mouthful of lukewarm water from a clay jug and hastily straightened his rumpled robe. He wanted to be at the entrance gate before the market opened, to keep an eye out for the little Arab. He would have to end his search no later than midday, because the Assassins wouldn't wait for an infidel Templar.

Before leaving, he glanced one last time around the room. The saddlebags containing the gold coins for the contract killers were safe enough hidden under his straw bed. It was only money.

He would fetch it later when it was time to leave for the dangerous meeting with the hashish people. His slipped his only weapon under his clothing – a sharp, pointed dagger.

But he couldn't possibly leave the precious cherub unguarded in his room. He stashed the figurine carefully in his pilgrim's sack, which he slung around his shoulders, and left the room.

VII

Harit was in a hurry that morning. Shortly after sunrise, he was already making his way to the sprawling suq. If he didn't find the pilgrim to whom he had sold the winged figurine the previous day, he would search for him at the Church of the Holy Sepulchre before he was due to start work at the Temple Mount. All pilgrims turned up sooner or later at the holy site where their God had been crucified and entombed.

He arrived in the Alley of Bad Smells, completely out of breath. It ran alongside the suq and its name was unjustified. Although it housed a few evil-smelling tanneries, the acrid smell of their lye vats was masked by numerous delicious-smelling, steaming food stands. Butchers offered their products not only fresh and raw – they also fried mutton, beef and chicken with onions and garlic in pots of simmering oil, and sold this fare very cheaply.

At one stand, pieces of mutton dripping with fat rotated on iron spits over an open flame. The aroma wafted temptingly past Harit's nostrils. But all he permitted himself for breakfast was a millet flatbread with honey, which he devoured as he walked, before posting himself at the northern entrance to the suq. There, he stood on an abandoned, upturned vegetable basket of hard willow and kept a lookout for the pilgrim.

He didn't have to wait long. There were few customers underway at this early hour, and the tall pilgrim stood out among the stalls, although he was trying to make himself scarce, walking slightly hunched. He too seemed to be searching for someone – turning his head this way and that and shading his eyes with his hand.

Relieved, Harit leapt down from his basket and ran to him, tugging gently at his robe.

"Nazarene! Thanks be to Allah! I'm glad I found you here. *Sabah al khair,* good morning!" Harit bowed subserviently to the man, who spun around in surprise and fixed him with his penetrating blue eyes.

"Good morning to you too. It's good we meet again. I was looking for you. You sold me a figurine yesterday..." Guillaume replied in Arabic, disregarding the disrespectful term 'Nazarene'. The Muslims applied it disparagingly to the Christians, because they prayed to a destitute carpenter from Nazareth as their saviour.

Harit was startled by the pilgrim's flawless pronunciation – yesterday he hardly seemed to understand a word – but he composed himself.

"I'll take it back!" He said quickly. "By Allah the Almighty, you paid me too much for the piece and I'm an honest man. I don't want anyone saying that Harit ibn Tharit takes advantage of devout pilgrims. It's on my conscience, believe me!"

Guillaume raised an eyebrow in surprise and smiled.

"I want to keep it, and I'll buy a lot more from you if you've found any other objects of its kind under the temple. The price was fair. Do you have more?"

Harit looked sidelong at the pilgrim. *It seems the Nazarenes are just as crazy for my junk as the Jews. Who would have thought?*

The man looked poor in his worn, tatty robe, and had nothing with him other than a pilgrim's sack of cheap, felted cloth. No comparison to the Jew Ishmael, who lived in a nice house with beautiful carpets and colourful silk cushions, and whom he knew was waiting for him with more silver. An ongoing business relationship with the rich goldsmith was surely much more worthwhile.

Harit shook his head and replied in a regretful tone, "By the prophet's beard, I have nothing more. I'll be honest with you, I passed on everything else I found to an old friend. He said he would be delighted to have the lead bird person that I sold you yesterday. You see, there's another figurine, which he has, and he sent me out to retrieve the second one for him. He's very fond of such pieces and the pair would complete his collection. So please, let me buy this thing back, which is surely worthless to you. I'll offer you double what you paid yesterday!"

"Ah... I see. Another statue. And it looks exactly the same?" Guillaume tried to sound as off-hand as possible.

Harit nodded hesitantly and Guillaume said casually, "Then go back and buy it from your friend and bring it to me. I'd like to have the pair for myself."

"Oh... no... that one's not... it's not as well-preserved as the one I gave you," Harit stammered. "Please! I'll pay five times what you paid me. What do you say? Do we have a deal?"

Five times. If Guillaume's suspicions were correct, all the gold in the world wasn't enough for the little sculptures. Apparently, the industrious Muslim had dug up other precious artefacts in the foundations of the Templars' former headquarters. Perhaps the complete Ark of the Covenant. The Muslim clearly had no idea of the significance of his find. But his supposed friend probbably did.

Guillaume quickly weighed up his options. He was to meet with the Assassins soon after midday. That left him enough time to follow the Muslim and locate this mysterious buyer.

"Show me the way to your friend. I want to persuade him myself to sell me the other figurine," he suggested.

Harit gestured dismissively and widened his eyes in a look of child-like innocence.

"Unfortunately he's... no longer here. He's a merchant and left yesterday... for Damascus," he lied, rubbing his smooth chin in agitation.

Guillaume knew Harit wasn't speaking the truth and decided on the spur of the moment to lay a trap for him. He would bait him with a considerable sum, so that the boy would lead him to his friend.

"Ten dirham. Give me ten times what I paid you and you can have it back. I suppose it's not worth as much to me, and the journey home will be long and costly – I could use the money. Decide quickly, I'm leaving the Holy City today." Guillaume frowned and pushed out his lower lip.

Harit was initially shocked by the inflated price. Then he came to his senses. He would receive much more for the statue from the eccentric Jew – twenty silver dirham. So he could still keep ten. *Not a bad deal,* he thought, proud of his arithmetic skills. He pulled a tortured face and scratched his ear.

"Pilgrim, really, you're robbing me! May Allah protect me in future from people like you!" He took a deep breath and paused, then said, "Agreed, you will have the money. Do you by any chance have the figurine with you?"

He had taken the bait, although it pained Guillaume to hand over the treasure.

Not for long, I'll get it back soon, you can count on it.

Guillaume gave an exaggerated sigh and took the sack from his back, pulled out the cherub and handed it to Harit, who quickly examined it and then hid it under his robe. He reluctantly drew out his money pouch and counted ten dirham into the pilgrim's hand.

"You shouldn't make a habit of these kinds of trades, or you'll never be a rich man. Live long and happily with it. And your friend too," said Guillaume with a smirk.

Harit bowed deeply. "You're right, Nazarene, truly, you're right. My heart is too big for me to succeed as a merchant. I'm better off reaching for the pick and shovel and earning my income with hard labour. That would be more lucrative. Thank you for your kindness. May God protect you on your journey home!"

Harit didn't wait for the pilgrim to reply. He turned and wove his way past the market's tightly packed stands toward the southern market entrance, before disappearing into a dark side street.

He was immensely happy and relieved to have found the Nazarene and persuaded him to hand over the figurine. Ishmael, the old goldsmith, would now reward him richly.

You think it's a bad trade, Nazarene, but I'll make a fortune today! I hope the Jew isn't a late sleeper, and is already awake.

Harit quickened his pace without looking back.

He didn't notice the pilgrim pursuing him at a distance like a hungry wolf stalking prey, not letting him out of his sight.

VIII

Harit knocked impatiently at the goldsmith's door.

The crazy old man had better keep his word and buy the second winged figure for twenty dirham, otherwise I really have just completed the worst deal of my life.

He would use the money to buy new sandals with leather straps, and perhaps two new linen robes. And he could afford to visit the *hammam*, the city's public bathhouse. When he still lived in Acre, he used to treat himself once a week to this fragrant indulgence. Now he was clothed in rags and reeked like a mule.

The heavy wooden door creaked open. A pair of dark eyes peered out at him from under bushy, white eyebrows.

"Ah, it's you. Do you have it? The statue?" Ishmael asked, his eyelids aflutter.

"Harit always keeps his word and..." The Arab didn't get to finish his sentence. The Jew quickly pulled him into the house by his rags and locked the door.

"Er, before I give it to you... you should know, it cost me a great effort to acquire it. I must confess, I had already sold the figurine to a pilgrim at the market. It wasn't easy to convince him to resell it to me, by Allah, I'm telling you. It was very expensive... Look, it's intact and matches the statue you already have in your possession – they're almost identical!"

Harit brought the cherub out from under his robe and held it up like a trophy.

"Jew, are you alright?"

The old goldsmith blanched, swayed and steadied himself on the door frame.

"Don't join your ancestors now!" Harit blurted.

Ishmael shook his head, composed himself and took a few deep breaths.

"I haven't drunk or slept enough, and it's early in the day," he explained. It had taken him the rest of the night to re-cover the cherub with lead and disguise the metal tablets under a layer of pale brown loam, which he made from a mixture of soil, water and fine sand. Finally, he imprinted the letters of the Ten Commandments into the soft surface with a stylus and fired them in the oven in his small kitchen. It was worth the effort. The precious items were returned to the condition in which he had received them.

Ishmael looked closely at the second figurine. His wildly beating heart almost leapt out of his chest. This was without a doubt the twin of his cherub. There was no holding him back.

"Give it to me!" He tried impatiently to grab the figurine from the Arab, who stepped back.

"Not so fast!" Harit held the object against his chest. "We haven't agreed on the price. As I said, it cost me a lot to get it back and..."

He faltered when he saw two gold coins glinting in the old man's hand. Ishmael held them up to his eyes.

Gold bezants! The most valuable currency in the realm of the Nazarenes. Harit was familiar with Frankish money. The two coins were equivalent to three hundred and sixty dirham. As much as he earned from a year of hard labour. A fortune for him.

"Yes, that... should suffice," he stammered incredulously, handing the cherub to the goldsmith, who closed his eyes and clasped it to his chest rapturously.

Harit looked at him for a while, but Ishmael made no move to give him the money, which was still clutched in his left fist. Harit cleared his throat and tapped the Jew lightly on the shoulder.

"My fee?"

Ishmael was startled. "Oh yes, wait... before I give you the coins, come here. Please, have a seat."

He placed the cherub on the cool tiled floor and quickly covered it with a cloth. Bewildered, Harit obeyed and sat on one of the cushions arranged on the carpet.

The goldsmith sat opposite Harit and scrutinised him. He had taken note the first time they met of the Arab's white teeth and slender, delicate hands, which were incongruous with the rest of his destitute, grimy exterior. This young Muslim had found the greatest treasure of Judaism and brought it to him, the rabbi of the congregation in Jerusalem. It was clearly divine providence. *The Lord must have something important in store for this person; he must carry some secret. I need to know more about him.*

"Thank you for your efforts. You kept your word and procured the second cherub for me," he said. "And you seem to be a prudent and enterprising man. But I believe you weren't always a day labourer. Your hands don't look as if they've been hauling heavy stones and rubble for years. Please, tell me more about yourself."

Harit looked at the goldsmith in amazement.

"You want to know something about me? Fine, but first my money, then I can speak freely." *For those two pieces of gold, I'll tell you every detail of my life and the history of all my ancestors too.*

"Of course, you shall have them."

Ishmael leaned forward and dropped the money into Harit's open hand. "Thank you again. Now speak!"

The coins felt warm and heavy. Harit fished out his money pouch and shook his head as he dropped them in almost tenderly.

What a fortune for such a small figurine. But these unbelieving *kafir* – Jews and Nazarenes alike – were known for their propensity for worshipping worthless splinters of wood and rolls of papyrus. Hundreds of splinters from the cross of their messiah, the dried fingers of their saints, and even rusty nails allegedly used in Jesus' crucifixion were sold to the hordes of pilgrims every year by resourceful traders in Jerusalem. Harit knew a few shady vendors who openly offered crude forgeries on their stalls and did very well out of it.

Who knows, maybe this winged figure is an effigy of some great saint of the scripture readers, or even their god, whose name they won't utter. The Nazarenes have three gods, which they call father, son and holy ghost. O Allah, I'm glad we true believers have it so much simpler, thought Harit with amusement. The old Jew seemed to be a good person, despite his insanity, so why shouldn't he talk with him? It had been a long time since Harit had told anyone anything about himself. No one was interested in the story of a day labourer living in the city without a family.

"As you wish, goldsmith, I'll tell you about my life. My full name is Harit ibn Tharit ibn Hamid. I was born in the port city of Acre as a free man and grew up there in a respectable, prosperous family. My father, Allah have mercy on his soul, used to manufacture brown sugar from sugar cane. He worked for a Frank, who owned the business. That was until our beloved Sultan Salah ad-Din, Allah protect him, reconquered Acre for Islam, shortly after the glorious Battle of the Horns of Hattin, and had all the infidels sold or killed. That included the Frank, who was too fat and old to be a slave. He lost his life for the glory of Allah. My father and all of our relatives pooled our money and bought the Frank's factory and the right to manufacture sugar from the Sultan's new governor. Our sweet wares went as far as Byzantium and Venice. The Nazarenes are crazy about sugar, as I'm sure you know – they only have honey as a sweetener."

Ishmael nodded. "I know. I lived for a long time in the realm of the red-bearded emperor of the Alemanns. Sugar was rare, coveted and expensive."

"Exactly, coveted... that describes it aptly," continued Harit. "Our product was coveted, my family industrious and very well respected. Our house on the waterfront was two storeys high and whitewashed so that it gleamed brightly from a distance. Inside, colourful tiles decorated the walls, the floors were covered in soft carpets that caressed our feet. There was a fountain of clear water in the courtyard, and on our roof were potted, shady palms under which we often held feasts on mild evenings. I was educated by a private tutor, learned reading, writing and even the language of the Nazarenes. That allowed me to actively help my father in the business."

Harit's eyes lit up as he reminisced about his home. He laughed happily, and again Ishmael saw his white teeth flash. Perhaps he chewed raw sugar cane daily, although it wasn't cheap to buy here.

"We even supplied sugar to the court of El Adil, our Sultan's brother. His officials always paid us generously. We were able to pay the farmers good prices for their harvest and often received gifts from them. Sometimes a lamb, or chickens, or figs, or fish from Galilee. I thought about marriage – there were plenty of eligible brides. Our good fortune lasted two years... and then..."

His voice grew quieter and his radiant eyes glazed over.

"...then came the day when the Almighty Creator turned his back on us. The Franks came back to Acre. The peoples from across the sea had joined forces. Led by King Richard, the dread of all true believers, Allah curse him and his offspring! The siege lasted two years. I thought it would never end. I helped out on the walls, hauling stones and boiling oil. The Sultan's brave warriors let it all rain down on the Franks who persistently stormed the ramparts. We suffered dreadful hunger and burning thirst. Illness and constant fighting decimated us. All the effort and hardship were in vain. The infidels conquered the city and the *shaitan* overcame us, in the form of King Richard. First, he had all the heroic defenders taken captive to demand ransom money from our merciful ruler Salah ad-Din. My family and all of our relatives were among them..."

Harit broke off and looked down at his stained, dusty sandals. The memory of the ordeal overwhelmed him and tears rolled down his cheeks.

Ishmael knew why he wept. Everyone in the country knew the story of the horrific slaughter of the two thousand hostages of Acre. King Richard received no money from the Sultan, so he had his people slaughter every man, woman and child. It was said that he hung a chain of severed heads around his horse's neck after the slaughter, to glorify the Christian god and to frighten his enemies. The goldsmith laid a sympathetic hand on the silent Muslim's shoulder.

"You managed to escape?" he asked with quiet empathy.

Harit nodded. "When they stormed into our house one night with torches, I ran terrified out onto the street. The Nazarenes were rampaging out there. Blood, screaming and death were everywhere. I collided with a huge warrior and fell at his feet in the dust. Expecting a deadly blow, I closed my eyes, but the giant picked me up like an empty sugar sack, shook me and gestured for me to keep quiet. Even in the dark, his eyes shone bright blue and I saw the goodness in them. He took me by the shoulders and I let him guide me. His incredible size and the bare sword in his hand protected me from the infidel soldiers, who fearfully gave him a wide berth. No one interfered with him as he took me to a breach in the crumbling city wall. He said something to me, it sounded urgent, but I didn't understand his language, it wasn't Frankish. So he kept pushing me gently down the rubble slope of mortar, stones and wood, waving his arms. I should flee, he was probably saying. May Allah bless this knight, I owe him my life. If I ever see him again, by the Almighty, I'll repay my debt to him!"

At the mention of the gigantic knight, Ishmael raised his bushy eyebrows and smiled at a distant but pleasant memory. He got slowly to his feet, fetched a jug of water for his guest and poured him a cupful.

Harit was oblivious. Eyes downcast, he continued, "I hid in the olive groves outside the city and saw the Christians execute my family and many of the other inhabitants the next day. All I could do was watch, powerless; no one could help them. I felt I was losing my mind, so I turned and fled into the mountains without any purpose or plan. One of our Sultan's patrols found me almost lifeless on a rocky plateau. They saved me from dying of thirst and I accompanied them to the safe city of Jerusalem. Thanks be to Allah, I found work and lodgings here, in the service of Izz ad-Din Yurdik, the governor appointed by our great Sultan."

Harit sighed deeply, then looked up. His face brightened and he spread his arms.

"And now you see before you an industrious worker doing his part to cleanse the Holy City of the infidels and cart the Nazarene's filth to the refuse trenches. I never thought this junk would make me rich. Allah's will is unfathomable! Perhaps the Nazarenes will even be driven out of Acre with the help of the Almighty. I would be glad to see my father's city again."

Harit smiled and wiped the tears from his cheeks, then whispered slowly and dreamily, emphasising every syllable, *"So dir Gott helfe!"*

"What? What did you just say?" asked goldsmith the, stirred again by a memory.

"Those were the last words I heard from the knight as he pushed me through the breach in the wall of Acre, saving my life. The words are burned into my memory. I don't know what they mean, but I hope one day I can repeat them to him in thanks, *so dir Gott helfe*," replied Harit.

Ishmael now had a hunch as to the identity of the Christian knight who had saved the Muslim's life. That was an Alemannic phrase, which he'd often heard uttered by a tall, Saxon warrior he once knew. Hartung of Scharfenberg was his name. He and his friend, Walter of Westereck, were to thank for the fact that Ishmael survived the long journey from Cologne to the Holy Land.

The two of them had led a large troop of armed pilgrims intent on liberating the Holy Sepulchre. Ishmael and ten dozen of his neighbours and friends were permitted to accompany them. This could not be taken for granted in a time when Jews were vilified as the murderers of the messiah, and massacred in their thousands by fanatical Christians in the cities of Alemannia.

The knights even borrowed a substantial sum of money from the Jews when their expensive venture was threatened with failure midway, due to a lack food and equipment. None of Ishmael's travelling companions thought they would ever see the money again. But after arriving in Palestine, the warriors accrued some wealth through theft and plunder, and repaid the debt.

Those two noblemen were powerful, fearsome fighters, but also generous and gallant. They always honoured their word, and protected the Jews from hostility. It had been almost two years since they parted ways outside the walls of the fiercely disputed city of Acre. Ishmael had continued on to Jerusalem and the knights had remained, presumably to serve in the army of King Richard the Lionheart. He was pleased to learn that they had survived the siege.

Ishmael was jolted out of his reverie when Leah entered the room and rubbed her bleary eyes in surprise.

"Uncle, we already have a visitor at this early hour? Why didn't you call for me?" she asked reproachfully, quickly covering her curly hair with a scarf and gazing inquisitively at Harit.

"You've already met our guest. He has brought me the second figurine, and I didn't want to wake you," replied Ishmael. "Prepare some tea for us, child, and perhaps some breakfast. He'll be staying a little longer. Won't you?"

He turned to Harit, who shook his head regretfully.

"That's not possible, I'm afraid. My work calls me, I can't be late. Perhaps I'll find more artefacts in the rubble under the temple. If so, I'll bring them to you this evening, and then I'd be glad to accept the invitation to eat with you," he said, rising to his feet.

"I look forward to it. Go with your god's blessing and bring me everything, no matter what you dig up. You won't regret it!"

Ishmael escorted the Muslim to the door, and Harit left the house with a cheerful disposition.

Goldsmith, you can be sure of it. You'll have everything I find, he thought, and whistled a joyful tune as he walked down the alley in the direction of the Temple Mount.

He didn't notice the huddled pilgrim watching intently from the other side of the street.

IX

Well look at that. You've sold the cherub to a Jew.

Guillaume sat across from the goldsmith's house in a shady gateway and watched Harit emerge through the door and hurry away.

After their encounters at the market an hour earlier, Guillaume had followed hot on his heels, never letting Harit out of his sight. This took him through the city's winding streets up to the northern wall protecting the Jewish quarter. There, Guillaume saw the Muslim knock on the door of a two-storey, whitewashed house in an empty street, and a weedy, white-bearded man wearing a dark felt skullcap and a black floor-length robe opened the door and let him in.

Guillaume was familiar with this quarter, its houses glued together as if holding each other up. Largely evacuated during the period of Christian rule in Jerusalem, it fell into disrepair. At that time, only a few money changers, healers and pawn brokers eked out an existence here. Now, many of the buildings appeared to be inhabited once more; they had been re-paired and some of the facades gleamed again in chalky white.

He had only been here once before. He was a squire at the time, in the service of his old Templar knight. His master suffered from bad colic, caused by overconsumption of fish, and sent Guillaume to find a doctor. Guillaume brought him a Jew-ish *medicus*, who got the vomiting Templar back on his feet with hot compresses and a herbal concoction.

Guillaume knew more about the Jewish people than any of the other Templars. During his time at the monastery, he read that Jesus was actually born a Jew, and that his preaching was based on the Jewish faith. And yet Guillaume shared the view of his Christian compatriots that these people had betrayed the

Saviour and allowed him to be nailed to a cross. They were outcasts, practised peculiar habits, and had an unfavourable reputation as usurers and misers. Which didn't discourage many high-born Christians from borrowing money from them or pawning their possessions during times of financial hardship.

Guillaume had chosen to wait and watch the entrance to the house until the Arab left. Then he would fetch his cherub, along with the second one, which he was certain the Jew had in his possession.

He crouched in the shade of a dark gateway, a stone's throw from the house, and pulled his hood down over his forehead.

After a while, a horde of children trotted into view, playing with a felt ball. They saw the ostensibly dozing man and tugged at his robe, begging for money. At first, Guillaume tried to shoo them away, but their shouts grew louder and they wouldn't leave him alone. Not wanting to attract attention, he flicked them a copper coin and asked them who lived in the house diagonally across the street.

"The pretty Leah lives there with her uncle, the old rabbi Ishmael," cried a small, thin boy with ears that stuck out. His companions nodded in confirmation.

"Come on pilgrim, more, give us more," begged the little boy, wiping his dripping nose with his hand.

Guillaume flashed his eyes dangerously at them.

"I don't have any more. Be gone, you little rats!"

He hid his face under his hood once more and hunkered down, ignoring the demanding tugs on his cloak.

The children hesitated a moment, then shrugged and left him alone, continuing raucously down the alley and disappearing around the next corner. It was quiet again, and he watched the Jew's door attentively.

Only an old man and a woman. This will be an easy robbery.

When the young Arab finally came out of the house, it seemed the time had come for Guillaume's raid. He got to his feet, but the door opened again and a dark-robed, veiled woman stepped out with a willow basket under one arm.

He froze and waited. But she was oblivious to him and skipped off toward the city centre. When she was far enough away, Guillaume glanced around warily, crossed the empty street and knocked on the closed door of the Jew's house. His dagger was clasped firmly in his hand, concealed in the sleeve of his robe.

Meanwhile, the overjoyed Ishmael took the second cherub up to his workshop. The industrious Harit had kept his word and been richly rewarded for it. Two bezants were a lot of money, but he had received three pounds of gold in return, so it was a ridiculously low price, especially considering the sacred significance of the sculpture.

Ishmael saw the generous payment as an advance on further finds that Harit may bring with him that evening. He had sent Leah to the market to shop for ingredients for a nice meal. He felt sorry for the young Muslim, whom fate had dealt a heavy blow, and who would be hungry when he came to them after work.

There was a loud knock at the front door. *Oh Leah, what have you forgotten this time?* he thought. She seemed quite flustered after the events of the last few hours.

He had locked the door behind her, as they had to be cautious with such a precious relic under their roof.

"Coming!" he called. He was about to lock his workshop, but the knocking intensified to an impatient thundering. He sighed and hurried downstairs as quickly as he could.

"Alright, alright, I'm almost there," he called loudly.

No sooner had he slid the bolt across than a rough hand reached for his throat – so forcefully and swiftly that he crashed against the wall of the little hallway and almost fainted.

"The figurines, where are they!" a voice hissed in Arabic in his ear.

He had no time to reply before he was grabbed roughly by his robe and flung into the centre of the living room. He hit the floor hard. A sharp pain shot up his right shin.

The attacker bent over him. The dazed Ishmael saw a glinting dagger waved threateningly in front of his face.

"Listen, Jew, I don't want to cause you any more pain. Just tell me where the statues are hidden and I'll let you live."

Ishmael tried to answer him, but his mouth suddenly filled with blood, which flowed over his trembling lips. His eyes rolled and he lost consciousness.

Guillaume grunted irritably, shook him, to no avail, and stood up. He had used too much force. The frail old man wasn't exactly a dangerous heathen warrior.

He surveyed the furnishings. There was nothing in the room but a carpet and an array of cushions. A wooden staircase led up to the second floor and he hastened up it, on a hunch. At the end of a small hallway, he found a heavy door, ajar, leading into a darkened room. Guillaume stormed inside, tripped over a stool and, flailing to steady himself, pulled a linen cloth off a workbench. He landed on his knees, cursing, and a cherub clattered to the floor in front of him.

My golden bird! I've finally found you!

He instantly forgot the pain in his kneecaps. His eyes adjusted to the dim light as he picked up the figurine and inspected it. Satisfied, he got to his feet and found the second cherub on the workbench. This sculpture was identical to his own figurine, down to the last hair, and its wings were held out over two dark grey tablets in front of it, as though protecting them. Guillaume stepped closer and noticed something engraved on them, in what looked like Hebrew letters.

"Holy Father," he breathed, crossing himself. It had to be them – the Lord's Ten Commandments chiselled in stone, received by Moses from the Almighty on Mount Sinai. They precisely matched the illustrations on the ancient parchments he had translated all those years ago in the monastery. Two stone tablets, two cubits long, a cubit wide.

The holiest of the holy! The origin of all faith. Before him were the actual contents of the Ark of the Covenant.

He felt the blood pulsing in his temples, and his mouth went dry from the shock. A shiver ran up his spine and he thought he could sense God's presence. He swiftly crossed himself several times.

I, Guillaume de Born, a bastard from the Pèrigord, former monastery student, member of the Order of Solomon's Temple, have been chosen as the one to possess the greatest and holiest relic of all time!

Breathing hard, he composed himself, picked up the linen cloth at his feet and carefully wrapped the tablets and the cherubim in it. Then he knotted it and slung the heavy bundle over his shoulder.

Meanwhile, Ishmael had regained consciousness downstairs. He was immediately gripped by fear. He tasted salty blood and heard his attacker cursing upstairs.

His first anxious thoughts were of the relic. He had to protect it, defend it with his life! But he couldn't get up. The shooting pain in his leg forced him to sink back to the floor, and he closed his eyes.

The Ark will disappear again, and there's nothing I can do about it. Who is this man? Did Harit put him up to this? He's no ordinary burglar, the man knows exactly what he wants. But I don't think it's the Arab's doing. Perhaps he carelessly bragged to someone about what he had sold for such a large sum, and they pursued the treasure for themselves.

Ishmael cursed himself for being so reckless and paying the Muslim two gold bezants for ostensibly worthless bronze sculptures. *Lord, don't let me die. Not yet,* he prayed desperately, as he felt the cold creep into his body.

He had to play dead – perhaps then the thief would simply leave him lying there. He did his best to suppress the pain and keep quiet when the robber thudded downstairs.

Ishmael tried to get a better look at him through half-closed eyes. He saw a tall, slender man with pale skin and a trimmed beard. A Frank, definitely. He wore a dark brown robe, and piercing blue eyes peered out from under its hood. On his left shoulder he carried a large bundle – evidently containing his loot. His right hand gripped a long dagger with a cross on its pommel. The cross formée of the Templars.

The Templar approached him. Ishmael stiffened, closed his eyes tightly and held his breath.

Guillaume looked down at the crumpled Jew and kicked him lightly in his side, eliciting a suppressed groan.

For a moment, he considered slitting the old man's throat just to be safe. But an inexplicable feeling of religious reverence arose in him and he rejected the notion.

A robbery in the house of a Jew wouldn't cause a stir among the Muslims in the city. He probably wouldn't even report it. What could he say? That the greatest treasure of the one true faith had been stolen from his house? No one would believe him. But to commit murder at the place where he had found the sacred artefacts could be an unforgiveable sin in the eyes of God. He had already piled enough guilt on himself to burn in hell for centuries. An act of mercy wouldn't do any harm, and after all, the goldsmith was the one who had united the tablets and the cherubim. That surely counted for something. Anyway, he was confident the old man couldn't identify him.

He bent over the rigid old man and whispered, "I know you can hear me. Forget all about this and you can continue living, and nothing will happen to your niece. Understood? It's only gold I'm taking from you. You'll get over the loss, won't you?"

Ishmael nodded faintly with trembling lips, his eyes still shut tight.

"Good."

Guillaume straightened up and slipped his dagger under his clothing, then hastened to the door. He looked cautiously up and down the street. There was no one in sight. He stepped out, shouldered the heavy bundle and walked at a leisurely pace toward the city centre.

Ishmael heard him leave the house and exhaled loudly. Tears welled up in his eyes. He couldn't be sure if they were tears of joy at surviving, or pain at the loss of the sacred relics. He tried to lift himself off the floor and managed to sit upright after a few painful attempts. Leaning against the wall near the front door, he gingerly pulled his robe up over his knees.

As he suspected, his right shin was broken. His foot lay limply and unnaturally twisted on the floor. His chin ached, and he wiped dark blood from his lips with a fluttering hand. He could feel with his tongue that he'd lost a tooth, and he gave an agonised groan.

Another one. At least I still have the leg, and hopefully it will heal without turning me into a cripple, he thought, gently feeling himself all over. He appeared otherwise intact. But what did he care about his frail body? The cherubim had been stolen. Probably by a Templar. The dagger with the cross on its hilt was a clue to the perpetrator's identity.

He was clearly no ordinary Nazarene; most likely a Templar disguised as a pilgrim. Ishmael had seen Templars before, outside Acre as they were preparing to storm the city walls. Their

Order was shrouded in sinister legends. They were said to unconditionally obeyed their leader's every command, and they were known to be exceptionally cruel and fearless when fighting the heathens. They were deadly enemies of Islam and therefore of the Sultan, who had them swiftly decapitated the instant he captured them.

The image of the man's angular face had burned into Ishmael's memory. He would never forget it. Those piercing eyes boring into him, the groomed beard and hissing voice. He shuddered again.

The Templar must have entered the city as a pilgrim to pray at the tomb of his Saviour, and somehow learned of the cherubim. Possibly from...

The goldsmith stiffened. Yes, Harit said that he bought back the second cherub from a pilgrim at the market – possibly the same man who attacked him.

If Harit did visit him again that evening with more of his finds, he could ask him about this pilgrim.

His head throbbed and his tongue explored the gap in his aching lower jaw. *A silver lining,* he thought, and a bitter smile crept across his swollen face. The molar that was knocked out had been throbbing slightly for the last few days. It probably had a tooth worm. So the brutal attack had at least saved him from the medicus' frightening pliers.

The instant he tried to move his right leg, he felt a shooting pain like a glowing poker in his shin. With immense effort, he dragged himself to the mound of cushions in the centre of the room and rolled onto them with a groan.

Ishmael was utterly exhausted. He closed his eyes and sank into a half sleep, from which he was startled awake by the rattling door.

"Uncle, I'm back!" Leah called cheerfully as she entered the room. "Why did you leave the door open, anyone could..." She faltered and then screamed in horror when she saw the old man with his blood-smeared chin laid out flat on the cushions.

She dropped her full basket of shopping and knelt down beside him.

"Uncle, what happened? Merciful God... what happened to you?" Her eyes filled with tears as she cradled his face in both of her hands.

Ishmael sniffed and swallowed a clot of blood.

"It's alright. I'm fine, Leah... don't worry... please, a sip of water, I... can't stand," he whispered.

"Of course, I'll fetch some!"

Leah sprang up and hurried to the water jug in the kitchen, treading carelessly on some figs and grapes that had rolled from her basket across the floor. She quickly returned with a full cup, from which Ishmael sipped gratefully.

"I was attacked, my child, I was attacked!" he explained. "My leg appears to be broken, nothing worse. And I lost a tooth. Otherwise I'm fine."

Only then did Leah notice the twisted leg. She clapped a hand over mouth, aghast.

"I'll fetch the medicus at once!"

"Absolutely not!"

Ishmael grabbed the sleeve of her robe and held her back.

"No medicus. No one in the community can know of the attack, do you hear me? No one! We're in considerable danger! The thief came for the golden cherubim. He knew exactly what he was looking for. You must treat the leg yourself, please... It appears to be a clean break, nothing too dramatic. Please go upstairs and see if the tablets are still in the workshop. Hurry!"

Leah looked into his troubled eyes, then rose and ran upstairs. She returned shortly.

"The tablets are gone. As far as I can tell, nothing else is missing. Even the golden bracelet for the governor's wife is still there," she said sadly, and Ishmael's eyes filled with tears.

He had expected as much, and it confirmed his fear that the intruder was indeed a member of the Templar Order, and that it wasn't just about the gold. The warrior monks were known for their relics. Many of these they had seized in the Holy Land and smuggled out before the Muslims reconquered Jerusalem. Probably to Acre, their present-day headquarters. It was alleged that they even had the shroud of their messiah Jesus in their possession, and they would certainly have knowledge of the old stories of the lost Ark of the Covenant.

Acre. Yes, that's where the disguised Templar must have fled with the treasure, he guessed. Only there, behind the fortress walls, would the stolen items be safe. He felt a glimmer of hope.

Leah looked at him with pity, then said decisively, "We must take care of this leg now, uncle. I need two thin boards, each a cubit long and not too wide. Where can I find something like that? In your workshop perhaps?"

Ishmael looked distracted. "Ah... no, in the courtyard; there's a stack of wood in the stable. What do you need them for?"

"I need to splint your leg and wrap it tightly with strips of cloth. And... I need another soft piece of wood," she replied.

"I understand, as a crutch."

Leah smiled wanly. "No, not as a crutch. For you to bite down on. The leg has to be reset, otherwise it'll heal crooked and you'll have a limp for the rest of your life. It will be very painful, believe me."

"If that's what must be done," Ishmael conceded. "But after that, with God's help, we'll try to retrieve the irreplaceable artefacts."

Leah shook her head. "I'm afraid you won't be able to walk for a few weeks. The holy relic is lost!"

Ishmael smiled weakly. "You're right. I can't do it myself. But I know someone who I'm sure will help us."

X

It was quiet and solitary on the stony, dry road that meandered gently southward around karst hills. Above him, the sky's canopy was a radiant blue. Small clouds scudded lazily toward the barren, brown mountain range on the horizon.

Low brambles clung to the ground at the sides of the road and tiny, grey lizards flitted into their meagre shade as he approached. Guillaume's dragging steps were the only sound in this wasteland. Everything around him looked calm and peaceful, but his senses were acutely heightened, and he clutched his dagger firmly in his right hand beneath his robe.

The Assassins were the most dangerous heathens he had ever encountered in the Levant. A notorious sect of murderers who risked their own lives to hunt down their victims. They killed in the name of their faith, but also for money. A meeting with them could easily end with a cut throat. He had to be exceptionally wary.

His thoughts kept returning to the contents of the Ark of the Covenant, which divine providence had led him to that morning in the old Jew's house. He wasn't sure he'd chosen a safe enough hiding place for the treasure. The ancient tablets inscribed with the word of God – the only true and original Commandments – would elevate him above everyone in the Order, and raise the brotherhood itself to be the leader of Christendom. No worldly ruler, not even the Pope, could challenge the might of the holy relic, the most precious possession in the world. And he had no better place to keep them safe than under the pile of straw in his room.

He would have returned to Acre with them immediately if he could, but he was determined to complete his mission for the Templars – if not quite in the way intended by Grand Master Robert de Sablé. Guillaume had plans of his own.

He glanced around warily and continued walking. Grains of sand and small stones kept finding their way into his sandals, a painful reminder that he had been forced to leave his mule in the stall at his lodgings.

The derelict monastery of the holy Lazarus, whom Jesus awoke from the dead, lay an hour's walk south of Jerusalem at the foot of the Mount of Olives, on the old pilgrim road to Bethlehem.

Guillaume squinted in the midday sun. He could make out the ruined house of God in the distance, its half-collapsed bell tower jutting like a charred, admonishing finger into the sky.

Those monks will never rise from the dead, despite their countless prayers to Lazarus.

Guillaume knew this road like the back of his hand. As a newly ordained Templar, his first responsibility had been to protect pilgrims from bandits and thieves on their journey from Jerusalem to Bethlehem, the site of the Ascension of Christ. That was many years ago, and a wistful expression stole across his face as he recalled those times. The road had been very dangerous. Thieving Bedouins frequently tried to rob the pilgrims, most of whom were unarmed. It was near here that he fought his first battle with them.

He was escorting roughly fifty Christians one day, when a dozen Muslim horsemen galloped down the road, brandishing swords, and charged at the column with terrifying howls. Guillaume impaled one with his lance, then drew his sword and split the skull of another. He knocked another two attackers from their horses with the help of his squires, who despatched them with heavy blows of their clubs. He rode fearlessly at the remaining heathens, bellowing, with a dripping blade, and they turned tail and galloped away.

Word of this battle must have spread quickly, because afterwards the mere sight of his white cloak with its blood-red cross formée was enough to discourage the infidels from attacking. As were the heads of the slain, which he had impaled as a warning on wooden spikes along both sides of the road, where they slowly decomposed.

The heads were long gone, and Guillaume was now travelling the same road disguised as a harmless pilgrim, to negotiate the murder of a Christian with the most terrible of all heathens.

He arrived at the agreed location before the sun had reached its zenith. Little remained of the monastery other than mounds of blackened stones scattered around the crumbling bell tower. Saladin's warriors were thorough in their devastation. There was nothing left to mark the grave of Lazarus. Even the village below the ruined monastery was desolate. Houses with crumbling walls crouched sadly on the lower slopes of the Mount of Olives.

Guillaume sat down on the crumbling wall of a fountain and peered into it. All he saw was sand at the bottom. The hole was as dry as his throat. He sighed, drew a water flask from his pilgrim's sack and sipped from it.

The sun was scorching and he began to overheat – under his earth-coloured robe he wore a chainmail shirt over a quilted, felt *gambeson*. He had had the foresight to purchase both cheaply from a Pisan merchant in Jaffa. The chainmail rings were rusty and a little worn, but still useful when negotiating with murderers.

Damn it, there are only two seasons in this land – winter and summer. Summer was fast approaching, even though it was only late February. The small palms around the fountain offered the only semblance of shade. He flopped down on the sand beneath them and gazed to the east.

That was the way they would come – the Assassins, or *Hashasheen* as they were also known, after their alleged habit of smoking or chewing intoxicating herbs. They were ascribed demonic strength, and suddenly he believed in their magical powers, when a curved, glinting dagger appeared out of nowhere before his eyes.

He stiffened with fear as a strong arm pressed against his throat from behind.

"You're looking for us?" a voice hissed in his left ear. Guillaume smelled the man's cloying breath.

They had arrived early. The blade reflected the midday sun and dazzled him. This wasn't the first time his life had been threatened, and he tightened his grip on the dagger concealed beneath his robe. He knew he could bite the hand in front of him, spin to the right and ram his weapon into the face of the man behind him.

"It seems I've found you," he replied casually in Arabic. The hold around his throat loosened slightly, increasing Guillaume's advantage by giving him a little more freedom of movement.

No trained warrior would make such a mistake. You're dangerously close to death, heathen.

Another Assassin swept into view and sat cross-legged in front of him. The man's red turban was wrapped around most of his face. Midnight-black eyes glared at Guillaume through a narrow gap. His robe was a brilliant white, and held together by a red cloth belt holding a silver dagger.

"What do you want, Frank?" the man asked curtly.

"My name is Almarich. I'm dragoman and servant to the Templars and I have an important message for your leader, Sheikh Rashid ad-Din Sinan," replied Guillaume.

"Ahh..." The Assassin nodded. "...the rich brothers of the white robes. I haven't heard from your people in a long time.

They were good to us and we were useful to them. They still owe us two lives."

A gesture from him and the arm holding the dagger at Guillaume's throat vanished. The Templar glanced behind him, but there was now no one in sight. All he saw were palms, ruins and sand.

"Sorcery!" he muttered in Frankish.

"Believe what you want to believe," said the man opposite him, also in Frankish.

He regarded the surprised Templar with amusement.

"As you see, we have many talents, including languages. Call me Hassan. I'm the right hand of Rashid ad-Din Sinan, praise be to the Lord. And you're not Almarich nor a dragoman, although you speak our language well. I recognise you, despite your clipped beard. Your name is Guillaume, the turcopolier of the Templars. You command the light cavalry. I saw you at the wedding of your king Henry to that whore Isabella last year. Disgraceful to remarry only eight days after her husband's death. And on top of that, she was pregnant to her dead husband. You infidels are veritable serpents!"

Guillaume smiled and replied, "And I know that the violent death of her spouse, King Conrad of Montferrat, was your work. Furtively stabbed in an alley in Tyre on the way home from his evening meal. Disgraceful for a king to die by an ordinary knife in his full belly. Unfortunately, the two murderers were killed too quickly after the act to name their employer. Was it really Lionheart, the English king, who ordered you to do it? Or was it Salah ad-Din?"

"We want nothing to do with the Kurdish sultan. We curse him – and that red-haired pig-eater Richard! You should know better," retorted Hassan evasively. "I already told you, you owe us two lives. Our brothers gave theirs after carrying out the deed, for the glory of Allah."

So I was right, thought Guillaume. He had guessed the new Grand Master of the Templars was behind the treacherous murder that had shaken the Kingdom of Jerusalem.

"Two lives..." Guillaume nodded. "I can offer you one life as recompense. And a thousand gold bezants. Enough to buy a hundred good camels or build a stone tower for your fortress. I think that's a suitable payment for... shall we say... the premature demise of a high-ranking man. What do you think?"

Hassan arched his back and smoothed his white robe. He surveyed the Templar, who held his gaze. *A very high sum. Too much for a knight, too little for a king.*

"To decide whether that's enough, I must hear the name," he replied shrewdly. "Do you have the gold with you?"

"Of course not. I wouldn't carry that much through the mountains alone and on foot. I've heard there are hordes of thieves and all kinds of rabble roaming out here on the pilgrim routes."

Guillaume smirked when he saw the Assassin's dark eyebrows furrow in anger.

"We're not thieves, Frank," he said disdainfully. "We are the fear and the terror of recusants who do not obey my lord!"

"Oh, I'm sure you are. I wasn't referring to you," Guillaume pacified him. He reached into his sack, pulled out a leather pouch and threw it at the Arab's feet.

"I brought with me five hundred gold bezants as an advance payment."

The Assassin opened it and let the chinking coins run through his fingers.

"This is good, Frank. Very gratifying. Now tell me who stands in your way."

Guillaume took a deep breath and held it for a moment. He knew that once he uttered the name there was no going back.

"The Knights Templar would like to rid themselves of a traitorous man who has sullied their honour and faith. No suspicion may fall on the brothers, and it must happen as swiftly as possible. The matter must not be delayed."

The Arab rolled his eyes impatiently.

"We'll hear our lord's decision and then obey his will. Now speak, who is it?"

After a moment's hesitation, the turcopolier answered in a low tone, "Tell your lord I want the Templar Grand Master, Robert de Sablé, to die."

The Assassin didn't seem especially impressed by the name. If Nazarenes wanted to kill each other, he was fine with that. And he was happy to help if they paid him well. Perhaps the Grand Master of the Templars would offer even more gold for his life to be spared. Or he could relieve this infidel now of the full sum of the blood money, which perhaps he was carrying with him after all. His sack looked full.

"For the leader of the Templars, the advance payment is too small," he said haughtily, with a dismissive gesture. "Surely you have more than that with you!"

Guillaume noticed Hassan's eyes flicker briefly. He swiftly drew his knife from under his robe, grabbed the Assassin who had suddenly appeared behind him and thrust his dagger over his left shoulder into the man's neck, while the attacker's dagger glanced off Guillaume's concealed chainmail. The man fell sideways and clutched his throat, blood spurted between his fingers and his feet scrabbled helplessly in the sand. He died gurgling beside the still seated knight, who watched impassively.

Horrified, Hassan reached for the dagger in his belt, but the Templar coolly shook his head.

"Don't even think about it," he warned, casually wiping his knife on the dead Assassin's robe while staring straight into

Hassan's wide eyes. "I don't believe in sorcery. I smelled him behind me."

Hassan swallowed. His dead companion was one of the best fighters in his troop. This Templar was incredibly dangerous.

"Alright, alright..." he croaked, raising both hands. "Please, spare me! It was worth a try, I'm sure you understand!"

"Yes, of course, you're professional killers. It's your livelihood," Guillaume replied tersely, getting to his feet. He slipped his dagger beneath his robe and added, "I'm a Templar. My role is to protect faithful Christians for the glory of the Lord Jesus. I'm sure you're aware that our Order has always fostered good relationships with you Assassins. I met your leader, Rashid ad-Din Sinan, at his castle a few years ago when I went to collect the tribute owed to us for our successful campaigns in your territory. I also have a long history with the fat potter in Jerusalem, Muhammad, who spies for you. A truly gluttonous, flabby man, but dependable if one feeds him enough money. Are you the same?"

The Assassin looked confused, nodded, then shook his head. "Gluttonous... no... but you can depend on me. Muhammad told me about you. But he didn't call you Guillaume, he simply spoke reverently of a 'blood Templar' with whom he had done good business before Jerusalem was taken by the Kurdish sultan. He said you were one of the most skilled and ruthless knights in your Order. I can now confirm that. But he also said you were a very generous man. I swear to you by the beard of the prophet, your enemies are my enemies from this day forth!"

Guillaume didn't think much of this promise, but extended his right hand nonetheless. Hassan grasped it hesitantly and allowed himself to be pulled to his feet. Standing up, he didn't even reach the knight's shoulders.

"Dispose of the body of your incompetent man and then hurry to your master with my assignment. He knows I'm a man of my word, and that payment is assured. Your fortress Masyaf is fifteen days from here, so make haste. The master of the Templars should be dead no later than one month from now. When it's done, find me in Acre and you'll have the rest of your money. Don't try to warn the Grand Master or negotiate a higher price for sparing his life. He won't be interested. Instead, he'll declare war on your territories and have you all slaughtered. You know too much about his involvement in the assassination of the former king. When de Sablé is dead, I'll be supreme commander of the Brotherhood, and I'll liberate you from the onerous tribute you pay to the Order, and maintain peace with you. You have my word."

He increased his iron grip and Hassan's knees buckled slightly at the pain.

"And remember this: if anyone other than your leader asks after me, you'll remain silent about our arrangement!"

"By Allah, I have already forgotten you. I never met a Templar," the Assassin gasped.

Guillaume released Hassan's crushed hand and smiled. *So they call me blood Templar.* The name appealed to him. He turned and climbed slowly down the stony slope to the road without a backward glance.

He felt deeply satisfied that his meeting with the contract killers had gone so well. De Sablé's days were numbered, and after his death, everything would be different. Guillaume de Born, the bastard, would become Grand Master of the Templars with the help of the greatest relic of Christendom. He wanted to return to Jerusalem as quickly as possible to retrieve the tablets and the cherubim before heading back to Acre.

The holy Lazarus rose from the dead in this place, thought Guillaume, taking a deep breath. That was surely a good omen for the beginning of his own glorious resurrection.

XI

It was as Leah had feared. The sacred relics brought bad luck. After resetting her uncle's broken bone, she bandaged his leg tightly with strips of linen. Ishmael didn't cry out, but the small piece of wood he bit down on during the procedure was covered with deep tooth marks.

Tears and spittle matted his white beard. He was pale, and his creased face was more deeply furrowed than ever by the pain. His compassionate niece handed him a towel, with which he dabbed his face distractedly.

"Leah, you should work as medicus for our community. Even my old friend Moshe ben Maimon couldn't have done better," he said, looking appreciatively at the neatly wound bandage.

She smiled at the mention of the Jewish scholar and personal physician to the Sultan, also known as Maimonides, who lived near the city of Cairo.

"So, you're feeling well enough to crack jokes again," she replied. "As you know, I grew up with my father and two brothers. There was no mother in our house – to take care of those three big children after accidents and through countless illnesses. That included a few broken bones. I often had to treat them, and learned a little about healing. Believe me, they kept me busy."

Ishmael sucked air through his teeth. He wasn't in the mood for banter. The relics from the Ark of the Covenant had been stolen. Having been lost for so many centuries, it could now have provided unity and hope for their persecuted people dispersed across the world. The blueprint for a new acacia wood chest was already sketched in his mind. If he interpreted the scriptures literally, the one true God could have appeared to him. It was said that the Lord's presence on Earth was located between the two inward-facing cherubim on the gold-plated lid of the Ark.

If the Ark were made whole again, perhaps it would reveal the unbelievable power ascribed to it – for example, burning all enemies of the Israelites in a single moment, in rays of fire, in preparation for the resurrection of the bygone Jewish kingdom.

He couldn't allow that to remain just a fairy tale. He alone had been called to make this dream a reality. The Ten Commandments and the two cherubim had to be found and retrieved at any cost.

Ishmael tried to sit up, but Leah pressed him gently back against the cushions.

"Stay there and be still. You need plenty of rest, or your leg will heal crooked. Now tell me, who did this to you, and why did he only steal the tablets and cherubim, and nothing else? Did he know their significance?"

The rabbi slumped. "Oh, Leah, I believe the damned thief was a Christian, in fact one of the most terrible Nazarenes of all – a Templar knight. His dagger had a cross formée on the hilt, and he knew of the cherubim in our house."

"A Templar? Here, in Jerusalem? Uncle, you must be mistaken."

She had seen the terrifying Templar knights once as a young girl. They were heading out from Jerusalem with banners flying, to confront Sultan Salah ad-Din at the Battle of Hattin. Some returned, but only with their heads impaled on the spears of the triumphant Muslim cavalry, who reclaimed the city after the battle. She remembered it well. Their stinking heads decayed for weeks on top of the walls.

She had heard gruesome stories about them. It was said that their bodies lived on in the desert, stealing the heads of lone wanderers to replace their own, so that they could continue to fight the Sultan. She shuddered at the thought.

"They're all dead. The Sultan purged them all, didn't he?" she asked.

"I'm not so sure. I know a Templar when I see one, and there are still a few of them left," said Ishmael with conviction. "This man was no ordinary thief. He was very tall and agile, with exceptional strength. Blue eyes, pale skin – obviously from the west. But he spoke Arabic surprisingly well. He asked me specifically about the cherubim and knew exactly what he would find here."

Ishmael groaned and massaged his temples. He frowned deeply and became agitated. "The holy relic! He stole it! That damned *goi,* that infidel, son of a dog, may his unclean, uncut cock turn leprous and fall off! I must have it back, Leah, do you hear me? For our people! It's our direct link to the Lord. His Commandments, his will!"

Leah tenderly pushed a strand of hair off his sweat-soaked brow.

"Calm yourself, uncle. Can I leave you alone? I'll go to our neighbours or to the synagogue and ask for help. Surely the thief is still in the city. Perhaps we can find him with their help."

"No, my child, stay here! No one may learn of the treasure! Not yet! I must make preparations – it must first be hidden in a safe place. Revealing the secret to the world now would bring misfortune on us all!"

As if it hasn't already, thought Leah. "It's alright, I understand." She pressed him gently back into the cushions. "You need rest. Please try to sleep. I'll watch over you," she said, covering him with a woollen blanket.

The goldsmith couldn't argue. The terrible events of that morning had taken their toll on his aged body.

"Don't go anywhere," he murmured, then closed his eyes and slept. Leah waited at his side a while, then got up quietly. She gathered the leftover bandages and the piece of wood. Then she slipped into the small pantry, where she absentmindedly put away her market purchases into the clay jars and wooden shelves.

She was in shock after the attack. What if her uncle had suffered worse than a broken leg? It didn't bear thinking about. The idea of being all alone in this city frightened her. She would have to hire herself out as a serving maid to members of the community. Or ask her brothers in Antioch for help. The feeling of being suddenly alone was all too familiar. When her partially paralysed father died suddenly two years ago, she had been presented abruptly with a similar predicament. A short time later, as if by some miracle, her uncle had arrived with several travelling companions from the west to live in the Holy City. He had immediately taken her under his wing and, with the consent of her relieved siblings, taken up residence in his brother's house and set up his goldsmith workshop there, so that Leah was able to remain in the house.

At the market, Leah had purchased a small bowl of salted sardines from the Sea of Galilee, which she distractedly placed on a shelf.

Fish, a symbol of fertility. She frowned. Sometimes she dreamed of a husband, her own household, laughing children, her own family, but there had never been room in her life for those things. It had always been filled with worry and care for her kin. Anyway, there were few suitors in the small Jewish community, and none she would seriously consider.

A knock at the front door made her prick up her ears. Thinking on her feet, she picked up a long kitchen knife and scurried into the living room. *Not the thief again, I hope,* she thought, glancing with concern at her uncle, who was snoring quietly.

But the soft rapping sounded too gentle for an intruder.

"Who's there?" she asked in a whisper.

"It's me, Harit. Let me in!"

Relieved, she opened the door a crack and peered out. "Please go, my uncle is indisposed."

"*As-salamu aleikum,* beautiful niece of the goldsmith. He is expecting me, it's important. I have more wares for him," urged Harit impatiently.

"I told you, he can't see you. Come back later."

"But he ordered these things from me! He just needs to take a quick look at them!" The Arab held up a dusty, felt sack for her to see.

"Who is it, Leah?" Ishmael called out behind her.

She turned in surprise. "It's the Muslim from this morning."

"Please invite him in. He's welcome." Ishmael sat up with a groan and rubbed his gummy eyes.

Leah concealed the kitchen knife behind her back and opened the door. Harit stalked past her, head held high.

"You see? He's expecting me," he said with a grin. "Greetings, Master Ishmael. I always honour my word. Look, I bring you more valuable things from the Temple Mou-..." He faltered and stared at the goldsmith's bandaged leg.

Ishmael saw the dismay in his eyes and waved his hand. "It's nothing. Sit with me. Leah, bring us sweet tea, I have something to discuss with my guest."

She frowned and left the room reluctantly.

Harit cheerfully watched her go, opened his sack and spread out the supposed treasure: two rusty spearheads, a pewter spoon, a tattered leather sandal and a cracked ceramic oil lamp imprinted with a cross.

Ishmael frowned. "Is that all?"

"Yes, unfortunately," Harit admitted. "By Allah, there is nothing else in that place. But these are worth something, surely?"

The goldsmith shook his head with regret and disappointment. "No, this is rubbish, nothing but useless, worthless rubbish."

Harit looked sorrowful. It was as he had feared, yet he hoped the Jew would pay him something for it.

"Then please give me just a little, as I learned today that my work at the Temple Mount has come to an end. The overseer no longer needs my services and he's let me go. I'm a poor man and I desperately need money. Please find it in your heart to buy these things from me." He bowed humbly several times, still seated.

A smile flickered across Ishmael's face. He had paid the Muslim a fortune for the figurines and stone tablets. Under different circumstances, he may have given in – after all, the Arab had discovered and brought him the holiest relic of Judaism.

An audacious plan began to form in his mind at the thought of the stolen treasure. He scrutinised the young man and said warily, "Harit, I can't pay you for these things, but if you can keep a secret and provide me with certain information, I'll reward you richly. What do you say?"

"By the beard of the prophet, you can trust me! That goes without saying. Tell me, what sort of secret is it, and what is it you want to know?"

"Listen closely. I was attacked this morning shortly after your visit. The two figurines you brought to me were stolen. By a Nazarene, I suspect. I wonder if perhaps you know him?"

Harit gasped, genuinely shocked. "By Allah, what terrible luck! It's true, I bought back the second figurine from a Nazarene at the market. Curse him! He must have followed me here!

What malicious *jinn* got into him?! Oh, forgive me, Master Goldsmith, it's all my fault!"

"It's alright, you're not to blame," Ishmael reassured him. "Can you please describe him to me? I want to be absolutely sure. And repeat every word he said to you. It's very important!"

Harit bowed his head and searched his memory. "He was tall. Very tall and slim. Less than thirty summers old, with a short, dark blond beard. I can still picture his cold, blue eyes. He was dressed like one of the countless pilgrims, with a walking staff and knapsack. He struck me as an educated man. He spoke to me in my language and shamelessly squeezed me like an orange when I negotiated to buy back the figurine. By Allah, a scandalous price! I had to give him ten dirham, even though I sold it to him for only one!"

Ishmael nodded. It was doubtless the man who had robbed him. Harit's description matched his recollection of the Templar.

"Tell me more. What else did he say to you?"

"He said he intended to leave the city today and return to his homeland. Then I said goodbye and left him in the middle of the market. He must have followed me to you, the monster, Allah curse him and all his offspring!"

Leah entered the room with two steaming cups of tea on a tray, and was startled by the Muslim's loud outburst. She now wore a light veil of the finest white cotton over her face, as it was inappropriate for her to show it to a strange man, even one so young.

"Not so loud! My uncle needs quiet," she said reproachfully, placing the drinks on the floor between them.

"Child, don't fret. Harit knows the Templar. But he's not to blame for the attack," Ishmael said in a soothing voice. "Sit with us."

She gladly accepted the invitation and sat on the edge of the rug.

"A Templar? Really?" said the Muslim, and he blanched and wrung his hands.

"Yes, a Templar. And I believe he's on his way to your father's city – to Acre," Ishmael said pointedly, and then sipped his tea.

A plan to retrieve the holy relics had taken shape in Ishmael's head during his conversation with Harit. It was a risky venture, which may even endanger the life of his niece. To have even the slightest chance of success, it had to be implemented quickly. Otherwise, the treasure could be lost again for a very long time, if not forever.

He leaned back in the cushions with a sigh, closed his eyes and pondered, while Leah and Harit sat in silence. They assumed the weakened man was falling asleep, and waited quietly.

But Ishmael wasn't asleep. Once he was satisfied his plan was complete, he opened his eyes and cleared his throat. He had to convince his niece and the young Arab to see it through under any circumstances.

"My friend Harit," Ishmael began in an ingratiating tone, at which Harit raised his eyebrows in surprise. "Would you leave me and my niece alone for a moment? I want to discuss something very important with her. Please take your tea out into our shady garden, just behind the kitchen. Make yourself comfortable on the bench out there. When I call you back in, I'll make you an offer which will solve your money troubles." Ishmael indicated the way to the garden.

Harit was perplexed, but could see in the old man's sparkling eyes that he was serious. He rose, bowed and went outside.

My prayers have been answered! He has money for me, even though I brought misfortune on his house. What a confused, good-natured man this scripture reader is. Allah has led me to him, so that I can finally be lifted out of poverty, he thought as he left the living room, excited to hear old Ishmael's proposal.

Perhaps he would be asked to track down that damned pilgrim, report him to the Sultan's soldiers and receive a high reward following his arrest. Or perhaps he would simply be asked to acquire some more artworks that others considered worthless. He knew several places around Jerusalem where large mounds of rubble had towered since ancient times. Surely he could find something of value to the goldsmith there.

Harit smiled, sat down on the small bench in the garden and slurped his tea appreciatively.

XII

"You must ride to Acre tomorrow to retrieve the holy Covenant."

Her uncle's words hit Leah like a slap in the face, rendering her speechless.

"I expect that damned Templar will take the relic to that city along the fastest route possible, or even get it out of the country on a ship. Time is of the essence – all is not yet lost, and if there's even the slimmest possibility of getting it back, we have to try everything in our power. I know two formidable Alemannic knights in Acre. They owe me a favour and they'll help you," Ishmael explained.

Leah's face flushed bright red. She tore the scarf from her locks, jumped to her feet and paced frantically back and forth across the room.

"Me? I'm supposed to pursue the Templar? Me, a mere woman? How do you think that will go? He'll kill me! Go to Acre?! The farthest I've been is the Sea of Galilee, and only once with my father to visit a market in Tiberias. That was many years ago, and only a day's journey! This is insanity! Uncle, you can't ask this of me, I'll never succeed!"

Ishmael leaned back in his cushions and spoke quietly and clearly. "Leah, it's the only way to bring the holy relic back to Mount Zion. None of our people is capable of overwhelming a Templar, because we don't know how to use weapons. And a Muslim warrior wouldn't dare attempt such a thing in the city of the Nazarenes, not for all the money in the world. Especially not on behalf of a Jew. The two knights I mentioned are truly generous and noble men. They protected me and many Jewish families from danger on our way to the Promised Land. Some of those people are now our friends and neighbours, and will take care of me while you're away. Listen, I would go myself, at once, but I can't go to Acre in my condition. You're my only hope, you *must* do it! For me, for our people, for our faith and for the Lord! Leah, I beg you!"

Leah's thoughts were in turmoil. Apparently, this was the end of her pleasantly peaceful existence. She was happy in her role as housekeeper for her uncle and deeply grateful for his kindness, but such a dangerous undertaking lay beyond her powers of imagination.

She understood the ineffable significance of the Ark to her people. But she still felt the shock in her bones after the attack on her home only hours ago. A feeling of panic crept up the back of her skull, and she desperately tried to think of a way out.

"But uncle, I don't know this Templar. I didn't see him. How am I supposed to identify him? And do you really think these... knights will help us? Us Jews? I don't speak the Frankish language. How am I to find and persuade them? A woman on a long journey alone – I'll be scarcely through the city gate before a slave trader abducts me or a bandit robs me, perhaps rapes or even kills me! Your plan is madness and – don't be angry with me – but it's impossible too! It's best we forget we ever saw the sacred relic!"

Ishmael gazed lovingly at his dismayed niece and fought hard to suppress a chuckle. *She has her Andalusian mother's hot temper, and the cool, calculating intellect of my brother,* he thought. He replied in a soothing tone, "Leah, we *must* get it back. Trust me, I've thought it through. Listen – Harit, the young Muslim in the garden, knows the Templar. He traded one of the cherubim with him. I'm about to persuade him and pay him handsomely to escort and assist you. He is fluent in the Frankish language and lived for a long time in Acre. I'm sure he'll be able to find the knights. He can pose as your husband, and if you dress as a Muslim, no harm will come to you. I would never let you go alone. And as for the knights, your father left us a considerable fortune in silver. I've also put aside some money over the years. So we can, and will, offer the warriors an exceptionally high reward. It will be a sum they can't refuse. If they do, then we must give up hope and accept that the Ark of the Covenant is lost to us again."

Leah knelt before him, looking small and lost. Rivulets of tears ran down her flushed cheeks and dripped from her chin. She made one last attempt to dissuade him.

"Uncle, please..." she sobbed. "I can't do it. This task is too big for me. Oh, uncle, at least give me time to think about it... please, just until tomorrow..."

Ishmael leaned forward and gently stroked her tousled hair. He knew he was placing a heavy burden on his niece. But he could see no other way. The sacred artefacts had to be brought back to the Holy City, and quickly, while their trail was still fresh.

"You know, Leah, you remind me of your mother. She was a strong, clever woman. Your father and I met her in Hispanic Cordoba where we grew up. She was the daughter of a highly respected jewel merchant. No sooner were they married than we had to flee from the Almohads – the Muslim Berber rulers. We separated; I went to Alemannia; she and your father chose the long journey to Jerusalem. She was already pregnant with your eldest brother. A ship took them to the coast of Egypt and they wandered for weeks on foot through blistering hot deserts to the city. Here, they built your family home with their own hands and had two more children. Your mother never gave up hope for a better life. She was always a loyal, proud and cheerful companion to your father. Her blood is in you, her strength and her unshakeable self-belief. You're capable of more than just running a household and bookkeeping – I know it, and you sense it too. Trust yourself and you'll see that you can do anything!"

Leah bowed her head and nodded timidly. Her mother was still very much alive in her memory, just as her uncle had described her. She used to swathe herself in a gentle scent of rosewater, warm and sweet. These days, expensive rosewater applied after a bath was the only luxury Leah permitted herself. It made her feel closer to her mother.

Her sudden death hit Leah and the rest of the family very hard. One morning she didn't wake up and no one knew how she had died. She was never sick, was always full of energy, gentle with her children and quick to laugh and joke. The medicus suspected a sudden stroke as the cause of death. Leah had little time to mourn. From that day on, it was her duty to organise the household for her father and two brothers.

"She was wonderful, wasn't she?" Leah whispered.

"Oh yes," replied Ishmael. "Extraordinary. Like you, my child."

He realised too late he had called her a child again, and bit his tongue. Fortunately, she seemed not to notice.

"Alright, uncle. I'll try, even though I'm not convinced it will work and I'm terribly nervous about such an adventure. But I'm not doing it for the sacred relics, I'm doing it for you and my family."

"I thank you, Leah. I thank you from the bottom of my heart. And our people will thank you for all eternity. If you're successful, you'll go down in the scriptures as the guardian of the Ark of the Covenant, I'll make sure of it!"

Ishmael breathed a sigh of relief. "Please bring the Muslim inside. I'll ask him if he'll help us. And remember – not a word about the holy relic. We simply want to get the cherubim back. He doesn't need to know anything else."

Harit relaxed on the wooden bench in the shade of the house, occasionally sipping his delicious tea and gazing, bored, at his dusty sandals. He could hear the loud voices of the old Jew and his niece inside the house, but couldn't understand them because they were conversing in Hebrew, which he didn't know.

What an unpredictable day this has turned out to be, he mused. That morning he had found the Nazarene at the market and succeeded in buying back the second winged figurine. He had received more money for it from the goldsmith than expected. After that, he had worked under the Temple Mount until midday, when the overseer had suddenly told him his services were no longer needed. The few objects he had dug up from the site turned out to be worthless to the Jew. And the old man had been robbed. Apparently by the same pilgrim he had spoken and traded with.

His frowned. The Jew's generous payment for the statues wouldn't last the rest of his life. Now that he was without work again, he had to find a way to earn a living. It wouldn't be easy. There were hundreds of poor day labourers like him in Jerusalem.

He banished these bleak thoughts with a wave of his hand. Allah had always been at his side, and would continue to ensure his wellbeing. *Inshallah* – God willing, he thought, with a confident smile.

A door creaked and Leah called him back into the house in a strained voice.

The goldsmith invited Harit to sit opposite him again, cleared his throat and said with an earnest expression, "Harit, you've learned of my misfortune and I of the loss of your work. I believe you to be a reliable and trustworthy man, so I'd like to employ you. I pay well, as you know, and if you agree, then you won't need to worry about money for a long time. What do you say?"

The Muslim straightened up and looked at the rabbi expectantly. Only minutes ago he had reassured himself that the Almighty would provide him with a way to make a living.

"It would have to be a lot of money. Working for a Jew isn't considered honourable by my compatriots," Harit replied hesitantly.

"Yes, I know. What if I told you that you wouldn't be working for me here in Jerusalem, but accompanying my niece on a journey to Acre? I'm sure you know the way. You'll see your father's city again and probably also the lofty knight who saved your life. What if I were to pay you..." Ishmael hesitated a moment. "What if I were to pay you a thousand silver dirham for it?"

"Then I would say, not only have you injured your leg, but your head was also affected!" blurted Harit. He could scarcely imagine such a sum – more than five times the amount a day labourer earned in a year.

"My head is fine and I'm serious. I must get the figurines back from the pilgrim, and you and my niece are the only ones who can help me."

"You must be mad, goldsmith, utterly mad! So much money!" Harit glanced questioningly at Leah, who sat motionless beside her uncle, staring at the floor.

Harit's mouth suddenly felt dry and he craved a mouthful of tea, but his cup was outside in the garden.

"Didn't you say it was a Templar who stole the statues? A Templar! They're butchers, merciless warriors! It's rumoured that they drink the blood of Muslims in the name of their many gods. I saw what they did to the true believers during the conquest of Acre. And you want to send out a weak woman and a lowly day labourer to steal back the spoils of a fierce Templar?

You must be out of your mind! Why are these figurines so important to you?" He shook his head in disbelief.

Ishmael raised his hands in a placatory gesture. He had expected these objections.

"Let me tell you my plan. The statues are sacred to my people. I dare not say more. Except that I must have them back at any cost. You and my niece will travel to Acre as a young married couple. You will disguise yourselves as cloth merchants – a very ordinary sight. You know your way around your hometown, and you speak Frankish. When you arrive, you must find two Nazarene knights who owe me a favour. Leah will persuade them with an extraordinarily high reward to take the stolen items from the Templar. You need only describe him, so they know who he is. Once they've done their part, you'll bring my niece and the recovered items back to Jerusalem. That's all you have to do."

Ishmael saw Harit stiffen in fear and his eyes grow rounder and rounder. He paused and gave him a reassuring nod.

"Don't worry, you won't have to meet that despicable pilgrim in person. These mighty warriors are skilled with weapons and fear no opponent. A single Templar won't stand a chance against them. Trust me, I've seen them fight. They protected me once on my way here from Alemannia. In fact, you've already met one of them, and you have him to thank for your life – it was he who protected you from the swords of the Nazarene mercenaries. I know him well – a giant whose body looks like blocks of stone, with hands as broad as shovels. I often heard him utter the phrase *so Gott dir helfe,* which means 'may God help you'. His name is Hartung of Scharfenberg and his friend, the noble Walter of Westereck, is his equal when it comes to heroism and combat experience. Together, they have always been invincible, and they'll face the Templar without fear. So, what do you say? Can I count on you?"

The ways of the Almighty are unfathomable. The goldsmith actually knows the man who saved my life! This is no coincidence, it's destiny!

Harit recalled the huge knight who protected him from the King Lionheart's bloody-thirsty soldiers. His mind flooded with images of his hometown and his affectionate parents. The whitewashed house near the harbour, the sugar factory with its unmistakeable aroma. How he yearned to return there.

But it was also a place of death. Some nights he woke in terror from dreams in which he heard the screams of butchered inhabitants and the roars of blood-thirsty Nazarenes.

He shuddered. Even though he knew that the Franks had negotiated peace with the Sultan, and that Muslims could now safely trade with them in Acre, the hairs on the back of his neck stood on end.

Harit tried to dispel his misgivings. He would never have another chance to call so much silver his own, if he didn't accept the goldsmith's offer.

These figurines – cherubim as the old man called them – seemed to be closely tied to his own destiny. He had found them, they had led him to this Jew, and now they were guiding him back to Acre. He would even have an opportunity to thank his rescuer. Yes, if he let them guide him, his life may take a turn for the better. The goldsmith's plan didn't really sound so difficult. And what did he have to lose, other than his lonely, impoverished existence?

Watching him closely, Ishmael misinterpreted Harit's thoughtful expression. "You'll receive the money when you both return unharmed. That's the best I can offer you," he said regretfully.

Harit looked up in surprise and shook his head. His decision was made. "A thousand dirham is a lot of money. I agree to your plan, as long as I don't have to face the terrible Templar myself. As Allah is my witness, I'll escort your niece to Acre and seek out the knights you speak of."

Ishmael wanted to embrace the young man, but instead spread his arms and bowed deeply.

Leah was less delighted by Harit's decision. She studied her new travelling companion distrustfully. The boyish Arab didn't look anything like the husband he was to impersonate, and she had serious doubts about his ability to protect her if they found themselves in a tight spot with thieving highwaymen.

But her uncle was brimming with confidence. He appeared to have forgotten his pain, and urged them to begin preparations immediately.

The journey to Acre could take four to five days, Harit estimated, and he listed off all the things he would need for it. Mounts, saddles, bridles, a small tent for cold nights in the mountains, a few blankets, food and, last but not least, plenty of water. He knew a drover, from whom he was sure he could buy three mules in the morning. A simple tent of black goat hide, like the ones used by Bedouins in the desert, could be found at the textile market in the city, as could some bales of cloth to pass off as sample wares.

Ishmael rejected the last suggestion with a wave of his hand. Heavy cloth would slow them down. And it might attract thieves, he pointed out. Leah and Harit should simply act as a cloth merchant couple on their way to visit family in Acre. That was inconspicuous enough. However, Harit needed to purchase himself a finer robe at the market, because his tattered rags were unconvincing attire for his supposed profession.

Leah volunteered to take care of the food provisions. She suggested bread, hard cheese, fruit and smoked fish. Harit agreed, additionally requesting dried lamb and dates.

They spent a long time planning thoroughly together. Leah marvelled at Harit's transformation from a naïve and obsequious waste disposal worker into a self-confident and insightful travel guide. His eyes sparkled as he put forward solutions for the preparation and implementation of their endeavour, astonishing Leah and her uncle with his shrewdness and foresight.

By the time dusk fell over the city roofs, they had considered every aspect of their plan and nothing stood in their way.

After a simple meal prepared by Leah, of flatbread, olive oil and fish, Ishmael gave a bulging pouch of silver coins to Harit. He was to spend it on animals, a tent and new clothes. He promised to return with the supplies no later than noon the next day. Leah would be ready by that time to load the animals and set off. Full of enthusiasm, Harit said a cheerful goodnight to his new friends.

Leah took the leftovers to the kitchen and began sorting the provisions for their journey in the pantry, while Ishmael tried to make himself more comfortable on his pile of cushions. The throbbing pain in his leg had subsided somewhat. He cooled his flushed cheeks distractedly with a damp cloth and ran his tongue through the new gap in his teeth. A small loss compared with the theft of the sacred relic.

He was aware that his plan to retrieve the Ark of the Covenant had a few weaknesses, but he hoped Leah and Harit would reach Acre safely. Whether the two knights were still there, he couldn't be sure. He had last seen them two years ago. It was possible they had long since departed for their homeland. If they were still in the city, he would have to offer an exceptionally high reward to convince them to go up against the Templar Order on behalf of a Jew. Not to mention the problem of how they were supposed to snatch away the spoils of a vicious Templar.

Sir Walter of Westereck was a destitute, homeless aristocrat, who would be prepared to take risks for good money; a calculating and foolhardy warrior, wasteful and pleasure-loving. But wealth meant nothing to his companion Hartung of Scharfenberg. The towering, sometimes melancholy man would rather be a mild-mannered monk than a sword-swinging warrior. The only thing keeping him from entering a monastery was his unshakeable friendship with Walter, who loved wine and women more than Christians loved their messiah and holy water.

But there were other ways it could play out. They may decide to keep the Ark for themselves – one out of greed, the other out of piety. And they could sell Leah to one of the corrupt pleasure houses he'd heard of in Acre, and cut off Harit's head.

Ishmael knew them both well, but not well enough, he admitted to himself with a sigh. These frightening thoughts made him shiver. He was taking an enormous risk. His entire fortune, his niece and his own future were at stake. But the sacred relic was more important than anything in the world. It was an onerous test, but he trusted in God to support his plan. And it was already decided, even if niggling doubts remained.

There was still one essential part of the plan to take care of.

The goldsmith recalled that the knight Walter of Westereck, unlike most of his peers, could read and write Latin. He had spent his boyhood in a monastery and learned these skills from the monks before becoming a squire and then a knight.

Ishmael called for Leah to bring him a quill, a few sheets of fine parchment and ink for a letter, which she would take with her. He hadn't used Latin since his time in Cologne. He made frequent mistakes and it took him a long time to write out a tidy, official-looking letter to the warrior. He hoped it was enough to explain why he needed their help so urgently, and to convince them to use their resources to assist his niece.

With tears in his eyes, he rolled up the finished document and tied it with a piece of raffia.

Ishmael was now convinced: there was no way the knights could refuse his extraordinary offer.

XIII

They came at sunrise.

Thundering hooves shook the small mountain plateau, instantly rousing Guillaume from sleep. Alarmed, he sprang to his feet, but before he could orient himself, someone rode over him from behind and knocked him to the ground. As he fell, he heard the hiss of a blade, which barely missed his head and sliced into his arm. He crashed down beside a boulder, writhing in pain.

This can't be the end of me! Not yet, he thought, then he heard the horse retreat. He rolled into the shade of the boulder and drew his dagger. But there was no second onslaught. He peered cautiously around the boulder toward the pilgrim's camp, relieved that he'd chosen to sleep a short distance from them that night, to escape their raucous celebration of the first, happily uneventful day of their journey home from the Holy City. He had joined the pilgrim train the previous morning in Jerusalem, to return to Acre undetected amongst them. His plan had now been thwarted by bandits.

About two dozen horsemen with glinting swords tore through the small cluster of tents and mercilessly mowed down the defenceless, unarmed pilgrims. Three Muslim soldiers – who had acted as escorts and guards to the group of roughly thirty Christians – lay lifeless on the ground, bristling with arrows. Dying screams and cries for help filled the air, drowned out by the attackers' harsh war cries. Through a cloud of swirling dust, Guillaume recognised the faces of some of the warriors, and a mixture of surprise and horror rooted him to the spot.

Turcopoles. His turcopoles! The Templar auxiliary troop, and in their midst, Nicholas de Seagrave, his temporary replacement. Guillaume recognised him at once, despite the black turban and grey Bedouin's robe he wore in place of his white Templar cloak.

Recoiling in shock, Guillaume wracked his brain to understand the reason for this slaughter. Why were his men raiding out here, over a hundred miles from Acre? Suddenly he heard slow, crunching footsteps behind him. He didn't turn around, but his senses and his muscles became as taut as a bowstring. He gripped his dagger firmly, ready to spin and thrust it into his opponent.

"Brother Guillaume? Is that you?" he heard an astonished voice say.

He slowly turned his head. Five paces away stood a turcopole, who lowered his bloody sword.

"Tigran!" Guillaume exclaimed. One of his most loyal and competent officers. Guillaume held out his dagger menacingly.

"Yes, it's me. Don't worry, I won't do anything to you, Commander. You saved my life. I'd never try to kill you," the turcopole assured him.

Guillaume lowered his weapon and nodded hesitantly. He had been at Tigran's side in the siege of Acre when a Muslim warrior knocked him down and then tried to finish him off. Guillaume protected his comrade with his shield and thrust his sword deep into the Saracen's chest. After that, the lanky, taciturn Armenian become one of his most devoted warriors – dependable and exceedingly loyal.

Guillaume liked him and considered him a valiant and upright man.

Tigran stooped, put down his sword and crept over to Guillaume's hiding place. He gave him a friendly pat on the back, then straightened up enough to peer over the rock at his comrades, who had dismounted and were finishing off the last survivors with spears, clubs and swords.

He ducked again, looked at Guillaume and whispered in his rolling accent, "Commander, listen to me. Brother Nicholas has ordered your death. We were told you fled the Templar fortress fearing punishment for your sinful acts, and that you're now conspiring with the heathens. He's searching for you and assumes you're travelling in disguise with Saracens passing themselves off as devout pilgrims on the old pilgrim's road from Jerusalem to Jaffa." He paused, then added, "Well, I suppose he was right about that."

"Nonsense, Tigran. Those pilgrims weren't heathens, they were Christians returning home to Jaffa. I was sent to Jerusalem by the Order to carry out an important secret mission, and was on my way home with these pilgrims. I swear by our Lord Saviour! Everyone is lying! There is no truth to the accusations against me," hissed Guillaume.

"It's alright, I believe you. You would never collaborate with the infidels. It seems there's a conspiracy against you, instigated by that whoreson Nicholas, who wants to secure his new position as turcopolier. Some of the brothers think as I do, but the Marshal seems to be on his side. We can't disobey his command, I'm sure you understand. I'm sorry about attacking you just now, brother. It was a mistake – I thought you were a heathen. But I'm afraid there's nothing I can do for you. Just one piece of advice: don't return to Acre, or you'll forfeit your life. May God protect you."

Tigran rose abruptly, retrieved his sword and glanced across at the massacre, his head held high. Guillaume quietly slumped down behind him and stared at the sand.

Nicholas de Seagrave caught sight of the Armenian and called out to him, "Is there someone there? Did you find him?"

"No, there's no one here!" Tigran yelled back. He strode casually to his horse, swung himself into the saddle and rode to Nicholas.

Curse that man, I can't fathom it. All this effort for nothing. Nicholas glowered at his men. "Has no one found the traitor?"

The warriors clustered around him, shaking their heads.

"Gather up anything that's worth taking and load it onto the mules. And hide the Saracens' bodies. We'll return to Acre!" he ordered.

"Those weren't heathens, Brother Nicholas. They had wooden crosses and rosaries, and they're fair-skinned. Some of the dead are even blond," said one of the men.

Nicholas spun around angrily and shrieked, "Satan lends the infidels a multitude of forms! They disguised themselves, fool! Now obey my orders and do your duty!"

He stomped to his warhorse, fuming.

That was the second group of pilgrims they had ambushed, and still no sign of Guillaume. He was sure they would find him amongst pilgrims returning home from the Holy City, or Muslim merchants. They had lain in wait for a week along the old pilgrim trail from Jerusalem to Jaffa. The men were grumbling and wanted to get back behind the safety of the fortress walls. It was dangerous out in the mountains. They could be surprised at any moment either by the Sultan's troops or belligerent, rapacious Bedouins – opponents who couldn't be so easily slaughtered.

Gritting his teeth, Nicholas decided to abandon the search, head home and try to intercept Guillaume before he reached Acre. He spat furiously on the dusty ground and mounted his horse.

From behind his boulder, Guillaume watched some of the turcopoles fling the pilgrims' bodies into a crevice and half-heartedly cover them with gravel and sand. Others herded the mules and tethered them together in a line. His own mule was among them, with the treasure. It had torn free of its hemp rope when Tigran attacked him, and then trotted aimlessly across the plain until two turcopoles herded it back.

He cursed himself. He'd left the relic and the sack of gold strapped to the animal in case he needed to escape quickly in the event of a raid.

What a thoroughly stupid plan. I should have tied the dumb beast's rope around my waist. Damn it, everything is lost and Nicholas, that scheming, ungrateful whoreson, has the sacred relic!

He balled his hands into fists. A sharp pain made him flinch. He had almost forgotten the wound on his arm, which was bleeding heavily. The left sleeve of his robe was already drenched in blood, but he could move the arm and fingers. Just a deep flesh wound. He used his dagger to cut a strip from the hem of his robe, and wound it tightly around his arm. That would slow the bleeding for the time being. Hopefully the wound wouldn't become inflamed. He didn't want to perish in this desolate place.

The perfidious Nicholas would pay dearly for this betrayal.

Right now, there was nothing to do but wait patiently for the turcopoles to finish their dirty work and leave the killing field.

Guillaume felt like storming across it and driving his dagger into the lying mouth of that two-faced sycophant. Instead, he drew his knees up under his chin and hugged his legs.

Alone against the turcopoles he had no chance. Tigran had told him some of them would back their former commander, but he didn't know how many of those loyal to him were in Nicholas' troop. Ultimately, they were mercenaries, who obeyed whoever paid them. And their wages were came from the powerful Order, not from Guillaume. Such a foolhardy skirmish was too likely to fail.

He rocked nervously back and forth and tried to organise his thoughts.

Nicholas de Seagrave was a crafty villain. Guillaume had been fooled by his obsequious manner. His motive for the devious betrayal was clear. The scoundrel wanted to keep his position as turcopolier, which gave him power and recognition within the Order. Nicholas had shamelessly exploited his loss of standing in the brotherhood – which Guillaume admitted he had brought upon himself through his own sinfulness – and set himself up as his successor. To secure his new post, Nicholas intended to kill him. He hadn't realised the lickspittle was capable of such abysmal hypocrisy and deceit.

At this point, Guillaume cared little about the cherubim and the precious tablets with the Ten Commandments. *He can take the relic back to Acre with him for all I care. That yellow-faced pumpkin-head may be able to wave a sword around, but he can't read or write. He won't even know what they are. He's too ignorant to recognise the significance of these things to Christendom, indeed to the whole world. He would probably hand over the lead-plated figurines to the Komtur as spoils and assume the tablets with their strange symbols were worthless, and throw them away.*

He sighed, looked up at the sky and rumpled his forehead. Tigran also said the Marshal was on Nicholas' side. So Raoul de Garlande must also know about this raid. A turcopole expedition into the Sultan's territory was impossible without the approval of the Marshal and the Grand Master.

At first, Guillaume tried to suppress the horrifying thought. *Not Raoul. Nicholas must be acting alone. We've been friends for so many years. I trust him blindly. And I know too much about him and his forbidden congress with Ruzan, the barmaid.*

All at once, the true extent of the conspiracy dawned on Guillaume and he saw the connections as clear as day. The

Marshal was collaborating with the Grand Master and Nicholas to destroy him.

De Sablé wanted to eliminate the witness to his insidious plan to murder Prince Bohemond, and Raoul – his friend Raoul – was seizing the opportunity to get rid of an unwanted accomplice to his sinful secret.

Raoul's betrayal was a heavy blow for Guillaume, and a dreadful realisation reverberated in his head: his time as a Templar knight was finally over. His death warrant was signed and he could do nothing about it.

He suddenly felt short of breath and overcome with nausea. His head spun and his world collapsed around him, grinding his future to dust.

Guillaume didn't notice the horsemen on the plateau behind him mounting and spurring on their horses and mules with whistles and shouts. His thoughts ground on like heavy millstones against his temples.

How could I fall so low? Why didn't I see it coming? Why didn't Raoul talk to me? Almighty God, what am I supposed to do now?

For the first time in his life, Guillaume questioned himself and his history with the Templars. His rapid rise from servant to knight and then commander of the turcopoles was unparalleled. He had come through countless battles unscathed. He even survived the bloody Battle of Hattin, when three quarters of the Templars perished and Jerusalem fell into the hands of the heathens – a transformative experience for him, after which he no longer believed in the possibility of a final victory over the Saracens.

Years later, during the gruelling siege of Acre, he saw countless brave men die. Princes, knights, men-at-arms, pilgrims, believers and non-believers. They expired from hunger and disease, were hacked to pieces, impaled, burned in Greek fire, or killed one another for a piece of bread.

In those days, he lost irreplaceable friends and comrades on a daily basis. Each day could have been his last, and the Almighty seemed to stand by and watch as his proud army of holy warriors was reduced to a ragged band of sick, marauding cutthroats.

The number of Saracens in the surrounding lands appeared to keep growing even after the conquest of the city.

When the walls of Acre finally fell, and King Richard's campaign to free Jerusalem failed miserably a short time later, Guillaume's faith disintegrated once and for all. He no longer saw any point in the strength-sapping battles or the Templars' holy mission. He began drinking and whoring. He had never taken the vow of celibacy seriously, and now he fucked his way through the port's whorehouses and taverns almost every night, indulging in orgies with mud-coloured wenches from Egypt and milky-skinned courtesans from France. But he was always careful to keep his binges a secret. The Almighty didn't seem to care about that either.

In lucid moments, he realised he couldn't continue this sinful life forever, but he didn't change a thing and carried on recklessly. He had always believed a carefully woven network of relationships, friendships, mutual dependencies and bribes would protect him from repercussions. Until that unholy night when his squire Pierre accused him of rape. The beginning of the end.

To Guillaume, it was like gazing into an internal mirror. At the moment when everything that ever mattered to him was lost, he didn't recognise himself.

He was a man with no serious purpose in life, without plans for the future. He had broken the Templars' Commandments a hundredfold and sealed his own downfall.

De Sablé, Nicholas and Raoul had deceived him, by the same means he often used himself to win privileges and ensure impunity from his depraved activities: guile, ruthlessness, hypocrisy and an unparalleled cold-bloodedness that didn't shy away from murder.

Guillaume shook his head incredulously and gazed at the sandy ground.

Impossible! I'm not really like that, am I? I never meant to harm anyone... By God! I am like that! I killed Pierre out of base motives, just to save my own neck. How pointless his death was – Raoul would have betrayed me sooner or later anyway. I'm beyond saving. I'm alone. Like before. A bastard. An outcast.

Almighty God was now punishing him for his unforgiveable sins. His time of reckoning had come.

His mouth felt dry. He tried hard to swallow and fought against the tickle in his nostrils. In vain. His eyes glazed over and the ground in front of him blurred.

Guillaume wept.

XIV

He woke with a shout and a shooting pain in his left foot. Guillaume kicked his legs wildly and a dark brown vulture with a red head and a hooked beak hopped sluggishly away from him.

He swiftly reached for his dagger and brandished it at the carrion eater.

"Begone, gallows bird," he tried to yell, but all that came out was an unintelligible croak. His throat was dry and his gums felt like old, torn parchment.

The vulture eyed him from two yards away, as if to ascertain whether this bloodied cadaver was actually still alive.

Groaning, Guillaume pulled himself up on the boulder that had sheltered him while he slept, and leaned his back against it. The instep of his foot bled a little. The wound was nothing more than a surface scratch.

The huge bird had evidently seen enough, and rose into the air with powerful wing beats. Guillaume looked up and saw half a dozen more of its kind circling in the sky.

He shook himself, rubbed his itching eyelids and hoped the assault on the pilgrim train was only a dream. But the vultures were real, and his memories of the massacre and the betrayal by his Templar brothers flooded back.

Curses, it wasn't a dream, the vultures have discovered the pilgrims' bodies. I'm lucky to still have both eyes.

He'd seen plenty of battlefields. Vultures and crows always took the soft eyeballs of the unburied first. He ran his hand involuntarily over his face and cautiously peered around the rock.

There was no trace of the massacre. Bare rock, sand and a few brambles scattered across the arid plateau where the pilgrims' camp had been.

He was alarmed to see two red-pelted animals not much larger than street mongrels. They crept along the edge of the crevice in which the hapless, naked pilgrims had been dumped by the turcopoles, stripped of their clothes. He held his breath. Jackals, the wolves of the desert.

They communicated with faint whimpers, then one gave a short bark. Trotting light-footed across the plateau, they disappeared into the surrounding hills. They were hunters, occasional carrion eaters, and fortunately hadn't caught his scent.

He turned back with relief. He knew he could stand up to two wild jackals with a knife, but their bites could be deadly if they became inflamed.

Glancing down at himself, he saw a dried pool of blood beside him in the sand. The searing pain in his injured arm went all the way up to his shoulder. The makeshift bandage and his sleeve were encrusted with dark brown blood. He guessed the wound had reopened while he was sleeping and that he had lost a lot of blood.

He didn't know how long he had been lying there. The sun was past its zenith and blazing down from a cloudless sky. At this time of year, it wasn't high enough to warm the cool valleys, and Guillaume shivered in the shade of his boulder. He carefully removed the bandage and inspected his injury. It was wet, with yellow pus around the edges. He needed to clean it, but had no water – not even saliva in his parched mouth. He cut a strip of cloth from the hem of his robe as he had done some hours earlier, and used it to tightly bandage his arm again.

That will have to do until I find water.

He got to his feet, his face contorting with pain. The blood loss and unspeakable thirst caused him to stagger, and he steadied himself on the boulder. The plateau appeared to tilt. He waited a moment and then shuffled unsteadily over to the pilgrims' mass grave. He hoped to find a discarded pack or at least a water flask, but there was nothing but plundered corpses carelessly covered with sand and stones. His approach disturbed a cloud of buzzing, black flies. He cursed the thoroughness of the greedy turcopoles and turned away in disgust. The smell of decomposition would soon attract more animals to the mountains.

I may as well lie down with them. Their company wouldn't be half as revolting as that of my traitorous Templar brothers. I've reached the end of my life. What do I have to live for?

Guillaume's hand gripped the hilt of his long dagger. No one would miss him; he had already been replaced. He sank slowly to his knees, aimed the tip of the weapon at his heart and closed his eyes.

But then his head filled with bristling rage and hate at Raoul's miserable deception. Satisfying, almost healing feelings of revenge rose in him, and he lowered his blade.

As terrible as his sins were, they didn't justify his Templar brothers' cowardly betrayal. He pictured Raoul, Nicholas and de Sablé before him; imagined them laughing at his naivety and going about their daily business as if nothing had happened. His death was to their advantage, whereas he, as a suicide, would only face hell and eternal damnation.

Guillaume opened his eyes. His sorrow had transformed into rage. Revenge – bloody, merciless revenge – would be his answer to their betrayal. Hell was waiting for him either way. He would never beg for forgiveness from the Almighty for his despicable sins, but the three conspirators would accompany him to that afterlife. He wasn't going to die pitifully by his own hand in the mountains only to become food for jackals and vultures. No, he wouldn't do the conspirators that favour. He wanted to look into their astonished, frightened faces when he personally sent them to their deaths.

I've lived through terrible battles and horrific diseases. I've looked death in the eye many times, even felt its hand. I won't throw myself into death's cold arms willingly!

His decision was made. He got slowly and tortuously to his feet. *I must find water.*

The thirst was almost unbearable. He couldn't take the old pilgrim route, half a mile to the west. Nicholas and his men were sure to be continuing the search for him there. Jerusalem was two days' away on foot. If he went east through the mountains, he could reach its walls without incident. Fat Muhammad would help him once he reached the Holy City.

Convinced he would find a spring, a water-filled wadi or a small stream on his way, he set out. Guillaume oriented himself by the position of the sun, left the little plateau behind him and searched for a way through the hills that rose into mountains to the east.

He made good progress at first, his thoughts vacillating between hunger for revenge and despair at his fate. He began to formulate plans of how he would exact retribution. In any case, he had to go to Acre. Perhaps the loyal Tigran and some of the other turcopoles could support him there.

Nicholas would be the first to feel his vengeance. Guillaume knew that the Templar suffered from chronic back pain. After riding in heavy armour, he struggled to get out of his saddle and walked around half doubled over in pain. Once a week, he visited a curative spa in the city, alone and in secret, where his muscles were kneaded and his misaligned spine was pressed back into place. It would be easy to ambush him there and crush in his yellow head.

He needn't concern himself with Robert de Sablé, because he was as good as dead. The Assassins could be relied on to fulfil their contracts. He didn't know how he would raise the large sum to pay the balance for the murder contract, but he didn't waste another thought on it. He was more preoccupied with how to confront his erstwhile friend, Raoul, and how he would kill him. He dismissed the idea of fair single combat. He didn't deserve that. An ambush was out of the question. He wanted to look into Raoul's cleft eyes when he finished him off. He could probably catch him at a rendezvous with Ruzan and slowly cut his throat.

After a few hours of strenuous marching through the dry, barren wilderness, over jagged rocks, steep mountains and along precipitous paths, hunger and thirst tore agonisingly at his innards. He found no water in the wasteland of rock, sand and dust. There were few trees offering shade, and he was easy prey for the sun's withering rays. His tears had long since dried up, as had his saliva, which he wanted to spit contemptuously in Raoul's face. His swollen tongue lay in his mouth like a piece of scabbed wood. His lips were split and burning.

It took immense effort to continue putting one foot in front of the other. Despite spells of dizziness caused by dehydration, he urged himself on, because to stop would mean certain death. Silence and solitude pressed in on him. The only sounds in the rugged landscape were his rasping breath and dragging steps. Confused daydreams began to swirl through his mind.

The Grand Master's face, contorted into a hideous grimace, swam before his eyes. Grinning gleefully, he held aloft a cup of wine, only to scornfully tip it on the ground a moment later. The wild war cries of Saracen's echoed in his ears, alternating with the lustful moans of sweating whores and their customers indulging in wild orgies. This was followed by the murmured prayers and powerful chants of the Templars. He felt a hot wind flap his cloak as he stopped on a mountain top to scan the terrain for enemies, and then felt the cutting chill of a winter storm freeze his chainmail.

Countless memory fragments from his life also surfaced. The abbot of the monastery he escaped all those years ago threatened him with fleshy fingers. Bare-breasted, giggling wenches beckoned him. Prostrate, bloodied heathen warriors begged him for mercy. He spoke to all of them, screamed at them, tried to banish them.

But the demons kept coming. The old Jew from whom he stole the relic gave a bleating laugh, stroked his beard, and was suddenly holding a golden cherub in each hand. The cherubim spread their wings, floated up and alighted on his shoulders. A sword was thrust through the Jew's body from behind, emerging from his chest dripping with blood, and Nicholas' yellow face peered over the Jew's shoulder, grinning.

After hours of wandering in the hot sun without water, Guillaume couldn't be sure if he was still alive or traipsing through hell. A raging headache hammered his skull, gradually driving out the hallucinations until he saw nothing but empty blackness.

He kept tripping in the sand, struggling to his feet, and dragging himself on. His eyes burned and his body began to shiver violently from exhaustion.

He staggered through the mountains until late afternoon. In a moment of clarity, he realised he was moving in the wrong direction.

By Almighty God, I'm going to die unless some miracle comes to pass. It's too late to change my sinful life, as much as I want to. I sincerely regret what I've done, but I doubt I can make up for it now. My end is near.

Utterly disoriented, he turned around and lost his way again in the confusion of rocky ravines and dry wadis.

As the merciless sun finally sank and a cold dusk settled in the valleys, he stumbled over a pair of deep wheel ruts, fell to the ground and crawled, groaning in agony and despair, into the shelter of a pair of large stones. Completely sapped of strength and close to dying of thirst, he passed out.

XV

The swaying motion of his docile mount and the monotony of the desolate mountain landscape made it hard for Harit to keep his eyes open and not fall asleep in the saddle. He gazed with disinterest at a dried, sweet fig in his hand, turning it this way and that before finally popping it into his mouth. He knew the road and surrounding area well, having travelled it many times with his father. They had transported and sold their highly coveted sugar as far as Nablus and Jerusalem. After the bloody conquest of his hometown by the Christians, he had fled on this very road to the safety of the Holy City.

Going from Jerusalem to Acre, there were only two routes to choose from. A well-worn road used primarily by pilgrims and merchants ran west through the cities of Lydda and Jaffa, then turned north up the Mediterranean coast, passing through Caesarea to Acre. Travelling that way without an armed escort was too dangerous. Roaming bands of mercenaries and thieving Bedouins were active there, frequently ambushing pilgrims and merchant caravans.

The other route was longer and more arduous, but less travelled and therefore much safer. It snaked in a north-easterly direction from the Holy City across the dry, stony mountains of Samaria to the city of Nablus. From there, the road ran through the fertile Jezreel valley to Nazareth. Acre was then just a day's ride to the west.

This was the route that Harit chose to take Leah safely to his hometown.

On the morning of the second day, they left the road and followed the stony trails that bypassed the old city of Nablus nestled between the high Ebal and Gerizim mountains. There, they attracted less attention and avoided Sultan Salah ad-Din's patrolling soldiers. Harit was anxious. He didn't feel comfortable in his cloth merchant disguise, and his supposed wife was obviously much older than he was. This was unusual for Muslims – men of faith only married younger girls, to be sure of producing offspring. But they couldn't pass themselves off as brother and sister, because they didn't look at all alike.

After a few hours, they found themselves back on the deserted road and followed it in the direction of Nazareth, the birthplace of Jesus.

Leah was unaccustomed to riding. The insides of her thighs were rubbed raw by the austere wooden saddle, padded only with a coarse woollen blanket, and her legs ached all the way up to her buttocks. She decided to go on foot, which Harit protested vehemently.

"Leah, your uncle warned us not to waste time. If you don't ride, we won't make it to Acre in four days. Your feet will swell and sand will get into your sandals and give you blisters!"

Harit sat imperiously on his mount, and she blinked up at him from below. "I couldn't care less. I can't sit any longer, it makes me unbearably sore between..." She faltered and lowered her eyes.

"By Allah, I know what you mean," said Harit with a grin. "When I was a child, my father took me on my first long journey to Tiberias, to the shores of the Sea of Galilee. I had never been in a saddle before, and at first, I was very proud to be allowed to ride alone on a donkey behind him, as part of the big merchant caravan. But after a few hours, it felt like I was sitting on burning coals that scorched my manhood. It was very painful. I found mutton fat to be very soothing."

"We have no mutton fat," she grumbled. "Unless you want me to render you."

He laughed and bowed mischievously. "I am entirely at your disposal, Princess. But I'm very lean, you won't get much out of me."

Leah smirked and considered other possible solutions. They had a small, clay bottle of olive oil for cooking. She seized the reins of Harit's mount and brought it to a standstill.

"You're not really going to put me in the pot?" he asked impishly.

"You're in luck, we have no pot," she replied cheerfully. "But we have olive oil. Wait a moment."

Leah searched through the packs on his mount and held up the bottle triumphantly.

"This will help. I'll rub some on, then I'm sure I'll be able to ride again soon. I'm going behind those rocks. Don't you dare follow me!"

She crossed the wide road purposefully and disappeared behind some tall stones.

"What do you take me for? I'm a chaste man, as Allah demands of true believers until marriage," Harit called after her reproachfully as he dismounted. The Jew was certainly pretty, but she was an infidel. He really wasn't interested in gazing lustfully at her.

Leah gathered up her *jilbab*, an outer garment of fine, dark blue cotton embroidered with a floral pattern. She crouched, uncorked the olive oil, poured a few drops of it onto her palm and applied it carefully to her reddened inner thighs. It felt soothing and cooling and she sighed with relief.

She was startled by a faint rasping sound behind her. She hastily covered herself, picked up the bottle and glanced around fearfully.

There was no one behind her. She looked back to the road and saw Harit sitting in the shade of his mount, drinking water from a leather flask. She heard the rasping sound again. It seemed to be coming from the huge block of stone to her right. She peered around it and discovered a man lying motionless in its shade.

His head was covered with a very dirty, once-white *kufiya*, held in place by a black *agal*. Grey dust coated his bearded face. His eyes were closed, and dry blood encrusted his cracked lips, which emitted an irregular wheezing sound. His cheap linen robe was tattered, only partially covering him, and his left arm was bandaged with a blood-soeaked strip of cloth. A black, wooden cross hung from a braided hemp rope around his neck, telling Leah he must be a Christian pilgrim. This man was no threat to her – he desperately needed help.

"Harit! Harit!" Leah cried at the top of her voice. "Come quickly. There's someone here! Bring water!"

Harit sprang to his feet and ran to her.

She tore the water flask from his hand, knelt beside the man and carefully dribbled a few drops onto his chapped lips, which trembled and opened.

"Shh, quiet now," whispered Leah. "Slowly, you must drink slowly."

The battered pilgrim briefly opened his eyes, looked at her in disbelief, and closed them again. His right hand reached for the flask.

"You can have more. But slowly, very slowly, otherwise you'll die!" Leah gently pushed his hand away and trickled more water into his mouth. He swallowed and moaned.

Standing beside them, Harit studied the man's face and suddenly stiffened.

"By the beard of the prophet! That's him! The Nazarene! It's him, I recognise him! Allah have mercy on us, the Templar!" he shrieked, stepping back in fear.

"Are you sure?" she asked, clutching the flask to her chest.

"Oh, yes! Absolutely! That's the man who robbed your uncle!" Harit shrieked, drawing from his belt the knife he normally used to cut bread and meat. Quivering, he aimed it at the pilgrim, who appeared to be regaining his senses.

"We should kill him now, while he's still weak, before he kills us!"

Leah stared transfixed at the man's blue eyes, which returned her gaze with a mixture of astonishment and curiosity. His hand rose feebly in a defensive gesture, then dropped onto his chest. He closed his eyes and lost consciousness again.

Leah placed the water flask on the ground and gently removed the knife from Harit's hand. In a quiet, coaxing tone, she said, "He won't hurt us. He's injured, almost dead from thirst. He's as weak as a small dog."

"Sleeping hellhound, more like it," said Harit mistrustfully. "Who knows how this happened to him? Maybe he attacked a band of robbers and lost the fight. We need to be careful. The safest thing would be to cut his throat, bury him and disappear from here!"

Leah shook her head vigorously. "We can't kill him. He has nothing on his person, and if what you say is true – that this is the man who robbed my uncle – then he's the only one who can tell us where the sacred statues are. We have to keep him alive, or our journey has been for nothing!"

Harit was unconvinced and shook his head. He didn't like the idea of saving the Templar. This was an extremely dangerous Nazarene. On the other hand, without his help, Harit could say goodbye to the rich reward for the return of the statues.

"I suppose you're right, he must know where the winged creatures are. But we should get away from the road and find a safe place where you can nurse him back to health. I'll fetch some ropes to tie his hands – he's still a bloodthirsty warrior, even in his weakened state. Remember what happened to your uncle... how badly he hurt him!" Harit raised an admonishing finger and hurried back to the mules.

Leah studied the Nazarene from two paces away, Harit's little knife in her hand.

She had never been this close to a Templar. When she and her brothers were children, their father sometimes teased them when they didn't want to sleep: "Eyes closed or the white Templar will come for you!" They used to pester him to tell them scary stories about the bloodthirsty knights until he gave in. The stories were full of wandering, headless warrior monks who had to atone for their murderous acts, and were damned to roam at night through the ruins of their mighty fortresses for all eternity. Or he told them tales of legendary treasures the knights had hidden beneath the walls of their fortresses.

This Templar didn't frighten her. He still had his head and didn't look anything like her father's descriptions of bloodsucking demons. He was exceptionally tall and powerfully built, but lying helpless on the ground in his tattered robe with a sunburnt face, he looked more like a Frankish wayfarer suffering from heat stroke. Nothing about him suggested he was a dangerous warrior. But she knew this man had lifted her uncle with one hand and thrown him to the floor. It would be wise to tie him up.

Harit came back with both mounts and the pack mule, and nervously bound the Templar's wrists with a rough hemp rope.

Satisfied with his work, he stood up, relieved, and pointed at a towering rock formation a hundred paces from the road, shaded by two tamarisk trees. "We can set up camp over there, and if it pleases Allah, no one will find us," he said, taking the wool blanket from his mount and spreading it out beside the Templar.

"Let's lift him onto this and drag him. It's the only way to move him."

He grasped the knight under his armpits and indicated with a nod for Leah to lift his legs. But the man was too heavy for them. He groaned quietly but didn't wake.

"He's a giant!" said Harit, panting and scratching his head. "Let's roll him onto the blanket, then we'll hold a corner each and pull him over there."

It took longer than expected. That had to pause several times to catch their breath and clear stones out of the way, so as not to add to their prisoner's injuries. Finally, they laid him in the shade of the trees and went to fetch the animals.

Leah was impressed by Harit's practical approach and asked him, "Do you do things like this often? I mean, wrapping a heavy man in a blanket to move him more easily? I would never have thought of it."

"No, no. By Allah, this is a first for me too. What do you think I am? A gravedigger? Moving heavy loads was part of my work as an assistant to the Sultan's construction workers. As I'm not blessed with strong muscles like this infidel, I had to think of creative solutions," Harit replied, flattered. He stood up and looked around.

It was the perfect location. The rocks formed a semi-circle behind which the ground sloped gently downward to a sheltered area not visible from the road.

Once the mules were unloaded, Leah tended the Templar, who still lay unconscious on the woollen blanket, breathing shallowly.

She used Harit's sharp knife to cut the filthy bandage from his arm. An acrid smell accosted her nostrils. She inspected the encrusted wound, which had split open and begun to bleed lightly. There appeared to be no broken bones, but the cut was deep. She had Harit bring water and a piece of linen.

She carefully cleaned out the wound, tore the cloth into strips and wound a tight bandage around the arm.

"And? Will he survive?" asked Harit, surprised by her healing skills.

"I think so. If it doesn't turn gangrenous, he'll likely just have a scar. Only the muscles are injured – his tendons and bones are intact," she replied quietly. She moistened a strip of cloth and squeezed a few drops of water onto the Nazarene's lips. He swallowed, but still didn't wake. Leah carefully removed the kufiya from his head and gazed thoughtfully at him as she washed the dust from his burnt face with slow, circular movements.

His hair was light blond and cropped very short. He had thick, narrow eyebrows and a high forehead. His eyelids were closed and she marvelled at his long, almost girlish lashes, which seemed out of place on a fearsome warrior. Below his straight nose, a neatly trimmed beard, surprisingly dark and coarse, covered his angular chin and sunken cheeks. His narrow lips turned up at the corners in a secretive smile, reminding her a little of her father. If it weren't for the patchy, red burns and scabs on his face, and if he were a little darker-skinned and not a ruthless Templar knight, she would have found him quite attractive and interesting.

"He doesn't look like a cruel butcher of the faithful, is that what you're thinking?" Harit's mocking voice jolted her out of her daydream. "I should tickle him with my knife, so he wakes up and tells us what he did with the figurines he so dishonourably took from your uncle," he suggested, sitting cross-legged beside her.

Leah turned away from the prisoner. Silent and lost in thought, they both gazed for a while across the stony terrain at the high mountains between them and the old city of Nablus.

They weren't sure how to proceed. They had found the Templar sooner than expected, but without the cherubim or stone tablets. Perhaps their journey was already at an end.

"I doubt he'll tell us anything about the leaden, winged figures," said Harit abruptly. "Even if he's tortured. I've heard these warriors love to die for their beliefs. They're not afraid of anything or anyone." He fell silent again. Leah sniffed and nodded.

"Who told you that?" said a strained, deep voice, shattering the silence.

Leah and Harit flinched in terror.

XVI

The Templar blinked up at the radiant blue sky. His bonds lay shredded on his belly and a long, straight dagger glinted in his right hand.

"You should do a better job of searching your prisoners for weapons." Guillaume's speech was laboured and he had to clear his throat several times. Lying on his back, he turned his head to the side to look at his two rescuers and saw the utter horror in their faces.

"Please... you have nothing to fear," he assured them hoarsely, turning the knife around in his hand and presenting them with the hilt. "Here, take it. I won't harm you. I swear."

Harit sprang to his feet, snatched the weapon from Guillaume without hesitation and aimed the point at him.

"I swear to Allah, I'll kill you if you move a muscle!" he snarled.

"Do you want to kill me too?" the Templar asked casually, turning to look at Leah. She was momentarily taken aback to hear the Templar speaking fluent Arabic, then was suddenly seized with unbridled rage and leapt to her feet.

"Only too gladly! You forced your way into our house, struck my uncle down, broke his leg and stole the sacred relic! We've been searching for you, and the only reason you're alive is because we want it back from you, cursed Nazarene!" she blurted.

"Er..." Guillaume looked at her in awe. Her eyebrows were drawn together, forming a deep crease above the bridge of her nose. Her dark, narrowed eyes seemed to shoot sparks.

My God, she's unbelievably beautiful. I thought you were only a wonderful dream, but you're really here. The sight of her made him forget his pain and woes for a moment, and a smile flitted across his face.

"The sacred relic, I see. So you know the significance of the cherubim and the Ten Commandments to the world and to me. And now a pretty Jewish girl and an adolescent Muslim think they can snatch back the precious prize from a Templar? I admit, you have gall," he said, wondering what fate had brought him and this mismatched pair together.

"What sacred relic?" asked Harit, confused.

"Never mind, I'll tell you later," Leah replied irritably, drawing her voluminous jilbab up over her curly hair. She had completely forgotten to cover herself, and was reminded by Guillaume's casual remark about her prettiness. Strangely, she didn't resent it.

"It wasn't my intention to harm your uncle. As you can see, the Almighty has already punished me for it. I, too, was attacked and my own Templar brothers robbed me of everything I had. I'm no longer a member of their Order. That treasure is cursed; it brings bad luck. Forget about it."

Disappointed, Leah studied his face. She heard genuine sadness and deep despair in his voice, but perhaps he was just a convincing story-teller.

Guillaume beckoned Harit and whispered hoarsely, "Stop waving that dagger at me. It's driving me crazy. You have nothing to fear from me; you saved my life. I beg of you, just give me a little water."

Harit lowered the weapon sheepishly and slipped it into his belt.

"If you say so," he said sulkily. "You should know, kafir, it's a custom in my faith that if we give water to a stranger, we may do no harm to him. So, if I give you something to drink, you needn't fear me."

Guillaume nodded and said earnestly, "I'm aware of that custom, and I'll take you at your word."

Satisfied by this response, Harit picked up the water flask and handed to the knight, who sat up awkwardly and drank from it in small sips.

He felt his spirits gradually revive, and with them the in-grained knowledge of precautions to be taken when choosing a campsite in heathen lands during times of war. He glanced around and assessed the location. The rocks around them formed a semi-circle opening out onto a broad, flat area. This meant they were well protected from an attack from behind, and could easily keep an eye on the expansive plain. A good defensive position if enemies approached. Satisfied, he corked the flask and gave it back to Harit.

"Tell me, where are we exactly, and how far are we from Acre?" he asked.

"Beyond those mountains lies the city of Nablus," replied Harit, pointing at the horizon. "A hundred paces from here is the road to Nazareth, which continues on to Acre. It's around three days' ride from here to the port city."

Guillaume shook his head incredulously. If that were true, he had strayed almost forty miles eastward across the moun-tainous landscape and completely missed Jerusalem.

At least this means Nicholas is searching for me on the wrong road. He'll never suspect I'm in the mountains of Samaria. Acre is closer than I thought. But that's not much use to me now.

He pictured the traitors' faces, and was once again over-come by a feeling of deep sorrow. His heady plans for revenge had long since evaporated. Without weapons or armour, with-out allies, and especially without money, he couldn't go up against the powerful Order. The conspirators had won, even though he still lived. He bowed his head.

Leah's initial rage had subsided, but her doubts about the Templar's story remained. She ignored the guarded expression on his face and fired questions at him like arrows. "It doesn't matter a damn where we are. I'm only interested in where the cherubim and tablets are. Are you telling us you were robbed? By your own people? And that the relic is gone forever? How do you know of its significance? And what's your name, anyway?"

Guillaume held up his hands, and his face immediately contorted with pain. The wound on his arm burned like fire. He glanced at the fresh bandage.

"That's a very good wound dressing," he remarked appreciatively. "Please sit down. I'll get a stiff neck if I have to keep craning to look at you. I'll explain everything."

Leah and Harit complied and sat on the sandy ground a respectful distance away. Leah looked at him expectantly and Guillaume struggled not to lose himself in those round eyes that reminded him of dark chestnuts.

"So many questions. Let's start with the last one. My name is Guillaume. And every Christian should know the story of the long lost Ark of the Covenant and its power. A gold-plated box of acacia wood, with two cherubim on its lid, containing the Ten Commandments chiselled in stone by God. It's mentioned in our holy scriptures. When your companion offered to sell me an apparently worthless cherub at the market in Jerusalem, I was reminded of the legend. When I discovered that the figurine could be genuine, I had to find out whether a second cherub existed. I followed him, attacked your uncle and found the second sculpture, along with the sacred stone tablets. I joined a troupe of pilgrims heading up the coast to Jaffa after visiting the Lord's tomb in Jerusalem."

He paused. His mind flooded with images of the massacred pilgrims, and the painful memory of his friend Raoul's betrayal.

"Not far from the city, we were attacked by the lightly-armed horsemen of my Order, the turcopoles, whom I used to command. They killed the pilgrims and looted everything, including the tablets and the cherubim. I survived only by the mercy of a warrior still loyal to me, who recognised me and spared me. All the others met their death because of me. The turcopoles were sent by the Grand Master of the Templars and his military commander to kill me, as I've become the victim of a scheming plot. My best friend, Marshal Raoul, wantonly betrayed me because I know things about him that could cost him his own head. The Grand Master evidently wants to wash his hands of me as a witness to a pact between the Order and the heathen Assassins. So in the end, I lost everything – the relic, my past, my future, my friends and comrades – and strayed aimlessly through the mountains. I'm an outcast who's been harshly punished by the Lord for my countless sins. My life is in ruins and means nothing to me anymore... You should have left me to die."

He lowered his eyes, overwhelmed by a sense of utter emptiness. He felt exhausted, burnt out and hopeless.

"So, if you want to use the dagger, I'm ready to leave this world and meet my maker. But if you can't bring yourself to do it, then give it back to me. I don't deserve to remain in this world," he whispered despondently to Harit.

The Muslim didn't know what to say and looked questioningly at Leah.

She felt dispirited and baffled by the knight's words. Grand Master, Marshal, Assassins. Words she had never heard, the meaning of which she could only guess at. *What an erudite, dangerous, maltreated and sad person,* she thought. Empathy welled up in her. She even felt an involuntary sense of affection, knowing what it meant to suddenly lose one's sense of security and belonging.

When her father died, she had no desire to go on living, but then her uncle had given her strength, confidence and a new purpose in life. Bringing the tablets and the cherubim back to him wasn't merely a question of obedience — she was doing it out of gratitude for his selfless generosity. This apparently broken man before her was her only link to the relic. She couldn't let him die.

She fidgeted with her jilbab and said in a harsher tone than intended, "Your death won't help anyone, not even you. You would be running away like a pitiful coward. I don't know much about Christians, but no matter what guilt you carry around, you can still do many good things and, in the end, I'm sure the Lord will forgive your sins. Self-pity really isn't becoming of a... mighty warrior... We should eat. I'll fetch bread and olives."

She leapt up and hurried to the mules that stood together in the shade of the trees, snorting quietly.

Surprised, Guillaume watched her go and rubbed his burning eyes.

"Exactly," said Harit drily, turning to the knight. "I'll keep your dagger for cutting bread. It's better suited to that."

The day gradually drew to a close. It grew cold in the mountains. So as not to draw attention, they refrained from lighting a fire, but wrapped themselves in wool blankets. They sat without exchanging a word, protected by the group of stones, and ate dry bread, salted fish and olives steeped in oil, until Leah broke the silence.

"Listen... Guillaume." The unusual name was hard for her to pronounce. "Now that you're no longer a member of your Order, you are free to do as you wish. You know what the Ark of the Covenant means to my people. It's the holiest thing ever created on his earth. The beginning of our faith – yours too. It was lost to us for so long, and now *you've* lost it. I'm sure you know where the men who betrayed you will take it. We've undertaken this journey to retrieve it. At any cost. Help us! Then perhaps God will forgive your sins."

She looked straight into his blue eyes.

Guillaume grimaced and spat an olive stone on the ground.

"You have no idea of the terrible things I've done. I can never be forgiven. The Ten Commandments that you're so eager to get back – I've violated them at least a hundredfold," he replied.

"Everything can be forgiven, if you sincerely repent and selflessly do good deeds," she retorted. Then she asked inquisitively, "What did you do that was so terrible it made you lose your faith in God's mercy?"

"You don't want to know," he replied, but he felt a yearning to answer her truthfully.

"Yes, I do want to know," she said resolutely.

"So do I," said Harit, adding, "Then I'll forgive you too, for sneaking after me to Leah's uncle's house and robbing him!"

Guillaume raised an eyebrow and nodded. "Very well. If that's what you want."

Perhaps the girl's beseeching eyes were what moved him to speak so openly, or perhaps it was just a desire to reminisce about his former life.

Guillaume spoke very slowly. Talking was still difficult for him. He shared with Leah and Harit rare insights into his life, opening up to them an utterly unfamiliar world of Christians, Franks and Templars, which frequently astonished them and occasionally made them shake their heads in disbelief.

They learned of Guillaume's time as a student at the monastery, his escape across the Mediterranean, his entry into the notoriously feared Order of the warrior monks in Acre, right through to his training as a squire and his knighthood in Jerusalem. He told them of the hard life of the Templars defined by prayer, asceticism and combat; of bloody battles and the horrifying cruelty practised by Christians and Muslims. They heard how he survived the murderous slaughter near the Horns of Hattin, after which Sultan Salah ad-Din crushed the Christian Kingdom.

"I found refuge in Tyre and later fought once again as a Templar knight at the siege of Acre, in the front lines. After the city was conquered, I was appointed commander of the turcopoles."

Guillaume interrupted his narrative and looked into his listeners' attentive faces. If he continued honestly with his life story, he would have to reveal his darkest side. He felt Leah's expectant gaze bore into his soul and exert a strange power over him that urged him on.

When he described the misconduct and hefty sins for which he lost his white habit, he lowered his voice, but left out no detail. He admitted to his immoral lifestyle of many years and even the murder of his squire Pierre, which no one could prove he had committed. He even told of how he had been sent by the Order to Jerusalem to convince the Assassins to murder a Christian prince, and how he had taken things into his own hands and altered the contract so that Robert de Sablé, the Grand Master, was now the target of their daggers.

He described his close friendship with Marshal Raoul, at whose side he had fought for many years, and the deep bond of trust that had existed between them.

"But he betrayed me, because I know too much about him. I know of his secret lover, a filthy whore from Acre's port district, whose services I introduced him to. I know of payments he sends to his children and wife in far-off France, which he regularly pilfers from the Order's coffers. He wants me dead.

So he allied himself with Brother Nicholas, promising him my post. That's why Nicholas ambushed the pilgrim caravan, assuming I was among them, and acquired the relic. I can never return to the Templar fortress. It would mean certain death. But perhaps I should go, face my fate and receive the punishment I deserve for my sins. Now you understand why I have no hope of forgiveness from the Almighty."

Guillaume leaned back, closed his eyes and sucked in a deep breath of the cold mountain air. He felt liberated. He had never spoken so openly and fully to anyone about his life. It felt like a confession. Except there was no priest here to offer him absolution, only a Jew and a Muslim to pass judgement on his deeds.

"Look at me!"

Leah's harsh voice snapped him out of his reverie and he opened his eyes.

"You've done truly terrible things. I wish I'd never heard them. But perhaps God can forgive you even for those, because his mercy is limitless and I believe that, deep down, you're a good person. You already regret your sins, otherwise you wouldn't have told us everything. You're an unusual Nazarene — a fearsome warrior, a linguist and even a schooled scripture reader and..."

"And a whoremonger, butcher, murderer and thief!" Harit exclaimed.

"Harit, not now!" she barked at him.

"No doubt he's right," said Guillaume with a straight face. "But keep talking."

Leah scowled at her travelling companion and continued. "A man with your skills and experience can't be allowed to die alone in the mountains. Perhaps the relic holds no meaning for you, but for my people it carries the hope of a direct connection to the Lord. I have my uncle to thank for my new life, and

I want to – I must – help him fulfil his dream by bringing it back to him. I believe it was fate that we found you and saved you from dying of thirst. This is the first step on your path to forgiveness."

She looked into his eyes and he met her gaze for a moment, then looked away and sighed. "Oh, Leah, I'd be only too happy to help you, and atone for the suffering I caused you and your uncle. But I have no armour, no sword, no steed and not a single copper coin. How am I supposed to retrieve the cherubim and tablets from the heavily guarded fortress with only a weak woman and a Muslim boy?"

He shook his head regretfully.

"Now listen to me, I'm not weak just because I'm a woman! I grew up with two boisterous brothers and I can handle myself! As you've discovered first-hand, I know a little about healing. I think that will prove useful. We've brought money with us. It will be enough, believe me. Harit knows his way around Acre very well, having lived there for a long time before you Nazarenes drove him out. And we won't be alone. My uncle knows two upstanding knights in that city, who I'm sure will assist us. In fact, it's our mission to find them and ask for their help. If you come with us, we'll have a much greater chance of success," said Leah petulantly.

"By all the saints, who are these supposed knights?" asked Guillaume doubtfully, rolling his eyes.

"Walter of Westereck and Hartung of... I don't remember the name. They're from Alemannia, my uncle tells me. So I suppose they're not Franks, but they are Christians. He lived in their country for many years before coming to Jerusalem."

Guillaume looked at her in astonishment. "I know those men. I fought alongside them at the siege of Acre. Sir Walter commanded an army for the Duke of Osterland. His comrade

Hartung was always at his side. Strong, battle-hardened, experienced warriors, almost invincible. Rumour has it that the two of them conquered one of the city gates, opened it for King Lionheart's troops and brought about the capitulation. Later, they placed themselves in the service of a hospital that cares for Alemannic pilgrims. If they agree to help you..."

"... then you'll help us too?" Leah interrupted impatiently.

Guillaume smiled and succumbed once more to the allure of her dark eyes. She didn't bat an eyelid. They held each other's gaze for a long time, until Harit could no longer bear the tension.

"By Allah, what happens now?" he asked. Startled, Guillaume tore his eyes away from Leah. This woman stirred his innermost feelings and filled him with warmth. He felt his heart beat faster and his face flush. He still couldn't quite fathom the Jewish woman. Leah seemed as naïve and vulnerable as she was self-confident, upright and proud.

She's... different. Different from anyone I've ever met. Clever and charming. And beautiful.

"I'll find the Covenant for you and retrieve it. With or without the help of those knights. You have my word," he said decisively.

XVII

Nicholas de Seagrave loved these grand entrances. Proud and solemn, he rode behind the Order's standard-bearers, leading the turcopoles through Acre's eastern gate. Inhabitants and visitors alike anxiously made way for them on the busy street that led through the market to the Templar fortress. Vendors hastily wheeled their carts aside, regarding him with a mixture of fear and awe. Some crossed themselves and bowed, others cried out blessings to the Templars, who were regarded as courageous and valiant. They were swathed in an aura of invincibility and godliness. Some believed the warriors were the living embodiment of the Almighty on Earth, permeated with his divinity and therefore immortal.

An exalted feeling of strength and power flowed through Nicholas, making him forget his chronic back pain, which was intensified by the weight of his heavy armour. It wasn't necessary to wear it, as Acre and the surrounding area were sovereign territory of the Christian Kingdom. Attacks by heathens were almost unheard of since the city was conquered two years earlier by Kings Richard the Lionheart and Philipp of France.

Before riding into Acre, Nicholas had the troops halt a mile out from their fortress, so he could change out of his Bedouin warrior disguise into the battle robes of a Templar knight. As the only knight among the turcopoles, he alone was permitted to wear the snow-white habit on his return. His arrival was announced by loud horn blasts, and he relished the reverence paid to his cloak with the blood-red cross. When he was within sight of the Templar fortress, its impressive walls towering into the sky at the northern end of the city, he spurred his steed to a gallop and crossed the lowered drawbridge, his lance raised.

The ministering brothers hurried to receive him and his men. Nicholas dismounted, threw his reins and lance to a sergeant, and adjusted his sword belt.

"I hope your success warrants such an illustrious entrance, with flying banners and highly polished chainmail."

The grumbling voice belonged to Raoul de Garlande, who leaned casually against a heavy, open gate. With a wooden toothpick, he freed a shred of meat from inflamed gums between yellow teeth – a remnant of his midday meal.

"Ahhh, Brother Raoul! Even the Marshal receives me in person," Nicholas joked. "We come bearing spoils that..." He noticed the Marshal's pinched face and faltered.

Raoul raised an eyebrow and eyed him disdainfully.

"So you didn't find Guillaume," he observed laconically, prying himself off the gate and striding toward Nicholas.

"Brother Marshal, we spent ten days and nights on the old pilgrim road, turned every stone, questioned every pilgrim and merchant we encountered and..."

"...and then robbed them," the Marshal interrupted sourly, pointing at the two dozen heavily laden mules and camels the servants were busily unloading in the courtyard. "It wasn't supposed to be a raid! Your task was to find and kill Guillaume," Raoul hissed quietly, leaning in toward Nicholas and assaulting him with his evil-smelling breath.

"I know, but why not take the opportunity to top up the Order's coffers?" Nicholas snivelled defensively. "It's godly work, despatching the heathens with our swords and redistributing their wealth for the glory of the Lord, as they say. I also gifted a few things to impoverished pilgrims, so that they might continue their journey to Jerusalem without deprivation," he lied, patting the Marshal on the back.

"You blockhead. I only backed your reckless venture because you assured me you could capture Guillaume before he returned to Acre. Instead you bring me a couple of camels!" Raoul's eyes flashed, and he held a clenched fist under the turcopolier's nose.

Nicholas bowed his head humbly and replied in a quaking voice, "I was convinced Guillaume would disguise himself amongst Christian pilgrims in order to travel undetected. I expect the Assassins have done the job for us and he's already dead."

"Nonsense! Guillaume wouldn't allow himself to be killed by heathens. He's far too shrewd and experienced for that. He's alive and well, you can be sure of it."

"You know him better than I do. You were friends for a long time. Do you think perhaps he suspects his life is forfeit and has taken off with the gold meant for the Assassins, never to be seen here again? It's enough to start a new life. What do you think?" asked Nicholas quietly.

Raoul grimaced at the mention of his former friendship with Guillaume, and replied sharply, "That God-forsaken sinner is not my friend! He's lied to us and cheated us for far too long. I want nothing to do with him! I'm just as horrified as you at his grisly trespasses. I hope I never see that whoreson again. May his degenerate soul burn in hell!"

Nicholas flinched and held up his hands apologetically. "Alright, Brother Raoul, I was only asking."

The Marshal boiled with rage and felt like punching Nicholas. The ambitious idiot had no idea of Guillaume's character. He may be a licentious, lazy sinner, but a thief? Never. There was no doubt in Raoul's mind that he would fulfil his mission and return. The trap must snap shut before he reached the walls of the fortress. The Grand Master's orders were quite clear.

"Guillaume is on his way here. He still considers himself a Brother of the Temple and he'll see his mission thorugh. Unlike you. You failed, Nicholas. But now you'll do as I command: you'll intercept him, preferably in the city. I don't care how you do it. Send out spies, bribe the guards at the city gates, or post yourself here at the entrance to the fortress until he appears. And then make him disappear forever! This is not a request! Don't you dare come back to me without news of your success, or you'll soon be an ordinary knight once more, not a turcopolier in dazzling armour!"

Raoul contemptuously spat out the bloody mucous that had collected around his rotting gums.

Nicholas nodded eagerly. "You can count on me. He's as good as dead," he replied with a submissive bow.

Raoul smirked, confident the overachiever would do whatever it took to keep his promise. This man coveted his new post. But it couldn't hurt to increase the pressure on him, and he added, "I depart for Tyre today with a dozen brothers. Philipp of Beauvais, the Bishop of the city, has been visiting King Henry and requested that we escort him home. I'll be back in two days and I expect Guillaume to be dealt with by then!"

He strode toward the Palace, leaving Nicholas standing in the courtyard.

What if the idiot fails again? Then I'll have to play executioner myself, damn it.

He never wanted to face Guillaume again. His friend had become a real threat to him and his position as Marshal since that ossified stickler Robert de Sablé was put in control of the Order's destiny.

Raoul had cautioned him several times to change his ways, but his friend had arrogantly disregarded the well-intentioned warnings and continued to push things to extremes.

The allegation that Guillaume had inveigled his squire into the most abominable and unnatural sodomy in a whorehouse was the last straw. There was also the fact that Guillaume was the only one who knew about Raoul's own sinful relationship with the barmaid Ruzan, which had to remain secret because he couldn't bring himself to let go of her.

Guillaume had become unpredictable. He had to be eliminated before he dragged Raoul down into the abyss with him. As soon as possible. That was why he had agreed to Nicholas' plan to capture and kill him before he returned.

Raoul arrived at the Palace and morosely barged the heavy entrance door to open it. The Grand Master would be displeased to hear that the hunt for the sinner was still fruitless.

Meanwhile, Nicholas trudged over to rejoin his turcopoles, who had gathered at the entrance to the stables. The elongated building beside the fortress gates housed almost one hundred horses. The walls were built from rough fieldstones. A gabled roof of wooden beams and thatched straw protected the valuable animals, saddles, bridles and costly oats from the wind and weather. Attached to the stables was a windowless storehouse, in which the brotherhood's food, clothing and armour were stored, stacked neatly on high wooden shelves.

In these buildings, the Order's *Komtur*, Brother Thibaut, had sole discretion. As the treasurer and chief administrator of the Templars, he held the second highest rank after the Grand Master, as his deputy.

The heavyset, self-assured man was known for his gruff manner and loud mouth. Standing legs apart and hands on his fat hips, he expertly inspected and counted the spoils from Nicholas' raid. A scrawny scribe stood behind a hastily erected lectern beside him, noting down the loudly enumerated items with a quill and ink on papyrus rolls. At the same time, ministering brothers and servants unloaded the plunder from the mules and stowed it in the storehouse according to Thibaut's instructions.

The turcopoles stood indecisively off to one side. They watched the Komtur at work and conversed quietly.

"What are you doing here?" snapped Nicholas. "Go home to your wives and children. I'll see you tomorrow morning at weapons training!"

The warriors fell silent and eyed him uncertainly. The lanky Armenian officer, Tigran, stepped forward, gave a quick bow and said calmly, "Brother Nicholas, you've only been our commander for a short time, so perhaps you're not aware that it's customary for each of us to receive a share of the spoils immediately after an expedition."

Nicholas blushed and looked in turn at each of the men, who nodded in agreement. He stifled the sharp retort on the tip of his tongue, realising he had missed something.

"You're paid well for your services," he said, covering his uncertainty with a forced smile.

"That's right. The Order pays us a wage. For that, and naturally also for the grace of God, we fight the infidels, but neither are sufficient to sustain our livelihoods. As I'm sure you know, we must cover the cost of horses, weapons and clothing ourselves. All we ask for is that which is due to us after a raid, according to the old custom. That way you can always count on our full commitment to the fight," said Tigran.

Damn you all! No one pays me even a copper for my difficult duties. I must be content with the good grace of the Almighty, thought Nicholas. And to think he was to lead these greedy, grasping cutthroats as their future commander. They were nothing more than unscrupulous mercenaries, whose loyalty to the Order was based on money and valuable spoils. It seemed he had to bend to their will, for better or worse. However, he would soon change this custom. He would abolish the existing rule of thirds, and introduce harsh penalties for defiance and appropriate individual reward for obedience and bravery. What impertinence, to embarrass the future turcopolier in front of everyone! He would take note of this impudent spokesman and give him a lesson in respect and humility at the next opportunity.

But it was too soon to crack down. As long as Guillaume was still alive and unconvicted for his sins, Nicholas was only his deputy. Marshal Raoul had informed the turcopoles of their former commander's alleged trespasses, but under strict confidentiality. Grand Master de Sablé couldn't announce his appointment as the new turcopolier until Guillaume had been dealt with.

Nicholas looked Tigran up and down contemptuously. "Suit yourselves," he said with feigned indifference. "Is Brother Thibaut aware of this rule?"

"Certainly. He's served as Komtur for a long time. We thank you, and please forgive the inconvenience." There was a mocking undertone in Tigran's voice, which didn't escape Nicholas. The dark Armenian waved to his comrades and they all relaxed visibly and made their way to the Komtur. Nicholas turned away, struggling to suppress his renewed anger, and strode to the block containing the brothers' quarters.

Brother Thibaut had overheard the conversation between Nicholas and the turcopoles, and watched him go with a disapproving shake of his head. *What an ignorant hothead,* he thought, wishing Guillaume was back – he knew how to handle his men and inspire their loyalty. It was a crying shame that he'd fallen out of favour. Thibaut didn't believe a word of the monstrous accusations against him. If all that were true, they would hardly have laden him with gold and sent him out on a delicate secret mission.

The Komtur returned his attention to recording the spoils.

"That goes over there... that one here... throw that on the rubbish heap in the corner!" he ordered the breathless servants hauling the items past him.

"By all the saints, this is by far your least successful raid ever," he said to Tigran, who now stood beside him. Thibaut summarised: "Three light saddle horses with bridles, a dozen mules, eight donkeys, four camels. A pile of tattered robes, some of them blood-soaked and unusable. Three baskets of bread, two barrels of dried fish, four clay jars of olive oil, five dozen leather water flasks, nine goatskin tents with poles, three dozen wool blankets, three leather saddles, two score clay pots. There are still a few linen saddlebags lying around here. Let's see what's in those..." Brother Thibaut bent and opened one of them. His eyes lit up.

"Look, this appears to be the only thing of any value. Three money pouches with... Hands off, you vultures!" he growled at the turcopoles, who had crowded around inquisitively. They recoiled. He reached inside and brought out a handful of gold coins.

"Who did you rogues attack? A Christian merchant or a prince on a pilgrimage? They bear the stamp of the Kingdom of Jerusalem!" The Komtur looked up inquiringly.

Tigran shrugged and stared pointedly into his men's faces. "Two merchant caravans were all we encountered. We didn't see anything unusual," he lied in a steady voice, and his comrades murmured quietly in agreement.

Brother Thibaut crouched down, shaking his head, and counted out the contents of the pouches painfully slowly, while the men waited impatiently.

"Exactly five hundred gold bezants and two hundred silver deniers. Quite a sum for an ordinary merchant caravan," he asserted finally.

"We still get our share, don't we, Brother Thibaut, even when it's such a high sum?" Tigran asked with concern.

"Of course. A third, as usual. But because it's so much, I'll only distribute the coins. The rest of the spoils and the animals go to the Order. Your claim to that is settled with this payment. Agreed?"

Brother Thibaut stood up amidst the nodding turcopoles. They preferred hard money. This solution spared them the trouble of selling the goods.

Under the warriors' watchful eyes, the Komtur counted out one hundred and sixty-six bezants and sixty-six silver deniers, tipped them into a leather pouch and pressed it into Tigran's hand.

"Here, Captain, share this amongst yourselves. Now go with God, but for goodness' sake go!" Brother Thibaut shouted jovially. He turned and went into the storehouse dimly lit by two torches. Outside, cheers erupted amongst the turcopoles. This unexpected boon of nearly seven bezants each was equal to an extra six months' wages.

The Komtur listened to their elated shouts as he swept his eyes over the carefully sorted and stacked plunder. His gaze wandered further down and stopped on two strange figurines that he hadn't previously noticed or counted. A servant had placed them facing one another on the hard mud floor. Their outstretched, feathered arms almost touched. Two dark grey stone plates had been flung down carelessly beside them.

Curious, he picked up one of the figurines. It felt heavy in his hand. *An angel with wings on a lion's body. Made of lead, perhaps, or copper. Pretty little artwork,* he thought. Suddenly he recalled an illustration he had once seen in an ancient psalter. This was a replica of a cherub. One of the guardians that sat on the Israelites' Ark of the Covenant and protected the Lord's Ten Commandments. He carefully put it down and inspected one of the ash-grey tablets. It felt unusually warm, and appeared to have letters engraved on its surface.

Brother Thibaut's face hardened. He had no doubt these were Christian artefacts – replicas of the tablets from the Ark of the Covenant. It was highly unlikely that infidel heathens knew their meaning. These objects must have been in the possession of Christians or Jews. A faint suspicion rose in him.

He reached for the leather pouch on his belt, took out a gold bezant and inspected it closely. Clearly minted in the Kingdom of Jerusalem. One side depicted the Church of the Holy Sepulchre. He returned it to the pouch, strode to the door and called out to Tigran, who had finished distributing the coins amongst his comrades and was about to mount his horse and ride out into the city. He stopped and led his steed to Thibaut.

"What is it, Brother Thibaut?"

"Tigran, I just have one more question," said the Komtur unusually quietly. "Earlier, you said you ambushed two merchant caravans. I believe that's not the whole truth. Am I right?"

The Armenian cleared his throat, blushed and scratched his chin. "I don't know what you mean," he replied warily.

"Well, some of these plundered goods suggest there were Christians among the merchants."

"That's possible. We suspected as much ourselves and reported it to Brother Nicholas. But he said they were all heathens disguised as true believers in order to spy."

"He said that? And you believed him?"

"He's our commander. There was no reason to doubt his word."

"I see... and what do you think? Answer me honestly. You have nothing to fear, I won't take the gold back."

Tigran stared sheepishly at the ground and said evasively, "You should ask Brother Nicholas. We simply follow orders, and he ordered us to attack the Muslims' camp. We thought it was strange that some of them carried rosaries and wooden crosses."

He kept the real reason for the ambush to himself. Before they rode out, the turcopoles had to swear on their lives to Marshal Raoul not to breathe a word to anyone about the hunt for Guillaume, due to the secrecy and importance of the mission for the Order. They were all afraid of the powerful Marshal with the cleft irises, and none would dare speak of it even on their deathbeds.

"Can I go now?"

"Yes, shuffle off. I'll speak to him about it."

The turcopole nodded, hastily mounted his horse and rode to the fortress gate, leaving the Komtur to mull things over.

The Armenian definitely knows more than he's letting on. Brooding, Thibaut walked back into the storehouse, took down a leather saddlebag and placed the cherubim and the tablets carefully inside it.

Their former owners must have been Christian. Possibly high-ranking pilgrims disguised as paupers. That would also explain the large amount of gold they brought back.

The Komtur shuddered at the thought. If it were true, then Templar knights had slaughtered innocent pilgrims. A deadly sin! And a terrible violation of the deeply rooted values of their brotherhood, which was originally founded for the purpose of providing all pilgrims with protection and safe passage to the holy sites of Christendom.

That damned Nicholas. I had a hunch about him. His ill-advised behaviour will bring calamity on our Order. I have no intention of speaking to him. I need more evidence before I can share my suspicions with the Grand Master.

Brother Thibaut sighed and began to search with painstaking thoroughness through the mounds of plundered goods.

XVIII

No, getting drunk won't bring me home, thought Walter of Westereck. He grunted and opened his eyes. He hadn't slept through an entire night in weeks. His thoughts kept returning to his doubtful future, and even more so to his past, which he tried to drown in barrels of wine.

He rolled off his straw bed with a groan, sat up and held both hands against his throbbing temples. His tongue felt as rough and dry as an old rag. The wine helped him get to sleep, but it didn't rinse away the nightmares of hissing crossbow bolts boring into the body of his beloved. Yolanda had been buried two years, after being killed in the battle on the walls of this city. He simply couldn't forget her, and he blamed himself entirely for her death.

Every evening, he lay down in the hope of waking the next day under a green tree in a lush meadow in Saxony, the castle of his forefathers visible in the distance. But every morning he opened his eyes here in Acre, in the house of the Brothers of the German Hospital of Saint Mary. Nothing changed.

He had joined the charitable monastic order, where he worked with three dozen men to care for sick and injured pilgrims primarily from his homeland. Needy pilgrims knocked daily on the gate of the small courtyard near the Tower of St. Nicholas in the city wall. There was a huge demand for medical treatment, spiritual counsel and alms from his compatriots. His friend and comrade-in-arms, Hartung of Scharfenberg, had brought him to the newly established monastic hospital after the murder of his beloved. There, he was supposed to process his painful loss and make peace with the world as a ministering brother.

But so far, his efforts had been in vain. He had found neither peace nor inner balance in this house.

A sliver of morning sun slanted through the narrow window of his small, sparsely furnished room containing a stool, a straw bed covered with a pale linen sheet and an almost drained pottery wine jug. A wooden, iron-bound chest held a few items of clothing, his chainmail and a longsword – his most valuable and only remaining possessions. He hadn't held a weapon in his hand in almost two years. He was no longer a knight nor a warrior.

Brother Walter, he was called by everyone in the hospital, and it still sounded strange to him. He had once had a brother by blood, who had lived with his father in Westereck Castle in Saxony. They were both brutally murdered by a cruel Count's son, Wilfried of Lauenau, in the course of an old feud. The murderer then destroyed his family's estate, kidnapped his bride Yolanda and fled with her to the Holy Land.

He followed his arch-enemy to the walls of Acre, where he finally took bloody revenge on him. Now the monster was rotting outside the city gates in the expansive cemetery, together with many other soldiers of fortune come to win riches and glory in battle against the heathens. Walter had realised a long time ago that it was impossible to acquire either in this country.

Often, all that awaited inexperienced pilgrims here was hunger, slavery or death. The infidels couldn't be vanquished. Not even the famous King Lionheart could do it, and he had slaughtered thousands of them, only to sail away unsuccessfully a few months ago.

Walter's stomach clenched. He let out a sour belch and scratched his itching chin. The brothers had to grow a beard and shave their crowns as a sign of their communion with God and their renunciation of all worldly things – as did the famous Knights Templar and the Knights Hospitaller, after some strange monastic tradition. He had steadfastly refused to shave his crown. Nothing in the world would convince him to part with his long, thick hair. The brothers had allowed him to keep his dark mop for a year, a month and a day, at which point he had to make a decision. This date had long since passed.

And I'm long overdue to leave here.

His decision was made. He was going to leave the brotherhood. He would tell his friend Hartung today. Walter dreaded the bitter disappointment of his faithful brother-in-arms.

He still hoped to convince him to leave the Holy Land and return home with him. But knowing his steadfast friend, he would refuse. He felt very much at home in the devout brotherhood, away from the turmoil of battle and worldly temptations.

A small cast-iron bell in the monastery courtyard plaintively called the brothers to morning prayer.

This won't be a cheerful morning. Neither for me nor for Hartung, Walter predicted. He got up, drained the wine jug and belched again.

Taking a deep breath, he straightened the simple hessian tunic with its black crosses sewn onto the front and back, and hastened to the brothers' chapel on the ground floor of the building.

The musty, windowless prayer room was sparsely lit by two oil lamp. Before the brotherhood took over the premises, it had been the property of a Pisan wine merchant, and this room was used to store wooden barrels. There was nowhere large enough to accommodate all the brothers at once, so they had chosen this room as the chapel.

Brother Hartung knelt on the floor, deep in prayer. He was alone, and his immense frame made the room look even smaller. He filled it up like a grey, stone monolith.

Walter knelt beside his friend. Harting acknowledged his punctual arrival with a surprised nod. They prayed together in front of the waist-high altar, on which stood a roughly hewn cross scarcely a cubit high.

The German brotherhood was relatively new. They were very poor and depended entirely on donations from pilgrims, who came to the Holy Land to fight the heathen Saracens for their own salvation and for the glory of God. Many of them ended up in the hospital, sick and in dire need of help. Some could be helped and a few gave their last, meagre savings as thanks to the charitable brothers. A grandiose church was out of the question.

After kneeling in silence for a while, Walter rose and patted his friend lightly on the shoulder. Hartung stood and turned to face him. His blue-grey eyes looked tired. There were dark circles beneath them. He stretched and rolled his shoulders. Walter felt small next to the enormous man, whose short-cropped hair and trimmed, dark blond beard made his angular accentuated the size of his head.

He gave the impression of being hulking and ponderous, but this was deceptive. Hartung was the most fearsome fighter Walter had ever seen, skilled with all manner of weapons, including sword, lance, dagger and mace, which he had employed mercilessly in countless battles. Walter had once seen Hartung send a heathen to his prophet Mohammed by cleaving him from head to navel with one mighty blow of his sword.

But he didn't enjoy killing. He was an honest, upright man, although somewhat simple-minded in his fervent devotion to God.

Walter swallowed, unsure how to share with Hartung what had been on his mind for weeks.

"My friend, I can't do this anymore," he began hoarsely. He couldn't think of a better way to break the news.

He looked into Hartung's questioning eyes and continued. "We used to be knights, we fought together gloriously in many tournaments in our homeland and won countless prizes. We led thousands of pilgrims on an armed pilgrimage from Alemannia to the Holy Land. We've lost many friends and comrades. We fought outside the walls of this city, suffered long, and were finally victorious. Our swords dripped with the blood of the heathens and our throats were sore from the clamour of battle. But we gained nothing. The Lord's tomb still belongs to the heathens. Jerusalem is lost and our homeland seems farther away than ever. Look at us – we exchanged our armour for grey habits and our steel weapons for wooden soup ladles!"

"I still have my sword, and it's well preserved. But our prayers have brought us closer to God and to our salvation than the sharpest weapons," Hartung replied in his booming voice, rubbing his snub nose. "By God, Walter, why are you telling me this? Have you forgotten that, as a reward for your toils, you were able to take revenge on your family's murderer? Your vengeance was the main reason we came to the Holy Land. I admit the price was high, perhaps too high. Yolanda is gone, but you honour her memory with your good deeds. Have you not earned the gratitude of the many pilgrims you've helped with your healing skills? You learned those in a monastery before becoming a knight. This is worthwhile, godly work. In the past, we sent many heathens to their deaths, but also Christians. For that, we must beg God's forgiveness. The work we do here is our only way to salvation, my friend."

Walter sighed. "God has forsaken me. And I won't find him again here. You have to understand, I'll never be a monk. I'm a knight and a warrior. I work with the sword and lance, not the rosary and the censer. You swore off fighting and chose a life here among the charitable brothers. But that's not my path.

By the Almighty, I can't do this anymore. I've made my decision. I'll go to Duke Leopold in Osterland and enter his service. He promised me a fiefdom back when I opened the city gate for him and brought about the fall of Acre. But the God-damned Sultan Saladin and his armies have conquered most of the Holy Land. It's almost entirely lost to Christendom. Only Acre and Jaffa are still in Christian hands, and these cities will soon fall to the heathens too. This is not our country. It holds nothing but misery. There's no future for me here. Be honest with yourself, there's nothing here for you either. I beg you, let's return home together."

Hartung stiffened and regarded his companion with sorrow. Walter's dark, wavy hair was streaked with grey. His bloodshot eyes were glassy and unfocused. His face looked old. But he was young – not yet twenty-four summers. Hartung knew he had been reaching for the wine of late, often drinking until he passed out. His shaking hands the next morning indicated the onset of addiction.

"Please, stay with us," Hartung replied in a measured tone. "Master Siebrand said to me only yesterday that he soon intends to change the rules of the brotherhood. Honourable knights will be accepted into our ranks, as they are with the Templars and Hospitallers. He wants to create a new Order with warrior brothers who take care of the wellbeing and safety of pilgrims from our homeland. Then I'm sure you'll be able to exchange the bone saw for the sword, as you desire. We need you here, as a healer and a knight!"

Walter waved his hand dismissively. "Old Siebrand has been promising that since Acre was freed from the heathens and we received this house from King Guido. The city has been Christian for almost two years now. And our brotherhood hasn't changed in that time. An Alemannic knight's order will remain a dream as long as there are no monarchs to make it a reality with gold. We beg for alms, as we always have, only to distribute them among the needy. There's little left over for us. Our entire savings are spent. We've already sold the warhorses and their saddles and bridles. A good sword is all I have to call my own!"

"We're not here to accumulate earthly wealth. The heavenly realm will be ours if we do good deeds for Christian people," said Hartung gently, full of conviction.

"You're repeating yourself. I appreciate your devotion, you know that. But this miserable, austere life is not for me. I miss the cool rains, the clear northern air, blossoming meadows and..."

"... and pomp and splendour and wenches!" finished Hartung in frustration. "You've done so much good here. Some of the pilgrims you've healed refer to you reverently as *medicus teutonicorum*. You can read and write Latin, you keep our books. That's a truly extraordinary blessing for the brotherhood. Don't throw that away for base, worldly profits and lust. Find the way to salvation and forgiveness with me!"

Walter shook his head. "I've already had simple folk describe me as the Warrior of the Lord when we led the Christian pilgrimage from Saxony. The Lord wasn't on my side then. Scarcely a third of them and only a handful of Jews survived the journey. And without the Jews' gold, the entire venture would have failed. Where was God's succour then?"

"With those surviving warriors, you helped to reconquer this city for Christendom, and with God's help you were even able to repay the Jews' borrowed silver. That was honourable and the Lord was on your side."

"Oh, I remember. In return for their coins, the Jews received our protection on their journey here, because they had to flee the cities of Alemannia from persecution and death. But their leader, rabbi Ishmael, must now be in the Holy City praying happily at the holy sites of his forefathers. We, on the other hand, will never set eyes on the Saviour's tomb. It was all for nothing. We should have kept the money and disappeared from this country. It's strange – you often see more honour in me than I actually possess. And as for lust, you can rest assured. Since Yolanda's death I haven't wasted a single thought on it."

Hartung wasn't ready to give up. He wracked his brain for a last objection that might dissuade Walter.

"You have no money to fund the sea voyage and the long journey through foreign lands."

"It's true, I don't. And there are no Jews left in the city from whom I can borrow money. They've all been killed or driven out," Walter retorted. "So I've spoken to the Templars. If we fight with them for three months as guest knights, they'll pay for our journey home. As you know, they're rich and have their own fleet. That's my plan."

"Definitely not!"

Hartung's eyes flashed furiously. "Those Templars are arrogant and devious and only out for their own gain. Every command from their superiors must be obeyed unquestioningly, no matter how preposterous. Many brave men have paid for that with their lives. For the glory of God, they say, but it seems to me they're more obsessed with blind hatred and foolish pugnacity. The merciless heathens spare none of them. They take no prisoners and kill every Templar that crosses their path, without exception!"

Walter was no longer listening. Hartung's misgivings merged with his headache into an annoying drone in his head.

"I've made my decision. I'll go to the Templar fortress at the other end of the city today. You have until midday to consider whether you want to come with me."

"Never! I beg you, take some more time to think it through." Hartung laid conciliatory hands on Walter's shoulders, but he shook them off and turned to go.

"Forget it. Come with me or stay. That's my last word on the matter," he said over his shoulder, then strode out of the chapel.

With a heavy heart, Hartung watched him go. He knew his friend well and understood his reasons. Their monastic existence was austere. They garnered no glory in battle, no riches, and they all had to follow strict rules. The brothers pledged themselves to godliness, poverty, chastity and charity. Hartung always observed these rules, having accrued a heavy burden of guilt in his past, for which he sincerely wanted to atone.

He cleared his throat and suddenly felt lonely. Life without Walter at his side would be cheerless and gloomy.

Sombre memories flooded back to him. He saw two bloodied, headless people on the floor in front of him, people he had killed in unbridled rage years previously.

He too once had a bride. She was beautiful, but she proved horrendously unfaithful, secretly cavorting with the bastard son of his feudal lord. When Hartung surprised her by arriving home early from a long military campaign against insurgent Slavs, he caught them making love in his house. Instead of showing remorse, she showered him with scorn and contempt, calling him simple and stupid. Ignoring Hartung's presence, her ravisher didn't even pull his cock out of her; but continued thrusting it into the wantonly giggling woman. Blinded by rage and disappointment, he lost all restraint and decapitated them both, still on the bed, with two swift sword swings.

It was a bloody crime with serious consequences. It didn't cost him his life, because the horny, feeble-minded bastard son was despised by his aristocratic father. But Hartung lost all of his possessions and was banished from his home forever.

He then battled his way through life as a death-defying mercenary and tournament knight, offering his services as a swordsman to numerous lords. At one of the tournaments, he met young Walter of Westereck.

They quickly became friends. Hartung taught Walter a range of new fighting styles, and Walter, three years his junior, taught him Latin in return. He went on to read the Bible countless times, devoured innumerable holy scriptures and found renewed confidence through his faith. By contrast, Walter seemed indifferent to the words of the Almighty after his family was cruelly murdered in the chaos of war in Alemannia between the Welf and Staufer houses.

From then on, Hartung remained steadfastly at Walter's side. He was convinced God had brought them together, and saw it as his destiny to guide Walter back to the faith, convinced this would earn him forgiveness for his own sins. As it was written in the Bible: *if even one sheep in a herd of one hundred strays, leave the ninety-nine and search for the one, and so please the Lord.* He was humbly forced to admit that, so far, he had searched without any real success.

Hartung left the chapel pensively and blinked up at the soft pink morning sky. The first rays of sunlight began to warm the chilly courtyard.

"I understand, my Lord. If it is your will, and if the Templars accept him, then I'll continue to stand at his side until he is finally enlightened by your grace," he whispered, crossing himself.

XIX

"So, you want to become a member of our Order?"

Robert de Sablé's voice was icy. He scrutinised Walter of Westereck, who stood defiantly before him, then leaned back in his chair and sipped wine from his goblet.

He doesn't look like a knight in that coarse, grey robe and little felt hat. More like an artisan or a servant.

But his proud, upright posture and the steady, almost haughty gaze in that angular face revealed his nobility. The Grand Master remembered this man, and was surprised by his request. He had never expected to see him in the Palace of the Templars.

"Yes, Grand Master," replied Walter tersely. He didn't feel like a true knight without so much as the dagger he had to surrender to Brother Gilbert upon entering the Templar fortress. Only members of the Order were permitted to carry arms inside the walls.

Brother Gilbert, the Preceptor of the Templars, stood at the knight's side, a quietly confident smile on his lips.

"I want to fight with my sword for a time, at the side of brave warriors of the cross against the heathens, for the glory of God, and then return to my homeland. I thought, about three months. Brother Gilbert here said that was possible and suggested I present my request to you personally today."

Gilbert the Pious, thought the Grand Master, grimacing as if the sweet wine in his mouth had turned to vinegar. As the respected religious instructor to the Templars and former provincial Komtur of Aragon, the Preceptor had been one of the applicants for the office of Grand Master three summers ago, and his toughest competition. But at forty, Gilbert was considered too young and impetuous, and he lost the vote to the more experienced Robert de Sablé, who came with a commendation from Richard the Lionheart.

As Robert had expected, Gilbert remained in the Holy Land, persumably waiting for the next opportunity to become the supreme leader of the Templars. The short, stocky man was exceptionally well liked among the brothers for his engaging manner, even temper, unshakeable faith and extensive knowledge of worldly and ecclesiastical things.

In addition to his role as Preceptor, he had also taken on the task of recruiting noble warriors to the Brotherhood. The Order had a constant need for new fighters in the relentless war against the heathens, which took a heavy toll on their ranks. His success at this increased his reputation and influence in the Order, much to the Grand Master's displeasure.

It's time to take him down a peg, Robert decided, asking slyly, "Now, is it true that you, Sir Walter, threatened King Richard of England shortly after the conquest of Acre and killed the commander of his bodyguard?"

Walter frowned and narrowed his eyes. The Grand Master seemed to be well informed. Everyone knew he had the English King to thank for his position in the Order. *Not a great start for me as a Templar.*

"Richard the Lionheart was never my enemy. But his bodyguard Wilfried of Lauenau was. He murdered my family in Saxony and laid waste to my estate. I pursued him to the Holy Land and exacted my revenge, curse his name for all eternity!"

De Sablé slowly stroked his beard and his mouth curved into a false smile.

"Yes, I remember. Wilfried of Lauenau. A shrewd fighter. I fought with him in Cyprus against the Greeks. Shame about him. We need men like him these days in the war against the infidels. What a disgrace – a Christian killing a Christian. I heard you put down your weapons after his inglorious demise, retreated to a hospital and haven't lifted a hand since to fight the heathen Sultan, while many of our fighters have given their lives in the holy war. That really doesn't recommend you for a membership in our renowned Order."

Walter struggled to maintain his composure. His face flushed and he breathed heavily. Brother Gilbert cleared his throat, laid a placatory hand on his shoulder, and said, "Sir Walter is an exceptionally skilled healer of suffering pilgrims and warriors here in the city. He learned the arts of healing, reading and writing in his youth at a monastery. He demonstrated extraordinary bravery in the siege of Acre. In a surprise attack, he was among the first to break through the city gate and open it for the Christians. Many infidels fell by his hand. He is skilled with weapons and an experienced commander of combat troops. I've no doubt he would be a boon for our army."

A boon for you, maybe. If the man doesn't even show respect to a king, he'll hardly fall in line under my command. He's too proud and cavalier, and probably temperamental. I'll put him to the test, the Grand Master mused with a disparaging glance at Brother Gilbert.

"All I see is a man who has insulted our Christian King Richard and murdered one of his trusted men out of base lust for revenge. That was neither godly nor chivalrous. There was also a wench, over whom the two of them were fighting. Wasn't her name Yolanda? And didn't she salaciously share a bed with Wilfried, even though he was her half-brother? I heard tell she tired of him, ran to you, and that you also lay with her in sin. She atoned for her whoring with her life when you crossed swords with Wilfried and the harlot tried to intervene. Oh yes, I know all about you and your nefarious deeds!"

Walter completely lost control. His right hand reached for his belt and, had he been wearing his weapon there, the Grand Master would have been slain in an instant. Instead, he roared with fury and raised his arms to lunge at Robert, but the quick-thinking Brother Gilbert grappled him from behind, slung his arms around his waist, and pulled him back with all his strength.

Robert de Sablé leapt to his feet in horror, his chair crashing to the floor behind him, and threw himself behind one of the massive columns that supported the hall's vaulted ceiling.

Beside himself with rage and oblivious to Gilbert's efforts, Walter continued to struggle forward. The pulsating veins in his temples looked like they might burst. Wide-eyed and grimacing fiercely, he bellowed, "You filthy dog! I'll kill you! I'll end you, whoreson! You have no idea! SHE WAS MY WOMAN AND SHE DIED FOR ME!"

Brother Gilbert clung to Walter like a heavy sack and screamed into the raging man's ear, "Get back! Back, I say! Have you lost your mind, what are you doing? Get a grip on yourself!"

Walter stopped, snorted, stretched up to his full height and tried to push Gilbert's arms off his hips.

But the Preceptor wouldn't let go. Instead, he dragged him with both arms to the door of the Palace.

"Get out, go!" he shouted. "That's enough! You must leave!" He turned and bowed to the Grand Master, who cautiously left the protection of the column to see them exit, his face white with fear. He spat contemptuously on the floor and Bother Gilbert was relieved that Sir Walter had already turned around and staggered like a drunkard to the door, so that he didn't see this last insult.

Outside, a fresh sea breeze blew through the fortress and cooled Walter's fierce temper a little. Gilbert closed the heavy door behind them and wiped droplets of sweat from his face. Sir Walter took a deep breath and shook his head, calmer now.

"I'm... I'm sorry, Brother Gilbert, I really am. I can't serve under that man."

"I doubt the Grand Master wants you to now. What got into you, Walter? Brother Robert is a powerful official, not some peasant! He is accountable to none but God and the Holy Father in Rome, and in that sense he holds the third highest position in Christendom! How could you allow yourself to be provoked so?"

"He deeply insulted me and dragged my honour as a knight through the mud! He never had any intention of considering my request!" Walter irritably adjusted his felt cap, which had slipped awry in the tussle. "I apologise sincerely. You spoke in my favour and I've put you in a difficult position. Forgive me."

The Preceptor waved dismissively.

"I should have known better. It's my fault too. Brother Robert was a loyal subject of King Richard before he entered the Order. You humiliated his king by killing the commander of his guard. I know he resents your new hospital brotherhood as a competitor for the favour of the Alemannic pilgrims. You should go now. Don't show yourself near the Temple for a while. The Grand Master bears a grudge and I don't want to see you in chains."

Walter nodded, bid a hasty farewell to the disappointed Gilbert and strode out of the fortress.

Well done. Wonderful! Now I have a new enemy and one more reason to leave the Holy Land. And no prospect of any money to make it happen, because I certainly won't be a Templar. Well, Hartung will be pleased when he hears I have to stay in Acre a while longer.

He stomped down to the harbour, scowling, and stopped in one of the many taverns to rinse away his rage toward the arrogant Grand Master with a few cups of wine. A little more relaxed, he wound his way through the city's convoluted alleyways.

Arriving at the hospital of the German brotherhood, he was surprised to see the gates unlocked. He pushed one of them open and stepped into the courtyard.

There were no monks in sight. They were all in the small chapel for their midday prayers at Sext. But he noticed some unusual-looking visitors resting in the shade of the main building.

Three mules stood there, two of them saddled, the third heavily loaded with provisions, with three dark-robed figures crouching on the ground beside them. Infidels, judging by their clothing. One of the figures raised its head and looked at Walter with wide eyes as he entered the courtyard. The other two kept their heads lowered under large hoods.

Walter approached them with curiosity. The man stood up at once and bowed to him.

"God be with you, sir," the said Muslim in Frankish with a strong Arabic accent. His voice was high and lacked confidence. He seemed very young – his face was smooth and his movements gauche.

"Greetings to you too," Walter replied with surprise, also in Frankish. It was unusual for an infidel to speak the common language of the Christian pilgrims.

"My name is Harit ibn Tharit ibn… doesn't matter, just call me Harit. We're looking for a famous Alman. Waltur of…" he turned questioningly to one of his seated companions, who whispered, "Waltur Westend, Westend…"

"Ah, *ana 'afham,* I understand, Waltur of Westend. Can I find him here?"

Walter grew suspicious. A heathen who knew his name. That was strange.

"Tell me, infidel, who let you in and why are you looking for an Alemann?" Walter's right hand slowly disappeared under his tunic and grasped the dagger he usually wore there. But not today, as he had forgotten to ask for it back from Brother Gilbert at the Templar fortress. He frowned.

Harit bowed again and replied evasively, "The gate wasn't locked. I opened... forgive our intrusion... do you know the... Alemann?"

Walter silently cursed Brother Heinrich, the gatekeeper. This wasn't the first time he had left the gate unlocked. A gregarious and pious man, but utterly useless as a guard.

He looked down at the Arab's companions still sitting silently in the dust beside him.

"You, get up and show yourself to me!" said Walter, nudging one of them with his foot. Harit hastily translated. The figure slowly stood up and removed its hood, and to Walter's astonishment, a female face appeared. Her lips were firmly pressed together. Dark brown locks curled out from under a blue jilbab, and her narrow eyebrows curved gracefully above eyes almost as dark as night. A straight, freckled nose, high cheekbones and a dimpled chin completed her delicate face, which looked far too pale for an Arab. She quickly lowered her eyes and covered her head again.

"Who... who are you?" stammered Walter, surprised and enchanted. The woman nodded nervously for her escort to answer on her behalf.

"This is Leah of Jerusalem, niece of the Jew Ishmael from Almanland. She doesn't speak your language. I'm her dragoman, here to escort her and translate her words and yours. We're on a very important assignment from her uncle, and must speak to Sir Waltur. We heard there are many Almans living here. Perhaps you can help us find him?"

Ishmael from Almanland. I mentioned him to Hartung only this morning. A strange coincidence, thought Walter, amused at the young man's pronunciation.

"I knew an Ishmael from Alemannia," said Walter, trying to catch another glimpse of the pretty Jew. "I'm Walter of Westereck. Not Westend. What do you want?"

Harit's eyes lit up and he flung his arms up to the heavens.

"Thanks be to Allah, we found him! It's him, Leah, did you hear? Waltur Westebeck!"

Leah understood and fell to her knees in front of the knight, an incomprehensible stream of words tumbling out of her. Walter stepped closer, touched her shoulders and gestured for her to stand.

"No one must kneel before me! I'm only a poor brother of the hospital, and my name is WALTER OF WESTERECK. Please tell her that!" he said to Harit, who immediately translated.

"Who are these people?" Hartung was suddenly standing behind Harit. He was on kitchen duty and excused from Sext. He had been preparing the midday meal for the brothers in the small kitchen in the refectory when he heard voices through the window and came out to investigate.

Harit stiffened when he heard Hartung's deep voice. He turned around to look at the tall knight and instantly fell to his knees, wide-eyed.

"My God," murmured Walter. "What is this new heathen custom of constantly throwing oneself to the ground? These two seem a little confused."

"So dir Gott helfe... so dir Gott helfe... so dir Gott helfe!" babbled Harit excitedly, pressing his forehead into the dirt.

"And now he speaks our language too!" Walter shook his head in wonder and looked at Hartung. "I just found them here. She's the niece of the Jew Ishmael from Cologne. We spoke of him this morning, remember? The leader of the Jews that joined our pilgrimage. Isn't that a strange coincidence? They say they're here on his behalf. And her self-prostrating companion is a Muslim named Harit. They were looking for me, but I have no idea what they want from me."

Hartung raised an eyebrow. "Strange, very strange. I'm sure it will become clear, my friend. They look hungry and thirsty. Let's take them to the dining hall and give them something to eat and drink, as befits good brothers of the hospital. Then we'll talk to them."

"Wait. I want to see who they've brought with them."

Walter stooped and threw back the hood of the motionless third visitor.

"By all the saints!" he exclaimed. "A Templar!"

XX

Komtur Thibaut strode across the noisy inner courtyard of the Templar fortress, a brooding expression on his down-turned face. He was oblivious to the clamouring throng of beggars who had assembled as they did every evening to receive charity from the brothers. There were a lot more of them than usual, as it was the one day of the week when meat was served. There were several huge pots full of tepid soup with small pieces of mutton and yellow beans floating it.

The earthenware vessels on the trestle tables emitted an appetising aroma that made some of the hungry strays and beggars quite frenzied. They pushed and jostled, pleading at the tables. Everyone wanted to be first. Sergeants filled small wooden bowls with the soup and handed out flatbreads, which were torn greedily from their hands. A knight with a surly expression and a long staff watched over the food distribution with two squires. Now and then, a scuffle broke out and he struck hard into the crowd.

Thibaut walked purposefully to one of the corner towers looming three storeys high in the northern fortification wall. That was where the archive was located, where Preceptor Gilbert went about his daily work.

Thibaut had wrestled with the dilemma of whether to share his suspicion that Nicholas, the new turcopolier, had attacked a Christian pilgrim train. If it were true, and the crime was made public, there would be serious consequences. Not just for Nicholas, but for the entire brotherhood. The Order's good reputation would be shaken to its foundations.

He hadn't found much evidence of such a crime amongst the spoils. A few rosaries, two small crucifixes in silver and

wood and a small parchment psalter with several pages missing. All these could have been stolen by heathens and kept as
mementos.

But he couldn't stop thinking about the gold and silver
pieces he had divided amongst the turcopoles without a second
thought. They were coins minted in the Kingdom of Jerusalem
– common currency in the Holy Land. It seemed too high a
sum for ordinary pilgrims to be carrying, which corroborated
his suspicion. The coins must have belonged to a high-ranking
Christian, perhaps a nobleman or a rich merchant wanting to
visit the holy sites incognito.

But the four items he carried in the saddlebag on his back
couldn't be attributed to either heathens or Christians. He
needed advice. He had decided it was wise to ask the Order's
head scholar about their origin before informing the Grand
Master. Brother Gilbert was a trustworthy, discreet man. Thibaut would make an objective decision based on his opinion.

The portly Komtur wheezed as he ascended the four long
flights of stairs in the tower. Out of breath, he knocked on the
unlocked door of the archive and entered without waiting for
a reply.

He was enveloped by an acrid smell of ancient, tanned goat
leather, which lingered in the air despite the open window. The
room was generously proportioned, but felt cramped because
of the multitude of shelves overloaded with stacks of papyrus
rolls, parchments and books. Locked wooden chests were
stacked around the room, and loose papers lay all over the
floor. In the farthest corner of the archive was the Preceptor's
bed. The neatly straightened covers and down pillow of snow-
white damask contrasted starkly with the chaos in the room.

Brother Thibaut hadn't entered this space since the archive
was relocated there a year previously. After the Holy City was

lost, the precious collection of knowledge comprising thousands of documents went through an eventful period. First, it was taken to Jaffa. But it wasn't safe enough there from the Saracens who, triumphant after storming Jerusalem, now threatened this city too. Great pains were taken to transport the archive once again, and it was sent on a ship to Tyre in the heathen-free north of the Christian realm. Then the brothers established their headquarters in the strong temple fortress in Acre after the conquest of that city. The documents, books and scriptures were now stored here, and Preceptor Gilbert had been trying to bring order to the chaos ever since.

Standing at a high lectern by the window, he dipped his stylus into a ceramic inkwell and looked up at the Komtur amiably.

"Brother Thibaut, nice to see you. Unfortunately, I can't offer you a place to sit, as you can see..." He gestured apologetically at the disarray. "What can I do for you?" His rolled pronunciation and dark complexion betrayed his Spanish heritage.

"It's alright, I don't need to sit. I'm not here to chat," said the Komtur, taking the heavy bag from his shoulder and setting it down on the floor. He cleared his throat self-consciously. "You're the most learned man among us and I'm sure you can help me. Brother Nicholas brought back a number of items from his last raid with the turcopoles. I'm wondering whether they once belonged to Christian pilgrims, and if they hold any value to us. These were among them..."

He bent and reached into the saddlebag, taking out the two cherubim and the clay tablets. "Look, there appears to be lettering on these panels, which I can't read. And these figures look like angels to me."

Curious, Gilbert stepped closer. He immediately recognised the items on the floor in front of him. His pupils dilated and he recoiled. "For the love of God, Brother Thibaut! Pack that away at once! Quickly put it outside the door and come back in!"

The Komtur gave him a baffled look, but the vehement request left no room for argument. He stuffed the items back into the saddlebag, took it out of the room and laid it beside the door.

"Close the door behind you, Brother!" The colour had drained from Gilbert's face and he leaned heavily on the lectern to steady himself.

"What's wrong? You look like you've seen the devil incarnate! Are you unwell?" Thibaut asked with concern, hurrying to his side.

"There's nothing wrong with me. Not yet." Gilbert took a deep breath and shook his head. "I never thought I'd see those ill-fated things with my own eyes. They bring death, Brother Thibaut!" Seeing the bewildered look on the Komtur's face, he continued, "Let me explain. I once served as a squire to Arnaud de Toroge, the Grand Master before last, and later I was his closest confidant in our chapter in Aragon. God rest his soul. Almost ten years ago, I accompanied him on his last journey to Verona, to request help from the German emperor in the fight against the heathen sultan. Brother Arnaud was already very ill at the time. I was with him in his last few hours and he confided in me a terrible secret, which until this day I couldn't believe. I thought he was delirious, but now I've seen it for myself!"

He paused, closed his eyes and tried to recall precisely his conversation with the former Grand Master.

The Komtur looked impatiently into his ashen face.

"I'm convinced that what you found brings certain death," Gilbert continued hoarsely. "Grand Master Arnaud told me that some of the brothers in Jerusalem had come across a supposedly precious find in the underground vaults of the Temple

Mount – more valuable than all the treasure in the world. The Ark of the Covenant, the holiest relic of the Jews. The words of the Lord engraved in stone, which Moses received from Him on Mount Sinai. The origin of all faith, but also death for anyone who holds them in their hands."

"I'm not convinced. These things don't look much like treasures to me. Two simple clay tablets and a pair of cast lead figurines can't be a sacred relic. And, as you can see, I'm still alive. You must be mistaken." Thibaut shook his head. He knew the story of the Ark of the Covenant from the holy scriptures. "The Ark was described as magnificent, gold-plated and full of miracles."

"Well, Komtur... I haven't finished the story. The Ark was indeed a gold-plated acacia wood casket with two winged cherubim. Inside were the ore tablets engraved with the Lord's Commandments. Some of the brothers examined the find, as no one believed in the miracle. It was presumed to be a fake or a replica. But the figurines were pure gold and the letters on the tablets were from an ancient Jewish script. Learned men were summoned to translate them, and revealed that they were indeed the Ten Commandments. Everything seemed to correlate with the scriptures, and the brothers realised the Ark may be genuine. But it didn't deliver miracles – quite the opposite. A few days later, several of the Templars began to lose their hair. Their bodies were suddenly covered in lesions, their skin flaked off and they died pitifully in unspeakable agony, one after another. They suffered terrible diarrhoea, their viscera liquefied and they bled from the nose and ears. Only those who had touched the holy relic were affected. Fear swept through their ranks. The Ark was reburied deep in the vaults under the Temple Mount in Jerusalem. All those who held it in their hands died a tortuous death shortly after. Including Grand Master Arnaud, who told me of these terrible events on his deathbed. He was among the men who spent a long time examining the supposed relic. The objects outside the door match his descriptions. I remember his words clearly. This is the devil's work, not a sacred relic! Now do you understand my agitation?"

The Preceptor sighed and looked inquiringly at the Komtur.

Brother Thibaut nodded incredulously. He had known Bother Gilbert a long time. There was no reason to doubt his story.

"I believe you, however unbelievable it sounds. But you're saying this plunder is that same treasure? The figurines clearly aren't made of gold, the tablets are clay and not stone or ore. And how is this... stuff... supposed to have found its way into the spoils from Nicholas' raid?"

"That I can't tell you. But the tablets were encased in clay and the cherubim in lead, as it was unclear whether they were imbued with something godly and the brothers were afraid to destroy them. In any case, they wanted to ensure no one would be exposed to them, so they were hidden. These things must have been dug up and sold by infidels. Maybe to knowledgeable Jews or even Christians."

Gilbert glanced at the Komtur, who pricked up his ears at these words and hastily rubbed his slightly blackened hands on his tunic.

"To Jews or Christians, did you say?" This information fed his suspicions.

The Preceptor shrugged. "Presumably. The heathens are ignorant of Christian artefacts. Since conquering Jerusalem, not a single stone of the Temple has remained in place. Pilgrims have reported that our former headquarters have been turned into a mosque by the Saracens. I've heard that many buildings were torn down or fell into disrepair. Everything our brothers had to abandon when they fled has been sold or destroyed. It's quite conceivable that Christians or Jews acquired some of it. Be that as it may, you must throw this unholy relic – or whatever it is – into the sea. At once!"

Thibaut held up his hands and shook his bald head. "No, not yet. Are you absolutely sure these things aren't of heathen origin?" he asked.

"I would be very surprised if the Saracens had any idea of the significance of the Ark of the Covenant. They consider it blasphemous to create images of their God or prophet. And that counts for any kind of idolatry. You'll never see paintings or statues of this kind in their houses of worship, let alone cherubim or tablets inscribed with Jewish script."

The Komtur suddenly felt very hot. He wiped sweat from his brow.

"Then these could be evidence of a nefarious act. Because if what you say is true, that the heathens consider these things worthless, then Brother Nicholas has killed innocent pilgrims and not heathen merchants, as he claims. I found these and other Christian items among the spoils from his last foray with the turcopoles. There was even a large sum of gold bezants, but no tradable goods of any kind," he said in a steady voice. He refrained from mentioning that Brother Guillaume was suspected to have been among the pilgrims and likely one of the victims.

Horror flashed in Gilbert's eyes. "That's a serious accusation. If it's true, it could plunge our Order into dire straits. The brotherhood of the Knights Templar was established to protect all Christian pilgrims. This would be a monstrous violation of all our ideals! Dear God. Are you sure?"

Thibaut frowned deeply and nodded. "After what you've told me about this supposed Ark of the Covenant, I'm quite sure. But please, Gilbert, keep this knowledge to yourself for now, because I want to consult with the Marshal on the matter.

He authorised the deployment of turcopoles in heathen territory. As you know, Brother Raoul departed for Tyre the day before yesterday to escort Philipp of Beauvais. He returns tomorrow. I want to talk to him before I take this to the Grand Master."

Thibaut's hands tingled and he was suddenly seized with fear. He crossed himself repeatedly and asked anxiously, "I won't die of that horrible illness like our brothers in Jerusalem, will I?"

The Preceptor shook his head. "I don't think so. That only happened to the men who spent a long time examining and touching the cursed objects. But please keep your distance from that dark enigma! I sincerely hope for all our sakes that your suspicions are not confirmed and that the Marshal has an explanation."

"We'll see. It's in God's hands. I'll keep the items safe in the storehouse, where no one but me is allowed to enter. Thank you, Brother Gilbert."

Relieved, the Komtur bowed and said goodbye, leaving the worried Preceptor alone in the archive.

Outside, he looked apprehensively at the saddlebag on the floor. Steeling himself, he picked it up and held it out in front of him as if it were full of poisonous adders. Then he stomped down the creaking stairs.

By God, what terrible news, thought Brother Gilbert as he listened to the stout Komtur's pounding footfalls. His mind drifted back to the past. *Those tablets are the devil's work. If they're ever found again, they'll bring calamity to our Order!*

Those were some of the last words his former Grand Master and patron, Arnaud de Toroge, had whispered to him on his deathbed. Gilbert hoped his ominous prophesy wasn't about to come true.

XXI

The unannounced visitors sat with Sir Walter, huddled in silence on rough wooden benches in the monastery's small refectory. The room was on the ground floor of the brotherhood's main, two-storey building, where Hartung was on kitchen duty that day.

He had laid out bread, jugs of wine and ceramic bowls on a table of pale pine boards. Today, the brothers would eat vegetable soup. It bubbled in an iron kettle over a flame in the kitchen and emitted an appetising aroma that wafted throughout the building. He wasn't a very good cook, but these days he could manage a simple soup of carrots, peas, onions and garlic without assistance.

Hartung brought a jug of water, poured it into cups for the guests, and sat down beside Walter.

"Eat and drink with God's blessing," he said peevishly, nodding at them.

Harit had been staring at him transfixed for some time and could no longer contain his excitement. He slid from his seat and fell to his knees before Hartung.

The tall knight rolled his eyes and asked, "What's all this? I'm not one of your heathen saints!"

"There is only one God for me, and that is Allah, and Mohammed is his prophet!" replied the Muslim, bending forward until his head touched the ground. "His grace led me to you, so that I may thank you! I owe you my life, benevolent warrior!"

Hartung looked at him cluelessly. "How so?"

"When the infidel soldiers under the command of the terrible King Lionheart ravaged Acre and took prisoners, you protected me from them and let me flee through a breach in the city wall. Your words were, 'So dir Gott helfe'! I've never forgotten them! I was able to escape the slaughter, when Sultan Salah ad-Din – Allah protect him and his offspring – didn't pay the ransom on time and the Nazarenes killed everyone."

Hartung's expression turned to one of loathing at the memory of the heinous massacre. Lionheart was impatient to move on Jerusalem after the fall of Acre, and the two thousand Muslim prisoners were a hindrance to him. He had them all unceremoniously slaughtered outside the city gates. An inglorious act by the exalted king, who then failed to conquer the Holy City anyway.

"It's alright, calm yourself. I only fight armed men, not defenceless women and children – whether heathen or Christian. You owe me nothing. Now get up, sit on the bench and eat!" he urged, and Harit quickly resumed his seat.

Silence prevailed once again. The three visitors made no move to touch the food, keeping their heads bowed.

Walter broke the silence, addressing the Templar, "I know you. You're Guillaume de Born, commander of the Order's turcopoles, and you fought against the heathens in the siege of this city. Why are you disguised and travelling with a Jew and an infidel? What do you want here?"

Guillaume didn't reply immediately. He filled a cup with wine and drank it slowly, savouring it. Then he leaned back with a satisfied sigh and looked at Hartung and Walter.

"I haven't had wine for a long time. You have my thanks. And I know who you are too. Sir Walter and his friend the invincible Hartung. Your reputation as excellent fighters is legendary. I saw you among the Duke of Osterland's men when this city fell."

He put down his cup and leaned forward.

"Listen, I'm not a Templar anymore. If I ever go near the Temple again, my life is forfeit. That's why I wear this humble robe. I no longer protect pilgrims nor do I fight for the Order – only for this mismatched pair on their truly holy mission. As strange as that may sound. They... er... we need your help."

"That does indeed sound strange," said Walter, gazing searchingly into his watery blue eyes. "You'll have to explain it to us."

Before Guillaume could reply, Harit held up his hand and said, "Wait, the goldsmith's niece has a letter for you from her uncle!"

He whispered something to Leah, who nodded and took the papyrus roll from under her jilbab, handing it to Walter with trembling hands.

Astonished, he took it, unrolled it and read its Latin contents out loud.

"Highly honoured and blessed Sir Walter, if you are reading these lines, you have found my niece Leah and her escort, the former sugar merchant Harit ibn Tharit ibn Hamid, in good health. I'm sure you remember me. I am Ishmael from Cologne, who has you to thank for my successful, safe journey to the Holy Land of my forefathers. With your help, and that of your loyal companion Hartung, I was able to start a new life in Jerusalem. May the Lord reward you for all eternity. But now I urgently need your help once again, and I know no one I can trust more than you. I was in possession of the greatest treasure of my people. The unsuspecting Harit found it in Jerusalem, in the vaults of the Temple Mount, and sold it to me. You and your friend Hartung, as readers of your Bible, will know of the sacred relic of which I speak. It was thought lost for centuries – the holy Ark of the Covenant with the Lord's Ten Commandments, handed down by God to our prophet Moses on Mount Sinai..."

Walter paused here and looked sceptically at the nodding faces of the visitors. Hartung, too, looked questioningly at them and shrugged doubtfully.

"That's impossible," murmured Walter. He read on. "I happily held in my hands the ore tablets inscribed with the Lord's Commandments, and two figurines, cherubim, winged creatures which you call angels, until they were robbed from me by a Templar. I assume he is on his way back to Acre with his spoils, to the Templar fortress there. He seriously injured me, so I'm sending my niece Leah and the Muslim Harit after him, to track down the holy relic. Noble Sir Walter, I beg you humbly, help my niece Leah to bring this treasure back to my people. Find the Templar and retrieve the sacred artefacts from him. For that, I will richly reward you. My niece will tell you the amount herself. I don't dare write it down here. I beg of you, help us! Yours gratefully, Rabbi Ishmael. May you be blessed by the Most High for all eternity!"

Walter puffed out his cheeks and let go of one end of the letter, so that it rolled itself up.

"By all the saints, I don't believe it," said Hartung after a period of silence. "I've read the story of the Ark of the Covenant. In the Book of Moses. It's part of my psalter. It's supposed to be very powerful, but has been lost for aeons."

"A legend," agreed Walter, wrinkling his nose. "I've heard of it too. One of the many fairy tales in the old Bible. Who knows what the little Arab really talked the old Jew into buying."

He looked at Harit, who held up his hands and defended himself vehemently, "By Allah the Almighty, I knew nothing of the significance of the tablets and statues. But Ishmael believes they're authentic, which is why we're here!"

Leah suddenly reached behind her held up a leather rucksack – the only piece of luggage she had brought into the refectory. She took from it two bulging money pouches, which she placed on the table before Walter. Then she spoke quietly to Harit, who raised his eyebrows. He hesitated, and didn't translate until she nudged him gently in the ribs. "Leah says this is three hundred gold dinar as an advance payment. You'll receive another seven hundred gold coins after you help us retrieve the holy relic and take it back to Jerusalem, whether you consider it authentic or not."

Walter's eyes lit up. This was it! The miracle he had been waiting and ardently praying for. A thousand gold dinar! A tremendous fortune, more than enough for the trip home. In fact, enough to rebuild his ruined estate in Saxony – more magnificently and better fortified than ever before. He looked at Hartung, who shook his head in disbelief and glanced in turn at Guillaume, who seemed equally astonished at the extraordinarily high reward.

"Well, faced with all that money, my belief in the authenticity of the relic is irrelevant. I'd happily take on the whole Order for that amount," said Walter. "Ishmael also mentions a Templar. Did these two pay you off, to help them? Did you betray your brothers for money? Is that why you're no longer a Templar?"

Guillaume held up his hand and replied without hesitation, "By God, all the money in the world means nothing to me, I swear to you. The rabbi was referring to me when he mentioned a thieving Templar. I was sent by my Order to Jerusalem on a secret mission, and there I happened to learn of the discovery of the Ark of the Covenant. I stole the treasure out of greed, as I was aware of its significance and I believe it truly is the long lost relic. I intended to return to Acre with the stolen items, but the Grand Master and his Marshal were already conspiring against me. On their command, my own turcopoles ambushed me and tried to kill me. But I escaped their duplicity and wandered, wounded, through the mountains of Samaria, until Leah and Harit found me half dead, and saved my worthless life. The Templars have the treasure now. But they won't recognise it as such immediately, because it's been disguised under layers of cheap lead and clay. I'm now helping these two because I owe them my life, because I want to rectify the injustice, and at the same time I plan to take revenge on my former brothers."

"Oh, Walter knows all about revenge," Hartung commented drily. "It's sweet, but has a very bitter aftertaste."

Guillaume looked questioningly at Walter, who waved his hand. "It's true. My desire for revenge led us here and earned me a squalid life as a healer of the sick. I too have an account to settle with the Templars, as of this morning. Your Grand Master is a scheming, dishonourable wretch!"

"Oh... is he now?" asked Hartung in a mocking tone, pouring himself a cup of water.

"Yes, he is. I'll never become a Templar. Hell will freeze over first!"

"Ah... I see. He turned you down," Hartung concluded laconically, unable to suppress a smirk.

"De Sablé deeply insulted me! He sullied the memory of... oh, it doesn't matter. I'll tell you later what happened." Red-faced, he turned to Guillaume. "Now you know I'm no friend of the Order. But I want to know the whole truth from you. Why were you in Jerusalem and why do they want you dead?"

Guillaume lowered his eyes in shame. It wasn't easy for him to honestly confess to these knights his story of sin, carnal lust, murder and treachery, but he resolved to leave nothing out. If, after that, the warriors declined to help, it was God's will, and he would have to find another way to the sacred artefacts. In a few words, he repeated the facts he had confessed to Leah and Harit in the mountains.

Walter and Hartung listened with a mixture of repugnance, incomprehension and astonishment. The treachery of the Templar Order was unprecedented. This became especially clear to them when Guillaume told them that the heathen Assassins had been commissioned with the murder of a Christian ruler. Not to mention the sinful transgressions of some of its high commanders. Guillaume was right to make the duplicitous Grand Master the target of the attack.

When the former Templar had finished his confession, Hartung blurted, "By God, Walter, and you wanted to lend your sword to those hypocrites! And you, Guillaume, you should be glad you're no longer a part of that fraudulent, traitorous mob! Your salvation from the dreadful sins you've committed is still a long way off, but you certainly wouldn't have found it amongst those blasphemers!"

The Templar's demeanour reminded Hartung of the way his friend had looked before Yolanda's death. Uprooted, full of sin and driven by thoughts of revenge.

Lord, is this another person I'm supposed to save?

Walter nodded. "How true. Guillaume, you should have turned your back on the Templars long ago. You're young and you're an experienced warrior. There must be barons or princes here in the Holy Land who'd be happy to take you into their service," he said. "It pains me that you were so disgracefully betrayed, although you deserve to be punished. But your brothers are burdened by no less guilt than you are."

"I'm very glad you see it that way," Guillaume replied, looking back and forth between the two warriors. "Will you help us take back the relic? The revenge part I'll take care of myself. That's between the Grand Master, the Marshall and me."

Walter was on board. He was already convinced by the prospect of all that gold. With Guillaume, who knew his way around the Templar fortress like no other, they had a good chance of success.

He elbowed Hartung. "What do you say? The Ten Commandments, carved in stone by the Lord Himself. And we can snatch them out from under the noses of those depraved Templars. Imagine that! It would be truly godly work!"

"Didn't you just say it was nothing but an old fairy tale from my Bible? Come outside with me. We need to talk."

An expression of irritation flickered across Hartung's face, but he said kindly to the visitors, "Please, fortify yourselves in the meantime. We won't be long."

Walter and Hartung rose and went out into the courtyard. The sound of soft singing drifted out of the small chapel. The Brothers were still in the middle of their prayer service.

Hartung glared at his friend and hissed, "Have you taken leave of your senses? Did the money addle your mind? First a fairy tale, and now a treasure bestowed by God! Maybe the stolen things are completely worthless and meaningless for all but the deluded Ishmael. The two of us with a fallen Templar, a snot-nosed Muslim and a Jewish woman against the most powerful Order in the Kingdom? It's ridiculous! The Templars are dangerous warriors, not ragged Bedouins. They live in the strongest fortress in the Levant. Those whoresons, to who Guillaume used to belong, will hack us to pieces the moment we enter the gates. We haven't fought in almost two years! How do you suppose that will go?"

Walter rolled his eyes and grabbed his friend by the shoulders. "I don't think we've forgotten how to use weapons; we were far too good at it. But I don't believe in coincidence either. We spoke of Ishmael only this morning. Now his niece is sitting here asking for our help. And she's with the Muslim whose life you saved. And then there was my fruitless visit to the dishonourable Grand Master of the Templars, who made a new enemy of me with his insults. And now one of his former knight is sitting inside, plotting revenge on the man for betraying him. That's divine providence if you ask me!"

Hartung pondered for a moment and realised he had to agree with his comrade. It couldn't all be mere coincidence. The Lord moved in mysterious ways, and seemed to have a meaningful plan for all of them. This supposed relic could be another sign from heaven. Their time at the hospital of the charitable brothers was evidently at an end, and the omniscient Lord was guiding them on new paths to forgiveness.

"You may be right. In a strange way, everything fits together," he ventured with a frown.

"If we help them, not only will we receive the rich reward, we'll also be able to return home and start a new life. And if the items in question really are the Commandments that the Lord engraved in stone, and which the despicable Templars will want to use for their own unholy purposes, then we would also be doing truly godly work by taking them out of their hands." Walter let go of Hartung and looked expectantly at him, hands on his hips.

"A truly blessed deed," agreed Hartung. "But one that requires a well-conceived plan. If we pit ourselves against the Templars, we'll be forced to leave the Holy Land and turn our backs on our lives here forever."

"So you're with me?"

"I have no choice. It appears to be God's will. You're my friend and brother-in-arms, and you'll never feel at home here. I'm convinced that only through good deeds will you be blessed with the forgiveness of your sins. And without me you're lost."

Walter embraced the warrior and they clapped each other on the back.

"You're a true friend! Don't worry too much about my salvation. With you at my side, everything will be fine!"

Hartung gestured toward the door to the refectory. Walter nodded and they both went back into the small room and sat down with their guests, who looked up at them impatiently.

Walter took the two money pouches off the table and placed them beside him on the bench.

"Alright, Harit. Tell your companion we'll help you. I don't know how, but my comrade and I will do everything in our power to bring the Ark, or whatever it really is, back to Jerusalem."

"Please, my lords, allow me to translate the good news," said Guillaume with relief. He spoke to Leah and her dark eyes lit up. She leapt up from her seat and dropped to her knees before Walter, a stream of Hebrew flooding out of her.

"What a silly custom, this knee-falling," said Walter again, touching her lightly on the shoulders. "Alright, alright, please sit!"

Guillaume pulled Leah back onto the bench by her jilbab. She beamed at him and he beamed back, which Walter didn't fail to notice. *Well, look at that, a fallen Templar and a pretty Jew in the tender bonds of love. Today is full of surprises,"* he thought.

"Hurry up and eat. The brothers will soon be here for their midday meal. We'll be hard pressed to explain if they find a heathen and a disguised Templar here, not to mention a woman."

Walter nodded at the food and drink laid out before them, and they began to eat in silence.

He studied the guests thoughtfully. Hartung wasn't wrong: Templar knights weren't ragged Bedouins. The Muslim and the Jew would be useless in a fight against them. The Templar looked emaciated and exhausted. But without him, the venture had no hope of success, as he was the only one who was familiar the Order and its fortress.

Walter's thoughts jostled in his mind. They would need weapons, armour and horses. Acquiring those should be no problem with Ishmael's gold. They would have to explain their sudden departure to the brothers, but their plan must remain secret no matter what. They must quickly find lodgings for their visitors outside of the monastery.

Finally, a new adventure worthy of a knight and warrior, and I'll be able to turn my back on this miserable place sooner than I thought.

XXII

Walter arranged accommodation for Leah, Harit, Guillaume and their mules and luggage at an inn he knew well, not far from the German hospital. A former brother-in-arms and trustworthy compatriot, Reinhold the Lame, ran the public house with his Syrian wife, having given up the soldier's life after the conquest of Acre, due to a knee injury. Reinhold was a gaunt Saxon with greasy, dishevelled hair, a grey goatee and bushy eyebrows framing cheerful eyes in a bony face. He was delighted to be able to do his former commander a favour.

He offered the group two rooms at the back of his property. Since the affable yet discreet innkeeper knew almost every tradesman in the city personally, Walter asked him if he could acquire a good sword and three light riding horses with saddles and bridles, without drawing unwanted attention and within two days. Everything was to be kept in a stable, ready to use at short notice. To pay for all this, Walter offered Reinhold a generous sum of gold from Ishmael's advance payment that he couldn't refuse, and he agreed immediately.

"You want to go back into battle, do you?" he asked, laughing as he counted the gold coins into his purse. "I'll gladly get you everything you need. I always knew you wouldn't last long with the charitable brothers. A warrior like you... although, your new army seems a little lacking. A pilgrim, a Saracen runt and a Jewish woman. Oh, I'd gladly come with you, but as you know, my gait has become a little ungainly over the years." He slapped his stiff right leg cheerfully, and gazed lovingly after his plump wife, who was leading the new guests to their rooms on the upper floor.

Walter sat on a stool and gazed around the barroom. The floor was freshly swept and strewn with reeds; long, dark wooden benches stood against the walls; and the small, open window let in scant daylight. The smell of stale beer and burnt oil lingered under the sooty, barrel-vaulted ceiling. He and Reinhold were alone. The barroom wouldn't fill up until late evening when journeymen, servants and wage labourers came to slake their thirst after a long day's work.

"How about a nice drop of wine? I have the red from Antioch in stock again, the one you like," said Reinhold, rising to his feet.

Walter held an index finger conspiratorially in front of his lips. "Only if you don't tell anyone. Especially the German brothers. Bring it on!" He grinned and Reinhold limped back with two full cups. They toasted and then drained them in a single draught.

"I'm counting on you, Reinhold. No one can know the identity of your guests, and if anyone enquires about them, tell me immediately. Get me those horses and everything else as soon as you can."

"Don't worry, Sir Walter. Always at your service. I'm in your debt, as you know. Without your healing skills, I would only have one leg after that damned Saracen rammed his spear into my knee. May he burn in the deepest pits of hell – where I sent him with a blow of my axe to his curly head!"

Walter stood and clapped the innkeeper on the shoulder. "It was an honour to fight at your side," he said earnestly. "But now I have to go. I'll look in on your new guests tomorrow morning. What do I owe you for the wine?"

Reinhold fingered the heavy pouch of money at his belt almost tenderly, straightened himself proudly and said, "This should cover it, Sir Walter. God be with you!"

"God be with you, Reinhold. I'll see you tomorrow morning," said Walter, and left the inn.

Meanwhile, Reinhold's wife had shown her guests to the narrow hallway at the top of the stairs. The heavy-set, round-faced hostess had climbed the narrow staircase surprisingly swiftly, and was now panting from the effort. Two doors led into low-ceilinged rooms. She directed Harit and Guillaume to one of them. Then she opened the door to the other room and led Leah inside.

"So, my dear. Here's a fresh straw bed with a clean linen sheet. On the window sill is an oil lamp, flint and tinder to use at night, and back there you'll find a pot for nature's minor calls. For major ones, you can go out into the yard by the stables. There's a wooden shack with a seepage pit. Oh, and you can close the window with a shutter if it gets cool."

Leah stood self-consciously in the middle of the room, happy to hear a woman's voice again, especially one speaking colloquial Arabic, a language she understood.

"Thank you, gracious hostess. The room is good and you're very kind," she said quietly.

"Gracious hostess, ha ha," chuckled the plump woman, clapping her hands together. "No one's ever called me that. Just call me Yeta."

"Pleased to meet you, Yeta. My name is Leah and I'm from Jerusalem," she said shyly.

"You're a Jew, aren't you? I thought so – your accent, the way you roll some of the words in your throat. Don't worry, everyone's welcome here. My husband is from Alemannia, I'm a Christian from Syria and our servants come from Egypt and Armenia. Now just a minute..." Her large-pored potato nose sniffed in Leah's direction. "By God, you stink like a herd of goats. You need a bath! I'll fetch you a tub of water, and I'm sure I have a piece of rose soap somewhere."

"Oh, that would be wonderful. May I help you?" asked Leah. The prospect of a bath elevated her spirits. She had five days of riding behind her, through the dusty mountains of Samaria on sweating mules, travelling with two men in whose company she could only wash her face and hands. She felt filthy, sticky, and ashamed that her hostess had noticed her strong body odour.

"Nonsense, you don't have to help. You're a guest here and I know Sir Walter will pay well for all of you. He's an honourable, generous man. As I said, we have servants and maids who'll take good care of you. Settle yourself in and have a little patience. I'll be back soon."

She bustled out of the room and Leah was astonished once again at how quickly the stout woman moved. Through the open door, she saw Guillaume carrying two saddlebags and a water skin into the room opposite, in which he and Harit were to spend the night. Their eyes met and a smile brightened his face, his blue eyes glinting at her. She smiled coyly, then lowered her head, ashamed at herself, and closed the door.

Guillaume felt an unusual tingling sensation all over his body, which was strangely foreign to him. His heart beat faster. This girl touched him. Even though she knew of nearly every sinful act he had committed, she was exceptionally friendly. He felt closer to her than he'd ever felt to anyone, and it seemed she felt the same. He didn't care what she looked like under her voluminous, blue jilbab – her dark eyes and those boldly arching eyebrows were enough to make him take leave of his senses.

He sighed and deposited the saddlebags and water skin in the room. Harit was already lying on his straw bed, his arms folded behind his head.

"Is your wound hurting again?" he asked, concerned.

"No, it's fine. It's healing well," replied Guillaume, then he said with a grin, "Let's see if we can stand being in the same room together. If you snore like a pig, I'll wring your neck or throw you out the window."

Harit wasn't sure how to take the joke and sat up. There was genuine concern in his eyes. "You know, I've never been alone in a room with a Nazarene before, let alone a Templar. I admit, I'm a little afraid."

"How many times do I have to tell you? I'm not a Templar anymore. Just call me Guillaume. I assure you, your fear is completely unfounded, and I don't kill people who save my life. It's new for me too, sleeping in the same room with an infidel. Snore as much as you like. Anyway, you have my dagger to defend yourself."

Harit scratched his dirty ankle and said nervously, "Yes, I have it, and I'm keeping it. Despite everything, you're still a dangerous... a dangerous Guillaume."

"Not to you, Harit ibn Tharit." Guillaume laughed quietly.

The Arab's features relaxed and he said light-heartedly, "Please let me go down and ask our hosts if I can wash. I may snore like a pig, but we both stink like one. It amazes me that you Nazarenes don't notice it. And you eat unclean animals, too, ugh... By Allah, you're not very hygienic people. I'll hurry down and find our hostess." Harit pinched his nose and winked, and Guillaume nodded.

Late that night, long after Reinhold had thrown the last drunken guests out of the inn and a cool stillness had settled over the city, Guillaume still lay awake. For a while, he listened to Harit's even breathing as he slept, then he quietly got up. He reached under the Arab's bed and carefully drew out the dagger. Harit grunted in his sleep and turned to face the wall.

Guillaume concealed the weapon under the dark brown robe Reinhold had given him to replace his filthy rags, and pulled the hood over his head. Then he opened the door and slipped out of the room.

A pale half moon hung over Acre, bathing the alleys and buildings in a pale, cold light, that made it easy for him to find his way safely to the Armenian Quarter. Guillaume's destination was a ramshackle mud house with an alarmingly slanted, gabled wall propped against the eastern city wall. On the ground floor of the house, an old, broken shutter hung askew on its hinges, and peered inside through a gap the width of his finger.

The person he sought lay on a straw bed, apparently asleep. A smoky oil lamp on the floor dimly illuminated the tall figure. Guillaume knocked and the man woke with a start, swiftly reaching behind him. A short sword flashed in the lamp's flickering light.

"Who's there!" he called, brandishing the weapon.

"Open up, Tigran. It's me, Guillaume," a voice hissed through the shutter.

"Brother Guillaume? What the devil..." Tigran lowered the sword, got up and opened the door. The visitor slipped inside and embraced the surprised Armenian.

"What are you doing here? By God, it's good to see you in good health. You must have multiple lives, Brother Turcopolier." Embarrassed, Tigran freed himself from Guillaume's embrace and leaned the weapon against the wall.

"I have you to thank for one of them, Tigran. If it weren't for you, I would have already met my maker."

"And I have you to thank for mine. I was only repaying the debt. Are you mad, showing your face in this city? We only returned yesterday from our fruitless search for you. Brother Nicholas is furious that we didn't find you. I happened to overhear the Marshal reprimanding him harshly. He told him to send out spies and bribe the city guards in order to bring you in. A lot of men are hunting you."

He gestured for Guillaume to sit, but he refused.

"I don't have much time and don't want to put you in a difficult position. But you're probably the only one who can help me win back my honour."

The turcopole shook his head and looked guiltily at the floor. "I can't raise my sword against our Templar brothers, as much as I'd like to. I have a wife and a small son asleep upstairs. They need me, and I can't risk my life for your honour."

Guillaume immediately raised his hands in a placatory gesture and replied softly, "Of course not. I understand. Just some information, then I'll disappear."

Tigran relaxed visibly and scratched his chin. "If that's all you need, ask me whatever you like."

"Good. You brought in a big haul after the attack on my little pilgrim train, didn't you?"

Tigran stiffened, nodded hesitantly and replied, "Yes, we did. There was an extraordinary amount of gold and silver in an old saddlebag. The Komtur found it after we returned, when he was sorting and counting the spoils. There's nothing left of it. We divided it all up amongst ourselves. It was yours, wasn't it?"

"Don't worry, I don't want the money," replied Guillaume evasively. "But did you see two winged figurines, about a cubit high? And two rectangular clay tablets with scribblings on them?"

Tigran turned his eyes to the ceiling and tried to recall. "I think so... Yes, I remember. Worthless pilgrim knick-knacks. Why do you ask?"

"Was anyone given those objects as part of their share of the spoils?" Guillaume probed, avoiding Tigran's question again.

"No, the Komtur kept them, as he did all the other items, and the animals. He said the gold should be enough for us."

211

"And the rest of the plunder? Is it still in the storehouse by the stables?"

"I expect so. Everything is stored there until it's sold or gifted. Why the devil are you asking me all this?"

Guillaume smiled secretively. A miracle – the treasure had apparently remained undiscovered. But time was of the essence. He knew the diligent, well-read Komtur Thibaut. It wouldn't be long before he learned the secret of the tablets and cherubim. Then the treasure would be almost impossible to retrieve.

"Can I trust you, Tigran?" he asked.

The turcopole nodded. "Look around you, Guillaume. I don't have much, but I have enough honour in my bones not to betray my commander. Because that's still who you are to me. Your replacement, Brother Nicholas, is a smug, vile bloodhound. If you're planning to take revenge on him, I won't stand in your way."

"I can't tell you what I'm planning. It's better for you if you don't know. And forget what we discussed here. Forget that I was even here."

"So be it. No one will hear it from me," Tigran promised gruffly as he fidgeted with his belt.

"I know you'll keep your word, you're a decent man. God protect you and your family."

Guillaume turned to go, but the Armenian held him back by his sleeve. Two gold bezants glinted in Tigran's open hand.

"Here, take these. I'm sure you can use them. Leave the city and don't come back. Revenge or not, you can't stand alone against the Order. They'll kill you if you even go near the fortress. Flee to somewhere far away and God be with you!"

Guillaume was taken aback and deeply moved. He'd never expected such a gesture of compassion from the lanky, rugged warrior. With both hands, he closed the turcopole's fingers around the coins.

"You have no idea what this gesture means to me, Tigran, but I can't take those. The Lord in heaven has already provided for me. I thank you from the bottom of my heart. God be with you."

Tigran shrugged with embarrassment. He walked Guillaume to the door and watched him go, until the tall figure was swallowed by the darkness at the end of the street.

He had the impression that a shadow was following Guillaume, and rubbed his eyes, but the alley appeared to be empty. Crossing himself three times, he closed the door.

XXIII

Hartung had never set foot inside an inn, and agreed only very reluctantly to a meeting with Guillaume in the tavern of Reinhold the Lame. He viewed such places as damnable cesspits of sin, in which vulgar men indulged their boundless cravings for food, drink and slovenly women. Walter had to work hard to persuade him, insisting there was no better place to discuss their plan undisturbed and without attracting attention. And the barroom was empty in the early morning, so Hartung's misgivings were unfounded.

Scowling, the massive knight sat down heavily on a wooden bench in the barroom. Above him was a tiny window overlooking the street, but the square opening in the porous mud wall let in very little fresh air.

"It reeks in here, like we're sitting in a trough of vomit," Hartung grumbled.

Walter pulled a face. "Don't be like that. It smells exactly the same when you cook soup," he mocked. "Have a little patience and you won't even notice the smell anymore. You get used to it."

He sat beside his friend and patted his broad shoulder. "Soon, you won't have to slave in the kitchen any longer. We'll take the relic back to the Jew, then board a ship and leave this miserable country," he said reassuringly.

Hartung ran a hand over his stubbled head and mused. "If it's true what that fallen Templar told us, then those things are much more than just a pair of ore tablets and gold figurines. We'll be closer than ever to Almighty God. The risky venture is worth that alone. Not the vile money or the journey home to an uncertain future. But I'm not so sure it's a good idea to take the relic back to the Jew. Who knows what we might set in motion? Maybe the end of the world! On the other hand, if the Templars learn its secret, they'll become richer, more powerful and more imperious than ever. I want to prevent that."

Walter filled his cheeks with air and exhaled noisily. "By God, you may be right. But maybe you're wrong, and a new golden age is about to dawn for all believers."

"We'll see. I'm interested in hearing the Templar's plan. Where is he, anyway? Still sleeping?"

His question was answered by a loud clatter on the wooden staircase that lead up to the guest rooms.

Guillaume had tripped over a wooden tub on the stairs and barely managed to keep his balance, cursing and bounding over the last three steps with a courageous leap.

"Who the devil put that tub of old beer on these narrow steps?" he thundered, shaking his head as he went to join Walter and Hartung.

"A tightrope-walking juggler couldn't have done better. You move well so early in the morning," Walter observed with a grin. "Greetings, Templar."

"Guillaume. Call me Guillaume, not Templar!" He slumped irritably onto the bench opposite the two knights. He hadn't slept much that night and his eyelids itched with fatigue. After his meeting with Tigran, he had slipped back into his chamber unseen, lain on his bed and begun concocting a plan to pull off a successful attack on the Order's mighty fortress.

"I visited an old friend in the city late last night. Tigran, the turcopole who saved my life in the mountains. I mentioned him to you." The other two nodded and he continued, "The treasure hasn't been discovered. It's in storage, along with the rest of the spoils. Tigran is confident that the figurines and tablets are in a storehouse beside the stables inside the fortress. Just behind the massive entrance gate. It's only locked with a simple wooden door and unguarded. So it'll be easy..."

"Sure," Walter interrupted in a mocking tone. "Child's play. Templar fortress, stable, wooden door. And only about two hundred armed Templar knights, sergeants and servants. We may as well leave right away and be back by midday for a good meal."

"Wait, I'm not finished." Guillaume shuffled restlessly on the bench. "But you're not wrong about midday. All Templar knights must attend prayer at Sext together in the chapel. There are no exceptions, according to their strict rules. So there won't be more than a couple of unarmed servants in the courtyard, going about their daily work. We approach the gate on foot, dressed as pilgrims. There will only be three or four guards there, who shouldn't pose a problem. You can take care of them while I fetch the tablets and cherubim. Then we leave. Our advantage is that no one will expect an attack during the day. The gate is always open at that time, because there are a lot of incoming deliveries. What do you say? Could it work?"

He looked expectantly at the two friends. Hartung frowned and Walter thought long and hard.

"That won't work," he said after a while. "They'll be on top of us before we're two streets away. We can take care of the guards quickly enough, but the servants in the courtyard will shout for help. The whole Order will pour out of the chapel and hunt us down. We'll have to attack on horseback. Then we flee the city immediately, preferably through the mountains of Samaria to Jerusalem. It's the longer, more arduous route and seldom used. The Templars will assume we're on the old, shorter coastal road to Jaffa. How long do you think it would take the knights to arm themselves, saddle their horses and give chase?"

Guillaume replied without hesitation. "No more time than it takes to empty a large jug of wine in a single draught, probably less."

216

"That won't give us enough of a head-start," said Hartung with a sniff. "We'll have to think of something else."

"No, no... I have an idea." Guillaume held up an index finger. "We use fire to prevent them from following us. A blaze in the stables! Saddles, bridles, straw and oats are stored there. I'll drive the horses through the gate and out into the city. Then I'll light the hay in the stables and their equipment will burn. That'll stall them by at least half a day, perhaps a whole day."

Walter nodded and Hartung pointed at a clay oil lamp on the window sill behind him. "Lamp oil. We fill a couple of leather skins, to fuel the fire. Burning oil can only be extinguished with sand. If you try to use water, the flames leap higher. I'm sure you remember the heathens raining oil and *naphtha* down on our warriors during the siege. Many brave men burned after failed attempts to put it out. Oil will buy us more time."

The others agreed and Walter looked solemnly at Guillaume. "If we act quickly and decisively, the plan could work. Hartung and I will take care of the guards, drive out the horses and stand guard while you start the fire and fetch the relics from the storeroom – if they're still there. If not, we go straight back to our hospital and leave you, the Jewess and the little heathen to your fate." *And I'll keep Ishmael's advance payment, which will at least cover the cost of a sea voyage.*

"I'm sure it will all be there," said Guillaume with conviction. At the mention of the Jewess, he thought of her dark eyes and added, "We can't forget Leah and Harit. They must come with us. We can't leave them here."

"Ahhh... yes. Your pretty rescuer," Walter drawled. He winked conspiratorially at Guillaume, whose eyes flashed and narrowed reproachfully.

Walter noted his displeasure, shrugged casually and said, "We'll take them with us, of course, and escort them safely back to Jerusalem. They need to be outside of the city during the attack, preferably waiting behind the hill a mile east of the city walls. You know the place – where our troops were encamped during the siege. They should travel lightly, with just enough water and food for five days and a couple of blankets. We need to ride fast and unnecessary ballast will be a hindrance."

They heard a scuffling sound through the small window, and listened out in silence. Hartung glanced at Walter, who waved a hand dismissively and said, "Probably just a mutt sniffing around for something to eat in the rubbish on the street."

A muffled whine seemed to confirm his guess. Walter turned and looked around the empty barroom. "Now everything depends on Reinhold the Lame bringing us horses and weapons. If he does so today, we could execute the plan tomorrow."

"Oh, you men! Always planning, planning, planning!" crowed their hostess from the top of the stairs. "Just like Reinhold! He's been planning to widen this staircase for ages and nothing comes of it! I can hardly go down it safely anymore!" she grumbled.

"Were you eavesdropping, woman?" Walter called, looking up at her with alarm.

"Nonsense," she replied, and the stairs creaked ominously under her weight. "I just heard something about a plan. But as I said, you men are always talking like that and then you forget about everything around you. The girl and the little man upstairs need to eat. That's *my* plan!"

She trod in the pool of beer at the foot of the stairs and slipped. Careening like an overloaded barge on high seas, she eventually regained her balance.

"God in heaven, who spilled all this beer?"

She put her short arms on her hips and bellowed loudly enough to be heard in the harbour at the other end of the city, "Eyla! Eyla! Where are you? Get out here and clean up this pigsty!" Then, with an apologetic glance at the bewildered warriors, she said, "It's not easy finding good maids these days. She'll clean this up in a minute – if I can track her down and the hussy isn't rolling in the hay again with the wine or vegetable delivery man. It wouldn't be the first time. Would you like something to eat?"

"Why not. We're finished, aren't we?" Walter looked at the other men, who nodded. "Good, then bring us a hearty breakfast," he said to their hostess. Then he waved to Leah and Harit, who had appeared at the top of the stairs. "Come, sit with us!"

"That's more like it," said the rotund Yeta approvingly, and she waddled to the kitchen, keeping her eyes on the floor.

Leah was enveloped from head to toe in a voluminous, black jilbab, which revealed nothing but her eyes. Yeta had loaned it to her while she waited for her freshly washed blue robe to dry out in the yard. Leah gathered up the oversized garment at her waist and cautiously descended the stairs.

Guillaume stood and offered her his seat. She shook her head almost imperceptibly and said quietly, "It's indecent for an unmarried woman to sit with men. I'll help in the kitchen and eat there. But thank you."

Her eyes smiled kindly at him, then she turned and followed Yeta, trailing a beguiling scent of rose soap.

Harit had followed Leah to the bench. He was about to take the seat offered to her, but Guillaume held him by his robe.

"Just a moment," he said, reaching under his own tunic and bringing out the dagger. "Forgive me, I borrowed it last night for safety, because I had to visit someone in the city. You can have it back now."

Harit looked at the weapon in surprise, and then at Guillaume's earnest face.

"It's alright, you can keep it," he said, adding in jest, "The cross on the hilt is distasteful to a true believer. And you'll need it in a moment to cut up your food."

Guillaume suppressed a smile, put the dagger away and they both sat down opposite Walter and Hartung.

Not long after, Yeta and Leah carried in a wooden tray heavily laden with food and drink. Panting, they set it down between the men on low wooden trestles. It was laid with fragrant millet cakes spread with honey, a bowl containing a salad of olives and pickled pomegranates, dried dates and juicy figs. For the Christians, there was also smoked ham and cold roast pork. Cured fish, sheep's milk cheese, black olives in oil, and sweet, hot tea in clay cups rounded out the sumptuous meal.

Their hostess had gone to great lengths to keep her well-paying guests happy. She bowed, wished them a good appetite and took Leah back into the kitchen.

The men ate copiously in silence. For a while, the only sounds were occasional satisfied grunts and loud lip smacking.

"By God, I haven't eaten this well in ages," said Walter, belching profusely and stretching his legs out under the table.

"Don't get used to it," growled Hartung. "A full belly doesn't like to fight."

"Then today won't be your day to ride into battle. I've rarely seen you devour so much," Walter retorted, farting loudly.

Hartung's mouth twisted and he raised an eyebrow. "It's late, almost midday. We should go. Our work awaits us at the hospital," he said sternly.

Walter nodded and said to Guillaume, "Tell Harit and Leah the plan. They should arrange food and water for the journey and skins filled with oil."

He stood and placed a hand on Guillaume's shoulder. "No more excursions – by day or night. It won't help us if you're discovered."

Guillaume replied calmly, "Don't worry, I'll stay in my room and catch up on sleep. God be with you!"

"God be with you," said the two knights. They promised to return in the evening, then left.

Guillaume and Harit called for Leah. She hurried out of the kitchen and was taken aback when she saw how little food remained on the table. Harit correctly interpreted her expression and raised his hands defensively.

"It wasn't me. The Nazarenes ate all that unclean pig meat. Bread and fish were enough for me."

Leah smirked and swiped a sweet fig from one of the plates. "It's healthy for men to eat a lot," she said knowingly, popping the fruit in her mouth. "Well, what is it?"

Guillaume couldn't take his glistening eyes off her. She felt the blood rise in her cheeks, and gazed back at him with a coy smile, chewing more slowly. An elbow to the ribs from Harit snapped Guillaume back to reality. He cleared his throat sheepishly and Leah lowered her gaze to the floor, disconcerted.

"Er... we have a plan for retrieving the holy relic." He struggled to recall it. It was as if her smile had evaporated his thoughts. *Lord in heaven, this girl is so lovely. I have no idea where this might lead...*

"We're listening, Guillaume!" Harit said impatiently.

The knight composed himself and apprised them of the plan in detail, explaining how they intended to pull off the theft and escape through the mountains of Samaria, to Jerusalem. They listened attentively and only interrupted him with an occasional question or exclamation of surprise. When he had finished, Leah clapped her hands quietly. But the expression on her face was one of concern.

"I know nothing about fighting, and I want to believe we'll succeed, but it sounds very dangerous. You could..." she faltered. "We could all lose our lives. Perhaps we should simply return home and tell my uncle we couldn't find the sacred relics. Or that you had already taken them out of the country. Or..."

"No, Leah," Guillaume interrupted. "I owe a heavy debt to your uncle. God has sent me this test to show me the path to the forgiveness of my sins, I'm sure of it. I'll retrieve the relic and return it to your people. No matter the cost. Nothing will stop me. And nothing will happen to you, trust me."

When the words crossed his lips, they sounded more solemn than he'd intended. Her concern for him was a soothing balm on his wounded soul and he looked at her lovingly.

"And nothing will happen to me either!"

Harit scowled and held his nose in the air in mock contempt. "By Allah, I'll just hide behind Leah. That sounds like the safest place to be!"

This snide remark melted the tension and they all laughed heartily. Leah wanted to go shopping for supplies and asked Harit to accompany her to the market. He agreed happily, hoping to catch a glimpse of his family home near the piers in the harbour, if it was still standing.

Guillaume couldn't go with them. There was too great a risk he would be recognised. He urged them both to exercise extreme caution, and got to his feet. His eyelids were heavy with exhaustion and the food sat like lead in his stomach. He said goodbye, exchanged a furtive glance with Leah and climbed the stairs to catch up on much-needed sleep.

Leah watched him go and felt strangely exhilarated despite the dangerous mission that lay ahead.

Everything will be fine as long as he's with us, I know that, she thought. She smiled at Harit, who winked back impishly, and she asked him to help her carry the table back into the kitchen.

XXIV

It took a while for Raoul's eyes to adjust to the semi-darkness in the storehouse. His vision was getting worse with age, and there were days when everything around him looked blurry. He felt weary and broken. The ride to Tyre and back in full armour had been a trying ordeal, and he longed for rest and quiet. The Komtur's request that he meet him in the storehouse immediately after his return was extremely inconvenient.

There were no windows in the storage room, only a long, narrow air vent in the wall bordering on the courtyard, through which a faint beam of the midday sun slanted, illuminating the iron-bound wooden chest that stood in the middle of the room. Its curved lid was open. It contained various objects that Raoul could only vaguely make out. Beside it, Brother Thibaut was rummaging in a linen sack. He turned when he heard the Marshal enter.

"Ah, Brother Raoul. Thank you for coming so promptly," he said, letting a rosary glide from his hand onto the lid of the chest.

"Brother Chrétien told me you wanted to speak to me urgently? I just returned from my journey and don't have much time. Why are we meeting here amongst all this clutter?"

He nudged a stack of pottery contemptuously with his foot, causing it to come clattering down.

The Komtur glared at the shattered bowls and then at Raoul. He assumed an overbearing stance, stretching up to his full height in front of the Marshal.

"Yes, Brother Cretien de Passarelle, one of the best knights in our brotherhood, wouldn't you say?" He ignored Raoul's question. "A truly devout warrior and knight of Christ, one couldn't wish for more. God-fearing, loyal, brave and above all trustworthy from the ground up. If only all the brothers were like him, then the Holy City would soon be back in our hands. There's a reason he's one of our honourable standard-bearers. But I know that there is a criminal, murder and liar among us. It's a damnable shame!"

The Marshal looked uncomprehendingly into Thibaut's scowling face. "You mean Guillaume?" he asked slowly, his eyelids fluttering nervously.

"By all the saints, no. I mean Brother Nicholas, your new turcopolier!" snapped Thibaut. "Look at what I found among the spoils of his last raid! The man attacked and slaughtered Christian pilgrims, not Saracen merchants! I'm telling you this in no uncertain terms. I have evidence!"

He pointed at the chest in which the tin and copper tableware for high-ranking guests was stored, and on the lid of which his evidence was now arranged.

"I found one wooden and one silver crucifix, three rosaries, a tattered papyrus psalter, a metal box engraved in Latin, and these two..." he paused and lowered his voice, "...angel figurines. No sign of any tradable goods! But that's not all."

The Komtur took a money pouch from his belt and let a few coins run clinking through his fingers. "Look, silver deniers and gold bezants. This is from the large sum of money I paid out to Brother Guillaume on the Grand Master's orders. I know these are the very same coins, because they were in the leather bag I handed to him!"

Raoul didn't let it show, but he suddenly realised what a grave mistake it had been to give in to Nicholas' insistence on intercepting Guillaume before he returned to Acre. That hot-headed brute had put him in a very difficult position. Nicholas evidently lied when he spoke of relieving Muslim merchants of their belongings. *That ass is going to drive me out of my position as*

Marshal and drive me out of my mind. He was supposed to kill Guillaume, not indiscriminately murder pilgrims. By God, I'll tear off his head for this.

He shook his head and feigned a friendly smile.

"Oh, Brother Thibaut, there are so many of these coins in circulation, and heathens hoard everything, whether it's gold or rosaries. They could have been thieving Bedouins disguised as merchants. Just a misunderstanding, I'm sure. Who knows..."

"Misunderstanding?" interrupted the Komtur, his voice cracking. "I'll tell you what this is. A crime! A crime against Christian pilgrims. THAT'S what your fine, new turcopolier has committed! He had them butchered and buried! Listen to me, Marshal, this is an utterly sacrilegious act that could drag our Order's reputation through the mud! I'm sure I don't need to explain that to you. We protect pilgrims. It's one of our core responsibilities here in the Holy Land. Protecting Christian lives is our mission! That idiot Nicholas probably also unwittingly killed Brother Guillaume, who was on a highly confidential and costly assignment, about which you still haven't revealed anything to me. It's monstrous! And you, Marshal, you're responsible for it, because it clearly happened with your consent!"

Raoul blanched, held up his hands defensively and said, "No, no... I only authorised a reconnaissance ride with the turcopoles. When Nicholas came back, he reported having encountered and robbed a number of Muslim merchants. I admit that was probably wrong of him, now that we have a truce with the heathen Sultan. Regarding Guillaume... you can be sure he's alive and well, and will soon return unharmed. You have my word. That settles the matter, as far as I'm concerned. Brother Thibaut, your time would be better spent selling the spoils."

The Komtur struggled to control his rage. Raoul was treating him like a subordinate and didn't seem to grasp the enormity of the allegations. He put his hands on his hips and snapped, "Oh no, nothing is settled! I won't let this go! Who do you think you're talking to? One of the lowly squires? I'm Komtur of this Order and the Grand Master's first deputy! This despicable act is quite clearly your responsibility and I won't tolerate such a violation of our rules! I questioned one of the turcopoles – the Armenian, Tigran, one of the captains. He confided in me that his men had confronted Nicholas about the possibility that they had attacked Christians. But he insisted they were spying heathens disguised as true believers. Ridiculous! You may be able to pull the wool over dumb mercenaries' eyes, but not mine!"

The Marshal snorted and gestured dismissively. "What's the word of a mercenary against that of a Templar knight? A fart in the wind, nothing more. Let it go, Brother Thibaut, nothing happened."

"I've heard enough, Marshal! You'll see how much I'm about to let it go!" snarled the Komtur, his eyes flashing. "I order you to appear before the Grand Master, the Preceptor, the *infirmarius*, the chaplain and I in the Palace this evening. I convene this meeting by the power of my office. Bring your turcopolier. The two of you will give us an account of the matter under oath! After that we'll decide who needs to let go!"

"It's alright. A meeting is unnecessary, as..."

"MARSHAL, THAT'S AN ORDER!" the Komtur thundered, conveying the full power of his rank. Raoul was taken aback. He never expected the hulking Thibaut to be so thin-skinned.

"No need to get excited, Brother. Of course Brother Nicholas and I will come. I'm sure he'll explain everything to your satisfaction."

Raoul looked at the wooden chest in front of him, outwardly calm, but inwardly alarmed. He feverishly considered the possible consequences for him if Nicholas were questioned. The new turcopolier was a scheming sycophant, always ready to trample those under him and grovel to those above. Nicholas would collapse meekly before high-ranking officials just to save his own skin.

If Nicholas played dumb at the hearing and it came out that Guillaume had been sent to commission the Assassins with the murder of a respected baron of the Kingdom – that alone could be enough to ruin Raoul and the Grand Master. And Nicholas wouldn't baulk at shifting the blame onto Raoul for the attack on the pilgrims, because he had unambiguously ordered that Guillaume be tracked down and killed at any cost.

Raoul resolved to speak to Nicholas immediately and compel him to maintain secrecy under interrogation.

Damn it, now Guillaume is not my only problem, I have to deal with that ferret Nicholas too. His silence will cost me.

Outside, the church bell chimed dully for Sext. Brother Thibaut surveyed the pensive Marshal, who was now standing before him in silence with slumped shoulders. He adopted a more conciliatory tone.

"Nicholas will soon be in the church. You can go to him there and personally convey the order to appear at the meeting this evening. I'm sure everything will be cleared up. I'll make sure of it. Let's go in peace and pray. There should be no rancour between brothers. Come."

Thibaut quickly stashed his evidence in the chest and let the heavy lid close with a bang.

Raoul nodded and left the storehouse without a word. The Komtur followed him, closed the creaking door behind him and bolted it by dropping a rough-cut length of timber into two iron brackets.

They both strode across the expansive courtyard to the church, where the brothers were already gathering to sing a hymn as they entered together.

Raoul sought out Nicholas, but couldn't see him in the crowd. He scowled as he stepped through the portal into the house of prayer and joined in the chorus.

The turcopolier had chosen not to attend the mass, and wouldn't appear at evening prayer either. He didn't want to face the Marshal or the Grand Master before he could report his success. He stood on the upper level of the fortress gatehouse and gazed down through a narrow embrasure at the access way.

There was still no sign of Guillaume, but he expected him to arrive soon.

Nicholas knew about the gold bezants Brother Thibaut had found amongst the plunder, and assumed such a large sum of Christian money must have been in Guillaume's possession. Perhaps the Assassins had rejected the contract to murder Prince Bohemond, or perhaps Guillaume hadn't been able to find them in Jerusalem in order to establish contact. It appeared that Nicholas had only missed him by a hair's breadth with his attack on the second pilgrim train. Guillaume must have miraculously escaped just in time.

That was over a week ago. If he was journeying back to Acre on foot, he could appear in the next few hours.

Nothing in the world will let you escape my sword again. Even if I have to spend countless days and nights here. Your head belongs to me, thought Nicholas decisively. He drank a large mouthful of wine from the clay cup he had the foresight to bring with him. Without taking his eyes off the empty drawbridge, he refilled it from a jug, placed it on the stony ledge of the embrasure and continued his vigil.

XXV

The three knights stood with saddled horses in the inn's courtyard, winding black kufiyas around their heads. They wrapped the long ends around their noses, mouths and chins, so that only their eyes were visible.

Walter and Hartung wore their old gambesons and heavy chainmail under their wide, brown habits. The chainmail had begun to rust. Their freshly sharpened longswords hung from leather belts lashed to their saddle pommels. Guillaume was only lightly armed, with a simple sword in his belt, because his role in the attack required speed and agility. He hoped the two well-armoured knights would provide him with enough protection.

He tied two oil-filled leather skins to his saddle and breathed deeply. The horses snorted restlessly, as if they knew what lay ahead. Walter stroked his horse's neck to soothe it, and Hartung tightened the flank strap on his saddle. The preparations for their daring venture were complete.

The two German knights had bid farewell to their hospital brothers the previous evening. The reason they gave for leaving was an urgent need to return to their homeland to attend to Walter's inheritance. Old Master Siebrand, the founder of the brotherhood, beseeched them to stay but couldn't change their minds. Although he deeply regretted losing the two men, he gave them his blessing with a heavy heart and told them they were always welcome to return. Hartung promised they would see one another again, but Walter wasn't so sure. He'd had enough of the Holy Land and hoped his loyal comrade would remain with him in Saxony.

Reinhold the Lame brought out a jug of diluted red wine and eyed the warriors with admiration. Hatung's tall, broad frame and the warriors' determined expressions inspired his respect.

"I wouldn't want to tangle with you. Whatever it is you're planning, may you succeeded."

Walter pulled the headscarf away from his mouth and bared his teeth in a grateful smile.

"A drink to boost courage. You're a true friend, Reinhold. Thank you."

He took the jug from the innkeeper's hand, drank a hearty swig and passed it to Hartung, who shook his head. Guillaume didn't hesitate to empty it in a single draught.

"I thank you too, innkeeper. You supplied me with a good sword and went above and beyond to help us all. God bless you," he said with a bow.

Reinhold waved away the compliment. "You paid me well for it. I'd gladly ride with you, like the old days. But I can't leave her alone." He grinned and inclined his head toward the inn, where his wife was loudly scolding the serving maid. "Give my greetings to the pretty Jew and the little heathen. God be with you!"

"God be with you," the warriors replied. They took their horses by the reins and led them through the gate.

At the mention of Leah, Guillaume sorrowfully recalled their parting. She and Harit had left the city at dawn with provisions for the journey loaded onto three mules. They were to hide on the hill a mile from Acre's eastern gate until the knights joined them there after their exploits at the Templar fortress.

"Please come back to me in one piece," she had whispered. Then, to Guillaume's surprise, she quickly embraced him before mounting her horse and trotting away. Harit shook his hand, but could think of nothing to say and simply followed her.

Guillaume rubbed his nose under his scarf and thought he detected the scent of rose soap. He shook his head and rode to the head of the small troop.

The Templar church bell rang out for Sext. Its low chime echoed impressively over the roofs as the other bells of the many churches and monasteries in the city joined it in chorus.

They trudged on foot, leading their horses northwest through the narrow alleys. They were eyed with suspicion by labourers, merchants and servants making their way down to the harbour. Masked men with swords on their saddles could be dangerous, and it was wise to keep out of their way.

When they were stone's throw from the Templar fortress, the warriors exchanged glances and stopped.

The gate was wide open. Two guards sat in the shade of the arch, their spears leaning against the wall. They languidly waved through a timber supplier with an empty, ox-drawn cart, who clattered out over the wooden drawbridge and turned right toward the harbour.

Then all was quiet.

Walter's blue eyes blinked nervously through the gap in his kufiya. Hartung gave a short nod and checked behind them.

"Now!" said Guillaume loudly.

They swung themselves up onto their horses, drew their swords and dug their stirrups hard into the animals' flanks. Walter's stallion reared up with a whinny of complaint, and the three of them charged toward the gate.

The unsuspecting guards had no time to retrieve their spears. Guillaume swept past them unhindered through the gate. Close behind him, Walter swung his sword and shattered the face of one of the guards. Brain and bone shards sprayed through the air, the sergeant twirled and dropped to the ground. Hartung simply rode the second guard down. The collision with the horse flung the soldier hard against the gate-house. His head cracked against the wall and Hartung thrust his sword deep into the man's chest. He died without a murmur, eyes bulging.

Walter reined in his horse hard and brought it to a standstill. He saw Guillaume leap down from his saddle, sheath his sword, tear the oil skins from his saddle pommel and hasten to the storehouse, his black kufiya coming loose and flapping around his neck.

Hartung trotted to Guillaume's horse, grasped its reins and guided it with the pressure of his thigh to Walter's side.

"Amazing," he said, gazing around the empty courtyard. His voice was muffled by the headscarf. "I thought the Templars would be better protected."

"It seems they're all in their church, as Guillaume predicted. And only two servants at the gate – no one else on guard duty. A careless bunch, this brotherhood," replied Walter, turning up his nose.

"We'll see," said Hartung, narrowing his eyes and scanning the fortress' abandoned battlements.

Meanwhile, Guillaume had thrown down the oil beside the stable door and arrived at the neighbouring storehouse. He lifted the heavy bolt barring the double doors, heaved it aside and kicked open one of the doors.

The storeroom was filled to the rafters with grain and firewood. A few towering shelves held vast numbers of garments, bales of cloth, folded tents and unsorted plunder. Camel saddles had been carelessly thrown on the floor beside stacks of broken and intact pottery.

Damn it, I'll never find the sacred relics in this chaos! It's madness to even try!

He glanced around desperately and a heavy wooden chest caught his eye. On a hunch, he opened it and saw in the half-light a cherub wing protruding from amongst old tin plates and copper pots. He rummaged frantically through the chest, found its twin and even the two stone tablets.

Thank God, it's all here!

He crossed himself, pulled the sack from his shoulder and stashed the treasures inside it. His heart pounded against his ribs and he took a deep breath. Then he flung the sack over his shoulder, hurried back out, swerved left and ran to the adjacent stables. He scarcely registered the knights keeping watch for him, swinging their swords slowly and calmly. All was still quiet in the courtyard.

Guillaume braced his feet, leaned back and pulled open the heavy, unlocked wooden door of the large stable. Picking up the skins of oil, he entered to find far fewer horses in the stalls than he'd expected. Only around a dozen magnificent warhorses and the same number of light riding horses – a third of the stock. The rest must be out to pasture outside the city.

However, Guillaume noted with relief that all the saddles and bridles hung tidily on hooks on the whitewashed mud walls. Sheaves of straw and sacks of oats towered in two piles almost reaching the twenty-foot-high roof of the stable.

He flung the oil sacks down in front of the piles before opening all the stalls, then drove out the restless horses with flailing arms and slaps to their flanks. They crowded together fearfully at the door at first, then surged out into the courtyard.

Guillaume fetched the oil skins, uncorked them and sloshed their contents over the straw. Then he took a flint and tinder from under his robe and crouched down. His hands trembled with nervous tension and the sword in his belt pressed painfully against his belly. He drew it out and laid it beside him on the floor.

Slow and steady, he told himself. It took three attempts before the mixture of dry cotton fibres and sulphur granules began to smoulder. He blew on it and added straw until a flame licked out, which he quickly fed with more straw. Once it was burning steadily, he flung the small torch into the sheaves of straw. At first, there were only plumes of dark smoke, then the oil ignited and long, hissing flames shot up.

Suddenly he saw the point of a sword in front of him, glinting in the light of the blaze. It was aimed at his neck.

"I knew you'd come. It was only a matter of time."

It was Nicholas' triumphant voice. He stood over Guillaume in full armour and white cloak, his mouth twisted into a wolfish grin and his eyes sparkling gleefully.

Nicholas had been at his post in the gatehouse when the three men on horseback charged across the drawbridge into the fortress. At first he assumed it was an urgent delivery, then he heard swords ringing out. He ran to the other side of the gatehouse and looked through the window into the courtyard. The masked men reined in their horses. One of them sprang down and ran to the storehouse, his headscarf slipping off his face as he did so. Guillaume!

Nicholas could hardly believe his eyes. He hesitated a moment, unsure if he should call for help, then decided against it. The Templar brothers would most likely capture Guillaume alive. But his orders were unambiguous. The former turcopolier must die.

Moments later, he saw Guillaume leave the storehouse, hurry to the stable, pull open the door and disappear inside. Nicholas sprang into action, rushing down the steps to the gatehouse door and peering out into the courtyard.

The two horsemen appeared to be waiting for Guillaume. They glanced warily around the courtyard. Nicholas quickly withdrew. Then he heard the sound of clattering horse hooves and frightened whinnies. He looked out again and saw dozens of horses bolting out of the stable and being driven by the two horsemen toward the fortress gate.

From where Nicholas stood, it was only ten feet to the small side door of the stable – the entrance used by stable hands and servants. He summoned his courage, drew his sword and covered the distance in three leaping strides. The horsemen were too busy with the animals to notice him.

He tore open the small door and rushed in to see Guillaume lighting a fire.

I've got you, finally, you whoreson!

"Surprised, are you? I was expecting you, bastard!" Nicholas lunged and thrust his sword at Guillaume's throat, but his opponent reacted swiftly and pivoted out of its path. The flat of his blade clanged against the Templar's, pushing it aside. Guillaume spun and landed a blow on Nicholas' back, which thudded dully and slid off his chainmail. Nicholas staggered. He regained his balance and held out his sword menacingly in front of him.

"Pathetic attempt," Nicholas said scornfully, and a swift blow hissed above Guillaume's head as he dropped to his knees and swung his sword ineffectually against Nicholas' armoured thigh.

"Give up. My armour will protect me from your feeble blows! It's time for your well-deserved punishment!"

"Oh Nicholas, you bragging fool. You think you're a hard man, but you were never good in single combat. Your strength lies only in your treachery. My sword is too good for a hypocritical traitor like you. I should strangle you with my bare hands," Guillaume retorted, re-establishing a firm footing.

"Ha, like your squire, you mean? Your demise was decided long before his death. You're the fool here! I've been secretly following you for half a year and reporting your countless transgressions and sins in minute detail to the Marshal. We know everything about you! You're an irredeemable sinner and a disgrace to the Order!"

Guillaume replied by aiming a blow at Nicholas' head, which he parried with his clanging sword and immediately reciprocated. Guillaume raised his weapon above his head just in time, but was forced to his knees.

"Enough talk! Now you die, you cursed dog!" Nicholas cried triumphantly as he swung his sword again. Guillaume sprang up and rammed his shoulder forcefully into his opponent's abdomen. The heavy sack on his back increased his momentum. He felt the partially healed wound on his arm split open with a shooting pain like red-hot coals. Nicholas fell backward into the blazing straw. Sparks flew, his robe instantly caught fire and he let out a shrill scream. Guillaume quickly got to his feet, held his sword in front of him and coughed as he watched Nicholas rolling on the floor, desperately trying to smother the flames enveloping his burning robe.

"Your armour may protect you against swords, but not fire!" Guillaume spat contemptuously at the shrieking Nicholas, whose flailing caused the blazing tower of straw to teeter and then tumble down, half burying him.

Guillaume wanted to be the one to finish him off, but the blaze held him back. This unexpected encounter had cost too much time. Nicholas' fate appeared to be sealed, so he turned and dashed out into the courtyard where Hartung and Walter were waiting with his steed.

They had herded the horses with shouts, whistles and swinging swords, and the animals had all fled in panic through the gate and out into the city.

"Where the devil were you?" Walter cursed. "They're coming out! Let's get out of here! Quick!"

Alerted by the noise, a crowd of Templars poured out of the church and across the courtyard. It only took a moment for the battle-hardened Templar knights to identify the three armed horsemen as the source of the commotion. Some of them hurried to their quarters to fetch weapons, bellowing orders to their squires to charge the attackers and prevent them from leaving.

Guillaume swung himself into his saddle and called, "I have it, I have it! Go! Go!"

The three warriors dug their spurs into the horses' flanks and the animals reared up, bolted forward and galloped through the fortress gate.

Raoul was one of the first to rush out of the church, and he instantly recognised Guillaume, who had lost his headscarf in the scuffle with Nicholas. Their eyes met as Guillaume galloped away, his robe billowing, and Raoul saw a flash of hatred in his old friend's eyes before he disappeared though the gatehouse. Raoul turned his attention to the fiercely blazing stables.

Nicholas stumbled on his knees through the door, his robe still smoking, and made it ten feet before collapsing to the ground.

Raoul ran to him and bent over the screaming turcopolier. Nicholas smelled of charred flesh and his entire head was hideously burnt. His hair was singed to the scalp, his skin blistered and black, scorched almost to the bone. His right eyelid was melted to his eyebrow in a blackened bulge. He wailed and tried in vain to hold the eye in its socket, but it had already burst, and fluid spilled between his scorched fingers.

"Help... help," he croaked, and his intact eye stared at Raoul from a horribly mutilated face.

The Marshal knelt with his back to the church and rested Nicholas' head on his thigh. He looked around to see if he was being watched, but the Templars were running frantically in all directions, calling for water, extinguishers and weapons, and paid him no attention.

"It's alright, I'll help you," he said quietly, drawing his sword out from under his robe. He held his hand over Nicholas' bloodied mouth and slit the incredulous Templar's throat, just above his Adam's apple. Blood sprayed from his jugular and Raoul quickly pushed him away, wiped his dagger on Nicholas' charred habit, and swiftly concealed it beneath his own robe. Nicholas lay dying at Raoul's knees, spluttering and spitting blood.

"I'm sorry, you've become a danger to us all," Raoul whispered, then he turned and yelled, "Come here, come here! Brother Nicholas is seriously injured! Quick, over here!"

A few sergeants and servants ran to him and pulled Nicholas' twitching body away from him.

"He can't be helped," said one of the men, glancing at his comrades and crossing himself.

"My God, it can't be true!" cried Raoul, clapping his hands over his face in feigned horror. "Dear God in heaven, they killed him!"

He got to his feet and looked down at the slackening body. Killing the unpredictable Nicholas was the solution to his problems. He would likely have succumbed to his burns, but Raoul couldn't take any chances. Now the incompetent fool could no longer testify before the heads of the Order, and Raoul could pin his death on Guillaume.

Nicholas' absence from the mass had made him very uneasy. He feared the ambitious schemer was with Grand Master Robert, who, uncharacteristically, had also failed to appear at mass. But he realised Nicholas must have been on guard at the gate and surprised Guillaume.

You may have found him, but you let him slip away again. You could never be relied on, you muttonhead.

Raoul snapped abruptly at the mute servants standing around him. "Don't just stand there, lock the gates and draw up the bridge, hurry! Do it!"

The men obeyed and Raoul dragged Nicholas' corpse over to the main building, beneath which the fortress' large water cistern was located, and out fo which the brothers swarmed with pails, jugs and wooden tubs to douse the fire. Behind it, the blazing thatched roof of the stable collapsed in a cloud of smoke and a burst of sparks.

XXVI

Dense swathes of smoke lay over the fortress, dissipating sluggishly on this windless day. The penetrating stench of charred wood and leather hung thick and acrid between the walls, making it hard to breathe. The Templar brothers couldn't prevent the fire spreading from the stables to the storehouse. Attempts to douse the flames with water from the cistern were hopeless, and only served to fuel the raging fire. The experienced knights and sergeants quickly realised that oil had been used as an accelerant. From then on, they only used water on the neighbouring buildings, to stop the fire spreading.

They allowed the stable and storehouse to burn down in a controlled manner. Burning beams were torn down with long hooks and the flames were then smothered with sand and soil. They stamped out the last embers or covered them with vinegar-soaked hides. Fortunately, the other buildings were spared.

The courtyard was full of people blackened with soot. Sweat-soaked and coughing, they gazed at the smoking ruins of the buildings gutted by the fire. Some of the brothers crossed themselves and prayed loudly to the heavens; others simply slumped down on the churned, muddy ground and wheezed. Sergeants and servants brought beer and weak wine for dry throats and treated burns with ointment and clean linen bandages.

Three corpses lay to the left of the locked fortress gate – the two guards and Brother Nicholas, shrouded with white linen sheets. The Marshal, the Preceptor and the Komtur stood solemnly beside them.

"What terrible luck for Nicholas," said Raoul, wiping away tears brought on by the soot and smoke.

"What good luck for him," said Thibaut calmly. "The Lord's punishment caught up with him before his interrogation. As I always say, God knows his own."

The Marshal scowled at him. "He fought bravely for our Order and loyally served our faith! He doesn't deserve your scorn!"

"He bravely killed innocent pilgrims," growled the red-faced Komtur, clenching his fists.

"I still doubt that. It's dishonourable to accuse him when he lies dead at our feet!" Raoul retorted.

"Quiet, Brothers," said Preceptor Gilbert, standing between the two antagonists with his hands raised peaceably. "This is truly unimportant right now. We have suffered considerable damage. The stable and all the saddles and bridles, and the adjoining shoeing shed have been burnt down, along with our supplies and tradeable goods in the storehouse. The more pressing question is, who attacked our Temple and why!"

"I know who it was. Guillaume de Born. He fought Brother Nicholas and killed him. I recognised him when he fled, with two other horsemen," said Raoul without hesitation.

"Nonsense," said Thibaut. "I know for certain that Guillaume is no longer alive. He was among the pilgrims that Nicholas had massacred. I have evidence... or I had."

He turned to look at the fire-ravaged storehouse, with nothing but its blackened limestone walls still standing.

"You may have seen it, Marshal. Unfortunately, everything is now reduced to a pile of ash."

Raoul shrugged. A bitter smile flickered across his sooty face. "If it was indeed evidence. I'll say it again: they weren't pilgrims that Nicholas had killed, they were heathens. Unfortunately, we can't question him now."

Fuming with rage, the Komtur was on the verge of a sharp retort when Brother Gilbert placed a soothing hand on his shoulder and hissed, "Is the... thing we discussed yesterday burnt too?"

"I put everything in a wooden chest in the storehouse for safekeeping. Now it's melted to a useless black lump of slag, but..."

Gilbert interrupted him. "It was only a suspicion, Brother Komtur. For the sake of the Order and in memory of Brother Nicholas, you should leave the matter alone. Throw the remnants in the sea. Believe me, it's better that way."

Oh, thank you, Lord! At least some good came of this fire. The ill-fated relic can't cause any more harm, thought the Preceptor.

Brother Thibaut sniffed, collected his thoughts and shot Raoul a poisonous glance. "Yes, I'll do that. And I agree – they were probably heathen bandits that our God-fearing turcopoles sent to their maker. There's nothing more to say on the matter."

Relieved, Gilbert turned to the Marshal, who was still smiling quietly to himself. "Brother Raoul, please explain to me what you meant when you said you recognised the former turcopolier? Was Brother Guillaume not punished for his weighty sins with the loss of his habit? I haven't seen him among us for a long time. I thought he was atoning for his transgressions in a cell. How could he have been travelling with a group of heathens? And why would he burn down our stable?"

The Marshall felt like boxing his own ears. How stupid and unnecessary to name Guillaume as the arsonist. He had no idea why Guillaume had attacked them.

"He's not here. He was sent to Jerusalem on a secret mission. But you'll have to ask Brother Robert about that," he said quickly.

The Komtur nodded in a rare moment of accord with the Marshal.

"Why? What does the Grand Master have to do with it? By God, what is it you're not telling me?" asked the Preceptor impatiently, looking from one stony face to the other.

A shrill, drawn-out scream echoed across the courtyard and made them all look up. On top of the northern seawall stood a white-clad man with a red belt and scarlet turban. In one hand, he triumphantly held aloft a bearded head outlined against the cloudless sky. Blood ran down his outstretched arm.

"Allahu akbar! La haula wa la quwwata illa bi-llah! Allah is the greatest! There is no might or power except through Allah!"

He flung the head down into the courtyard, turned and leapt from the battlement into the sea.

The Templars watched in horror as the head flew through the air, thudded against the cobblestones and rolled right up to the feet of the speechless Preceptor.

"That's... Brother Robert!" Gilbert gazed down in horror at the Grand Master's bloody head.

"For the love of God!" Komtur Thibaut cried, falling to his knees before the severed head. "It really is him!"

Raoul was the first to gather his wits. He dashed to the nearest stone steps leading up to the battlement. On the way, he bellowed to the other knights and sergeants, "To the walls, quick, man the walls! Archers! I need archers!"

A few sergeants had propped their weapons against the church wall during the efforts to control the fire. Two of them responded immediately, seizing their longbows and arrows and hurrying after the Marshal. They reached the top of the battlement and joined Raoul, who was staring down into the clear water below.

"There he is! Shoot, now!" he bellowed at the sergeants, pointing at the swimmer, whose white robe billowed out around him like a cloud in the turquoise water. The archers aimed and hit their mark. Two long arrows bored into the heathen's back. His robe bloomed red as he slowly sank.

The Marshall called down to the courtyard. "We got him, we got him! Pull the wretch out of the water!"

The fortress gate was opened, the drawbridge rattled down and half a dozen sergeants stormed out, followed by two heavily armed knights.

Raoul leaned over the battlement, breathing heavily, and watched the brothers fish the lifeless body out of the water with spears. It was undoubtedly an Assassin.

His heart pounded, he felt light-headed and his thoughts were a swirling maelstrom at the centre of which Guillaume grew steadily larger. He must have somehow learned of the plot against him and was now on a path of vengeance. Raoul was sure he had met with the Assassins, commissioned the murder and had them help him with the arson attack. Except their target was not Bohemond, the Prince of Antioch, but Grand Master Robert de Sablé.

I'll be next on his list.

Curiously, he was not afraid of Guillaume's wrath, but he blacked out and collapsed nonetheless.

"Brother Marshal, what's wrong?" cried one of the archers in dismay, gripping him under the shoulders. Raoul got up with a groan and shook him off rudely.

"I'm fine! A momentary lapse... stay here and guard the walls," he replied, walking stiffly to the steps. He made his way down on unsteady legs. Indistinctly, as if through a mist, he heard the Preceptor calling to him, but he was in no state to respond. His head throbbed, he felt ill and he staggered straight toward the men's quarters.

Preceptor Gilbert watched him, bewildered. The Marshall appeared to be in a trance.

245

"What in God's name is he thinking? Has Brother Raoul taken leave of his senses?" he asked Komtur Thibaut, who was staring dumbstruck at the Grand Master's head in his hands. Gilbert shook him by the shoulder and repeated his question, pointing at the absconding Marshal.

"I... I don't know... it's too much for him... for all of us. What a terrible calamity!" stammered the stunned Komtur.

"By all the saints, he's the commander of our troops! He needs to restore security and order in the fortress, he can't just leave!"

The Komtur bowed his head and shrugged helplessly.

Brother Gilbert felt compelled to act. The rattled Templars had been hit hard and needed clear orders and direction. He assembled the captains and delegated the most pressing tasks with a commanding tone.

He put the entire army on high alert. Every brother was to arm himself immediately; a dozen sergeants were sent out into the city to corral the costly horses and at the same time round up the turcopoles who lived in the city to come to the fortress immediately, fully equipped for battle. He had the bodies of the two guards and Nicholas carried into the church and laid out respectfully.

He gave the visibly shaken and indecisive Komtur the task of going to the Grand Master's chamber to search for his headless corpse. Finally, he sent the ministering brothers of the Templar hospital to Raoul's quarters, to tend to his wellbeing and offer help if necessary.

The Preceptor's decisiveness enabled the Templars to swiftly reorganise themselves and restore the customary discipline and unity to their ranks. They carried out his orders eagerly and obediently.

Brother Thibaut found the body of Robert de Sablé in a pool of blood in his chamber, punctured with numerous stab wounds. Two knights helped him carry the body to the church. They passed Brother Gilbert, standing in the courtyard beside the Assassin's corpse. He nodded sadly at Thibaut.

It wasn't the first time Gilbert had seen a dead Assassin. Only a year ago, two members of the murderous sect had stabbed to death the newly crowned king of the Holy Land, Conrad Montferrat, in an alley in Tyre. One of them was immediately slain by the king's bodyguard, and the other later admitted under torture to being an Assassin, but didn't part with any other information, and died with a smile on his lips.

Gilbert was in that city at the time, overseeing the transportation of the Templar archive, and was present at the distressing interrogation. The murderer was dressed in exactly the same clothes as this wet corpse at his feet.

The Assassin wore a snow-white robe, bordered with fine braiding embroidered artistically with heathen script, and a blood-red belt of the finest sheep's wool tied tightly around his hips. In his belt was a long, curved dagger in a silver sheath.

The Preceptor had heard the rumours surrounding the assassination of King Conrad – that the Templar Order and the English King Richard were embroiled in it and had hired the Assassins to commit the murder. But he had always refused to believe it. However, he suspected there was a connection between that incident and today's events. Perhaps Robert de Sablé had angered the sect by not paying the fee for the king's murder. Or perhaps the heathen Sultan Saladin wanted to inflict damage on the Templar Order and had commissioned the murder despite – or because of – the current truce with the Christians.

As much as he brooded over it, Gilbert could think of no logical reason for the Assassins to target Grand Master Robert de Sablé. *Who knows what macabre, unholy secrets de Sablé will take to his grave. And there they shall remain. The Order's high standing in Christendom must be preserved.*

The Marshal claimed to have recognised the former turcopolier, Guillaume, and Gilbert needed to find out what role he had played in the assassination. He would consult Brother Raoul as soon as he was in a fit state.

Disgusted, he turned his back on the Assassin's corpse and ordered two servants to remove the body and burn it outside the fortress.

The sergeant he had sent to Raoul returned to report that the Marshal had merely fainted and was now resting, and that he would soon be on his feet again.

The Preceptor was relieved to hear this and, sending the sergeant to resume his duties, he sat down with a sigh on an abandoned wooden tub that had been used to douse the fire. He gazed at the wet ground in front of him and tried to organise his thoughts.

The Templar rules stipulated that, if the Grand Master was captured or died, a Grand Commander – a temporary supreme commander – had to be elected to guide the fate of the Order in the short term. That meant convening the grand chapter, a gathering of all the brothers in an administrative council. This usually took place every five years, or was scheduled by the Marshal in an emergency. Later, a new Grand Master was appointed by delegates from branches of the Order in each country.

This time it was an emergency. But the Marshal seemed presently incapable of carrying out this duty. Gilbert thought back to the Grand Master election two years earlier, for which he put himself forward, and lost. He bore no grudge against the winner and chose to remain in Acre. But during de Sablè's time in office, there had been some serious disagreements between them.

Gilbert was now convinced he would have been a better Grand Master than the overly strict but recklessly wasteful Robert. He would apply for the esteemed post a second time.

His contemplation was interrupted by the sound of shuffling footsteps. He looked up and was surprised to see the Marshal's pale face.

"Brother Raoul! I'm surprised to see you! I was told you needed rest. How are you?"

"I'm alright. I suddenly felt faint. I've no idea what came over me. Please excuse my absence. I shouldn't have abandoned the brothers at such a difficult hour," he replied contritely.

He was acutely embarrassed at his failure as a commander in one of the most dangerous situations the Order had ever found itself in. The death of the Grand Master hit him surprisingly hard, but that wasn't the only reason for his fainting spell.

Lately, there had been so many things to decide, weigh up and re-evaluate that his brain struggled to process them all. Komtur Thibaut's accusations, his dangerous insistence on interrogating Nicholas, Guillaume's sudden appearance and his inexplicable raid on the Temple, which clearly had something to do with the Grand Master's death. And then the arson and Nicholas' murder. These events stirred up his thoughts into a roaring cacophony in his head, ultimately causing him to lose control of his body.

In his chamber, after a jug of wine and some rest on his bed, he had composed himself and realised the day had brought about a massive advantage to him personally.

Guillaume had caused the greatest possible detriment to himself by attacking the Templar fortress. The man was now an outlaw. He could hunt him with the backing of the entire brotherhood and eliminate him permanently – even if it meant they had to face one another in the end, which he hoped to avoid.

His role suddenly became clear to him. Feeling as if a great weight had been lifted off him, he left his cell and sought out the Preceptor, whom he found sitting by the church.

"I see that you've ordered whatever was necessary to restore security, which should have been my responsibility. I thank you." Raoul bowed and Gilbert gestured dismissively.

"It's alright. I'm glad to see you in good health. Unfortunately, not everything necessary has been done, we still have to..."

"...convene the grand chapter," Raoul finished his sentence and nodded. He sat down beside the Preceptor and said quietly, "Yes, a Grand Commander must be chosen. Will you put yourself forward? I can think of no better man among us."

"I'm sure there's someone better than me," replied Gilbert humbly. "But I'll gladly prove myself worthy of the honour. We have no time to lose. The longer we wait, the greater the danger to the Order. After these disastrous events, we must pull together and stand united behind a leader. The election must take place this evening immediately after vespers. Will you take charge and lead the assembly?"

"Of course! As you know, I've had the honour once before, when Grand Master Gérard de Ridefort lost his life outside the walls of Acre. I'll spread the word immediately, rest assured."

"Very good. You said you recognised Brother Guillaume amongst the murdering fire-starters. What kind of mission was he supposed to carry out in Jerusalem?" Gilbert asked abruptly. Raoul was expecting this question and had prepared himself.

Only he, the Grand Master and Nicholas knew the details of Guillaume's mission to meet with the heathen Assassins and arrange the dispatch of the Christian Prince Bohemond. Komtur Thibaut was never let in on the secret. He had merely supplied Guillaume with a large sum of money, on the Grand Master's orders, and was forbidden from asking questions. De Sablé and Nicholas were dead and could no longer testify to Raoul's involvement in that thorny conspiracy.

"I have no idea," Raoul lied. "The Grand Master only told me that there was no way of proving the sins Brother Guillaume was accused of. He was given a final test and sent to the Holy City to carry out an assignment. Upon its successful completion, he was to be reinstated as turcopolier."

"I see. Then why did he show up here, apparently in league with the murderers?" Gilbert probed.

"By God, I can't tell you, I really can't."

The Preceptor nodded and rubbed his hands pensively. "Then Brother Guillaume is the only one who can tell us. You know him better than anyone. Pursue him, drag him out of hiding and bring him back to us alive. But it must be done quietly and under the strictest secrecy. Our Order has already suffered enough harm from his attack. A member of our brotherhood has turned murderer of his own brothers. That could seriously damage our reputation!"

"I'll depart this evening after the election and take five turcopoles with me to track him. They won't ask questions. I'll avoid taking any overly inquisitive knights, sergeants or squires. I assure you, he won't escape me," Raoul promised resolutely.

Gilbert got to his feet and patted the Marshal's shoulder. "Good idea. Go now with God's blessing. Let me know as soon as preparations for the election are complete. I'll retire now to the archive to document today's events."

Raoul nodded and watched with mixed feelings as the Preceptor hurried across the courtyard toward the corner tower in the north wall.

Guillaume, that bastard, would bitterly regret going against him. He was Marshal of the mighty Templar Order. An ostracised, outcast knight was no threat to him.

Fortes fortuna adiuvat, fortune favours the bold. My motto always proves itself true, thought Raoul. He would personally send Guillaume to hell; there was no way he would botch it like Brother Nicholas.

XXVII

Harit stood on the barren mound about a mile east of Acre that the Christians called the *Hill of Turon*, and looked wistfully at his hometown, with its houses snuggled safely behind the high defensive walls on the headland. Around the port city, expansive green areas spread out to the north and east. The sun was almost at its zenith, its light reflecting off the glittering turquoise sea. Only a few carts and ox-drawn wagons were underway at this hour. Most people avoided the unshaded plains at midday.

The weather was clear and dry, so that he could see almost to the far end of the crescent-shaped bay of Acre, which stretched fifteen miles southwest to the fishing village of Haifa. The little Belus river snaked around the bottom of the hill, forming a shallow, reedy delta as it approached the sea.

For three years before the conquest of Acre, this hill was the central encampment of the Christian armies. A few half-buried trenches and the collapsed remains of palisades were all that remained. The hill was stripped of trees – all felled to build the massive defence systems that protected them from the Sultan's army. Many warriors died in battle here, but thousands also died of hunger, illness and pestilence.

Blood-soaked ground... My family and friends were slaughtered near here, thought Harit, gazing sorrowfully down the slope to where Leah sat on the grass in the shade of their mules.

The previous afternoon, he had showed her the outside of the house in Acre where he was born. It was still used for manufacturing sugar, but now it belonged to a Venetian merchant, as he learned from a Syrian worker employed there.

It pained him deeply, because he knew there was no way back to that life. His future lay in Jerusalem, and in the hope that the three knights would retrieve the sacred artefacts for the Jew and they could all return to the Holy City unscathed. The high fee he was promised would enable him to start a new life. It wouldn't be enough to buy his own sugar factory, but perhaps he could go into business as a sugar trader.

He looked back at Acre, shading his eyes with his hand. To the northwest, he saw a dark grey column of smoke rising straight up into the sky.

"Leah, Leah! Look!" he called, pointing at the city. "The smoke! Over there! They've started a fire and, if Allah wills it, they'll soon be here!"

Leah jumped up and peered across at the city as Harit scampered down the slope. She was filled with dread when she heard the sombre chiming of the midday bells resonating through the clear air, signalling the attack on the Templar fortress. She'd been unable to think clearly since parting with Guillaume that morning. She was as surprised at their embrace as he was. She could still feel the firm pressure of his arms, and fondly recalled the tender look in his blue eyes. He simply had to return to her, with or without the Ark of the Covenant.

She squinted and strained to make out Acre's eastern gate, through which the knights would escape if the risky venture were successful.

"Harit, do you think they'll succeed?" she asked quietly without taking her eyes off the city gate.

"*Inshallah,* if God wills it... I think those men know what they're doing," Harit replied confidently. "And I've been praying continuously for Allah's blessing on the Nazarenes. Although I'm not sure if the Almighty has an open ear for prayers on behalf of infidels. So I also prayed to their three Gods to put your wondrous relics into the warriors' hands, so that we can return to Jerusalem. Surely that can't hurt – the more the better, don't you think?"

Leah smiled to herself. "They pray to the father, the son and the holy ghost. That's one entity to them. I've prayed to my eternal, gracious Lord and..." she broke off. A movement at the eastern gate caught her eye. She made out two dark-robed horsemen, bent forward, heads lowered, galloping along the dry, deserted trade road in the direction of Haifa.

"Harit! They're coming!" she cried. "Get in your saddle. They're riding like the wind and they'll soon be here!" She mounted her mule and gripped the reins firmly.

Her heart hammered in her chest. *Only two horsemen... I hope Guillaume is one of them,* she thought anxiously.

The riders dashed toward them and reined in their whinnying horses. A dust cloud swirled around them as they came to a standstill.

"We have your treasure!" Walter cried, patting the saddlebag behind him. "It was easier than we thought!"

Hartung pulled the kufiya away from his face, nodded and noticed the horror dawning in Leah's eyes.

"It's alright, the Templar is unharmed. He saw someone at the fortress with whom he has a score to settle, and wanted to stay in the city to claim his debt from the man. I'm to tell you that he'll come to Jerusalem later and meet you at your uncle's house," said the broad-shouldered knight, beckoning Harit to translate his words for her.

When Harit spoke, Leah nodded sadly and looked away.

"Don't worry," he said consolingly when he thought he saw tears in her eyes. "The Nazarene's a tough man and a powerful warrior. He'll keep his word. These two knights have the holy relics! You can be happy!"

Leah nodded and managed a small smile.

"You're right, Harit. Please thank them for me."

Harit did as she asked and the knights bowed in their saddles.

Walter reached for the water flask hanging from his saddle, uncorked it and took a long draught. Then he turned back toward Acre and looked at the smoke column above the city.

"Enough talk," he said decisively. "We need to move on. I don't think they'll follow us today, but we need to give ourselves a head start. We'll take the less travelled trade road to Nazareth. If I remember right, we can ride east on that road to the mountains of Samaria and then on to Jerusalem. I hope you two know the way."

"Yes, we took that road from Jerusalem to Acre and we can guide you, Sir Knight," said Harit.

"Then let's go, ha!" Walter spurred his horse and the small troupe followed him. They rode around the hill to the road and increased their pace to a quick trot. Harit took the lead, followed by Walter and Leah holding the pack animals by the reins. Hartung fell back a little to bring up the rear.

After three miles, they reached the forested hill of Saladin, from which they could see the entire plain around Acre, all the way to the sea. This was where the Sultan's troops were encamped during the battle for city.

The sun was high and the knights sweated profusely under their chainmail and thickly padded gambesons. Walter called for a short rest. In the shade of a pine, they changed their clothes and stowed the heavy chainmail in saddlebags. Then they wrapped their swords in pieces of clothing and hid these on one of the mules.

The troupe moved off again and Walter manoeuvred his horse to Hartung's side.

"Well, my friend, the first part of the plan wasn't so difficult. We have what may be the greatest treasure of Christendom, the weather is fine, the sky is blue and we're uninjured. If God continues to be so merciful, we'll be in the Holy City in four days, to pray at the tomb of our Saviour. Isn't that what you've always wanted?"

Hartung blinked in the dazzling sunlight. He sneezed loudly, startling Leah, who turned around. He waved apologetically. "I often sneeze in the bright sunlight. I can't help it!" he called to her. She didn't understand, but smiled and turned to face forward again.

Hartung sneezed violently twice more and wiped his face with the sleeve of his robe, then finally answered Walter's question.

"Yes, you're right, Walter. It was always my most ardent desire to stand at the tomb of our Saviour. Whether these alleged relics really are part of the Ark of the Covenant, I can't say. But they haven't brought about any blessed miracles so far. Quite the opposite – we've left the safety of the German brothers in Acre, the Templar knights are hot on our heels and we're riding through hostile Saracen territory. All this is happening under contract to a Jew, planned by an outcast Templar, in the hope of receiving a high reward for the robbery and murder of Christians. We've committed more grave sins and I fear it will only get worse."

"Stop looking at everything in the darkest colours," Walter retorted. "In Jerusalem, at the tomb of the Lord, we'll receive forgiveness for our sins old and new. The Almighty will look kindly on us when we bring his Commandments engraved in stone back to the city where his son suffered as a martyr."

"Perhaps you're right. I hope so. But we're mad to ride alone through heathen territory. We'll be recognised as Christians, slaughtered and left to be eaten by vultures in the mountains."

Walter laughed mischievously. "By God, Hartung, your giant body would be a veritable feast for those birds of death. Although you'd probably be too dry and tough for them. Our disguise is sufficient – we've already discussed that at length.

We're simply pilgrims on the way to Nazareth. Once we've passed that city, we'll be pilgrims on the way to Jerusalem. We happened to meet a Muslim man and wife and asked them to guide us. No one will suspect anything. Anyway, there's an agreement between King Richard and the heathen Sultan. Christians can visit the holy sites, and are under Saladin's protection on their way there."

"An agreement is worth nothing out here in this wasteland, and honestly, I shit on the dubious promise of protection from a heathen Sultan. We must be extremely vigilant and keep a close eye on the mule carrying our weapons!" Hartung replied.

"Yes, yes. Don't worry, the Lord is with us," Walter asserted confidently. *Courage and serenity, that's the motto of my house and I'll abide by it,* he thought, adjusting his position in the saddle.

Hartung's face was impassive, but he was pleased to observe the change in his friend. This new adventure had finally wrenched Walter out of his melancholia. He was almost transformed back into the cheerful, optimistic knight he had once known. Perhaps he could come to terms with his unholy past and actually find his way to God at the Lord's tomb.

They rode without pause until the sun disappeared behind the grey mountains. A little way from the road, Harit found a small valley with a pond that was still filled with the rains from the previous winter. Cedars, tamarisks and a few palms stood around the water. Narrow strips along the shore were carpeted in thick grass. They decided to camp there for the night.

Leah was exhausted. Her legs felt as if they were made of wood, and she had difficulty dismounting. Harit was no different. He walked stiffly over to help her unload the sacks of provisions from the mules.

The knights seemed unaffected. They quickly unsaddled their horses, led them to the pond and let them drink their fill.

Then they tethered the animals and refreshed themselves in the little lake.

Once their provisions were piled up on the ground, Harit gathered wood for a fire and Leah began preparing food.

Later, they all sat around the crackling fire and enjoyed a meal of dark bread, smoked fish, olives and dried figs. Leah made sweet tea in a small copper kettle and poured the hot beverage into two clay cups. She shared one with Harit and handed the other to the knights.

As he drank, Walter eyed the baggage piled ten feet away in the circle of firelight. "I'd like to know what it looks like – the world's greatest treasure that we looted today," he said, elbowing Hartung in the side.

Hartung shrugged and raised his eyebrows. "Then have a look."

Harit translated Walter's wish. Leah's eyes widened and a torrent of words tumbled out of her.

"She says to be careful. The Ark kills anyone who gets close to it. It's written in her scriptures," said Harit, raising his hands beseechingly.

"Nonsense. If that were true, we'd all be in the ground already," argued Walter. He stood up and fetched the heavy sack containing the relics. But he felt a slight sense of foreboding when he opened it. He gingerly took out the objects and placed them by the fire.

Hartung's curiosity was aroused, and he sidled up to them on his knees.

"What, is that all? Two angel statues and two clay tablets with scratchings on them?" The corners of his mouth drooped with disappointment and he rubbed his nose. Walter crouched beside him and commented sarcastically, "Looks unbelievably precious. No wonder the whole world sees the Jews as misfits if they pray to such worthless junk."

Leah read the peevish expressions on the knights' faces, tugged at Harit's robe and asked him to translate for her.

"You should know that my uncle is a renowned scholar and rabbi of the congregation in Jerusalem. He examined those things thoroughly and judged them to be authentic. The cherubim are pure gold, but covered in a layer of lead. The Lord's Commandments are chiselled into some unknown ore. My uncle covered them with worthless clay to disguise them..."

Harit interrupted her, incredulous. "By Allah, the figurines are made of gold? If I'd known that, I..."

Leah frowned and waved irritably. "Yes, yes, then neither of us would be here. But please keep translating... It's only part of the Ark. The evergreen staff of Aaron and the holy pot of manna are missing. This is most certainly the long lost sacred relic! I believe that with all of my heart!"

Walter listened attentively and cocked his head sceptically. "I grew up in a monastery, I had to copy many old scriptures and I clearly remember the story of the miraculous Ark. Aaron's rod was an almond branch and the manna pot dispensed endless amounts of food out of nothing. I wished I had a pot like that. I was always hungry when I lived with the devout but impoverished monks. Faith, pretty Leah, faith always has something to do with belief. I believe the relic existed, but I don't think this is it. Even if the angels are pure gold."

"My uncle told me that you Nazarenes worship the true cross of the messiah Jesus, on which he was nailed in ancient times. Even though wood is known to rot and doesn't last a thousand years. And yet you consider it genuine and prayed to it until Sultan Salah ad-Din took it away."

Leah's eyes flashed with suppressed anger and Harit struggled to translate her rapid speech faithfully into Frankish.

Hartung sat up, shot her a disparaging look and growled, "That's going too far, woman. Don't compare your idolatrous rubbish with the cross of the Lord who died for our salvation!"

"Leave it be, Hartung," Walter soothed him. "She's a woman, and a Jew. She doesn't know any better. It doesn't matter what these objects mean to her. I know what *I* believe in – the high reward we'll receive from Ishmael. Even if his sacred relic were nothing but a sack of threadbare rags, I would protect it with my life and take it to him." He turned to Harit. "Best you don't translate that part."

The Muslim nodded. He shared the knight's perspective. He had never considered the objects sacred, even after hearing for the first time that the winged creatures were pure gold. They were simply marketable refuse that he pulled out of the rubble of the Temple Mount.

By the beard of the prophet, I could be sitting in the bathhouse in Jerusalem now, being washed with scented soaps and oils.

Harit scratched himself behind the ears and gazed absentmindedly into the crackling campfire. This find had changed his life dramatically. Even in dreams, he could never have imagined the events of the last few days. He was united in a covenant with Jews and Nazarenes – one of which was a fearsome Templar knight.

For the first time since his family's murder, he felt a sense of belonging again; that he was needed and appreciated. Yesterday, he had seen the house where he was born, and today he sat beside the man who saved his life, breaking bread with him. In a way, that was worth more to him than all the gold in the world. But Ishmael's fee would also secure his future, and he would only receive that if the treasure reached Jerusalem intact.

He decided to pray again to the Almighty for the success of their mission, and got to his feet. "May I be excused? I've only prayed once today, and I'm supposed to do it five times a day, or I won't receive Allah's mercy."

"Yes, we've talked enough. Take these things and put them away," grumbled Hartung, returning the cherubim and tablets to the saddlebag.

Harit did as he was asked, then he took out his small, worn prayer mat and disappeared into the darkness. Leah tidied away the remains of the meal and rinsed the cups and pot in the pond. When her work was done, she returned without a word to sit by the fire.

Walter looked at her and smiled. "You should sleep now," he said slowly, pressing his hands together against his cheek. "Sleep, do you understand? We'll keep watch."

Leah understood. She wrapped herself in a dark woollen blanket, lay down and closed her eyes.

A light evening wind rose and ruffled the surface of the little lake, carrying the sound of Harit's singsong prayers to the knights sitting in silence.

Hartung reached for his sword, laid it across his legs and nodded to his comrade. He would take the first watch.

Walter patted his friend's shoulder, wrapped himself tightly in his wide robe and lay down on his side.

Harit soon returned, saw the slumbering Leah, acknowledged Hartung with a wave and lay down too.

The knight narrowed his eyes and gazed across at the grey mountain slopes bordering the little valley to the south, which were now gradually fading into darkness. Everything seemed peaceful, but he felt a strange restlessness within himself.

This place has eyes, he thought, gripping the hilt of his sword tighter in his right hand.

XXVIII

The hasty election of the Grand Commander proceeded smoothly under Marshal Raoul's leadership. He would have gladly put himself forward as a candidate for the esteemed post, but he was shrewd enough not to, his reputation having taken too much of a blow after recent events. One more reason to want Guillaume in the deepest abyss of hell.

As expected, Brother Gilbert Heràil was voted in by a huge majority as the interim leader of the Templars. Once the chapter hall had cleared, Raoul quickly recruited five dependable, discreet turcopoles to assist him in the hunt for Guillaume. They were to be ready to depart from the fortress the following morning.

Raoul himself wanted to scout around Acre first, hoping to pick up the trail of the three horsemen who started the devastating fire. With Brother Gilbert's permission, he left the fortress late that evening and headed down to the harbour.

Now he was sitting on a low bed, looking down at a dark head of hair bobbing up and down between his legs. The smell of stale beer and burnt fat rose up from it and assaulted his nostrils.

He folded his arms behind his head, sank back comfortably and tried to ignore the filth and disarray of the attic room. Dozens of unwashed, stained garments hung from slanting beams amidst smoked sausages and legs of ham. There were stacks of wooden plates with leftover food and half-full wine jugs in every corner of the room. Two smoky oil lamps stood on a stool by the bed, bathing the room in a forgiving, yellow light. Ruzan, his secret Armenian lover, was not exactly known for her tidiness.

He often wondered why he was so attracted to her. Perhaps it was the way she spoiled him with motherly tenderness, in strange contrast to her rough demeanour. She often had to contend with drunk, clamouring guests in the tavern, and had a reputation as an energetic, confident woman, uninhibited in her dealings with men. But she could also be very brusque if necessary.

Or perhaps it was her boyish body, which almost drove him mad with desire. After so many years of carnal abstinence in the Order, her candid sensuality made him feel like a real man again. And her round eyes, brown hair and skinny frame reminded him of his wife, whom he had left many years ago, and who now lived near Paris with their two half-grown daughters at his expense.

Guillaume had introduced him to Ruzan shortly after the conquest of Acre, and he was immediately captivated by her. No one else knew about Raoul's secret lover, and he had to ensure it stayed that way. Chastity was a fundamental rule among the Templars. Transgressions were punished harshly, with the loss of the white habit or even expulsion from the Order.

He bought Ruzan's silence with large payments of silver deniers, which he pressed into her hand at the end of each visit. As far as he knew, she used them to pay for her overpriced lodgings inside the city walls near the harbour, and for the upkeep of her daughter who lived with relatives in the countryside.

"Relax and stop thinking so much," Ruzan grumbled between his thighs, spitting on his semi-erect cock. He felt her take him back into her warm mouth and hum softly. *She does that so well,* he thought, enjoying the tingling sensation that spread through his body as she tongued his glans. She slid a finger into his anus. He groaned softly.

"I knew it. He likes that," she said in her deep, husky voice. She gazed proudly at his bulging, veined manhood, slithered up his body and kissed him behind the ears. Then she sat on him and let his cock glide into her moist loins. She rocked her hips and Raoul looked up at her lustfully. Her small breasts barely jiggled. He gripped her bony, sinuous body by the hips, lifted her up and down and watched, aroused, as his member plunged into her tight, hairless vulva, slippery with her juices. It wasn't long before he spurted into her with a loud moan and closed his eyes contentedly.

She felt a tightening in her thighs, lifted her right leg and let his manhood slide out of her with a smacking sound. Then she rolled onto her side and laid her arm across his chest.

"That was quick. You're distracted," she murmured reproachfully, running her fingers through his sparse chest hair. "Is it because of the fire at the fortress? The whole city's talking about it."

Raoul opened his eyes and blinked. She was right. Guillaume's attack, the Grand Master's death, Nicholas' murder and the election of Brother Gilbert to the post of Grand Commander had all affected him. He feared his head might explode at any moment like an overripe melon.

He couldn't resist the urge to tell her what had happened. Ruzan was very discreet and one of the few people he trusted. She knew of his plan to destroy Guillaume, and endorsed it wholeheartedly, as it had originally been her idea to silence him as quickly as possible. She saw him as a constant threat that could put an abrupt end to her lucrative life with the rich and powerful Marshal.

"Could be. It was a horrible day," he replied. "Three horsemen set fire to the stables and the storehouse. One of them was Guillaume."

"Guillaume?" Ruzan sat up, startled. "I thought you sent him on a long journey to the Assassins, from which he was unlikely to return?"

"I did. But he was definitely the arsonist, and that's not all that happened. He killed Nicholas, and a heathen killed Grand Master Robert de Sablé during the attack. He simply hacked off his head. The damned Saracen jumped off the battlement after committing the act. He's dead too. A new supreme leader was elected only a few hours ago – Brother Gilbert Heràil the Pious. He's now my superior and sent me out to search for Guillaume. If I don't capture him, my days in the Temple are numbered. I have no idea how to go about it, but I have to find Guillaume at any cost."

Ruzan's eyes widened. She shook her lank, shoulder-length hair in disbelief. She had met Nicholas. At the time, she still earned her living as a whore amongst the tents of the besiegers of Acre. A slimy, deceitful, cocky Templar, who was as brutally lecherous as he was self-confident. She shuddered to remember his blows and the dark blue marks he left on her one night. That was their only encounter. She had never told Raoul about it. She really wasn't sorry about Nicholas, and she had never had anything to do with the Grand Master.

"That sounds like a truly horrible, unlucky day. Are you sure it was Guillaume? I thought you said he had no idea. But he must have been targeting you with his attack. Thank God you escaped him! Your plan was so well laid. Sending him to a fateful meeting with the fearsome Assassins, which should have cost him his life. How did he figure it out what you were up to?"

She pressed her body against his and squeezed him hard. Losing Raoul would be very unfortunate for her, her adolescent daughter, her frail father, her idiot brother and her countless kin in the mountains of Galilee. His money kept her impoverished peasant family alive, and it meant she no longer had to sell her body to other customers. Icy fear crept up her back and bit into her neck.

"How should I know? Before he left, Guillaume seemed as gullible and trusting as ever. I thought that, if he survived the meeting with the Assassins, Nicholas would take care of him before he made it back to the Temple. That was why I sent Nicholas out looking for him. But he failed completely. I on the other hand, must and will deal to that blaggard. But it would be a mistake to underestimate Guillaume," he replied.

They were silent for a while and Ruzan contemplated how she could best help her lover.

"Three horsemen, you said? It may be nothing, but my master, Reinhold the Lame, bought three horses with saddles and bridles for some of his guests. His wife mentioned it in passing. The animals were out in the courtyard when I left the tavern late last night."

Raoul sat up and leaned his back against the cool mud wall at the head of the bed.

"What kind of guests?" he asked, looking sharply at Ruzan.

"A small group of travellers who stayed two nights at the inn. I heard it was a merchant from Jerusalem with his wife and a Christian pilgrim. But I never saw them in the barroom, even though I worked there from vespers until late into the night. Thinking about it now, that seems a little strange."

"What a mismatched party. Very unusual. Do you know anything else about the pilgrim?"

"Only that he was very generous with his money. Does that help?"

"Perhaps... sounds suspicious. What did they need expensive saddle horses for? Without an armed guard, they'd lose them as soon as they left the safety of the city walls. There's enough rabble waiting out there, only too glad to relieve defenceless pilgrims of their belongings," said Raoul. "I'll ask the innkeeper about it tomorrow morning."

"Yes, do that, but you didn't hear it from me!"

Ruzan rolled onto her back, spread her slender legs and reached for a corner of the bedsheet. She deftly wiped herself clean with it and got up. "I'm hungry. The food is ready. I expect you could use some too, my big strong man."

She skipped naked across the room to take down one of the grey dresses hanging from a nail on the back of the door, but she never made it that far.

The door suddenly splintered in its frame, swung open and crashed into Ruzan's head, flinging her against the wall. She fell unconscious to the floor.

A large, darkly swaddled figure stormed into the room. The man went straight for Raoul, who quickly turned to reach for his sword, but instead received a hard kick in the belly. He buckled in pain, then another strong kick to his ribcage flung him back against the wall.

He gasped for air. His vision blurred and he was overcome with nausea. He vaguely registered the glinting point of a sword aimed at his right eye. Then he heard Guillaume's voice.

"Why, Raoul, why? You damnable shit!" he snarled. The hilt of the sword smashed into Raoul's temple. The room around him rapidly faded to the deepest black and the Marshal lost consciousness.

XXIX

Hartung was woken by someone gently shaking his shoulder. He blinked and saw Walter holding an index finger to his lips.

"There are six of them. Bedouins maybe. On foot. They don't seem to have bows and arrows," Walter whispered, pointing toward the pond.

Day was breaking, the sky was fading from black to dark grey and a few orange clouds were already reflected in the smooth surface of the water.

The knight peered across it and saw several stooped shadows moving slowly between the rocks on the opposite shore of the pond, creeping toward their camp.

"Wake the others. But not a sound."

Hartung winked at Walter and slithered on his belly to where Leah lay rolled tightly in her blanket. He put a hand over her mouth. She woke with a fright, eyes wide, and tried to scream, but the knight motioned reassuringly for her to be quiet. Leah nodded and he took his hand away from her lips. Then he woke Harit in the same way.

"Six men are approaching," he whispered. "Tell her that, then protect her with your knife as best you can."

Harit nodded, slid over to Leah and hissed the warning into her ear. Frightened, she tried to sit up, but Hartung pushed her gently back to the ground and gestured for them both to be still.

He crawled back to Walter, who was looking out over the water, motionless and alert.

"They're almost here."

They quietly drew their swords from their sheaths. Not a moment too soon. A shadow lunged at them, followed by a second. Both ran into the knights' swords, which pierced their bodies. Shrill screams shattered the silence and were answered with loud battle cries from the other grey figures. *"Allahu akbar! Allahu akbar!"* They charged at the knights with glinting swords and daggers.

Walter and Hartung wrenched their weapons out of the twitching bodies of the first two attackers and sprang to their feet. Blades clashed and strenuous fighting ensued.

Hartung stooped low and lunged at the next enemy, brining him down with a hard body thrust and slicing deep into his thigh, through veins and sinews to the bone. He side-stepped the next heathen's attack, spun around and brought his sword down between the man's neck and shoulder from behind. Blood sprayed and he thudded to the dry ground.

Just before his opponents reached him, Walter dropped to his knees. With a powerful swipe of his sword, he separated one heathen's foot just above the ankle. The Muslim toppled, shrieking with pain and surprise, and fell into a thick tamarisk bush. From a kneeling position, Walter straightened up to meet another charging attacker, thrusting his sword deep into the man's throat. It split his larynx, scraped past his spine and jutted a cubit out the back of his neck. Terror-stricken eyes stared at Walter in disbelief before the man buckled and fell sideways.

The two knights quickly positioned themselves back to back, breathing heavily and circling slowly, their swords at the ready in front of them.

"Is that it?" asked Hartung breathlessly.

"Think so," replied Walter. "I didn't see any more of them."

The Muslim in the tamarisk bush screamed loudly for help. The other heathen with the gash on his thigh sat whimpering in the sand, trying in vain to stem the flow of blood from his artery. The four other attackers lay dead in the sand.

Hartung trudged over to the incessant screamer, who frantically tried to untangle himself from the bush when he heard him coming. Hartung split his head open with a single powerful blow. Then he crossed himself and looked warily toward the pond, where a light morning breeze created ripples that glittered in the light of the rising sun.

Walter turned to Harit and Leah, who had watched the short but horrifically bloody fight, clutching one another like helpless children.

"Harit!" Walter cried. "Come here! Don't be afraid, they can't hurt you anymore. I want to question this one and I'm afraid he doesn't understand me. Do you?" He kicked the last living attacker in the side, but the man didn't seem to notice. He rocked back and forth, whimpering, and tried to staunch the bleeding by binding his leg with his blood-soaked robe.

Harit approached, shaking from head to toe. He held the small knife in his trembling hand.

"Calm yourself," Walter said gently, standing behind the heathen with the point of his sword aimed at the man's left shoulder. "It's alright. Ask him if there are more of them, where their camp is and whether anyone is guarding it."

Harit translated hesitantly. He had to repeat his questions several times before the badly wounded man answered him with a stammer.

"He says they were out alone on a raid. Their unguarded camp is behind the hill at the end of the pond."

"I see. Bandits who ambush merchants and pilgrims," Walter scowled. "Anything else?"

"Yes. He begs for forgiveness and mercy. For Allah's sake, we should spare him. He admits it was a mistake to attack Frankish warriors, and he'll never do it again. Never again."

"Oh, he's right about that," Walter said drily, and without warning he shoved his sword between the bandit's collar bone and shoulder blade, deep into his heart. The Muslim toppled sideways without uttering a sound and died.

Harit stood rooted to the spot, his face ashen. He looked with dismay at the knight wiping his sword clean on the dead man's stained robe.

"I didn't believe him," Walter explained. "There may be more of his kind roaming through these mountains. We should leave quickly. He would have bled out anyway."

He put a comforting hand on Harit's quaking shoulder. "It's alright, young man. It was necessary. We can't take prisoners. Now go to Leah and help her pack. Hartung and I will take care of the bodies. Then we'll ride to the thieves' camp. We might find something usable there."

Harit nodded and staggered to Leah, who had followed the exchange in disbelief.

"Harit... what kind of men are these?" she whispered, getting to her feet. "They're... they're so vicious!"

Harit took a moment to calm himself, then he looked into her fearful eyes. "They were robbers, Leah. If the knights weren't with us, by Allah, we would now be lying in pools of our own blood. They're warriors and killing is their profession."

"But... but six against two. It scarcely took them the blink of an eye to kill them all. Is Guillaume like that too?"

"You heard what he told us about his life when we found him. I don't know, maybe he's even worse." Seeing Leah's horrified expression, he corrected himself. "No, not worse. But he was a Templar. They're said to be the cruellest of all. True believers are warned to avoid them, because it's rare to survive an encounter with them."

"You did. Guillaume was good to you."

Harit forced a smile. "We saved his life. And... he's not a Templar anymore. Anyway, he only has eyes for you. What does he care about an insignificant little sugar merchant? Come on, we need to pack."

Leah blushed and turned away in embarrassment. She felt caught out – even the inexperienced Harit had noticed Guillaume's attraction to her. Thinking of the knight made her heart beat faster.

She hurriedly gathered up her blanket and helped Harit to load the animals. Finally, they loaded the saddlebags containing the sacred treasure. She shuddered with dread when she felt one of the cherubim through the rough sackcloth.

Since its rediscovery, the holy relic of her people seemed to bring about strange occurrences.

Now it was protected by Nazarene knights, and she was longing with every fibre of her being for an outcast Templar knight.

Yes, it can work miracles. And bring death, she thought, glancing at the two warriors.

Hartung and Walter dragged the corpses of the six bandits into a pile and covered them with brushwood. They threw the robbers' swords and daggers into the pond. Then they washed their blood-smeared hands and mounted the horses Harit and Leah had saddled. None of them could contemplate breakfast in the small battlefield. There would be time for that later. They had to leave.

The troupe circled the pond. Tracks in the sand led them to a few silver rings, knives and copper coins, which they took. They loaded sacks of grain, dried figs and three bottles of olive oil onto the mules. Hartung commented disparagingly on what unsuccessful thieves they were, and Walter sneered in agreement.

The knights dismantled the tent of felt and goat hair, and tied it to one of the horses. Then Harit rode out ahead, followed by Hartung, Leah and the mules. This time, Walter brought up the rear.

On the way back to the road they passed the site of the bloody skirmish and Hartung grew pensive.

They had easily overwhelmed a few lightly armed thieves. But their journey had just begun. Three long days and nights lay ahead of them before they reached Jerusalem. The Holy City was full of battle-hardened Saracens, and it would be difficult to move around among them undetected.

Oh Lord, if these really are your tablets with the Ten Commandments, then you must protect us. We'll take them to the city where your son died on the cross, thought Hartung with a quiet sigh.

They trotted slowly east, where the sun had now banished the dark night, bathing the chalky white mountain slopes in a surreal rosy light.

XXX

Raoul came to his senses and slowly opened his eyes. His temples throbbed painfully and he tasted blood. He was lying on his side on the bed, facing the wall. Directly in front of his face, a huge cockroach scuttled down the mud wall and disappeared into a crack.

He tried to turn away in disgust, but his hands were bound at his back, and a piece of hemp rope was a tightly knotted around his ankles. He rolled onto his other side with a groan and saw Guillaume sitting on the floor, his sword aimed at Raoul's neck.

"What... what do you want?" the Marshal asked hoarsely. He ran his tongue gingerly over his split, burning gums. His eyes darted to the door, where Ruzan kwasnelt, tied in a bundle on her knees, breathing noisily through her nose, her eyes wide with fear. Her mouth was gagged with a large rag and long strings of saliva hung from her chin.

"I want to know the reason, although I've had my suspicions for some time. But I need to hear it from you. Why did you betray me, Raoul? We've been through so much together. How many times did I protect you from evil? I was always a true friend and served loyally under you. I was at your side in countless battles, and we saved one another's lives many times. All because of her?" Guillaume spat contemptuously in Ruzan's direction, and she snorted and shook her head vehemently.

Raoul's mouth twisted into a tortured smile.

"The blame is on you," he croaked, avoiding the question. "I warned you time and again to be careful. Not everyone in the Order appreciated your debauchery. I had to protect myself. But I'm still your brother, so untie me and we'll find a solution together."

"I know your solution," growled Guillaume. "You had Nicholas hunt me with a troop of turcopoles as soon as I left Jerusalem. He'd never have dared without your permission. You and de Sablé orchestrated my downfall because I'd become too much of a danger to you. The Grand Master wanted to be rid of me as a witness to his wicked plan to kill Prince Bohemond. And you fear for your lucrative post as commander of the army. Because I know what the God-fearing, straight-laced commander of the Templar warriors does in this filthy attic room with a sordid whore week after week!"

Guillaume's sword moved dangerously close to Raoul's neck.

"But I don't understand. After all these years, you throw our friendship away like an old rag. You even ordered my death! Your secrets were safe with me; I would never have given you away. But you... you're a dishonourable, self-serving traitor who deserves to die. And after that, de Sablé gets his just punishment. I've made sure of it!"

Raoul flinched and shook his head vigorously.

"Don't make it worse than it already is. My death won't help you. I was only acting on the Grand Master's orders. What could I have done differently? You know the rules of the Brotherhood – I must obey him. And he's already dead. You had him assassinated at noon today, did you not? Your attack on the Temple and the fire in the stables was an excellent diversion. A superbly devised plan, I have to admit. And you took the opportunity to send Brother Nicholas to hell. Now all of your enemies are out of the way. So untie me – we'll go to the Temple and..."

"Stop... What did you just say?" interrupted Guillaume. "De Sablé is dead? How... how did he die?"

"You don't know? Well, your revenge is complete. While you were attacking the fortress with your men, an Assassin cut off his head. We killed the murderer when he tried to escape, but that didn't help the Grand Master. Don't look so surprised. Congratulations!"

Guillaume lowered his sword and stared dumbfounded into Raoul's expressionless eyes. It appeared the Assassins had carried out their contract to kill de Sablé simultaneously with his theft of the holy relics.

What an incredible coincidence, he thought, privately marvelling at the reliably executed assassination. Hassan, the fiery-eyed representative of the Old Man of the Mountain, was worth every bezant of the advance payment.

"It's news to me. I never thought the hashish eaters would act so quickly. Yes, I commissioned his murder, with the money I was to pay them for the murder of Prince Bohemond of Antioch. De Sablé would have had me killed as soon as I returned, and I had to prevent that. I only handed over the first payment; unfortunately, Nicholas robbed me of the rest. I was hoping to retrieve the money during my attack, but no such luck. The spoils from his raid had already been distributed," said Guillaume.

He remained silent about the real reason for his surprise attack. There was no need to tell Raoul of the cherubim and tablets.

To his dismay, Guillaume sensed a certain familiarity with the Marshall returning. He wasn't here to chat; he was here to kill him for his villainy.

"It doesn't matter; the details of my plans for revenge are no concern of yours now. The sight of your lying face disgusts me! You don't deserve to live another moment, you Goddamned whoreson!"

Guillaume sprang to his feet with resolve raised his sword. Raoul drew up his trussed legs, pushed himself back against the wall and tried to sit up.

"For the sake of our friendship, don't let me die trussed up on a whore's bed," he hissed.

Guillaume paused and rested his sword on his shoulder.

"Ahh... so we're friends again? You're nothing but accursed scum, deserving of a dishonourable death!"

"No more than you," Raoul retorted coldly. "You'll be hunted down and painfully executed for your despicable crimes. The Order is powerful and you won't escape it. Let me live and I'll help you flee to safety!"

Guillaume looked at the defenceless knight with a mixture of admiration and sadness. Faced with death, he wasn't begging for his life. Treacherous and deceitful as ever, he was actually making a tempting offer. He had no word of apology or remorse, only more lies. Raoul would never help him. He had already betrayed Guillaume for the sake of his sordid harlot; why would he protect the murderer of Nicholas and de Sablé? To Raoul, he was an unpredictable risk who would stab him in the back at the next opportunity.

Despite everything, he still felt close to his former friend and comrade. He was suddenly flooded with memories of their time together. Firm embraces after winning a battle or happily surviving a skirmish, merry drinking bouts, long nights planning their ascent to important posts in the Brotherhood. Not to mention their secret, sinful relations with lascivious women, which they related to one another down to the smallest details.

Tears of grief welled up in Guillaume's eyes and he lowered his sword helplessly. No, he couldn't kill Raoul.

The Marshal saw the weapon slowly sink toward the floor. A quiet sigh escaped his swollen lips. Guillaume was too weak to slay him. Raoul himself wouldn't have hesitated a moment.

"I always knew you were a sensible man. Untie me and we'll straighten everything out with our Templar brothers."

Guillaume stooped and laid down his sword without a word. Then he tore a strip off the linen bed sheet and gagged the surprised Marshal with it.

"I'll spare you. But don't let me see your face ever again. If you do, know that I'll kill you... and her too," said Guillaume in a husky voice. He picked up his weapon and pointed it at the naked, bound and gagged Ruzan, who looked back at him out of a terrified, tear-stained face. She was now kneeling in a large puddle. Disgusted, Guillaume turned back to face Raoul.

"The Order is no longer my home. I'll leave this miserable country and take your secrets with me. But I warn you: don't search for me, or you'll die. May all the torments of hell seek you out while you still live, you ignominious, treacherous Judas!"

Guillaume spat on Raoul with utter contempt, then turned and strode to the door, his head held high.

Raoul snorted with relief and rested his head against the wall behind him. *What a drivelling idiot.* Of course he would go after Guillaume and kill him. His own future in the Order depended on it. The laughable threats of an outcast Templar didn't bother him. But the warm saliva on his face did.

First, he had to free himself. His eye was caught one of the flickering oil lamps on the floor near Ruzan. He should be able to burn through the ropes around his wrists with that. He slid off the bed and rolled over to it.

I'll get you, bastard son, he fumed, as the flames singed his wrists and the room filled with the acrid smoke of burning hair, skin and rope.

Guillaume stepped out onto the dark street and drew in a lungful of the fresh, salty sea air. He scanned the harbour district, but no one was out at this late hour. And yet he couldn't shake the feeling of constantly being watched since arriving in Acre.

He concealed his sword under his wide robe and pulled the hood over his lowered head.

He knew it was a mistake to leave Raoul alive after telling him about his pact with the Assassins to murder Robert de Sablé. The Marshal now had confirmation of his complicity in the Grand Master's death, and would inform the other brothers.

They'll hunt me like a wild animal. From now on, I won't be safe in any country in which even a single Templar lives.

Strangely, he felt no sense of satisfaction knowing the Grand Master was dead. He pictured Raoul's cold eyes again. He couldn't kill him because his long-time friend and comrade was not the cause of his downfall. It was his own fault, and he had been righteously punished by the Almighty for the unforgiveable sins of his past, which he now deeply regretted. Killing Raoul would only burden him with more guilt.

How his future would look, only God knew. But He seemed to be pointing the way with His Commandments engraved in stone: Jerusalem. The relic must return to that place, to the old Jew. And Guillaume wanted to see Leah again. She had given him new hope, and that long-forgotten feeling of pure, honest affection.

Guillaume gathered his robe around his neck and made his way quickly to the inn of Reinhold the Lame, where he had again sought refuge after the attack on the Templar fortress. He would saddle his horse there at daybreak and ride as fast as possible through the mountains of Samaria to the Holy City.

XXXI

Guillaume didn't sleep that night. At sunrise, he left his little room at the back of the inn.

It was an unseasonably cold morning, and the knight shivered in the courtyard as he tied provisions to his horse – water skins, a felt blanket and saddlebags containing bread and apples.

Reinhold the Lame was had also risen early. His stiff leg was often very painful, and walking slowly around the yard brought him some relief. He heard Guillaume in the stable and hobbled to greet him.

"God be with you, good knight," he said.

Guillaume turned around. "Ah, our faithful host. God be with you too. Already up and about?" he asked, tightening his saddle strap.

"On one and a half legs," replied Reinhold wryly. "I didn't sleep well last night. Probably the weather. I've never experienced such a long, cold winter here. It's mid-March and there's still frost on the roof in the mornings, even though the sun blazes down from a cloudless sky by day. The cold doesn't seem to do my bones any good. They pinch and twinge in the joints. So, you mean to follow your friends?"

Guillaume nodded and, seeing a glint of curiosity in the innkeeper's eyes, chose his next words carefully.

"Yes, my work here is done. I'll ride along the coastal road to Jaffa. That's where we all plan to meet," he lied. It was best Reinhold the Lame didn't know that he planned to take the road through the Samarian mountains.

Reinhold chuckled and raised his bushy eyebrows. "The whole world is talking about a madcap attack on the Templar fortress, a fire and many dead. I've heard tell the Assassins were responsible for it. The brothers spent all day trying to round up their escaped horses in the city. So they couldn't pursue the supposed heathen attackers. It was you, wasn't it?" asked the innkeeper with undisguised admiration in his voice.

"It's best you don't ask," Guillaume answered quietly. "We owe you a great debt of thanks."

Reinhold waved it off. "I was glad to help. You should know, I was there from the start, when Sir Walter and his friend Hartung led the pilgrimage to the Holy Land. Together we saw many good days and terrible days, all the way here from distant Saxony. I owe them my life. They're both generous, noble men, whom I was always glad to serve. And if they're helping you, then believe me, you must be worth it."

Guillaume clapped his hands on the innkeeper's shoulders in farewell, then took his horse by the reins. "I'll pass on your greetings, God willing. And don't forget: not a word about any of this or me!"

"No one will learn anything from me, I'm not suicidal," replied Reinhold, suddenly serious. He limped to the gate, raised the crossbar and slowly opened both gates, which creaked loudly in the still morning.

"God be with you. I hope we meet again one day, in better times," he said.

"I doubt it. God be with you," replied Guillaume, sure he would never see the gaunt innkeeper again. From now on, Acre was a forbidden city to him. He'd never return.

Guillaume left the inn and led his horse on foot through the quiet alleys to the eastern gate, which was already open for the early arrivals – farmers and traders from the region. They were in a hurry to get into the city to set up their market stalls. Two tired and bleary watchmen propped themselves up on their spears. They let him pass without question.

As soon as he was outside the city walls, Guillaume mounted his horse and trotted a mile down the coastal road toward Haifa.

When he reached the Hill of Turon, he scanned his surroundings to make sure no one was following him. Satisfied, he turned his steed southeast and rode cross-country until he found the old trade road from Acre to Nazareth. A short while later, he reached the forested hill of Saladin.

There, he unexpectedly encountered a number of heavily armoured Christian horsemen. They carried shields painted in bright yellow and Guillaume could see no way of avoiding them on the narrow forest trail, which broadened out into a small clearing behind them.

One rider trotted slowly up to him, his lance lowered. The man's tanned, beardless face was framed by a chainmail cowl over which he wore a Norman helmet with a nose guard. He looked a similar age to Guillaume. A red, welted scar ran across his right cheek. He looked Guillaume up and down with grass-green eyes from a distance.

"If you're a Christian, identify yourself! If not, then shuffle off, heathen!" he cried in an unpleasantly high voice.

Guillaume realised with relief that he knew the short-sighted man. It was young Bohemond, the Count of Tripoli, second son of Prince Bohemond of Antioch. The name was passed down as part of a family tradition, which often led people to confuse the two rulers.

"God be with you, Lord Bohemond. It's me, Guillaume de Born, former turcopolier of the Knights Templar. I hope you and your father are in good health?" called Guillaume.

The Count raised his lance and rode nearer. His escorts stopped a short distance away, hands on their swords.

"Good heavens, it really is you! I didn't recognise you without your white robe, Brother Guillaume. It's been a while since we last saw one another at the King's wedding in Acre. You almost drank me under the table!"

Guillaume smiled and winked at him. "You must be mistaken, my Lord. Templars are not permitted to drink."

"Right, I forgot. My mistake... I'm glad to see you." The Count laughed and signalled his men, who took their hands off their swords. The two dismounted and shook hands.

"What brings you out into the forest alone? With no armour and only a sword at your side? Are you on a leisure ride or reconnaissance?"

Guillaume shook his head. "It's a long, sad story. Too long to tell you standing here. But what brings you here? I thought the way from Tripoli and Antioch to Acre was blocked by the heathens?"

"No longer," replied Bohemond, removing his helmet. "We're on our way to bring glad tidings to Acre. Last night we made our last halt outside the city gates here in the forest. The heathen sultan, that Godless Saladin, was summoned by the prince of darkness a few days ago. He's dead, thanks be to God!"

"By the Almighty! That is truly good news!" Guillaume was surprised, and quietly rejoiced. The deadly enemy of the Christians, slaughterer of Hattin, conqueror of Jerusalem and spoiler of the Christian Kingdom had finally received his just punishment from the Lord.

"Who killed him? Was he slain by our hand or did one of his many sons help him along?" he asked.

"No, listen to this, he passed away in his bed like an old woman. God sent him an illness that rapidly weakened him. May he burn in hell!"

They were interrupted by thundering hooves, and two dozen horsemen broke through the dense pine forest into the clearing.

"Ahh... my father... and his wife," said Bohemond. Guillaume heard the disdain in his voice. He joined the other horsemen, who formed a semi-circle to make way for their Lord.

The Prince of Antioch, Bohemond III, rode a horse with a pelt the same ash grey as its owner's hair. The man's eyebrows bristled below a creased and weathered forehead, and his close-set eyes intently studied the tall man at his son's side. The massive Bohemond was encased in chainmail that was too tight for him, and sat stiff as an oak on his magnificent warhorse.

Beside him rode his third wife, Sibylle, whom Guillaume had met almost ten years ago in Antioch. Proud and beautiful, she sat enthroned on her light riding horse, her dark brown hair in a thick braid that swung between her well-formed breasts, which were only half covered by a tightly laced bodice of gold brocade. Her dark blue silk dress fluttered in the wind for a moment, then caressed her body like a second skin. The cool morning air gave her cheeks a slight flush, and there was a look of boredom in her long-lashed eyes.

If temptation had a name, it would be called Sibylle, thought Guillaume as he recalled his first night with her, when she came to his chamber in secret all those years ago. He had been in the entourage of the old Grand Master, Arnaud de Toroge, who was conducting negotiations in Antioch with the eternally cash-strapped Prince Bohemond.

Sibylle had taken a shine to the young Templar and taught him, over three clandestine nights, things he still couldn't forget. Never again had he had such a charming, depraved and scheming woman. He had jokingly called her snatch an oil press. It was she who taught him that other orifices could also give endless pleasure.

Guillaume felt hot at these recollections, and the blood shot into his loins. She had fallen utterly in love with him, and even wanted to leave her newly wed husband for him. She would doubtless have dragged him with her into ruin. It wasn't easy driving the fanciful notion out of her head. But in the end, he impressed upon her his lack of means as a bastard son without an inheritance, and his even more precarious future as a poor Templar. Miraculously, she was suddenly cured of her folly and of him.

After that, he occasionally heard wild stories of her exploits. The Prince had left his second wife for her. She was close with Saladin for a time. Rumour had it, she even spied for him, and that if it weren't for her intercessions, the Christian principality of Antioch would no longer exist. She was involved in negotiations and state business, and was said to have given herself over anonymously to countless suitors in the brothels of Antioch.

Sibylle instantly recognised Guillaume. Her eyes lit up and she gave him a friendly, slightly mischievous nod.

Prince Bohemond greeted him from his horse.

"W-w-what a-a-a sur...surprise," stammered the high-born knight, his head jerking with each word.

"I re...recognised you im-im-immediately, Guill....Guillaume!"

Now I see how he got his nickname The Stammerer, thought Guillaume. Perhaps his speech impediment was what had turned him into one of the cruellest barons in the Holy Land. Married three times, he had discarded his previous wives without just cause. He had been reprimanded in a personal letter from the Pope, and even excommunicated by the Patriarch of Jerusalem for bigamy. After that, he retaliated against the Church, raiding monasteries, torturing and massacring priests, until finally the Church gave in and reversed the ruling. But he never separated from his Sibylle. And Guillaume knew why.

"Ha-ha-have you f-f-f-finally parted ways with the T-T-Templars? You-you-you're not wearing your ha...habit. It never suited you."

"It's true," Guillaume admitted candidly. "The strict life of a monk is not for me. I'm going back to Jerusalem as a pilgrim, and later I'll seek out a new Lord whom I can serve with my sword."

Sibylle listened attentively and sidled closer on her horse. "You're no longer a Templar? How wonderful..." Her velvety voice enveloped Guillaume like a warm summer wind. "Bohemond, we should employ this brave man in our entourage. He has the same name as our son, after all." She smiled secretively and added, "He's already ten years old and should become a squire soon."

Guillaume was shocked, but didn't let it show. *Is she trying to tell me I'm the father of her son?* The child's age was about right. But he was certain he wasn't her only lover back then. He studied her face, and she drew her full lips into a pout.

"Of course! Y-you're right as always!" Bohemond nodded and turned to Guillaume. "W-w-w-what do you s-say?"

"I thank you for the very generous offer and I may well accept," replied Guillaume. "But first I must fulfil my Christian duty and atone at the Lord's tomb. If it is His will, I will then gladly come to your court."

"Suit yourself." Disappointed, Sibylle leaned back in her saddle, guided her horse with a squeeze of her thigh past the two men, and left the clearing. Guillaume caught a whiff of lavender as he watched her go.

Bohemond noticed his attention and said, his breast swelling with pride, "W-w-w-what a woman, eh?"

"Oh, yes, you can count yourself lucky. I'm sure she makes you proud."

"Nonsense. She makes me happy with her m-m-mouth, ti-ti-ti-tits and sp...splendid arse. And has done so fff-f-for years!" said the Prince with a bleating laugh.

Guillaume smiled peevishly back.

"Well yes, you're blessed, my lord. Your son tells me the cursed heathen sultan is finally dead. Praise the Lord! And I have news of a death too. The Templar Grand Master has died. Murdered by the Assassins, it appears. Perhaps that will help your negotiations. I know about your credit with the Templars. They're terribly indignant about your tardiness in paying back the loans."

And wanted to have you killed because of it. You have me to thank for your life, Stammerer. Now let me be on my way!

The Prince's face darkened. "Ahh. Assassins... my c-c-c-crazy neighbours. G-g-good job, I c-c-c-could never stand old de Sablé. That d-d-d-damned usurer. The Brotherhood won't g-g-get a single c-c-c-copper coin. As you know, the Ba...Baghras Fortress was once the... the headquarters of the T-T-Templars in my c-c-c-country. It was taken by Saladin and... and then fell into the hands of the Arm-mmm-menians. I want to g-give it back to-to-to the Templars. That's the mmm...main reason I'm tra-tra-tra-travelling to Acre. I think... that should c-c-cover my debt."

Guillaume prudently refrained from mentioning his own negotiations with Saladin regarding Baghras, which was now in the possession of the Armenian Grand Duke Leo, whom he also owed money. Leo wouldn't dream of giving up the fortress.

"If you want my advice, talk to the Preceptor of the Order, Brother Gilbert. He's an approachable man. I think he would appreciate your efforts."

Prince Bohemond nodded with pleasure and beckoned his men. "Forward! Enough d-d-dallying!"

He leaned toward Guillaume and grinned. "G-G-God be with you. You're always welc-welc-welcome in my c-c-c-court."

Guillaume bowed and mounted his horse. "God protect you and your spouse. Good luck with your endeavours and thank you for your kind invitation."

Two heavily loaded, ox-drawn wagons rumbled out of the forest into the clearing and the Count's entourage formed a train behind them.

Without looking back, Guillaume continued northeast and found the trade road that led through the mountains to Nazareth. The smell of Sibylle's lavender water was still in his nostrils and his member stiffened when he recalled their nights together. *What a crazy, lustful woman.*

Her comment about naming her son after him echoed in his head.

"The hell I'll go to Antioch. Far too dangerous. That whore will use me as a pawn and my head will end up impaled on the parapets of the Stammerer's citadel," he growled under his breath.

These thought made him uneasy. He much preferred picturing Leah's innocent face. Strangely, that made his cock even harder, so that it was now pressing, bony and painful, against the pommel of his saddle.

It's too long since I had a woman under or on me. I must explain to the Jew that I'm almost going out of my mind with longing for her. If not her, then no one.

Guillaume straightened up in his saddle, spurred his horse and trotted into the rolling foothills.

Hidden in the forest undergrowth, dark eyes watched him vigilantly.

XXXII

Reinhold the Lame sat on a large chopping block in his shady inner courtyard. At his feet stood a willow cage containing a dozen excited, clucking hens. He would soon slaughter them so that he could offer his guests roast fowl for their evening meal. Peering at his left hand, he cursed quietly and tried to find the splinter of wood driven under the skin when he rolled the heavy chopping block out of the stable. Fortunately, it was large enough for him to see with his cloudy eyes and pull out with his fingernails.

He sucked the drop of blood from the small wound, stood up and drew a hatchet from his belt. Then he heard someone hammering loudly at the gate.

New guests? I've done very well lately with overnight stays, he thought. It was late morning, a little too early for enquiries about lodgings. More likely the servant of the Venetian merchant Enzo, who was expected today with another delivery of Cyprian wine.

He swung the axe into the chopping block, hobbled slowly to the gates, lifted the heavy crossbar and opened them a little.

Outside stood a very tall Templar knight in full armour. His face was flushed and he quickly jammed his foot between the gates.

"God be with you, innkeeper," he muttered, rudely pushing past him into the courtyard. Reinhold bowed humbly, alarmed to see the Marshal of the Templars standing before him.

"God be with you too, good knight. It's an honour to greet such a high-ranking brother of the Templar Order in my house. How can I be of service?"

"You know me?" asked Raoul, walking past him into the courtyard. He saw the axe in the chopping block and wrenched it out.

"Of course. I saw you in the battle for Acre. I fought in the army of Duke Leopold of Osterland."

His eyes followed the axe, the head of which the Marshal was now examining with a professional air. Reinhold's throat tightened. He hoped the Templar knew nothing of his involvement in the attack on their fortress.

"Sharp, very sharp," said the knight appreciatively. "I expect you can behead chickens with that very swiftly and easily. Or cut off hands."

Reinhold looked at him, confused. "Why would I cut off hands with it?"

Raoul laughed quietly. "No, not you. I would do that... to men who lie to me, for example..."

Without warning, he raised the axe and struck it forcefully into the hard wood. The blade sank halfway in. He surveyed the courtyard.

"Our fortress was attacked yesterday by three horsemen, as I'm sure you've heard. I was informed that you procured horses and bridles for three of your guests. I wonder if there's a connection between that purchase and the attack. What kind of people were they?"

Reinhold looked into the Marshal's expressionless, reptilian eyes. *God in heaven, where did you hear that?* He had been so careful when procuring the horses. Maybe his wife Yeta had blabbed, or the verbose horse trader couldn't keep his mouth shut.

"By the Almighty, I heard about that calamity; a truly terrible turn of events. But I had nothing to do with it. I often procure things for long-distance travellers who don't know their way around the city – from new robes to camels and horses – a lucrative side business. I purchased two ancient nags for a Syrian and his wife in Acre on business, who wanted to return quickly to Jerusalem. They left yesterday. The third I bought for a Frankish pilgrim who paid me this morning before leaving the city."

"They must have been in a great hurry if they purchased costly horses instead of camels or mules."

"The hacks were old, but they paid well, so I didn't ask questions." Reinhold shrugged and scratched his head nervously.

Raoul sensed the innkeeper was keeping something from him and grew impatient. "But now *I'm* asking *you* questions, and things will go better for you if you answer me truthfully." His hand went to his sword and he slowly drew it halfway out of its sheath. "What was the pilgrim's name?"

Sweat broke out on Reinhold's brow. He stared at the Marshal's glinting weapon and hesitated.

"Speak! My patience is finite. Or do I need to cut it out of you with my blade? His name was Guillaume, wasn't it?" Raoul growled.

"Ah yes, that's what he called himself. But I don't know anything else about him," Reinhold stammered in surprise.

"You do know more. If you keep lying to me, I'll split you open from top to bottom like one of your hens. Where is he now?" Raoul drew his sword fully and aimed it at Reinhold's neck.

"Alright, I'll tell you everything! The pilgrim wanted to follow the Syrian and his wife to the Holy City. I don't know why. I heard him say to them he would stay one more night in Acre, to settle old debts. As I said, he set out for Jaffa this morning."

Raoul slid his sword back into its sheath. "That sounds like him," he muttered, scrutinising the frightened innkeeper. The supposed Syrians were probably Guillaume's accomplices in his attack on the fortress. When the three riders fled, he recognised Guillaume, but only saw the other two from behind. One of them could have been a woman.

Half a day's head start, but he has only one horse and will take at least two days to reach Jaffa if he doesn't want to ride it to death. The turcopoles and I can catch up to him with relay horses before he gets to the city.

There was no time to lose. He had heard enough, and the his hand-picked trackers had been waiting for him at the Templar fortress since dawn. He was right to follow up on Ruzan's tip and question her employer about the horses he bought for his guests, before chasing after Guillaume aimlessly. As for the nervous innkeeper, whom he was sure was mixed up in the attack, he would deal with him later.

Rivulets of sweat streamed down Reinhold's temples. Raoul looked him in the eye and said, "You should be more careful about whom you do favours for, or one day your greed will be the death of you. Today you got off lightly."

The Marshal strode to the gates and opened one of them, then turned back. "Don't stand in the way of the Temple ever again. I've committed your face to memory."

Reinhold nodded earnestly and bowed repeatedly as he closed the gate behind the knight. Then he leaned against it and breathed heavily.

He heard his wife scolding one of the maids, the hens clucking in their cage and his own rattling breath. The shock had penetrated so deep into his bones that he scarcely noticed the chronic pain in his leg.

The encounter with the terrifying Templar reminded him how fleeting life was. One could never be too careful. But he was also proud of himself for not confessing everything. The Marshal hadn't the slightest idea of the planning and preparations that had taken place in his inn prior to the attack on the fortress. And he seemed to know nothing about the knights Walter and Hartung.

Reinhold was determined to find out how the Templar knew he had purchased horses for his guests. He couldn't let it happen again. When it came to his lucrative secret deals, confidentiality was essential to his survival.

"Yeta! Yeta!" he shouted to his wife, as he hobbled across the yard toward the kitchen.

Meanwhile, Raoul hurried through the city to the Templar fortress, rubbing his unbearably itchy, scorched wrists. It had taken a long time to burn through his bonds with the oil lamp, and it was extremely painful. After he freed Ruzan, she smeared soothing pig fat on his burns and bandaged them with strips of cloth. But they would scar.

You'll pay for this, Guillaume! I'll burn the soles of your feet to charcoal. The new Grand Commander ordered me to bring you in alive. Like hell I will. You'll die a thousand deaths!

Thinking of Brother Gilbert dampened his spirits. He should have gone after Guillaume hours ago. It would be hard to explain his wounded wrists and the delay caused by Guillaume's surprise visit to Ruzan's room. He hoped to gather up the waiting turcopoles unseen by Gilbert and depart immediately for Jaffa.

He quickened his pace, ruthlessly shoving aside anyone who wasn't nimble enough to get out of his way.

His fear was unfounded. When the Marshal arrived at the fortress, Grand Commander Gilbert was already kneeling with most of the Templar brothers in the church at Sext, praying for the soul of Robert de Sablé and the other victims of the attack.

Raoul's select group of mercenaries sat bored behind the gatehouse with their horses, flipping copper coins. When he appeared, they rose to their feet with disgruntled faces.

"You said yesterday we should be ready to leave at daybreak. Now it's midday," grumbled Silenus, a heavyset, bull-necked Greek with dark, greasy locks that hung in his face. The others nodded.

Disrespectful vulture. Unfortunately, I need you, or I'd break your nose with my fist for your insolence!

Raoul eyed the warriors with contempt. The wiry Armenian Ruben – whom everyone called 'the Eye' because he never missed a target with his bow and arrow even at full gallop – stood idly beside a pair of full-bearded, Syrian twins. Johannes and Jacobus had converted to Christianity under Richard the Lionheart and fought in his army as scouts before joining the Templar light cavalry. The spokesman of the small troop, the muscular Silenus, had served the Order for years as a tracker and a translator.

Raoul had asked each of them the previous evening whether they were prepared to hunt down their former commander Guillaume for an additional three months' wages. They all agreed without hesitation. They weren't part of Nicholas' unsuccessful search party. However, word had spread quickly amongst the turcopoles of how rich the spoils of that raid were. Pursuing the former turcopolier seemed worthwhile, especially as it was rumoured that he was involved in the attack on their fortress.

"You obey my orders, even if it means waiting until vespers! It's none of your concern, is that clear?" Raoul asked sharply. "We set out now. We'll each take an additional relay horse from the pasture outside the city. We must be fast, or the target will escape us."

"No target on two legs has ever escaped me, even on horse-back," Ruben the Eye remarked confidently.

"Maybe, but Guillaume has half a day's head start. He's on his way to Jaffa and means to ride from there to Jerusalem. In your saddles!" Raoul commanded.

"That won't be a problem, Marshal. We're faster than the turcopolier, you can count on us," said Silenus, signalling his men to mount their horses.

Catching up to him probably won't be a problem. But some of you will have to pay for it with your lives. Guillaume will fight back like a cornered rat, Raoul thought grimly as he climbed into his saddle and spurred his steed.

XXXIII

"Jerusalem," breathed Hartung, full of awe. He shaded his eyes with his hand and gazed out over the Holy City sprawled across a mountain saddle in the morning light. They stood holding their snorting horses by the reins on a mountain Harit called *Scopus,* to the east of the city.

"Yes, Jerusalem," Walter echoed. "I pictured it differently. Golden rooftops with towers and walls of ivory, full of wondrous sites. But it's scarcely bigger than Acre, much uglier, and the fortifications seem rather weak by comparison."

Hartung dropped to his knees. After three years of energy-sapping privation and heavy losses in battle, he finally felt he had arrived in the Holy Land. He could see the dome of the Church of the Holy Sepulchre, the place where Jesus was resurrected after the crucifixion, and where he himself would find forgiveness for his many sins.

Walter eyed the city doubtfully. The holiest city of Christendom, for which thousands of pilgrims and Saracens had given their lives, appeared to harbour vast numbers of heathens. He watched hundreds of them surge through the gates and bustle along the convoluted alleys. All the city's towers flew green banners with golden crescent moons. A troop of almost two hundred white-clad horsemen armed with shields and spears trotted north along the ancient pilgrim road toward Jaffa. A grey dust cloud billowed behind them, merging with the haze that hung over the city.

Harit broke the silence. "You need to be careful," he said. "Pilgrims are only allowed into the city unarmed, and are checked thoroughly. I advise you to hide your weapons here under these bushes, and retrieve them later."

Hartung nodded, but Walter shook his head. "I'm not going into a city full of infidels without my sword!"

"You must, otherwise you'll be siezed at the gate. Your swords will betray your nobility, and high-born Nazarenes bring in high ransoms. Or you'll be enslaved. In the worst case, you'll be beheaded in the market by an executioner's sword," Harit said in an imploring tone. "There's something else you should know. It's true that Nazarenes are now allowed to visit their holy places in the city, but few Muslims will be friendly toward you. Except perhaps the relic vendors and innkeepers. They might..." he faltered.

"Might what?" Hartung probed.

"Well, they might jeer at you, throw stones and dirt, strike you or even spit on you. There's little tolerance for Nazarenes since the Sultan retook the city from the infidels. You must be prepared for that."

The two knights drew themselves up into a proud, overbearing posture, their eyes glinting dangerously.

"Are you out of your mind! I'm a Knight of Christ! A pilgrim blessed by God incarnate. I don't allow myself to beaten or spat on by heathens!" Hartung's temples pulsated and the veins in his neck swelled and throbbed.

Harit saw this and bowed deeply. He summoned his courage and said, "By Allah the Merciful! My lord, I owe you my life. Let me now protect yours. I know you're a strong, fearless warrior. But you'll die if you don't heed my advice. You must enter Jerusalem dressed as pilgrims with your heads bowed!"

The knight inhaled deeply through flared nostrils. He reluctantly admitted to himself that the little Arab was probably right. Hartung glanced at Walter, who nodded slowly.

"We're almost at our destination, my friend. It will be humiliating, but we've endured worse."

Harit was relieved. He pulled out two tattered robes and shawls that he'd found in the Bedouin bandits' tent and had the foresight to bring with him. The knights grumbled as they changed their clothes to resemble impoverished pilgrims. They wrapped their swords and armour in felt blankets, and Harit hid them under a dense tamarisk thicket.

To complete their disguise, they cut two long staffs from fallen branches. But the warriors wouldn't part with their daggers. They refused to enter a city full of heathens completely unarmed.

Harit warned the proud warriors apprehensively that it was inadvisable to ride on horseback and that they would have to enter the Holy City on foot, as was customary for pilgrims.

"Oh Lord, what other tests do you have in store for us before we're finally allowed to pray at your tomb!" Hartung moaned. Walter smirked.

They chose two strong horses and two mules and loaded them with the treasure, some provisions and their tent. The animals they had taken from the Bedouins' camp were set free. The scrawny nag immediately ran off, and the two donkeys trotted after it. But the mule that had carried the holy relic all the way from Acre had blood trickling from its nostrils and putrid faeces dripping down its hind legs. It staggered away slowly. Leah watched it go, with pity and concern.

What if the Lord's Commandments really do bring death, as it says in the scriptures? The other animals are fine, she thought.

Harit noticed her worried expression.

"It probably has worms. Or ate a poisonous plant. If Allah wills it, it'll survive. We couldn't have taken it with us in that condition anyway."

"They all had the same food and water. Strange, isn't it?" said Leah.

"Perhaps a nasty insect or snake bite... forget it."

He placed a reassuring hand on her shoulder, then shuffled over to the waiting knights, who were once again gazing across at the city.

Leah tied the few saddlebag to one of the remaining mules, keeping a respectful distance from the already loaded relics, and looked at the knights. She hadn't understood the conversation, but she couldn't help smiling to herself at the way Harit fussed over the loudly protesting warriors, straightening their clothes.

Earlier, when they reached Mount Scopus, she had felt almost sapped of strength. Battered, exhausted and dirty from the strenuous journey, she was disgusted to smell her own sweat clinging to her dusty clothes, and she was worn down by the constant pain in her thighs, rubbed raw from riding.

But seeing Jerusalem from this vantage point made her forget her cares. It put her in a strangely elated and fearless mood. They were at the end of their long journey, she was unharmed, and she was bringing the treasure of her people back home. She never thought all this would be possible, and yet it had happened. Joy welled up in her at the thought of seeing her uncle again.

A miracle, a truly unbelievable miracle. Please, Lord God, grant me one last wish. Let Guillaume come back to me in good health!

She flinched when Harit called out to her, "It's time to go! Get in your saddle. I'll ride ahead, you behind me, and the two..." the Muslim smirked, "...pilgrims will follow us on foot with the mules. If it is Allah's will, we'll soon be at your uncle's house. We'll go through the eastern Josaphat gate, the fastest route to your house."

Leah nodded. Her heart hammered in her chest – whether at the excitement of returning home or her thoughts of the Templar, she couldn't say.

The little group set off. They cautiously picked their way down into the valley where the Kidron River, still knee-deep with the winter's rainfall, snaked around the rocky base of the Temple Mount.

They saw a colourful swarm of people in front of the Josaphat gate. It was early morning and the heavy gates had only been open for half an hour. The city, with its many markets, was just waking up.

Streaming toward this bottleneck were traders with ox-drawn wagons, peasants with baskets of field crops on their backs, a caravan of two dozen heavily loaded camels, and countless day labourers from the surrounding area, with tools over their shoulders.

A wagon heavily loaded with cedar beams stood to the right of the gate with a broken wheel, obstructing free passage. The wagon driver shouted instructions to his three companions, who levered up the wagon with a long wooden plank so that one of them could attach the spare wheel. The endeavour failed, the plank snapped with a loud crack and the wagon crashed onto the road again. A large cloud of dust enveloped the waiting crowd of people, who berated the poor driver in a cacophony of outrage.

Harit and Leah dismounted, took their horses by the reins and squeezed past the broken-down wagon with the other shouting and gesticulating arrivals.

The five guards with pointed helmets and spears had long since abandoned the inspections. The crowd pressed them against the sides of the gateway and flooded into the waiting city. The small group around Harit didn't attract any attention. They allowed themselves to be carried along in the throng, which dispersed into small groups and individuals about thirty paces from the gate.

"By the beard of the prophet," sighed Harit, wiping the irritating dust from his streaming eyes. "We were very lucky. It's market day, so the whole city and the surrounding region is out and about today. Everyone wants to buy or sell something. What about you, Sir Hartung?"

Hartung was staring incredulously at his surroundings and Harit tugged at his robe. The warrior's gaze swept back and forth across the square with several alleys branching off it. He marvelled at the chaotic, tightly packed, squalid-looking houses of brown loam and pale limestone. Some had once been whitewashed and now looked as if the paint was all that was holding them together.

"It's alright. Take us to the Jew's house," Hartung replied peevishly.

Like Walter, he had expected the Holy City to look quite different. It had been described to him as vibrant, magnificent, the centre of the world; surrounded by rich greenery, colourful fruit gardens and crystal-clear streams; full of marvellous holy sites and places of significance. He saw none of that here.

"We need to turn right up there. That's the way to the Jewish quarter. We're close," said Harit, leading the way.

Walter's attention was on the people in the streets. He saw no weapons, and hoped it would remain so. He had still clutched his dagger tightly as he went through the gate. When he pushed past the guards, his heart leapt into his mouth, but they didn't give him even a passing glance in the jostling crowd.

Relieved, he followed Harit and Hartung, with Leah running ahead excitedly.

They reached Rabbi Ishmael's two-storey house and Leah knocked repeatedly on the door until it creaked open and a dark brown, creased face with thin, white hair nervously peered out.

"Uncle, it's me, Leah!"

Ishmael raised his eyebrows and his eyes lit up. The door swung open and Leah fell into his outstretched arms.

"Thank the Almighty! You're back!" he cried, embracing her tightly.

Tears of joy streamed down Leah's cheeks. She stepped back and looked with concern into his emaciated face. "Uncle, what's wrong with you? You look so thin and your hair is... it's so... light. How's your leg? Is it healing?"

"Come in, come in! My leg is fine. If only that was the worst of my woes... I'll explain later," he replied, pulling her through the door by her sleeve.

Walter appeared behind her. Ishmael was initially shocked, then he bowed deeply when he recognised the man.

"Lord in heaven, it's you! Sir Walter! How happy I am to see you again. Shalom, come in!"

"God be with you, Ishmael. It's a long time since we parted ways outside Acre. I never thought I'd see you again." Walter stepped aside and Hartung's tall frame filled the doorway.

"Sir Hartung! I can't believe it! You're here too! Please, step inside my humble home!"

Ishmael bowed deeply several times, then lost his balance and fell forward. Walter quickly stepped up and caught him before he hit the ground. He was as light as a feather and as scrawny as a chicken. Ishmael glanced gratefully at him and explained in a frail voice, "I... I'm a little weakened... forgive me..."

"It's alright," said Walter, standing him on his feet like a doll and keeping a hand on his arm to steady him.

"Don't fall out of your sandals with joy!" Harit crowed happily in Arabic, pushing past Hartung. "It's enough if you give my men some water and bread. We've travelled a long way!"

Hartung and Walter looked quizzically at the little Muslim.

303

"He said I should give you something to eat and drink," Ishmael translated, then he wagged a finger at Harit and said jokingly, "Be glad the knights don't understand your language – your men! A warm welcome to you too!"

Harit was still chuckling when Leah asked him to lead the animals through the side door into the little inner courtyard and help her unload the baggage and the relics. She couldn't wait to see her uncle's face when he realised she'd actually succeeded in bringing everything back.

Ishmael invited the knights to sit amongst the mounds of colourful cushions on the carpet in the centre of the room, then he limped slowly to the pantry to fetch wine and water.

He was trembling from head to toe – whether for joy at his niece's return or for fear she may have actually brought back the artefacts, he wasn't sure. A few days ago, he had discovered the real reason for his wretched state and constant bouts of diarrhoea and vomiting. It was all to do with the holy relics.

Hartung and Walter made themselves comfortable and glanced around the room. It was the first time they had been in a Jew's house. The ceilings were low, supported by heavy, half-round beams. The plain, whitewashed walls made the large room seem even more spacious. Through a small, round window, the morning sun shone on the compacted dirt floor and filled the room with warm light. The heavy, reddish-brown carpet they were sitting on seemed to be the only thing of value in the otherwise sparsely furnished room.

"I thought goldsmiths were rich. I'm starting to doubt we'll actually receive our reward," grumbled Hartung, gazing around the room again. "And it smells like rancid vomit in here. Looks pretty haggard, the Jew. I hope he's not sick, he might infect us."

Walter dismissed the sentiment with a wave of his hand.

"Always the pessimist. What did you expect? A palace? Remember when Ishmael and ten dozen of his brethren joined our pilgrimage from Saxony to the Holy Land? What a bunch of worn and tattered strays they were, and yet they covered more than half our army's expenses, only so that we would take them with us and protect them. They don't like to show their wealth. Don't worry, he'll pay us. He promised us seven hundred gold dinars for the holy relics."

They were speaking loudly and Ishmael could hear every word from the adjacent pantry. He nodded sadly to himself, picked up a corked wine jug and hobbled back into the living room.

"Here, my esteemed gentlemen. Sweet red wine from the mountains of Galilee. Please drink, I must go to my niece in the garden."

Walter uncorked the jug with the tip of his dagger, put it to his lips and drank greedily before passing it to the thirsty Hartung. Ishmael smiled with pleasure at the huge warrior's satisfied belch, then bowed and went out into the little courtyard where Harit and Leah were still unloading the animals.

"Harit, please be so kind... in the pantry you'll find bread, smoked fish and olives. Take food to my guests and fortify yourself too. I need a moment alone with Leah," he said haltingly.

The Arab understood immediately that the goldsmith wanted to see the relic. He pointed at the saddlebag containing the treasure still tied one of the mules, and left the two of them alone.

Leah went to lift down the bag, but Ishmael said with uncharacteristic sharpness, "Don't touch it, Leah! Ever!"

She was startled and took two steps back. Ishmael heaved the sack off the animal's back and laid it on the sandy ground. He opened it with fluttering hands.

Two tablets and both cherubim. The Ark of the Covenant has returned! He knelt down and tears welled up in his eyes.

"What good fortune. What misfortune," he murmured, rubbing his face with both hands.

Leah stood behind him, a little disappointed. She tapped him on the shoulder. "What's wrong, uncle? We brought it back! We did it! Everything will be alright now, won't it?"

"Please, child, step back a little. I need to explain something to you. Sit down on the bench."

She reluctantly obeyed. Ishmael hastily closed the sack over the relics, struggled to his feet, shuffled over to the bench and flopped down beside her.

"It's incredible that you and Harit managed to find Walter and Hartung and retrieve these things from the fearsome Templars. I'm so grateful to you... I... can't find the words. I'm sure you have much to tell and I'm excited to hear of your experiences. But first listen to me. These objects bring death. Especially the tablets. They're made of some unknown ore that causes degeneration. After you departed, I fell terribly ill for three days. I had dreadful diarrhoea and couldn't keep down any food or drink. I felt constantly hot and nauseated. Then suddenly I felt better. As if by magic, I seemed to have recovered. But then, inexplicably, my hair started falling out in clumps. I can pull it out without pain."

To demonstrate, he slowly pulled a strand out of his thinning goatee and held it up to Leah's incredulous eyes.

"I've been feeling unwell again for the last two days. My belly feels like a pit of churning stones, and I'm light-headed and continually have to vomit. Death is creeping up on me! There is a curse on the tablets, and now I carry it in me. The renowned physician, Maimonides, confirmed this and explained the root of my illness."

Leah looked up in astonishment. "Moses ben Maimon? He was here in our house? What... what did he say? ...You must be mistaken! You can't be dying!"

Ishmael nodded sadly and took his niece's hand in his.

"Yes, he's in the city. As you know, in a few days we celebrate Passover to commemorate the exodus of our ancestors from Egypt. Maimonides takes this opportunity every spring to visit his relatives in Jerusalem, and this time he wanted to speak to the new rabbi of the local congregation. So he came to me personally. Because he is one of the wisest men among our people, I told him about the contents of the Ark of the Covenant. He thinks the objects are forgeries, even after I described them to him in detail. He's convinced the Ark was destroyed thousands of years ago by the Babylonians. He has ancient scriptures in his possession that he says prove this. During our conversation, I had to throw up several times. He examined my body and discovered that I was suffering from a rare disease he had heard of, which sometimes affects miners. It's occasionally seen deep in the south of Nubia, where the black people dig for gold, silver and copper in the mountains, and pile up worthless rock in huge, dusty heaps. Some of the workers become terribly ill and feverish – presumably from inhaling the dust. Then they feel better for a few days and seem healthy, but they soon fall ill again. They suffer from diarrhoea and their skin flakes and festers with pus. Toward the end, their hair falls out, and death catches up with them soon after. I know I only have a few days left in this world, because there's no cure. Maimonides believes the fake tablets contain these dangerous ore residues, and that I was too close to them when I was working on them. I probably breathed in the deadly dust."

He sighed deeply and squeezed Leah's hand. She shook her head in denial. She didn't want to believe it, and desperately sought another explanation.

"What's this about deadly rock dust? The tablets are made of metal, aren't they?"

"The cursed stone residue must have been melted and cast in this form so that it looks like metal." Ishmael shrugged weakly.

Leah wasn't convinced.

"But why would anyone cast the Lord's Commandments in such a deadly substance?"

"Maimonides and I thought long and hard about that. The loss of the Ark of the Covenant in the distant past must have deeply unsettled our people. Our ancestors probably created a faithful copy, and used this dreadful stone to mimic the deadly effect described in the Book of Moses," Ishmael surmised.

"Nonsense. You're not dying, you just ate something bad," whispered Leah hoarsely. But, looking at the clump of hair in her uncle's hand, she knew what she was saying made no sense. Her head spun. Moments ago, she had been overjoyed, and now the world seemed to be crumbling around her.

"You... you can't leave me alone..." she rasped, tears streaming down her cheeks. The cursed relic brought nothing but misery – as she had suspected from the moment she saw her uncle lying helpless on the floor with a broken leg after Guillaume's attack. Now she had certainty. She sobbed uncontrollably.

Ishmael took her in his arms and squeezed her as hard as he was able.

"Don't be afraid, Leah. When you were away, I made preparations. There's enough money here that you'll never want for anything for the rest of your life. Maimonides promised to take you into his household in Cairo as your new guardian. You'll do well there, much better than here. But I'm not dead yet, and today I feel good. We have guests and... and they're waiting for their reward, which of course I'll pay them despite everything."

They sat huddled together in silence for a while. Finally, Ishmael let go of her and stood up. Leah swallowed hard, dried her tears with her wide sleeve and looked at him with red eyes.

"Will we all die? Harit and the knights too?" *And the Templar?*

"No, I'm sure you won't. If you haven't had an upset stomach yet, you shouldn't worry. That was the first sign of the illness. But keep your distance from this... unholy stuff."

"I will, absolutely. But how can I help you?"

Ishmael smiled. "If you want to help me, prepare food and beds for the men."

Leah irritably waved away his suggestion. "No, no, that's not what I meant!"

"I know." Ishmael sighed and kissed her forehead. "Even in the most difficult moments of our life, we must praise God. Everything is at his mercy, and this is his will. Trust in God, and all will be well. Come, let's go inside – and not a word to Harit or the knights. I don't want to worry them. After we eat, my child, you can all tell me about your journey."

XXXIV

Marshal Raoul and the five turcopoles allowed themselves and their horses no rest in pursuit of Guillaume, except to stop and ask farmers, merchants and pilgrims along the coastal road if they had seen a tall man with blue eyes, riding alone in haste toward Jaffa. But no one had seen such a man.

By early evening, they reached the small Templar fortress Le Destroit, which overlooked the road to Jaffa from a rocky elevation about a mile inland. The fortress consisted of a two-level, thirty-foot-high defensive tower, and three outbuildings partly cut into the hill, surrounded by a square stone wall. Six Templar knights and a dozen sergeants served there. On the horizon to the left of the fortress rose the dark Carmel mountain range, and to the right, the sea shone a deep blue in the light of the setting sun.

Twenty miles in half a day and no sign of Guillaume, Raoul thought morosely.

His troop dismounted inside the fortress walls and were immediately received by three brothers in black smocks. Raoul dismounted his own sweat-soaked horse and threw the reins to a sergeant who had hurried to his aid. His back was in agony and his legs felt as if they were filled with lead.

The turcopoles didn't seem bothered by the long ride. They calmly walked their horses to the stables and unsaddled them. Two servants took care of the feeding, watering and grooming while the newcomers followed one of the brothers who invited them to dine in the slanting, thatched, wooden building that served as the kitchen and refectory.

Raoul was greeted by the fortress commander, Brother Eric. The short, burly Templar had fought for King Richard at Acre and joined the Order after the city was conquered. The young

Norman became commander of the little fortress after only five months, and took this role very seriously.

His angular, bearded face brightened when he saw the man stretching his back and rotating his arms in the courtyard.

"God be with you, Brother Raoul! It's an honour to receive such an esteemed guest. What brings the Marshal of our brotherhood here? With no squires or banners?"

He bowed. But Raoul turned first to the sergeant holding his horse's reins. "Leave us and go and make preparations for our mounts to be saddled and ready at first light."

The boy nodded obsequiously and left. Raoul rubbed his itching wrists and scrutinised the commander.

"God be with you too. I'm in a hurry, Brother Eric, and I don't have time for explanations. We'll only take advantage of your hospitality tonight, as we're in pursuit of a wicked criminal and traitor on his way to Jaffa. You know him, Guillaume de Born. Have you seen or heard word of him lately?"

"Guillaume? A traitor? You must be mistaken, Brother Marshal, I just can't imagine it. What crime is he supposed to have committed?" Eric asked with a frown.

Guillaume had taught him the rules of the Order when he first joined the brotherhood, and later strapped his Templar sword to him during his induction ceremony. He considered Guillaume one of the most faithful, upright men in the Order.

Raoul's face darkened for a moment, then his mouth twisted into a cold smile.

"I can't tell you that. It must remain secret for now. He's fleeing his just punishment. But I assure you, I'm as shocked as you are by his nefarious betrayal. His trespasses are serious – so monstrous that *I* was sent out to bring him in."

He refrained from mentioning the death of Grand Master de Sablé, as the news would cause great upset and prompt further awkward questions.

"Speak, have you or any of your men seen him? Was he here? He's riding alone, or possibly with a Syrian and his alleged wife toward Jaffa."

Baffled, Eric shook his large, shaven head.

"With a Syrian? An infidel? What the devil has he done? No, he wasn't here, and he won't make it to Jaffa. The coastal road has been blocked for the last two days. A thieving Bedouin tribe with almost two hundred horsemen have besieged the port city of Caesarea, between here and Jaffa. We were informed by merchants who were lucky to escape their swords. So I quickly sent out scouts, who confirmed it. I believe they're acting on behalf of the damned Sultan. The city will most likely withstand the siege; its walls are thick and the garrison there is made up of experienced fighters. But the heathens are roaming the entire length of the road, greedy for spoils. You'd have to be invisible to get past them."

"So Guillaume would have no chance of reaching Jaffa and be forced to turn back?" asked Raoul.

"That's right. Or he's already fallen into their hands. Why would he be in the company of a Syrian and...?"

The Marshal cut him off with an angry gesture. "I already told you, I can't talk about it. Stop asking questions! That's an order! Go and inform your guards and scouts to keep a lookout for Guillaume and capture him immediately if they see him. He's disguised as a pilgrim. I want him alive. Have beds prepared for my men and I, and prepare fresh victuals and water for us. We'll depart first thing tomorrow. Now I need to eat. Show me the way!"

The commander was dismayed by Raoul's sharp, overbearing tone. He hadn't known the normally amiable, well-liked Marshal to behave in this way. He bit his tongue to stop himself asking which direction Raoul intended to ride the next morning, in light of the fact that the road to Jaffa was teeming with heathens. Striding stiffly ahead of the Marshal, he led the way to the refectory.

Two wooden tables stood between roughly hewn benches in a low-ceilinged room dimly lit by two oil lamps. Four resident knights sat at the table on the left, and on the right were the serving brothers, who shared their table that evening with the turcopoles.

As Raoul entered with the commander, the brothers of the local fortress stood and bowed. The Marshal greeting them with a nod and sat at the knights' table, and they all resumed their seats. Two sergeants served him bread, meat and wine. He ate in silence, grimacing at the intense pain in his inflamed gums, which plagued him so often of late.

After he had finished his meal and the heavy, undiluted red wine gurgled in his belly, Raoul relaxed. He belched loudly, got to his feet and went to join his men, without even a glance at Brother Eric. With an imperious jerk of his head, he banished the seated servants, who quickly picked up their cups and bowls and left the room.

He sat down amongst the turcopoles, explained the situation on the road to Jaffa and scanned their perplexed faces.

"Two hundred Bedouins or more... We must abandon our search," said Ruben the Eye, brushing bread crumbs from his stained jerkin. "Or wait until they withdraw. That may be soon if there isn't much to plunder or if they're met with harsh countermeasures. Then they often show themselves to be cowards and vanish."

"He's right, Brother Marshal," advised Silenus the Greek. "We're better off waiting. Guillaume isn't suicidal. He wouldn't pit himself against such numbers. He's probably already on his way back and will walk straight into our arms of his own accord."

Raoul picked up a wine goblet, took a long draught and gazed thoughtfully at his bandaged wrists.

"No, I believe Guillaume is on his way to Jerusalem. He knows the place and is safe there from the Order's retribution. He knows he's being pursued and would never turn back. He will have taken some other route after discovering the pilgrim road was blocked. I wonder if he even..."

"...took the coastal road in the first place, rather than riding into the Samarian mountains from Acre," Ruben finished for him. "Via Nazareth and Nablus to the Holy City. Many years ago, I used to hire myself out as a guide to a spice trader from Bethlehem who delivered wares to Acre, and I know that route well. A difficult journey, slow going. High mountains, deep valleys, not much water and a lot of dust."

I'm a damned fool, Raoul thought. *The lame innkeeper lied to me, or Guillaume misled him as to where he was going.*

No sensible Christian would choose the route through unsafe Saracen territory. But Guillaume couldn't afford to be sensible. He was a fugitive, and few would dare follow him on that dangerous path.

"How far could he have got? After a day's journey with only one horse?" Raoul asked the men.

Ruben leaned back and thought for a moment with his eyes closed.

"He should have reached Nazareth this evening. In another day, he'll be in Jenin with its many springs, at the foot of the Mountains of Gilboa. I was born and raised there. From there it's a day's ride to Nablus."

"Could we cut him off before he reaches Jerusalem?"

"From here? Let me see... East over the Carmel mountains to the Megiddo plains, then southeast to the road to Jerusalem, which runs from Nablus through the mountains. That would take two days, I think, but we should be able to intercept him well before the city," answered the turcopole.

"Slow down," growled Silenus. "Marshal, we agreed to hunt the man through Christian lands. But the mountains of Samaria have been heathen territory since the Battle of Hattin. It's bordering on suicide to pursue him there."

The other men nodded in agreement.

"Two hundred deniers for each of you, whether we find him or not." Raoul made his offer without hesitation, counting on his warriors' lust for money. The sum was equal to half a year's wages for each of them.

"By God, Brother Raoul, that's very decent of you. Let's call it three hundred, and we'll ride to hell for you!" Silenus looked at the Templar expectantly.

"Done. You'll have it. You have my word as Marshal."

It wasn't about the money for Raoul. Without Guillaume in hand, his days as a high-ranking Templar commander were numbered. He vividly pictured the punishment he would receive from the Grand Commander for his failure. Guillaume could resurface at some point and accuse him of grave transgressions in order to vindicate himself. For many years, Raoul had secretly hoarded silver coins for emergencies, hiding them under the floorboards in his lover Ruzan's squalid quarters. For emergencies such as this.

The turcopoles didn't disguise their pleasure at this unexpected pay increase. They toasted one another, grinning, and Silenus elbowed the man beside him – the twin Johannes.

Only Ruben the Eye had misgivings. "Unfortunately, I don't know the route through the Carmel mountains to Megiddo. We need a guide to take us that far."

"Alright. I'll ask the fortress commander."

Raoul rose and went back to join Brother Eric, who sat at the head of the other table with his knights, slowly chewing a piece of mutton spiced with expensive pepper and cinnamon. He nodded when Raoul asked about a local guide, and commanded one of his brothers to lead the Marshal and his people through the mountains the following morning.

The commander asked no further questions – neither about Guillaume nor the reason for the change of direction. Brother Eric was glad he only had to spare one man from his small garrison. He was very eager to see the tense and unfriendly Marshal swiftly on his way.

Once everything was arranged, Raoul ordered his men to retire for the night and had Brother Eric lead him to a little room in the fortress tower, where a simple bed had been made up for him.

Despite the day's exertion, Raoul scarcely slept on that moonlit night. He tossed and turned on his bed, his thoughts revolving around Guillaume and his bloody attack on the Templar fortress, his own murder of Nicholas, and de Sablé's beheading by the Assassins.

All these men dead for the sake of a horny barmaid who's fucked me out of my right mind. When I find you, Guillaume, you'll be the next to die. Otherwise all efforts to protect my secret were in vain.

It suddenly became clear to him that Guillaume was not his only problem – Ruzan was too. He had fully confided in her; she knew everything about him – far more than his former friend. In fact, she presented the greater danger, especially as she constantly lured him back onto the path of vice, which in the end had brought him to the edge of this abyss. His flesh wasn't weak. She was a sinful temptress and the root of all evil.

He held his breath momentarily and glanced at his sword lying beside him, its pommel gleaming silver in the pale moonlight that slanted through the open window. He exhaled loudly and was disgusted to smell the foul breath emanating from his diseased gums.

Ruzan will go to hell right after Guillaume, I'll make sure of it. Then a new life will begin for me. Oh yes, Almighty God, I swear, from that day on, I'll obey all of your Commandments and those of my Order to the letter.

XXXV

Walter, Hartung and Harit looked up expectantly at the pallid, emaciated goldsmith when he returned from the garden.

"Well, did you verify our success?" Walter asked impatiently. "Did we bring back what the Templar stole from you?"

Ishmael bowed his head in affirmation. "I didn't dare hope that my bold plan would bear fruit. My heart overflows with gratitude, and now you must tell me how you achieved this miracle."

He sank to his knees with a grunt and touched his forehead to the floor.

"God in heaven," said Walter with a sigh. "Another person falling to their knees in front of us. This is getting tedious. Get up and let's discuss the reward for our efforts."

"Exactly," Harit concurred. "By Allah the Almighty, I have to agree with the knight. The journey was immensely difficult and we survived extraordinary dangers. You'll never guess whom Leah and I met in the mountains soon after we departed. The Templar! His name is..."

"Be quiet!" Walter interrupted impatiently. "You can tell him about that later. Look, Ishmael, you have what you wanted. Now give us what you owe us. You promised us seven hundred gold dinar. That's what your niece told us."

The goldsmith sat down and pointed at a colourfully embroidered bolster cushion on which Hartung was resting his right arm.

"The gold is in that. Take it, you've earned it!"

Hartung looked at him in astonishment and lifted his arm.

"So that's why this thing is as hard as wood. I was wondering."

He quickly tore open a seam with his rough hands. Seven bulging leather pouches fell out of the cushion. Walter grabbed one, opened it and let a few gold coins run through his fingers.

"There are a hundred dinar in each pouch. Leah has already given you three hundred. This brings it to a thousand coins, as agreed," said Ishmael, fighting the urge to retch.

Walter felt around behind him surreptitiously, in the hope that he was sitting on more cushions full of gold, but all he could feel in them was soft down.

"That's too little," he said, frowning. "From the money your niece gave us, we had to pay for accommodation, equipment, horses and food. Add another hundred and we'll be satisfied."

Ishmael felt the bile burning his throat and swallowed hard, but this didn't impair his mental arithmetic. For that sum, one could buy fourteen pounds of the most expensive pearls, or two artisan's houses like his own. He doubted Walter had spent that much on expenses.

"I'll add two dozen dinar, that's all I can manage. I still have to pay Harit."

The Arab nodded vigorously. "Yes indeed, a thousand silver dirham. That's what we agreed if I brought Leah and the treasure back to you."

"That corresponds to three, almost four gold dinar," said Ishmael, reaching into his robe and bringing out a small money pouch.

"I'll give you four coins. Thank you, Harit, for everything."

He counted the gold pieces into the Muslim's open hand. Harit suddenly felt hot. He had never had this much money to call his own. It was pitiful compared to the monstrous sum the knights received, but he didn't mind. With this money, he could finally start a new life. He could already see himself in his own house, surrounded by stacks of sugar sacks waiting to be transported to Jaffa, Acre or even Cairo, which would then bring him considerable profits overseas – possibly in Venice or Genoa. Then, perhaps he would even have chests full of spices such as cloves, cinnamon, or even saffron. He wanted to be a merchant, just as his father would have wished.

"Alright. Add two dozen gold dinar and we have a deal," said Walter. "What do you think, Hartung?"

"Fine by me. I'll leave the business of money to you, you understand it better," replied the knight, drinking a deep draught of wine.

Ishmael's face turned dark grey. "Please forgive me... I must leave you for a moment."

The goldsmith clapped a hand over his mouth, stood up as fast as his splinted leg would allow, and hobbled to the outhouse in the garden.

Leah was still watering the animals. She watched with concern as he disappeared into the wooden shack beside the stable. Then she heard loud retching sounds and a rasping cough.

I wish those tablets had never entered this house, she thought, more tears welling up in her eyes. She looked with foreboding at the fake relics inside the saddlebag that lay in a dusty corner of the courtyard.

A little later, she prepared a midday meal for the men. Ishmael was feeling better and sat once more with the knights and Harit, who described in detail how they rescued the treasure. Harit loquaciously recounted the astonishing of events after he and Leah rescued the thieving Templar in the desert, and he assisted them in retrieving the relics from the Templar fortress.

Ishmael could scarcely believe it. A Christian Templar knight going against his brotherhood to help a Jew he had recently attacked and robbed.

The unholy treasure truly seemed to bring about wondrous and terrible things.

When Guillaume's name came up, Leah flinched and blushed. The men were speaking Frankish, and as she understood almost nothing, she didn't contribute to the narrative. She was flooded with blissful memories of Guillaume and hoped he would return to her in good health. She stole a glance at her uncle, who looked pale and strained as he tried to listen attentively to the travellers' account.

To see Guillaume just one more time... before I have to leave Jerusalem forever.

Hartung also contributed little to the conversation. He was preoccupied with thoughts of the Holy City. He never believed he would see it. He had been told one could physically feel God's grace within its walls. Now he was sitting in a Jew's house with bags of gold in front of him, and he had no sense of divinity.

He listlessly chewed a piece of millet bread to pulp. Walter, on the other hand, seemed quite relaxed. He cheerfully embellished Harit's account of their journey, and the more sweet, rich wine he drank, the more lascivious his glances at the pretty Leah. Fortunately, she was too distracted to notice, but Hartung wasn't. He elbowed Walter roughly in the ribs, leaned in and whispered in his ear, "Pull yourself together. We didn't come all this way for that."

Walter was taken aback and plastered on a smile, which looked more like a grimace. He didn't really want the Jewish woman, but now – watching her nimbly and lithely caring for their physical wellbeing, her robe stretching across her buttocks as she placed the food on the floor – he was reminded that there was more to life than food and money.

Embarrassed at being caught out, he quickly rounded out Harit's narrative with the fact that the former Templar had promised to follow them to Jerusalem a day later.

Ishmael looked up in fright. "He... he means to come here? To my house?"

"He probably will. He said he wanted to atone for his crime and ask your forgiveness," Harit confirmed. "Don't be afraid, he was sincere, wasn't he, Leah?"

He translated and Leah nodded. "Yes, Harit speaks the truth. The man has changed. He'll never do anything like that again, I know it."

"What... Why would a Templar want forgiveness from a Jew?"

Ishmael was unconvinced. He pictured the robber's piercing blue eyes, cold and dispassionate. It had been a close scrape with death.

"He's a Nazarene, who sincerely regrets all of his sins and wants to beg for forgiveness at the tomb of their saviour. The list of his terrible crimes is long, by Allah! He told us about all of them, and I still shudder to think about it," said Harit, shaking his head. "But he was very grateful to us for saving his life and he always treated Leah like a high-ranking lady. He'll be good to you too. You don't need to be afraid anymore, trust me."

Ishmael sighed. Unfortunately, he knew the gratitude of Christians only too well. You could buy it with money, but not with words. He felt ill again and got slowly to his feet.

"If you say so, Harit. I'm not afraid. Not anymore." He turned to the two knights. "My lords, I'm not feeling well today. Too much excitement for an old man like me, and I'd like to retire. My house is yours. Leah will arrange somewhere for you to sleep."

"Yes, go and rest. We'll only stay one night. Tomorrow we'll ride to Jaffa. Then, if God wills it, we'll leave this country and return home," said Walter.

"To Saxony? To your ruined castle?" asked Ishmael.

"That's right. I'll reclaim my ancestors' estate and rebuild it. Stronger and more beautiful than ever before, thanks to your reward."

The goldsmith smiled weakly, bowed and shuffled out into the garden. They heard him retching again, and Leah hurried after him.

"God in heaven, I hope it's not infectious. He vomits as if he's sailing through a storm," said Walter. "Maybe we should leave today."

"Forget it, Walter! No. First we must go to the Lord's tomb and pray there together for our salvation. Then all the sins we've committed will be forgiven by His grace," Hartung insisted. "We'll never be this close to the Lord again. Think of all the terrible things we've done. In this city, we're close to heaven. I think." Hartung wrinkled his nose and added, "Although it doesn't look much like paradise."

"Of course, my friend. We can't leave Jerusalem without having stood at the tomb of our Saviour. Harit, I assume you know where the Church of the Holy Sepulchre is?" asked Walter.

"I do, but I must warn you, the inspections there are much stricter than at the Josaphat gate, and you'll probably have to pay to pray there," replied Harit. "I'm happy to take you there, but I won't go inside."

The knights decided to seek out the holy sites immediately, then depart very early the next morning for Jaffa. They told Leah of their plan, and she agreed to arrange food and water for their journey.

After the warriors and Harit had left the house, Leah went up to her uncle's bedchamber. He was awake. His brow was covered with sweat and his breathing was shallow. Beside the bed stood a wooden pail, in case of another bout of vomiting. It was empty, but a sour smell of decay hung in the air. Leah

323

opened a window and a mild breeze banished the unpleasant odour.

"Sit with me, my child," whispered Ishmael, beckoning her feebly. "I must speak with you about the relics."

"What is there to discuss? I knew they would bring death and ruin to our house. Oh, Uncle, you can't die!"

"It's God's will! Be firm in your faith, my child. As you know, Maimonides believes the tablets are fakes. God's presence on earth can't be situated between two small, gold cherubim, he says."

"Authentic or not, what does it matter? They're deadly, aren't they?" Leah asked sadly.

"Maimonides is convinced of that. He warned me of the evil effects of the tablets and cherubim. They emit some force that slowly and insidiously decomposes everything in the body. An unprecedented danger to our people! Whether it really is the sacred relic or a fake, who knows? But Jews and Nazarenes alike will fight for possession of the objects if they ever learn of them. That will lead to war and persecution. People will die... Oh, Leah, I saw it in a dream!"

He strained to sit up and grasped his niece by the shoulders. His eyes darted around the room, and she noticed clumps of damp hair on his pillow.

"I won't give the Ark of the Covenant back to our people! It must be hidden – no, destroyed – or it will be the ruin of all of us!"

"Calm yourself, Uncle," said Leah gently, pushing him back onto his bed. His skin felt like hot, dry desert sand. "You have a fever, and it's making you see terrible things when you're between sleeping and waking. I'll fetch cold water and wrap your calves in cool, moist cloths. That will alleviate it, you'll see."

"Leah, I'm serious. Those things down there in the garden must go. They'll be the death of us all! And *I* must get rid of them, because I'm already sick... not you! You mustn't touch them!"

"I won't touch them, I promise," she said, getting up. Ishmael could no longer keep his eyes open, and he began to doze. "The Templar... Give them to the Templar when he comes... *He* must destroy them," he whispered. Saliva dribbled from the corners of his mouth.

Leah soothingly stroked his cramping hands, but said nothing. She was certain Guillaume was now indifferent to the cursed relics. Given everything she knew about them, she didn't want him to ever lay eyes on them again.

XXXVI

Heavy, ice-cold rain drenched him to the skin. Guillaume watched grey clouds sluggishly drift across the dark sky, so low they appeared to touch the tops of the tall pines clustered around the forest clearing. At the edge of the lush, green grass, he spied a dark-robed horseman, almost camouflaged in the thick underbrush. Loud calls echoed back and forth. The rider drew nearer. His huge warhorse tore up clumps of damp soil from the forest floor as its heavy hooves thundered toward him. There was a lance wedged under the horseman's arm, aimed at Guillaume.

He roared with fear and rage, raising his sword in both hands, ready to cut through the horse's front legs. But the rider abruptly swerved and disappeared into the forest. A quiet sound of snapping twigs caught his attention. Guillaume turned to see Raoul swinging his sword and crashing it down on his hastily raised shield.

He woke with a start, breathless, and glanced around frantically. A dozen mountain goats were climbing a nearby rocky slope. Stones loosened under their hooves and clattered down into the valley. His heart still pounding, he rubbed his eyes with relief and took a deep breath.

A dream! Thank God it was only a dream, thought Guillaume with a sniff.

After a while, he rose and hitched up his robe to relieve himself amongst the rocks bordering the small wadi that flowed a short distance from the pilgrim road. Lost in thought, he listened to the splashing stream, which was greedily absorbed by the dry sand. The sun hadn't yet risen; the sky was changing from black to deep blue. The third day of his journey to Jerusalem began with a cool morning breeze blowing across the mountains from the east.

When he was finished, he straightened his robe, shivering from the cold, and returned to his campsite. He picked up the saddle that had served as a hard pillow and swung it up onto his horse, which suddenly began to snort restlessly.

He froze and his hand moved slowly to the sword on his left hip. Drawing it rapidly, he spun around to look into the dark, smiling eyes of a man standing five feet away from him, arms folded behind his back.

"The longer you spend in the mountains, the more careless you become, Templar."

Hassan the Assassin. Guillaume raised his sword higher and drew his dagger. Then he scanned his surroundings.

"I'm not alone. Put your weapons away." Hassan slowly raised his right hand and beckoned. Three more Assassins rose from their hiding places behind grey boulders.

By God, I almost pissed on their heads and didn't notice them! A dozen horsemen appeared up on the road and steered their horses down to join them. They were armed with round shields made of hard reeds, and long spears, the tips of which flashed in the rising sun.

They all wore red kufiyas wrapped around their heads, covering everything except their eyes, which were fixed coldly on the lone knight.

Guillaume took two steps back, ensuring no one could attack him from behind. He couldn't win against their superior numbers, but he could still send a few of them to their prophet before he had to die.

"Surrender, I'm not out for your head. You know what I want." Hassan waved again and the horsemen dismounted and sat down in the sand, forming a semi-circle around the two of them. Their leader also sat cross-legged on the sand.

Guillaume lowered his sword incredulously, stabbed it into the soft sand and threw his dagger down beside it. Then he sat down opposite the Assassin, who nodded contentedly.

One of the men brought a leather water flask. Hassan handed it to the knight, who took it without hesitation. He knew this gesture assured him protection and the promise that he wouldn't be harmed – as long as these were honourable heathens. But he couldn't be sure, so he only drank a little.

"Well, Templar..." Hassan began, then corrected himself, "Former Templar, I should say. We had an agreement, and I've already fulfilled my end. We carried out your wish. The Grand Master lies in two pieces in the church of your Order. Now we want the balance of the sum you promised us."

Guillaume shrugged and placed the water flask before him on the ground.

"I don't have the gold with me. But rest assured, I'll fetch it and settle my debt," he said in a steady voice to disguise his insecurity. The money was long gone. This was belated revenge on the part of Nicholas, into whose hands it passed during the attack on the pilgrim train.

Guillaume had no idea how he could possibly raise the monstrous sum of five hundred gold bezants that he still owed the contract killers.

"Oh... you don't say. Didn't you rob it from the Templar fortress? And aren't the two knights who assisted you carrying it to Jerusalem as we speak?"

Guillaume's brow creased in surprise and he shuffled his feet in the sand. "How do you know about the knights?"

Hassan smiled. He nodded his head rhythmically in time with his reply, speaking each word very slowly, "Because nothing remains secret from us, infidel." He leaned forward and picked up the water flask. He sipped from it and smugly watched the knight's face turn grey.

"After you commissioned us with the murder of the Grand Master, I sent a messenger pigeon asking permission from my commander. The reply came quickly and, alas, it was bitter. My master, Rashid ad-Din Sinan was dead. We were all overcome with grief. However, as his first deputy, I had to assume the mantle of responsibility for our brotherhood. I decided to grant your wish and left for Acre myself, with three brave warriors, to execute the mission. By divine providence, I saw you go into an inn accompanied by a woman, a Syrian servant and two Nazarenes. From then on, I followed you unseen. I was behind you when you sought out the house of the turcopole that night, and I sat under an open window outside the lame innkeeper's tavern as you forged a plan with the knights to attack the Templar fortress."

"So you decided to take advantage of the robbery as a distraction while you murdered de Sablé!" Guillaume exclaimed with a hint of admiration in his voice.

"That's right. In the chaos that ensued after you lit the fire, no one saw my men creep into his chamber and fulfil their mission. Two escaped after the deed, and the third displayed the severed head of your Lord to the fearful Templars, for the glory of Allah, and then died with a happy laugh as he leapt from the high wall into the sea. He went to paradise with the blessing of the gracious Lord of all true believers."

Hassan spread his arms, closed his eyes and raised his face to the sky.

So I wasn't mistaken. I often felt I was being followed in Acre, but noticed no one, thought Guillaume with a queasy feeling.

"Yes, your gold is on its way to Jerusalem. The knights have it with them and will protect it with their lives. They'll only hand it over to me. Let me go in peace. We'll meet in three days at the ruins of the Lazarus monastery. I'll give it to you there," he lied.

Hassan's eyes widened and he fixed Guillaume with a piercing gaze.

"Perhaps you'll do that, and perhaps you won't. I don't care about the money anymore. I don't even believe you have it. But you have something much more valuable. You'll give me the... treasure, which is so unspeakably precious that a Syrian, two Nazarene knights, a Templar and a Jewess will work together to acquire it. There's no use lying. I heard with my own ears what you discussed in the tavern. It's made of pure gold, isn't it? A legendary sacred relic of the scripture readers, I know. Far more powerful than the true cross that the Sultan took from you, which is of supreme significance for your faith."

"If you know so much, then get it yourself. You have enough men to kill two knights," snarled Guillaume.

That I have. But not enough to search for two Nazarenes in a city full of stinking Sunni Kurdish servants. The danger of being discovered would be too great, thought Hassan, grimacing involuntarily.

Franks couldn't distinguish between Shiites and Sunnis – two seemingly irreconcilable branches of the Islamic faith. Muslims could. Salah ad-Din was a sworn enemy of his former master, Sheikh Sinan, who followed the Shiite teachings. According to his convictions, only Ali, the prophet's stepson, and his descendants were the true leaders of the faithful and the foundation of the religion. The Sultan, on the other hand, adhered to the Sunni perspective – that the prophet did not name any successors, and therefore a supreme leader – a caliph – had to be elected from the ranks of Muslims.

Countless Shiites fell victim to his Kurdish soldiers' swords in religious wars, and were slaughtered in the mountains like cattle. Many members of the Assassins' Sect also lost their lives. A truce had been observed for many years, but Jerusalem was a forbidden city to Assassins and Shiites.

Hassan cleared his throat and said in a conciliatory tone, "I don't desire the deaths of those knights. Nor yours. We only spill blood when our faith and absolute necessity demand it. Look, Templar, at this moment we're even protecting you, so that you reach your destination in good health and give me the treasure as payment for your life and the death of the Grand Master."

"What is it you need to protect me from? Yourselves, if anything," sneered Guillaume.

"No, we're not your enemies, but the Marshal of the Templars is. He's been pursuing you since you visited him at his skinny whore's house. He's riding fast, accompanied by five well-armed turcopoles."

A sharp hissing sound made them both listen out. One of the Assassins sitting motionless in a semi-circle behind Hassan suddenly started spitting blood. He spluttered and toppled sideways, the tip of an arrow protruding from his neck. The other men shouted and leapt to their feet, holding their shields protectively over their heads as they dashed to their horses.

"Ahhh... yes," Hassan said calmly, sneering at Guillaume. "He's found you."

XXXVII

Three turcopoles dashed into the small wadi on horseback and fired long arrows into the midst of the startled Assassins, precisely targeting the Muslims' unarmoured bodies. They galloped to the end of the valley floor, turned their whinnying horses, drew fresh arrows from the quivers slung around them and attacked again instantly.

Guillaume darted forward from his hiding place to pick up an abandoned shield, which he held in front of him as he ran backward to tear his sword out of the sand and kneel in the shelter of a large rock.

More arrows honed in on the lightly armed, fleeing Assassins, and they fell screaming to the ground before being mercilessly trampled by hooves. Guillaume heard their bones snapping, then watched the turcopoles exit the valley in a cloud of dust s they made for the road. Under different circumstances, he would have been proud of his former soldiers, but today he was sure there would be another deadly onslaught targeting him alone. He got to his feet, established a firm footing and braced himself.

He swung his sword in slow circles.

The dust settled, but they didn't return. A few severely wounded Assassins wailed wretchedly, writhing on the ground soaked in blood. Others with arrows protruding from their chests and backs were no longer moving.

What a bloodbath! Ten out of sixteen, Guillaume counted. He scanned the area for Hassan, but couldn't see him. Then he heard hoof beats again, growing louder. A rider was approaching from the road, his chainmail glinting silver in the rising sun. He wore neither helmet nor shield, holding only a bloodstained sword in his hand.

Guillaume's muscles relaxed a little when he recognised Raoul. The Marshal slowly rode toward him and stopped his horse within earshot.

"So, you've joined forces with heathens, you traitor!" he bellowed, holding his sword above his head. "I've finally found you! Your journey ends here! I'll send you to the devil once and for all!"

He spurred his horse, which reared up with a whinny, then shot forward.

Caught off-guard, Guillaume hesitated a moment, then flung up his shield and ran at the charging Marshal. Just before they collided, he sprang to the left and thrust his sword with all the strength he could muster into the side of the horse's neck. Horse and rider fell to the ground.

Raoul curled up like a big cat and thudded down in a cloud of dust beside the animal. His armour protected him from serious injury, but he lost two teeth. He instantly leapt to his feet, spat blood and pulled his sword out from under the dying horse.

Guillaume turned to face him, lowered his shield and walked slowly and warily toward the Marshal.

"Raoul, let me leave. I spared you in Acre because you were once my friend. We have no business with one another. You'll never see me again."

"You're a fool and always have been!" Raoul contemptuously spat another lump of bloody mucus on the ground. "Why do you think I pursued you through these damned mountains? To wish you all the best on the way to your heathen whore? You've always been a reckless simpleton. You didn't see the signs of your impending doom when de Sablé became Grand Master. And then your squire accuses you of sodomy! You horny imbecile! You came within a hair's breadth of dragging me down into the abyss with your heedless, irresponsible behaviour. I won't let that happen again!"

"You crawled up the Grand Master's wrinkled arse! Out of fear of losing your high position, because you're a heinous sinner too! We could have commanded the Order's troops together – you as Marshal and I as turcopolier. But your fear of me got the better of you. I never wanted to usurp your rank as senior commander, let alone spill your depraved secrets!" Guillaume retorted, lowering his sword. "But none of that matters now. I'm not, and never was, a danger to you. Let me be on my way."

"Quiet! You would have gone against me sooner or later, because you're erratic, arrogant, and you act impulsively without considering the consequences. The real danger to me is your unpredictability. I saw through you long ago, and your actions since have proven me right. You turned away from the Order, turned your faith into a steaming pile of shit and conspired with heathens. You're without honour, a disgrace to our Order. You attacked the holy Temple of Acre, killed Nicholas and had the Grand Master beheaded by filthy, infidel contract killers. Your guilt is proven and the only punishment for your sins is death!"

"What about your sins? You're a fraud and a fornicator! How many fictitious transactions did you orchestrate, with my help, for weapons that never reached our army, only to steal money from the Order's coffers to send to your wife in France? Around two hundred bezants, I estimate. And how long have you been romping with that whore Ruzan? More than a year, I think, several times a week. Don't talk to me about guilt! I'm prepared to answer before a court of our brothers! Then we'll see which of us is fundamentally to blame for all these disastrous events!"

Guillaume stood tall and resolute, holding his shield close to his chest. Raoul scoffed and gripped his sword in both hands.

"I knew it! What drivel... You think you can turn the tables and betray me? I always knew you were an asinine fool! I'll change my ways, but *you'll* never have that opportunity again. Your death will be the start of my new life. You should have killed me in Acre, but you missed your one chance. Today, *I* put an end to *your* pitiful existence!"

He leapt forward and his sword crashed down on the shield Guillaume had swiftly raised above his head. Another forceful blow tore the leather arm straps, and the shield arced through the air.

Swords clashed and they pushed against one another, blades together. Their straining faces were so close Guillaume could smell his opponent's rotten breath and clearly see the clefts in his pupils.

Like a snake, he thought, shoving Raoul away from him.

They circled each other, crouching low. Guillaume calculated his chances of defeating the Marshal. They had never fought as opponents, but he was aware of Raoul's unusual physical strength and stamina, and that he wielded his longsword in both hands with exceptional skill and speed. He was a head taller than Guillaume and was wearing a short-sleeved, fine-meshed chainmail shirt over a thickly padded leather jerkin. His reptilian eyes sparkled with merciless resolve.

Guillaume, on the other hand, was unprotected under his earth-brown linen robe, with nothing but a simple, roughly forged sword in his fist. As if guessing Guillaume's thoughts, Raoul slowly raised his sword above his head.

"Surrender and I promise you a quick death!"

"I don't want any favours from you," Guillaume hissed, and lunged at him. A powerful blow hissed past Raoul's head as he hastily retreated. The Marshal nimbly deflected the next two blows with his broad blade. They both fought doggedly. Many of Guillaume's well-aimed blows bounced ineffectually off Raoul's armour. Raoul's own thrusts often met with nothing but air. His opponent was much more agile without armour, and circled him like a hungry wold.

Raoul panted and sweat ran down his temples. His heart was racing in his chest, and his right hip hurt like hell after the fall from the horse. The last time he fought in a battle for life and death was outside the walls of Acre. That was two years ago and his lack of practice was showing. He was glad to be wearing armour.

Guillaume's arms grew tired. Parrying the longsword's heavy blows cost him as much energy as evading them in a light-footed dance. He felt himself slowing dangerously.

Put... an... end... to... it! The words hammered in his brain with each sword stroke, and he couldn't say whether he was willing himself or Raoul.

A brief moment of inattention and a blow hit Guillaume's right thigh, causing him to cry out in pain. He staggered back and fell to his knees. Raoul instantly followed through, raising his sword for the final, deadly blow, but Guillaume curled up and rolled into Raoul's feet. The Templar, sure of victory a moment ago, now lost his balance and fell flat on his belly, his weapon spinning out of his hands. Still on the ground, Guillaume spun around, gripped his sword in both hands and summoned the last of his strength to lop off the Marshal's left arm at the elbow.

A shrill scream echoed off the rocky walls of the valley. Raoul writhed in the sand and bellowed, clutching his splintered upper arm with his right hand. Blood sprayed from the stump, spattering his chest in powerful spurts.

Guillaume leapt to his feet, breathing hard. He pointed his sword at the other knight's face. Raoul clenched his jaw in unspeakable agony, his veins and sinews bulging like hard, gnarled tree roots.

"You cursed dog... you hacked off my arm!" Raoul wheezed through gritted teeth, shaking violently in response to the searing pain. He glared hatefully at Guillaume, who stood beside him, seemingly enjoying his revenge.

"Go on, do it! Kill me, you bastard!" he croaked as his streaming eyes searched for his weapon. "My sword, give me my sword! I don't want to die like a helpless swine!"

Guillaume limped numbly around Raoul and kicked his sword to him. Raoul let go of his arm stump, rolled onto his side and felt for his sword.

"It doesn't have to end like this," said Guillaume in a monotone, but he knew better.

"Oh really? Shit and damn it... you want to leave me to rot as a cripple? Damned whoreson, hurry up and do it, you coward! Do the right thing for once!" Raoul shouted hoarsely, gripping the hilt of his sword.

"DO IT!"

Guillaume's blade plunged deep into his neck. Raoul choked and spluttered, bloody foam spewing over his trembling lips. The blood from his carotid artery mingled with his last desperate, gurgling breaths, then his eyes rolled back in his head and his body slackened.

Guillaume wrenched out his sword and threw it down in the blood-stained sand. Then he felt to his knees, exhausted, and pressed his trembling hands against his body.

He felt neither the pain of his leg wound, nor the warm blood soaking his thigh. There wasn't a single thought in his head. He felt profoundly empty. Sitting dumbstruck beside Raoul, he watched the pool of blood beneath his head slowly seep into the dust.

Far off, as if through thick velvet curtains, he heard muffled applause. The five turcopoles had returned. They sat on their horses in a semi-circle around him and the dead Marshal. Ruben the Eye was the first to start clapping, and the others gradually joined in. They didn't stop until Guillaume looked up blankly at them.

"Do your duty. Whatever the Marshal commanded," he said apathetically.

The stocky Silenus shuffled awkwardly in his saddle. "You were once our commander. For good reason, as we've seen again today. You fought excellently and honourably. Tigran sends his greetings. He asked us to pass them on in the event that we actually found you. And he said we should protect you from the Marshal if he tried to kill you."

"Unfortunately, we failed to do that," Ruben chimed in with a sheepish grin. "We were busy with the remaining heathens in their camp behind the red mountain." He pointed toward the road. "But it turns out you were quite capable of taking care of yourself."

"What now? Will you take me to the Temple as a prisoner? I expect there'll be a handsome reward."

"Oh, turcopolier, if those heathens really were your friends, then you had very rich allies," replied Silenus, patting his bulging saddlebags.

"We found a lot of gold in their leader's tent. Much more than the Order would ever pay us. Enough for us all to live comfortable lives to the end of our days, far away from this country's killing fields. Look!" He reached into one of the saddlebags and threw a piece of gold to Guillaume. It bounced off his chest and fell into the sand.

A gold bezant. One of five hundred. My advance payment to the Assassins.

"Keep it. And we'll leave you two nags. When we return to Acre, we'll say Bedouins killed the Marshal. If we ever go back there. We never found you, turcopolier." Silenus grasped his horse's reins and added, "And... you never saw us either. God be with you!"

The warriors inclined their heads, then rode their mounts toward the road.

Guillaume watched them go, speechless.

Miracles really do still happen, he thought. His gaze wandered across the mountain slopes and down to the scattered corpses in the wadi. There were no more wounded. The turcopoles had finished them all off with well-aimed shots. Only now did he register his painful leg wound. He undid his sword belt with trembling fingers and tied it tightly around his thigh above the wound. It would stop the bleeding for the time being. The wound was wide but not deep.

Not as deep as the wound of a betrayal or the loss of a friend. It'll heal, but a large scar will remain.

He decided to load Raoul's body onto one of the horses and bury him in a peaceful place. Far from this bloody scene. He was overcome by deep sadness when he saw Raoul at his feet, holding the hilt of his sword loosely in his hand.

How did it come to this?

He looked up at the cloudless sky and closed his eyes. His many years in the Holy Land seemed like a bad dream from which he was finally waking.

Now I'm free. Free of the Temple, free of false friends, free from fear. I'm Guillaume de Born, a simple knight from Périgord, no more, no less. The Lord hasn't entirely forsaken me, and perhaps He will guide me on my future path.

He no longer hoped for the forgiveness of his grave sins. But there was one injustice he had committed for which he still had to apologise and atone.

Jerusalem wasn't far now.

XXXVIII

It was remarkably crowded in the square in front of the Church of the Holy Sepulchre, whose grey limestone walls towered defiantly into the sky. Dozens of Christian pilgrims had gathered there, recognisable by their hiking sticks and the wooden crosses and rosaries strung around their necks. They were hemmed in by numerous gesticulating street vendors loudly touting their wares.

There was a considerable selection on offer. On wooden stands and carts, they saw mounds of oranges, melons and pomegranates. Flat cakes spread with honey stood in towering stacks alongside various types of smoked, salted fish. One vendor carried in his hands skewers of grilled mutton dripping with fat, which he held temptingly under the visitors' noses.

Beggars shuffled on their knees through the dust, holding up their hands to receive alms from the pilgrims. Half-naked, emaciated children darted between the stands looking for edible scraps on the ground or opportunities to steal food. The babble of languages was diverse. Pilgrims and merchants alike, from all over the world, haggled, shouted and laughed. Some of the pilgrims sang devotional chants and gazed ecstatically at the sky.

"Here it is. The place where your prophet supposedly rose from the dead," Harit said with a flourishing gesture the Church of the Holy Sepulchre.

Walter cleared his throat and raised a disdainful eyebrow. "That? It's not at all what I was expecting. Perhaps a solitary stone tomb surrounded by olive groves, with white-clad women praying for the Saviour... or a cloistered courtyard with monks and a burial mound at its centre. But this looks like the quay walls of Acre on market day."

"We're close to Him," whispered Hartung with an exalted look in his eyes. "Keep your scorn to yourself. This here is the centre of the world. The Saviour died in this place and rose again to save us all from our sins. Can't you feel it?"

His friend looked ashamed and tried unsuccessfully to search within himself. A cloud of oily smoke from a cooking stand wafted past him. He restrained himself from voicing the cutting remark on the tip of his tongue. Faith was no laughing matter for Hartung, and Walter respected that greatly.

"Yes, I feel... somehow... different," he replied haltingly.

"See! You just have to give in to it! I knew it." Delighted, Hartung patted Walter's shoulder, then said to Harit, "Let's move closer."

The Muslim shrugged and led the knights in a beeline to the church entrance. It had two levels and was crowned by a huge stone dome. There were originally two portals, but the Sultan had bricked up one of them shortly after conquering the city, to humiliate the Christians. Three pale marble columns stood on either side of the open portal, supporting an arch of finely hewn sandy limestone. Standing in front of it, controlling admission, were two sombre-looking Muslims in grey robes with daggers displayed in their belts.

"You have to pay them. Give them a piece of silver and they'll let you in quicker," said Harit, tugging Hartung's sleeve. "I won't come in, obviously, but I'll wait here for you."

Harit hung back and the knights pushed their way through the milling pilgrims. Despite his enormous size, Hartung struggled to move through the dense crowd to the guards, with Walter in tow. He passed a silver dirham to them over the heads of the waiting throng, and they were instantly waved through.

Meanwhile, Harit sauntered across the square, bought two oranges and sat down within sight of the church entrance, in the shade of a wall. He felt tired and wanted to go back to the goldsmith's house to fetch his money, so he could return to his lodgings in the south of the city. He hadn't been there for weeks. It was possible the owner, a miserly old fishmonger, had already rented out the empty room to a new tenant. *If so, inshallah, I'll simply buy my own house outside the city walls,* he thought, savouring the unfamiliar feeling of independence. A piece of juicy orange disappeared into his mouth. He squeezed it pleasantly against his gums and closed his eyes blissfully.

"Can I have some?"

The voice belonged to a young girl, who unceremoniously sat down beside him. Harit blinked in surprise, and turned to look at her. Her hair was covered by a dark blue scarf. She had a high forehead, thick, brown, arching eyebrows and a long, narrow nose. Her complexion was bronze-coloured and smooth. She waved at someone on the other side of the square and a little dimple formed in her right cheek as her full lips smiled broadly.

Without a word, Harit passed her a quarter of his fruit. She took it, popped it in her mouth and chewed quickly.

"Thank you. That's my father over there. We sell mutton with onions on palm leaves to the infidels. We've been standing here since early morning. Now my feet hurt and I can't stand the sight of meat anymore, let alone the smell. I always need something fresh and sweet when I take a break," she babbled.

"Aha," said Harit.

"You don't talk much, do you? Father always says people who talk a lot are good at selling. So you're not a salesman, are you? You look like you'd make a good guide for the kafirs here, in your fine cotton robe. But you smell a bit horsy. Are you a stable hand? For a high lord maybe? No, stable hands don't earn enough to buy oranges. So what are you?"

Harit was flummoxed and only managed to say, "A... a... guide." *I've been accused of a lot of things, but not of talking too little.*

"Thought so. I'm telling you, I'm a good judge of character. Have you come a long way? Some guides escort the infidels all the way to the coast, to make sure they get through the mountains safely."

Harit arched his back and said with pride, "You guessed right. I've been to Nablus, Nazareth and Acre as a guide to Nazarene warriors. One of them was even Templar. I fought Bedouins and had to spend weeks in the mountains of Samaria!"

She widened her dark eyes and looked at him in astonishment.

"Really? A Templar? You'll have to tell me about him, I love adventure stories – the scarier the better. But now I have to go. Look at all those people crowding around our stand. By Allah, the Nazarenes are a real blessing for our business, especially on market days like today! Come back tomorrow. We're always here at this time. Agreed?"

Without waiting for an answer, she jumped up and ran to her father.

Harit got to his feet and shouted after her, "I'm Harit! What's your name?"

"Saadia!" she cried cheerfully over her shoulder.

The happy one. The name suits her. He sat down against the wall again and smiled as he watched her go. He would definitely come back tomorrow. There was a lot he could tell her.

Harit waited for a long time. The day was nearing its end and the clear sky turning blood-red when the two knights stepped through the church portal.

He hobbled over to them. His right leg had gone to sleep, and perhaps he had too, because he couldn't remember his new acquaintance and her father leaving the square, which was now almost empty.

"How was it? I was starting to worry you'd been buried in there too, you were gone so long." When he noticed the men's pale, blank faces, he felt like biting off his glib tongue.

Walter was the first to gather his wits, replying quietly, "It was... unbelievable. It's all real! His tomb, the site of crucifixion, the stone of anointing on which the Lord was prepared for burial... it's all real!"

He kept shaking his head, inspired and filled with a profound sense of faith. "A priest led us around and explained everything. Until now I believed, now I know. I saw the tomb with my own eyes, even touched it."

Hartung was equally awestruck. A blissful peace filled his soul. His friend had glimpsed the Lord, just as he himself had carried Him in his heart for so long. Today, they had finally arrived, after many years of pilgrimage.

He hooked his arm through Walter's and they walked together to join Harit, who led them silently to the Jew's house.

The rest of evening also proceeded in silence. The knights went straight to bed without eating anything. Leah asked Harit to stay until morning, to translate any requests the warriors' might have before their departure. He was happy to oblige.

Very early the next day, the knights saddled their horses and strapped food, water and the pouches of coins to the animals' backs. They chose not to say goodbye to Ishmael. He lay upstairs in his bedroom, speaking incoherently in a feverish delirium, and they preferred to keep their distance.

Before they set out for Jaffa, they wanted to retrieve the weapons and armour they had hidden at Mount Scopus. So Leah and Harit didn't take them to the city's northern gate where the old pilgrim road to the coast began, but back to the square by the Josaphat gate in the east. There, they paused briefly and Leah bowed deeply to the knights.

"I thank you from the bottom of my heart. You did a great service to my people, my uncle, Harit and me. I'm very sorry he can't bid you farewell in person, but he's too weak and only has brief moments of clarity. But know this – to him and to me, you're neither Nazarenes nor infidels; you're noble men who will always be welcome among us. We wish you a good journey and, at the end of it, may you find what you're looking for in your homeland. Good luck. I'll pray for you."

She sank to her knees and touched her forehead to the hard, dusty ground. Harit had tears in his eyes as he translated. He couldn't think of any of his own words of farewell, so he simply stammered, "*So dir Gott helfe... So dir Gott helfe,*" then he dropped to his knees too.

The warriors gripped them both by the shoulders and pulled them up.

"As we've said again and again, kneeling before us is not necessary. Don't let this annoying custom become a habit," said Walter in a husky voice.

"God be with you, Leah." Hartung gave a slight bow. "And also with you, Harit ibn Tharit ibn Hamid," he added, winking conspiratorially at Leah, who had secretly and painstakingly taught him the young Arab's full name during their travels.

Harit was honoured and bowed too. Then, unable to hold himself back, he embraced his rescuer. Hartung laughed, shook him off and gave him a friendly pat on the head.

The knights led their horses to the gate, which was less busy today.

It was very early and the city was still waking up. There was no one at the gate but a guard vociferously scolding a cloth merchant whose camels were loaded so high that they didn't fit under the archway and had to be unloaded first. He paid no attention to the knights, being responsible for controlling entry only, so they walked past him without a word.

Leah and Harit watched in silence as they passed through the gate unchallenged, mounted their horses and slowly rode away.

They both turned in their saddles and looked back at the city.

"I'll always remember Jerusalem fondly. Do you think the fallen Templar survived and will return?" asked Walter.

"Do you mean to the city or to Leah?"

"Both." Walter smiled with a twinkle in his eyes.

Hartung took a while to answer.

"We'll never find out if we leave the Holy Land forever. His fate is in God's hands, just like ours. I hope for his sake he does. And for hers."

XXXIX

Guillaume gritted his teeth and sucked air through the gaps between them. The wound on his thigh was now as painful as if Raoul's sword had freshly cut it to the bone. The three-mile hike from the little village of Anata to Jerusalem had been overly ambitious.

Groaning, he leaned against the unplastered wall of a house, whose shadow reached more than halfway across the alley in the afternoon sun. The rabbi's house stood opposite.

At daybreak, he had left his horse, armour and sword with a goatherd in a settlement outside the city for a scandalously high price. The ancient and enterprising man had told him, chest swelling with pride, that the famous Salah ad-Din had set up camp beside his derelict property before taking back the Holy City. Meaning it was sacred ground blessed by Allah, and infidel Nazarenes had to pay an inflated price for a place in his stable.

The devout Muslim clearly probably his guest was no ordinary pilgrim, but for a gold bezant, he would have housed stinking pigs in his stable, and Guillaume was satisfied with the arrangement.

Not wanting to attract attention, he had entered the city on foot with nothing but a gnarled walking staff. He almost regretted this decision when he lifted his robe and looked at the bandage on his leg.

Blood had seeped through the wide strips of cloth in a dark red stain the size of his palm.

Grimacing, he covered it again with his robe and squinted at the goldsmith's house.

Only a dozen more steps.

He had stood in almost this exact spot a few weeks earlier, waiting for the Jew's niece to leave the house, before attacking her uncle and robbing him of the greatest treasure in the world.

Now he hoped the treasure was once again safely hidden behind that door. And Leah too – he still had no idea whether she had returned home safely under the protection of the two Alemannic knights.

His mouth was dry, and thinking of the enchanting Jewish woman made his heart race in a way that was now becoming familiar. He tightened his grip on his staff, hobbled to the house and knocked.

Nothing happened.

After a moment, he hesitantly tried again.

"Who is it?" someone called loudly from inside.

Leah!

His eyes lit up and he answered with a smile on his face, "It's me. Guillaume!"

There was a crashing sound behind the door and he heard a muffled cry.

"Is everything alright?" he asked, listening out anxiously.

The lock rattled in answer and the door creaked open. Leah had hastily wrapped a scarf around her head and was nervously smoothing her black robe. She beamed at him with her dark eyes and bowed her head.

"Shalom! Please, come in," she said, a slight quiver in her voice.

Guillaume stepped over the threshold and closed the door behind him. They gazed at each other without speaking, then, before the knight had time to reply, she embraced him tightly. His staff clattered to the floor and he closed his eyes, put his arms around her and deeply inhaled the scent of rosewater that he had so missed. They remained like that for what seemed like an eternity. He gently pried her away and looked lovingly at her, wiping a glittering tear from her cheek as tenderly as he could with his large hand.

"It's good to see you looking so well," he said haltingly. His throat was parched and he had to swallow hard.

"I prayed for your return," she whispered shyly. "Please, have a seat and some water. Or wine. I have some, I'll fetch it now."

"No, water is fine. Thank you."

Without warning, she thumped his chest with her fist and glowered at him a reproachfully, a deep frown line forming above the bridge of her nose.

"How could you do that to me?! I was so worried when the knights rode out of Acre without you. What kept you? Who did you see in the Templar fortress?"

"An old..." Guillaume hesitated, "...enemy. He had to pay with his life for his loathesome betrayal."

Leah saw his eyes glaze over and immediately regretted her emotional outburst.

"The Marshal? You told us about him in the mountains. Your friend who betrayed you. I'm so sorry."

"You needn't be. He's nothing but a malignant shadow from my former life. Nothing else remains of him."

Leah nodded sympathetically. She gestured for him to make himself comfortable and went to the kitchen to fetch a jug of fresh water.

He grunted as he sat down cross-legged on the carpet. Leah heard him as she came back into the room.

"What's wrong? Are you injured?"

"It's nothing. Just a scratch. It'll heal."

"Let me see."

Guillaume shook his head.

"Maybe later. Just give me some water."

Leah passed him the jug, sat opposite him and watched him drink large gulps and sigh contentedly. He put the vessel on the floor and asked, "Where's your uncle? I need to speak to him. I want to ask his forgiveness for what I did."

He noticed a cut in her robe above her right breast, a hand's width in length. She saw him glance at it and covered it with her left hand, her eyes glittering with moisture.

"You can't speak to him anymore. We buried him yesterday."

Guillaume blanched.

"The tear in my clothing... it's one of our traditions, to show our grief. I was with him in the last few hours and know that he forgave you, as he forgave everyone."

"Leah, I regret my actions so very much. I'm sure it's my fault – I injured him too severely when I..."

She shook her head and interrupted him, "No, you're not responsible. He was already sick internally," she said vaguely.

"By God, how terrible this must be for you! You have my sympathy. What about the knights and Harit?"

"The warriors received their reward and left for Jaffa two days ago. They're going home. They both seemed well. Harit was here this morning to look in on me. He's in good health and has big plans. He wants to buy himself a house and become a sugar merchant."

Relieved, Guillaume stretched out his painful leg and leaned back in the cushions. Leah saw his mouth twitch.

"Where are your... sacred objects... now?"

"Still in the courtyard, where we unloaded them on our return. My uncle left them out there. In a sack in the stable. I'm afraid to touch them."

"That's understandable. Those relics don't bring happiness. Only death and suffering, I'm sure of it. There's an evil curse on them. Many men have died since the first cherub came into my possession. Innocent pilgrims, servants, Templar knights and Assassins. If you'll allow it, I'll take them out of this house and throw them in the deep refuse trenches outside the city gate. They won't cause any more harm there, God-willing."

She breathed a sigh of relief and looked at his leg.

"Not today. I'll heat some water now and tend to your wound. And... you must be hungry."

She got up, smiled at him and scampered into the kitchen.

Guillaume gazed after her, admiring her delicate figure, and feeling wonderfully safe. He closed his eyes and recalled their first meeting – the moment he regained consciousness when she found him almost lifeless in the Samarian mountains after he had evaded Nicholas. The way her eyes flashed with fury when she reproached him for his cowardly attack on her uncle. His confession, during which he divulged his life so frankly to her and the little Muslim. And what she said when he'd finished – that killing himself was unbefitting, and that there were so many good things he could do to receive forgiveness from the Lord for his sins. This delicate but by no means weak woman had restored his confidence and hope.

A loud sound of shattering crockery wrenched him back to the present. He smiled to himself. Apparently her excitement at seeing him again hadn't yet subsided. But his smile vanished when he saw her in the doorway to the kitchen.

Leah's eyes were wide with terror, and there was a long, sharp knife at her throat. A hand covered her mouth and a figure slowly emerged out of the gloom behind her.

Hassan the Assassin.

He sneered maliciously and nodded at Guillaume, who still sat frozen amongst the cushions.

"Don't move. I know you're fast, Templar, but you're injured and my dagger is faster."

Guillaume slowly raised his hands in a pacifying gesture.

"Easy now. She's not responsible for the deaths of your men. You should take your revenge on me. Take my life, let her go!"

The Assassin laughed quietly, removed his hand from her mouth and slowly pulled down her headscarf. Her dark brown, shoulder-length hair fell loosely around her face and he sniffed it appreciatively.

"I don't care about my men. They're enjoying themselves in paradise with a dozen delightful *houris* like this one here. I don't care about you either. I could have taken your life long ago, on your journey out of the mountains into this city. I followed you because I knew you'd lead me to the all-powerful relic of Judaism. And you'll give it to me now!"

Guillaume shook his head, ignoring Leah's wide, incredulous eyes.

"If I give it to you, you'll kill us both anyway. It's too precious to put in the hands of a murderous sect. I'm the only one who knows where it is, and I'll take that knowledge to my grave."

"By Allah, are you completely mad?" The Assassin rolled his eyes and yanked Leah's hair, forcing her head back and revealing her long, vulnerable neck. His dagger glinted menacingly.

"You still owe me for the Grand Master's death! Give me the damned relic and I'll let her live. I swear it by Allah the Almighty! I already told you – we only kill for our faith. And our faith will spread throughout the world once we finally possess this sacred relic. What do I care about the lives of an outcast Templar and a little Jewish whore?"

"Do I have your word? You'll let us live if I hand it over? Your word as leader of your brotherhood and to your god?"

"I swear by Allah and his prophet Mohammed, and on my honour." Hassan let go of Leah's hair. She lowered her chin slightly, but the dagger was still close to her face.

Guillaume looked searchingly into Hassan's dark eyes. Then he got up. The Assassin moved out of the doorway, pulling Leah with him.

"If you don't keep your word, I'll kill you, make no mistake! I'll go now and fetch what you want. Then you'll let her go and vanish," said Guillaume in a steady voice.

"No games, Templar. Or she dies."

Guillaume limped cautiously past them and out into the yard. The garden was surrounded by a six-foot wall, which provided protection from neighbours' prying eyes, but not from Assassins.

Evening was falling over the city, bathing the little courtyard in a reddish light. Two mules snorted contentedly in their stalls as he entered the stable and looked around. He found the bag containing the treasure on the ground in a corner. He eyed it apprehensively, then picked it up gingerly. The heavy cherubim clinked together softly as he turned and went back into the house.

"Show it to me!" commanded Hassan as soon as he entered the room. Guillaume fumbled with the sack and held it open under the Assassin's nose.

"They're solid gold, aren't they?" His eyes shone greedily.

"Yes. They're worth much more than I owe you. Let her go."

The Assassin shoved Leah hard and she stumbled into Guillaume. Hassan quickly tore the sack from his hands and leapt sideways, holding the dagger defensively in his outstretched arm.

"I'll keep my word. Pray to your three gods that we never see each other again, Templar!"

Hassan slowly backed out onto the street and disappeared.

For a long while, all was silent in the room as they held each other tightly and listened out into the evening. Leah gradually relaxed as Guillaume gently stroked her hair. The cursed relics were finally gone.

Guillaume eventually broke the silence. "He's gone. The treasure is once again lost to your people," he said quietly.

"Hopefully forever... There's something I have to tell you," Leah whispered, pressing her head against his shoulder. "The relics are what made my uncle sicken and die. A renowned physician was here and confirmed it. Moses ben Maimon, whom the world calls Maimonides – the wisest scholar among my people. He said the cherubim and the tablets were ancient forgeries, imbued with a terrible evil. Anyone who is exposed to them for too long dies the most tortuous death. Uncle Ishmael locked himself away with those objects for days, examining them, before they went on their long journey and then returned."

She paused and withdrew from the embrace. Guillaume said nothing. Leah's face suddenly darkened.

"You can't imagine how he suffered. It was as if his innards consisted of nothing but blood and water. It oozed out of every orifice. Death was a release for him. I suspected from the start that the so-called treasure would bring devastation."

You're right about that. A deadly forgery then, thought Guillaume, his lips twisting into a bitter smile. If the wisest Jewish scholar described the cherubim and tablets as forgeries, there was no reason to doubt his words.

He had been chasing an unfulfillable dream. The real Ark of the Covenant would probably never be found.

He wished he could speak to the man he once was, when he believed the greatest mystery on earth would help him attain power and glory. He would advise him to take the Templars' blood money for the murder of the Christian prince and return to France to start an honest, humble life. Far away from betrayal and malevolence, from false friends and devious Templars.

"If what you say is true, how much time do we have? We all touched the figurines and the tablets," he said with an anxious frown.

"The objects only kill those who are very close to them for an extended period. It starts with diarrhoea and fever, then you recover for a few days. After that, the illness comes back worse than before. Your hair falls out, and it ends with another bout of dreadful diarrhoea and pain throughout the body. I haven't experienced any of that. I feel fine. What about you?"

"I've never felt better," replied Guillaume, taking her gently in his arms. He deeply inhaled her scent again and closed his eyes.

"There's something else I shouldn't and don't want to keep from you..." Leah said in a fragile voice. "I leave for Cairo tomorrow morning with Maimonides. His family will take me in. I can't stay here."

She felt his heart pounding in his broad chest. Guillaume was stunned and said nothing for a while. A despised Christian Templar knight and a Jewish woman could never build a future together in this country. She had clearly realised this long ago.

"What will... *you* do?" she asked, nestling closer to him.

He took a deep breath and she felt his lips on her hair. A shiver of pleasure ran through her body.

"I had a lot of time to think in the mountains. I'll leave the Holy Land, follow the Alemannic warriors Hartung and Walter, and offer them my services as a liegeman. I've never met such upright, noble knights in my life. I'd be honoured to follow wherever their paths might lead."

She pulled out of the embrace and looked up into his pale blue eyes. "They'll be good friends to you. I'm sure of it..." She gave him a bittersweet smile. "So we'll just have this one night?"

"We'll have much more than just this one night," he replied.

--- *THE END* ---

Glossary

Adonai – one of the names for God in Judaism

agal – cloth cord holding a headscarf in place

al Aqsa mosque – the mosque on the Temple Mount in the Old City of Jerusalem, considered the third most important place of worship in Islam

Alemann – Arabic word for Germans in the early Middle Ages, borrowed from the French name for the West Germanic people

al haram ash-sharif – the Arabic name for the Temple Mount, a flat-topped hill in the southeast of the Old City of Jerusalem. The Temple of Solomon and later Herod's Temple once stood on it, where the Dome of the Rock stands today

dinar – Islamic gold coin. At the time of the Crusades, it was worth roughly two gold bezants

dirham – Islamic silver coin. Converted to today's value, one dirham would be about five euro

dragoman – interpreter, translator and guide in the Middle East

goy – Jewish term for a non-Jewish person

gold bezant – gold coin minted in the Kingdom of Jerusalem. Converted to today's value, a bezant would be about two hundred euro

Grand Master – supreme dignitary of the Templar Order with almost limitless authority

habit – the white cloak of the Templar knights, a symbol of their purity, made of heavy loden and adorned with a cross formée on the left shoulder

jilbab – a head-to-toe garment worn by women in the Islamic world

jinn – in the Islamic faith, a demon of smoke and fire that could harm humans

kafir – Arabic term for 'infidel' or 'non-believer'

Komtur – treasurer of a house of a religious order

kufiya – in the Arab world, a scarf traditionally worn by men as a headdress, sometimes wound around the head and face as a turban

Marshal – highest military commander in the Templar Order, who commanded the entire army, including fortress garrisons and turcopoles

naphtha – incendiary made from distilled crude oil. Mixed with resin, sulphur and bitumen, it was almost impossible to extinguish

Preceptor – high-ranking religious instructor in the Templar Order

Sefer Shemot – Hebrew name for the Second Book of Moses, or Exodus, meaning 'Book of Names'

shaitan – an evil spirit in Islam comparable with the English word 'devil'

suq – a merchant quarter or marketplace in an Arab city, equivalent to 'bazaar' in Persian and Turkish

Tanakh – also known as the Hebrew Bible, the collection of Hebrew scriptures, comprising twenty-four books

turcopolier – Templar knight and commander of the turcopoles. The turcopoles were Christian mercenaries recruited in the Holy Land, who fought in the style of the Saracens, primarily as archers on horseback

Index of persons

This index is not exhaustive, but includes all main characters and most of the supporting characters in the book. Information in *italics* is fictional, not historical.

ARNAUD DE TOROGE, Grand Master of the Templar Order from 1179–1184. Before that, he fought in the provinces of Aragon and Provence against the Moors. Died 1184 in Verona.

BERTRAN DE BORN, born ca. 1140 at Born Castle in Périgord. Famous 12th century troubadour. Fought in France on the side of Richard the Lionheart against King Philip of France. Had four sons and a daughter from two marriages. Entered a monastery in 1196 and died ca. 1215. *Father of illegitimate son Guillaume de Born.*

BOHEMOND OF ANTIOCH, 1144–1201, nicknamed the Stammerer, was married four times. In his third marriage (1181–1199) to Sibylle he had a son and a daughter, Guillaume and Alix. Kept his principality out of the conflict with Saladin and retained his property after the Battle of Hattin in 1187.

GÉRARD DE RIDEFORT, Grand Master of the Templar Order from 1184–1189. Was taken prisoner by Saladin after the Battle of Hattin, was freed, and died in 1189 during the siege of Acre.

GILBERT HÉRAIL, Grand Master of the Templar Order from 1193 until his death in 1200. Lost the Grand Master election in 1191 to Robert de Sablé. Preceptor in Acre until de Sablé's death in 1993, succeeded him as Grand Master.

GUIDO OF LUSIGNAN, King of Jerusalem 1180–1192, lost the throne to Conrad of Montferrat and afterward ruled Cyprus until 1194.

GULLIAUME DE BORN, *born ca. 1162. Bastard son of Bertran de Born, famous troubadour and Lord of Hautefort in Périgord. Grew up in the Cistercian monastery of Dalon, fled in 1180 and joined the Templar Order in Jerusalem in 1181. Became commander of the Order's light cavalry after the Battle of Hattin in 1187.*

HARIT IBN THARIT IBN HAMID, *born ca. 1178 in Acre as the son of a Syrian sugar manufacturer. Fled to Jerusalem after the conquest of Acre in 1191.*

HARTUNG OF SCHARFENBERG, *born ca. 1163. Son of Otto of Wettin, standard-bearer to the Margrave of Meissen. Killed the Margrave's youngest son and was outlawed. A well-known tournament knight, travelled with Walter of Westereck to Palestine in 1191.*

HENRY OF CHAMPAGNE, titular king of Jerusalem 1192–1197 by virtue of his marriage to the widow of Conrad of Montferrat, after Conrad was killed by Assassins. The wedding took place eight days after the murder.

ISHMAEL OF COLOGNE, *arrived in Palestine in 1191 as part of Walter of Westereck's small pilgrimage. Moved to Jerusalem and became rabbi of the Jewish community there, and goldsmith to governor Yurdik.*

YOLANDA OF LAUENAU, *born ca. 1168, daughter of a ministerial of Archbishop Wichmann of Magdeburg with a large estate. Stepdaughter of Count Konrad of Lauenau.*

YURDIK, Izz ad-Din, Emir of Jerusalem after its conquest by Saladin in 1187.

CONRAD OF MONTFERRAT, Lord of Tyre, became King of the Holy Land with the help of King Philip II after the conquest of Acre. Killed by Assassins soon after, in April 1192. Various sources attribute the murder to King Richard, and Templars were supposedly involved.

LEAH OF JERUSALEM, *born ca. 1175 as daughter of Esau of Jerusalem, a Jewish money changer. Niece of Ishmael of Cologne.*

MAIMONIDES, a.k.a. Moses ben Maimon, 1135–1204, famous Jewish scholar, philosopher and physician. Lived near Cairo, personal physician to Sultan Saladin.

NICHOLAS DE SEAGRAVE, *born ca. 1170 in Seagrave, Leicestershire, son of Sheriff Lord Gilbert de Seagrave. Arrived at the siege of Acre in the entourage of Richard the Lionheart in 1191, then entered the Templar Order.*

RAOUL DE GARLANDE, *from an important family of politicians in France, born ca. 1163 at Castle Gournay-sur-Marne near Paris as the son of Guillaume de Garlande. In 1181 he left his family, went to the Holy Land and entered the Templar Order. In 1187 survived the Battle of Hattin and was promoted to Marshal of the Templars in Acre.*

The Commandments of the Templar

RICHARD I, a.k.a. 'Richard the Lionheart', 1157–1199, King of England from 1189. Conquered Cyprus and Acre during the Third Crusade. Married Berengaria of Navarre in 1189 in Limassol. Insulted the banner of Duke Leopold V during the conquest of Acre. Left Palestine in October 1192 and was captured by Austrian Duke Leopold on his way home, near Vienna. Freed in March 1194 in return for a high ransom.

ROBERT DE SABLÉ, Grand Master of the Templar Order 1191–1193, previously Admiral of Richard the Lionheart's fleet, and his vassal. Died 1193, *murdered by an Assassin.*

SALADIN, Sultan of Egypt, 1138–1193, a.k.a. Salah ad-Din. Ruler of Egypt and Syria, defeated King Guy of Lusignan in 1187 at the Battle of Hattin, then reconquered Jerusalem and most of the Crusader-occupied cities in Palestine.

SIEBRAND, Magister of the Brothers of the German House of Saint Mary in Jerusalem. Probably from a northern German trading town. Founded the German hospital (the nucleus of what became the Teutonic Order) outside the walls of Acre.

SINAN, Rashid ad-Din, a.k.a. the Old Man of the Mountain, leader of the Assassins – an Islamic sect headquartered in the Masyaf fortress in Syria. Died 1193.

SIBYLLE OF ANTIOCH, third wife of Bohemond of Antioch from 1181–1199, with whom she had two children, Guillaume and Alix. Chroniclers describe her as a loose woman. Hated by the nobility for her lifestyle and for meddling in politics. Arabic chroniclers claim she was a spy for Saladin. In 1194, she seduced Leo I of Armenia in order to secure her children's succession in Antioch, betraying her husband, who was captured by Leo in 1194.

THIBAUT, *Komtur of the Templars in Acre ca. 1193, of Alemannic heritage.*

WALTER OF WESTERECK, *born ca. 1170, youngest son of Saxon knight Hugo of Westereck, raised in a Cistercian monastery. Later became a tournament knight and led a pilgrim army to the Holy Land in 1191.*

WILFRIED OF LAUENAU, *born ca. 1165, son and heir of Count Konrad of Lauenau. Spent time at Loccum Monastery with Walter of Westereck. Later knighted, fought in the Wendish wars. Went on a pilgrimage to Palestine and rose to commander of the bodyguard of King Richard the Lionheart.*

Afterword and thanks

The Ark of the Covenant is still lost without a trace. Generations of treasure hunters have searched for it in vain. There is no evidence that it ever existed. The Bible describes many wondrous things and occurrences that have so far eluded a strictly scientific explanation. As Sir Walter said to Leah in this story: faith always has something to do with belief.

Before I come to the historical background of this book, I would like to make one comment. My characters act and speak in the context of their times. They represent the attitudes and prejudices toward people of different faiths that were common at the time. Regrettably, there are alarming parallels in today's world. It seems that humanity must continue to repeat history and learn little from past mistakes.

To be clear, I distance myself expressly from antisemitism, islamophobia and racism. These are remnants of ancient times, which caused endless misery and suffering, and continue to do so. They no longer fit into a modern-day framework of democracy, international understanding and scientific progress.

It has been established that over a thousand years ago the inhabitants of the Holy Land, despite their different faiths, found ways to live together, often peacefully.

Around 1120, a good twenty years after the bloody conquest of the Holy City by the Christians, the chaplain of the King of Jerusalem, Fulcher of Chartres, wrote: "For we, from the Occident, have now become Orientals. One who was a Roman or a Frank, in this land becomes a Galileean or a Palestinian. One from Reims or Chartres has become a citizen of Tyre or Antioch. We have already forgotten our birthplace; many of us no longer know it, or it is no longer mentioned."

The process of assimilation for westerners in the Levant happened exceptionally rapidly, but it was not all-encompassing, and was a long way from a harmonious, multicultural society. Among other things, tangible economic motivations to live peacefully amongst people of other faiths were a decisive factor. There was a need for a workforce, a desire to trade in exotic commodities and collect taxes. The amenities offered by an oriental way of life contributed significantly to the convergence of cultures. Muslims, Jews and Christian benefited one another in the most diverse ways.

However, this didn't lead to lasting equilibrium between religions. Intolerance on all sides often brought about new, violent conflicts. The Crusader spirit of the Christians was continuously revived by newcomers from overseas, just as jihad never left the minds of the resident Muslims.

The year 1193 was one of the most peaceful years in the Holy Land. The Third Crusade had ended, King Richard had left Outremer, and the Latin Kingdom had shrunk down to just a few, pitiful outposts along the coast. All sides were war-weary and exhausted. After Jerusalem was lost to the Latin Kingdom, Acre became its capital. Only the strips of land around Jaffa, Tripoli and Antioch remained in Christian hands. To this day, it's puzzling that Sultan Saladin didn't muster the strength to wipe out the fragmented remnants of the Crusader States.

He died in March that year and left behind seventeen sons, who quarrelled hopelessly over his legacy and therefore posed no serious threat to the Christians for a very long time. The feared leader of the Assassins, Sheikh Sinan, also known as The Old Man of the Mountain, followed him to the afterlife soon after, as did the Grand Master of the Templars, Robert de Sablé.

The Commandments of the Templar

Sources state vaguely that the Grand Master perished in February 1193 in a battle with the heathens. De Sablé could have been around seventy years old by this time, so it was unlikely he still went out on the battlefield on horseback. Therefore, I took poetic licence and had him killed by Assassins. His successor, Gilbert Hérail, is historically documented, holding the office of Grand Master until 1200. He was a man who brought balance between Muslims and Christians, but unfortunately, conflict intensified under his leadership between the Templar Order and their perennial competitors, the Knights of St John.

There are vast numbers of publications about the Templar Order itself that could fill whole libraries on their own. All I'll say is this: it was the first knights' Order to combine a monastic life with chivalrous ideals. Founded by Frankish aristocrats between 1118 and 1123, this elite force was invincible in battle against the Saracens. Their reputation as fierce fighters was legendary, as was their wealth, gifted in abundance by believers from all over the world. But they also paid by far the highest death toll in innumerable skirmishes.

The Order's statutes were compiled around 1129. Initially, they consisted of two rules, which were expanded to an incredible 686 provisions by 1260. They set out in minute detail the guidelines each member had to observe, awhat they must avoid doing where possible, in order to partake of the grace of God. One can only conclude from the unbelievable number of threatened punishments for transgressions that there must have been a lot of sinners in the Order.

The character of Templar Guillaume de Born is fictional. There was a Bertran de Born – a well-known troubadour and brawler from Périgord. It's quite conceivable that the well-travelled, fun-loving knight may have sired a number of bastards, and that one of them may have soared to a career as turcopolier in the Templar Order.

Nor was there a Raoul de Garlande. The noble house of de Garlande had many branches and held influential official posts in the royal court of France. So it's possible that one of its numerous offspring may have moved to the Holy Land and, thanks to his noble lineage, become Marshal of the Templars.

The Assassins were undisputedly dangerous murderers, feared by Christians and Muslims alike. Even Sultan Saladin twice escaped their daggers only narrowly.

They were responsible for the sensational assassination of the titular King of Jerusalem, Conrad of Montferrat, in March 1192. On his way home from visiting a friend, he was ambushed by two Assassins in an alley in Tyre and stabbed to death. Conrad was a declared enemy of King Richard the Lionheart, and some contemporaries attribute the murder to the English king. But there are various other possible sponsors, for example, Saladin or Conrad's old rival Humphrey of Toron.

King Richard was captured on his way home from the Holy Land by Austrian Duke Leopold, and one of the pretexts was this accusation. It was never proven.

The Duke was probably deeply offended when Richard seriously insulted his person shortly after the capture of Acre. The power-hungry Richard refused to share the spoils with him, even though the Austrian had been the primary commander of troops outside the city throughout most of the siege. The King had the Duke's banner thrown down into the trenches, after which Leopold returned home fuming with rage and swearing to take revenge. This he did, very successfully in fact. King Richard was only released after an enormous ransom was paid two years later.

The Templars probably had nothing to do with Conrad's murder, but it seems quite plausible to me that they could have commissioned it. They certainly maintained good relationships with the Assassins for a long time, and Richard the Lionheart was known to be very favourable toward the Order.

It is well documented that Robert de Sablé was one of his admirals, and that the King pushed for his instatement to the post of Grand Master. Richard sold him the island of Cyprus, which he had casually conquered on his way to the Holy Land, for one hundred thousand bezants, and received a deposit of forty thousand bezants. Robert de Sablé sent a handful of Templars to the island, who immediately alienated the local population by raising taxes to an intolerable level and scarcely managed to suppress an uprising. He gave the island back to the King after only a few months.

The enterprising monarch kept the deposit and promptly sold the island to Guido of Lusignan, the hapless former king who lost the Battle of Hattin to Saladin in 1187, and almost the entire Kingdom of Jerusalem along with it.

This little episode shows the close ties between Richard and de Sablé, and the vast resources at the disposal of the Order, which appears to have easily written off this financial loss. At a rough estimate of the current value, the Grand Master invested almost ten million euro in the sand off the coast of Acre. According to historical sources, Richard left the Holy Land soon after on a Templar ship, dressed in the garb of the Order so as not to be recognised as a king.

These intrigues would certainly provide entertaining, even comical material for another novel. As would the character of Bohemond of Antioch, the Stammerer – a ruthless contemporary whose third marriage was to the *Mata Hari* of the Crusades, the beautiful Sybille. She is alleged to have spied for Sultan Saladin, betrayed her husband with her lover King Leo of Armenia and was, according to chronicler William of Tyre, a godless whore.

Bohemond was reprimanded for this marriage by the Pope, and later excommunicated by the Patriarch of Jerusalem. This didn't intimidate him. He proceeded to attack monasteries, rob church treasures and torture clergy until the punishment was meekly reversed. He was also in conflict with the Templar Order over possession of their former fortress of Baghras, which once lay within his territory. Reason enough, in my view, for them to make him the target of an assassination.

There's almost nothing recorded of the Jewish community in Jerusalem after the Third Crusade. After its conquest by Sultan Saladin in 1187, the city was depopulated and the ruler encouraged Jews to resettle there. It's likely that some heeded the call, but their numbers probably weren't great. Three small congregations formed there, with synagogues, but they disappeared again in 1219 after one of the Sultan's grandsons had the city walls torn down, and Jerusalem faded into insignificance for many years.

Jews lived much more peacefully under Muslim rule than they did in Christian lands. Islam characterised them as 'scripture readers' and wards deserving of protection, referred to as 'dhimmi'. One of the hadith (transmitted reports of the words of Mohammed) stipulates, "He who does injury to a dhimmi does injury to me, and he who does injury to me does injury to Allah." Jews paid an additional tax, and were permitted to live largely undisturbed amongst Muslims.

The characters of Rabbi Ishmael and his niece Leah are fictitious. But the famous rabbi and scholar Maimonides existed – a renowned scholar, medicus and personal physician to Sultan Saladin.

Walter of Westereck and Hartung of Scharfenberg have their own fictional history, elaborated in my novel *The Warrior of the Lord*. In this book, they're described as Alemannic knights, which is inaccurate. They come from what is today

Lower Saxony. However, in the Levant, Germanic people were all referred to collectively as 'Alemann', just as all other Christians were lumped together under the term 'Frank', regardless of whether they were French, English, Italian or Spanish. The Christians in turn generally referred to all Muslim Arabs, Syrians, Turks and Kurds as either 'Saracens' or 'heathens'.

The Crusaders only held out in the Levant for around two hundred years. A comparatively short period in the course of the long and turbulent history of the region. But they have left their mark to this day – both in surviving architecture and in the memory of the people. Despite the brutality of the religious wars, often fuelled by a thirst for wealth and power, this epoch has inspired the imagination of generations.

It was in the myth-enshrouded Holy Land that the mystical Templar Order arose, with its alleged hidden treasures and its inglorious downfall on Friday 19th October 1307.

Emperor Barbarossa lost his life during one of the Crusades, and legend has it that he will one day return to the Kyffhäuser mountains in Germany if there is ever a need.

Another legend was very popular in the Middle Ages: Richard the Lionheart, the swashbuckling king, fought the noble Sultan Saladin and was humiliatingly captured on his way out of Palestine. No one knew where he was being held, and his faithful troubadour, Blondel, searched for him and found him in Trifels Castle in Germany, where he was finally released. Other stories say that Robin Hood was involved.

The reality of the Crusades in these times had little to do with the fairy tales and legends. There were vicious battles, gruesome deaths, cowardly massacres and sinful conduct. But historical sources tell of rapprochements between the warring sides, and there was certainly some level of chivalry and honourable conduct.

I conducted extensive research while writing *The Commandments of the Templar*, in order to create a realistic picture of the era. A novel can't illuminate every facet of daily life in the Holy Land in the year 1193, but the intent was to come close to historical accuracy.

A great help in this regard was my good friend Gerald – a passionate medievalist and an established authority on medieval ways of life.

On reading the finished book, he said it brought to mind many ideas for sequels that I should definitely consider. Perhaps there is more to tell of Leah and Guillaume's story. We'll see. *Inshallah,* as Harit would say.

My exceptionally knowledgeable, patient and conscientious proofreader Franka also deserves my heartfelt thanks. I tend to be overzealous with commas, and at the same time terribly ignorant of correct punctuation. Without her, this book could have been a few pages thicker, but by no means more readable.

My biggest thanks go to my partner Andrea. She read the work many times through, with incredible energy and endurance, until it satisfied her expectations. I wrestled with her over many paragraphs, sentences and words, and I often lost. The manuscript definitely won.

And I hope I've won the affections of the people most important to an author: you, the readers!

Tom Melley

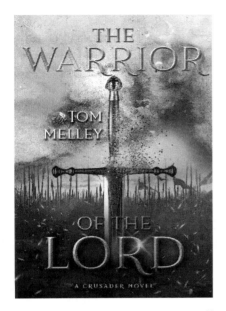

Tom Melley

The Warrior of the Lord

A crusader Novel

Paperback 314 Pages

6 x 0.79 x 9 inches

877477649844030

Saxony in the year 1190.
Walter of Westereck, the youngest offspring of a knightly lineage, is obligated to compete in his first tournament, hosted by his family's arch-enemy, Count Konrad of Lauenau.

The Count's troubled daughter Yolanda beseeches Walter to free her from the clutches of her sadistic brother Wilfried.

Walter disbelieves her story and moves on, while her hate-fuelled brother razes Westereck Castle to the ground and executes Walter's father in cold blood.

Swearing revenge, Walter pursues Wilfried and Yolanda, who are suddenly forced to embark on a pilgrimage of penance to the Holy Land after being convicted of incest and kin slaying.

Walter takes up with a troop of armed pilgrims until he reaches the city of Acre in Palestine, where Christians and Muslims have been warring mercilessly for years.

There he encounters his mortal enemy, only to find he is under the protection of the powerful King Richard the Lionheart ...

Printed in Great Britain
by Amazon